Rocking HORSE HILL

CATHRYN HEIN

About The Author

 A South Australian country girl by birth, Cathryn loves nothing more than a rugged rural hero who's as good with his heart as he is with his hands, which is probably why she writes them! Her romances are warm and emotional, and feature themes that don't flinch from the tougher side of life but are often happily tempered by the antics of naughty animals. Her aim is to make you smile, sigh, and perhaps sniffle a little, but most of all feel wonderful.

Cathryn was born horse mad, which is little wonder with three generations of jockeys in the family. After scoring her first horse at age 10, upon whom she bestowed the eternally romantic name of Mysty, Cathryn spent the rest of her teenage years in equine bliss riding pony club and hunt club, and competing in eventing, dressage and showjumping until university beckoned.

Armed with a shiny Bachelor of Applied Science (Agriculture) from Roseworthy College she moved to Melbourne and later Newcastle, working in the agricultural and turf seeds industry. Her partner's posting to France took Cathryn overseas for three years in Provence where she finally gave in to her life-long desire to write.

Cathryn currently lives in New South Wales at the base of the Blue Mountains with her partner of many years, Jim. When she's not writing, she plays golf (ineptly), cooks (well), and in football season barracks (rowdily) for her beloved Sydney Swans AFL team.

Contact Cathryn via

cathryn@cathrynhein.com

or the contact form on

cathrynhein.com

You can also follow her on social media at:

Facebook:

https://www.facebook.com/cathrynhein/

Instagram:

https://www.instagram.com/cathrynheinauthor/

Twitter:

@CathrynHein

Goodreads:

www.goodreads.com/author/show/5137697.Cathryn_Hein

For Jim

One

Car headlights shot yellowy-orange streaks over the slick bitumen of Levenham's main street. The footpath remained empty, bar the occasional person dashing for their car, head obscured by a rain jacket hood or low-held umbrella.

Hunched against the wind, Emily Wallace-Jones tucked her leather satchel tighter under her arm and finished locking PaperPassion's shop door. If it weren't for her innate sense of duty she'd have closed up and headed to Camrick and a hearty gossip with Granny B an hour ago, but customers had unexpectedly come in and Em still had rent and other expenses to cover. Nor did she want to develop a reputation as unreliable. Levenham might be home to seventeen thousand people, but word spread just as fast here as it did in a small village, and being a Wallace put her at a big enough disadvantage as it was. In a town where hardship and wealth maintained an uneasy coexistence, old resentments and jealousies lingered.

Rain sleeted the windscreen of Em's four-wheel drive as she turned into Camrick's drive. The Wallace's 125-year-old manor, where Em's mother, Adrienne, brother Digby and Granny B resided in their distinct quarters, was built on a slight rise several streets back from the centre of town. Night cloaked the property's full grandeur but the lights illuminating the old carriageway exposed part of its handsome front. Compared to some of the rendered brick mansions cropping up around Levenham, Camrick wasn't overly large but, where they had modernity and size, Camrick faced the world with history and majesty.

The house was two storeys. A large bay extended out the left side, decorated columns splitting the three delicately arched windows of each floor. From the bay, the walls sank inwards, protected by a large bull-nosed verandah that wrapped the remaining front and side of the house. The iron-laced second-floor balcony was Granny B's favourite perch. No matter the weather, each evening after dinner she could be found surveying the land and sky through her one good eye, thin cigar in one hand, cut-crystal tumbler of whisky in the other.

The lights in Granny B's rooms were out. Em braked and leaned forward to inspect the stables. The entrance to Digby's lodgings was dark, the wall lights either side of the converted stables' pale blue door unlit. A dull yellow glow peeked from between the blinds of the far right upstairs window – Digby's bedroom. Warmth began to fill her. He was back.

Tuesday-night dinners were a tradition in the Wallace family, an anticipated and fun event. A chance to keep them knitted together, to quickly catch any pull or hint of familial unravelling. When one of them was missing, they all felt it. Even during Em's years at university, no matter what adventure or stress was occurring, Tuesday night would bring a wistfulness for Camrick. Wistfulness soon followed by a crushing yearning for her beloved Rocking Horse Hill.

A gust of wind rocked the car. Granny B's elegant outline was silhouetted against Camrick's rear door. Her grandmother beckoned, the gesture impatient. Em grabbed her bag and the carton of fresh eggs she'd made up before work and made the dash.

Granny B held out a powdery cheek for a kiss. She wore her short hair in its usual style, set crimped and parted on one side, with the waves held in check by half a can of hairspray and a pale metal clip that blended in with her silvery-white hair. She was tall, Em's height, straight-backed and as skinny as a film star. All length and bone with a solid air of haughtiness and privilege. Em had been advised her entire life that she took after her grandmother and had not once minded the comparison. Granny B oozed old-style glamour.

'Ghastly weather, isn't it?' said Granny B. 'How's Muffet coping?'

'A little stiff but the tablets seem to be helping. She's settled in to the house pretty well. If she needs to go outside she comes and wakes me, but that's only happened twice so far. Must have a good bladder.'

'Unlike the rest of us oldies,' said Granny B with a sigh.

Em hooked her arm through her grandmother's. 'You're not old. You're grandly mature.'

Granny B smiled. 'I am rather, aren't I? Incontinence pad and all.' She patted Em's hand. 'Now, come. Digby's got his knickers in a twist about something and your mother and I are anxious to discover the cause. Refused to answer any questions and then scuttled off to the front lounge when we wouldn't be put off. What does the boy expect? Away all that time without once coming home. Barely even rang.'

'Maybe he met a girl.'

'Or boy?' asked Granny B, lasering in on Em with one of her special looks. Chronic open-angle glaucoma had destroyed all but the central vision in Granny B's right eye, causing her to peer at people with unnerving sharpness.

'Would it matter?'

'Not to me.' Her eyes sparkled. 'In fact, it'd be rather serendipitous to see the family wealth pass down the matriarchal line again. Wallace men have had it too easy for too long.'

Granny B steered Em down the softly lit hall, their footsteps echoing off the polished floorboards. A worn Persian runner had once carpeted the hall, which ran the width of the house before hitting a T, one turn leading left to the front wing, the other to the upper floor, but Adrienne had declared the runner a relic of the past and pulled it up. There were plans for carpet and a repaint. Em had always loved Camrick's old-fashioned classicism but her style-conscious mother hankered for modernity, and since Uncle James's death had been slowly transforming the decor.

'Here she is,' announced Granny B as they turned into the kitchen.

Adrienne was at the stove, stirring a pot of something that wafted savoury deliciousness. A light sheen of moisture disturbed her make-up and caused the fine tendrils of her piled-up dark hair to hang limp around her face.

Like all Wallace women, bar herself, Em's mother had an 'A' name. Granny B's was Audrey but a clash with Em's other grandmother, who shared the name, led the children to refer to their grandmothers as Granny A and Granny B. The titles had stuck. Em would have been Amelia except for a last-minute quarrel between her parents – one of many until their divorce – saw the name tradition forfeited, and baby Amelia was instead christened Emily, much to most of the Wallace family's displeasure.

'Sorry I'm late. I got caught up in the *Ballad*,' said Em, referring to her latest calligraphy project, an illuminated edition of G. K. Chesterton's epic poem, *The Ballad of the White Horse*.

Em's handmade books helped while away quiet hours in the shop and winter-deadened nights at Rocking Horse Hill and, though it had never been her intention, her hobby was beginning to make money. The last book she'd put up for auction on the Internet – a beautifully scripted and illustrated leather-bound edition of Jules Verne's *Around the World in Eighty Days* – had fetched close to a thousand dollars. People were asking for more, pressing for commission work. So far she'd refused, afraid the pressure would spoil the creative pleasure. Books would come, but at a pace of her own choosing, and driven by inspiration instead of behest. While the extra money helped, Em had proven for several years now that life was survivable on the shop's small profits and income from the share portfolio she'd inherited from Uncle James. Digby allowing her to live at Rocking Horse Hill rent-free assisted a great deal too.

She set down the eggs, smiling as she walked over to her mother. The height gene had skipped Adrienne and Uncle James' generation, though the Wallace's famous fine bone structure remained. Em inspected the pot of mushroom sauce simmering at the back of the stove, breathing it in. 'Porcini?'

'A few. It's a mix, mainly. Dansley's had some Swiss browns so I threw a handful of those in with the flat tops.'

'Smells amazing.' A ridged cast-iron grill plate was heating on the front hobs, ready for the fillet steaks that were warming to room temperature on a plate nearby. Em counted them. Her mother's boyfriend, Samuel, must be coming. 'Anything I can help with?'

'It's all done. Go through and say hello to your brother while I cook these steaks. See if you can't worm whatever secret he's hiding out of him. Your grandmother's fit to burst.'

'And you're not?'

Adrienne smiled as she left.

Her brother was sitting sideways on the wide sill of the bay window with one leg drawn up and hugged to his chest, staring vacantly outwards as rain pelted the glass and slid in glittery streaks down the pane. The open fire was crackling enticingly, filling the room with warmth and the smell of wood. At the door's opening, Adrienne's drowsy Siamese cat Peaches slid from Uncle James' wingback leather chair — a piece so handsome and well made even Adrienne couldn't bring herself to dump it — to resettle near the hearth.

Em leaned against the doorjamb with her arms crossed, wondering if Digby had even registered her presence. 'Very Heathcliff.'

Digby turned his head. 'Is that good or bad?'

Unlike Em, who had always adored reading and gone on to gain an Honours degree in English from Flinders University, Digby was a left-brained science nerd, who would rather read a paper on plant pollination than *Wuthering Heights*.

'Depends how crazy you turn.' Em crossed the room to join him on the sill. She pushed his leg aside and settled down, pressing her shoulder affectionately against his. 'So, dear brother of mine, I'm guessing good times were had in Adelaide?'

A flush crept up Digby's neck and bloomed pinkly across his cheeks. He crossed and uncrossed his legs at the ankle, tilting forward as if unsure whether to stand or stay sitting. 'They were.'

Em studied him closer. He'd been away on an intensive course at Adelaide University's Roseworthy campus, north of the city, for three weeks. Not an unusual occurrence. As a horticulturalist with the Department of Agriculture, professional development was an important part of his job, but this was the first time he'd not come home for weekends. Adelaide was only four hours or so away, Roseworthy perhaps an hour further. A reasonable drive, but that had never stopped him previously.

He glanced at his watch, twisted the band and frowned at the rain-striped window. Two words for three weeks away. This was going to take some effort.

'Care to fill me in?'

Digby's gaze flicked across the room. Em followed suit and smiled as she spotted Samuel, paused and slightly stooping beneath the doorframe.

'Not interrupting, am I?'

'No,' said Digby, 'not at all.' He leaned closer to Em, his voice low and tainted with smugness. 'All will be revealed after dinner.'

'It had better be or you'll have Gran to contend with.'

Samuel poured himself a drink from the trolley beside the back wall and together they stood near the fire, bemoaning the weather and discussing Samuel's service club's initiatives. He was an attractive man, with salt-and-pepper hair and a rangy body kept fit by morning jogs and golf. He was also a consummate facilitator. The sort of man who went out of his way to relax people – confident and charismatic, but without Em's father's overconfident swagger – and his love for Adrienne was unwavering.

Sadly, the adoration in his blue-grey eyes for Em's mother was tempered by unhealable sorrow. Years before he'd lost his only son to meningitis. For any man the sense of helplessness would be acute, but for a retired radiographer, a man who'd lived his life surrounded by medical science and its wonders, the loss must have held a sharper edge. Which was why, Em supposed, he gave so much of his time to children's services.

Granny B called them to dinner, lingering beside Em to ask if she'd discovered Digby's news. Her mouth puckered upon learning they'd all have to wait.

In an unusual display of fortitude, Digby ignored his grandmother's unsubtle prods and kept his counsel throughout the meal. Samuel filled in the conversational gaps with details of his upcoming trip to Timor-Leste, before discussion moved on to Adrienne's favourite topic of local arts funding, ensuring a lively debate with Granny B and Em over what field should take priority. Em allowed herself a glass of red wine, noting, as did her mother and grandmother, that Digby drank nothing and that his attention was constantly flicking to the dining room's cherry wood mantel clock.

'Well,' said Granny B, dabbing at her mouth with her napkin and looking at Digby, 'we have now finished dinner. What's this news of yours?'

Digby glanced at the clock again. Nearly eight. Em would have to leave for Rocking Horse Hill soon. Even with her heavily blanketed porch basket her darling collie, Muffy, would be feeling the cold. Plus Em needed to lock up the chooks and Chelsea, throw a few sheaves of hay to her horse Lodestone, and check on Kicki and Cutie. The tough little donkeys usually looked after themselves but they didn't have cold-beating rugs like Lod. With the weather this inclement she might need to bring them in.

'Digby?' asked Adrienne, sliding her hand across the table towards his. 'What's the matter?'

The clock began its Big Ben toll. Granny B glared at it as it struck the hours down.

Another sound joined the chime.

Frowning, Em looked at her mother. 'Is that the doorbell?'

'I'll answer it,' said Samuel, laying down his napkin and half-rising.

'No!'

Samuel stilled. Everyone's gaze fixed on Digby who quickly scraped his chair back and jerked upright, his napkin falling from his knees to the floor, unnoticed. He stared towards the dining room door with an overexcited, almost fearful look in his eyes.

The clock ceased its chime.

He swallowed, cast around the room and gestured towards the exit. 'I'll get it.'

For a few seconds, Em, Adrienne, Granny B and Samuel could only gape at the empty doorway before regarding one another with acute puzzlement.

Samuel was the first to speak. 'Well, whoever our visitor is, I'm guessing they're for Digby.'

'Shh,' ordered Granny B, her head cocked to listen.

Voices drifted. One deep, the other soft and barely audible. Then Digby and his guest ceased talking, leaving the sound of the ticking clock, the distant drum of rain on the roof, and footsteps on the timber floor, slowly coming closer.

His cheeks blooming with colour, Digby stepped into the room and halted, alone, then inhaled deeply and straightened his shoulders. 'I'd like you all to meet someone.' He took another breath and turned slightly, his arm held out. 'Someone very special.'

A few heartbeats passed, then a small slim blonde woman with her long hair pulled back into a girlish ponytail stepped into his embrace, and together they took another few steps into the room. She smiled hesitantly at Adrienne, then around the table at Granny B, Em and Samuel. Finally her gaze turned back to Digby.

He smiled at her for a moment, holding her like a fabulously rare, priceless and prized piece of art: covetous, careful and proud.

'Mum, Gran, Em, Samuel, I'd like you to meet Felicity Townsend.' He raised his chin. 'My fiancée.'

Two

Em held her steaming cup to her lips. She blew gently before taking a sip, then continued mulling over the previous night's drama.

Digby, engaged. Both a shock and a complete delight.

She wished she could have stayed at Camrick longer, learned more about Felicity, their wedding plans, but Rocking Horse Hill had called, as it had so often in her life, and Em had to depart just as Felicity began to relax into the meeting with her future in-laws.

Still, there'd be plenty of time. Perhaps Digby could bring her out to the farm as soon as she was settled. Em could walk her around, show her where it all began for the Wallaces, tell embarrassing tales about Digby as a boy. Sister stuff.

Em smiled and raised her eyes to the view. Through the massive floor-to-ceiling windows of the living area the landscape sprawled with soothing familiarity. Winter etched the sky pewter, darkening the shadowy sheer western slope of Rocking Horse Hill, its abandoned quarry a sad scar in the volcano's side. To the south, the sinkhole-ridden plain extended to the sea. Even on a day as dull as this the scene flushed Em with deep pleasure.

So much to tell. So much that Felicity needed to learn about their heritage to preserve and pass on to Digby's children, as Adrienne, Granny B and Uncle James had done for them. She needed to understand the responsibility that came with marrying Digby. Not so much the wealth, or even the community standing, but the history.

Em turned at the sound of Miss Muffet's nails clicking across the slate floor and her smile faded. Arthritis had weakened her beloved Smithfield collie's gait and made it stiff, particularly in the mornings. Muffy now slept inside; her aging body eased by the warmth of a freestanding slow-combustion wood heater and sheepskin-lined bed. The dog pressed her fluffy black-and-tan side against Em's calf, before looking up with dark, still-bright eyes.

'Hello, Miss Muffet, who sits on her tuffet.' Em caressed the dog's silky ears.

Muffy pressed her nose into Em's palm, earning her another loving pat. The smile returned in full to Em's face, her heart warming. She straightened, only to yelp as a huge grey hairy head banged against the window. Her fingers fanned in fright. The mug slid from her grip and shattered on the stone floor, only just missing Muffy who raced to the window with her hackles up. Her sharp barks stabbed the silence and jangled Em's nerves.

Em lifted her flared fingers to her chest and stared at the window. 'How the hell?' But the answer to that question would have to wait.

Heart still thumping, she grimaced at the snotty smear greasing the window where the donkey's nose had impacted, called Muffy back and crouched to stroke her, the contact as much for herself as the dog. Muffy trembled a little under her hand, although Em suspected it was more from outrage at being ambushed by her nemesis than shock.

'Shh. It was just Kicki.'

Em rose to fetch paper towels before the spilled tea leaked into the cream shag rug beneath her desk. She loved that rug. There was nothing quite as lovely as squelching her bare feet through the thick pile when she sat down to calligraphy work, her toes curling to tug the threads like summer grass.

She tsked as she cleaned, casting Muffy annoyed glances. She adored her but the dog shed hair in swathes and no matter how many times Em swept or mopped, Muffy's presence crept into every corner, forming hair-webs and spidery knots. When she'd finished with the floor, Em pulled on her boots and trudged outside to hunt down her errant donkeys. If Kicki was out, then his girlfriend Cutie wouldn't be far behind.

The porch timbers creaked under her step, as though moaning about the cold. She breathed out, the puff of air turning opaque in the frigid early morning. The weather bureau had forecast another day of scattered showers, perhaps rain periods, and a maximum in the low teens. Normal for June in this south-eastern corner of South Australia.

The chooks and Chelsea the Indian runner duck were out foraging, picking at plants and slumberous insects and grubs; flashes of golden-brown and white among the damp, drooping foliage of Em's vegetable garden. She'd unlatched their coop when she'd let Muffy out to conduct her secretive morning ablutions. Since puppyhood, Muffy hated being watched while going to the loo. She'd wander off to who knew where, leaving not a trace. On the rare occasion Em accidentally stumbled across the dog, Muffy regarded her so reproachfully that Em quickly backed away, muttering apologies.

The donkeys were hock-high in Em's vegetable garden, delicately probing a juicy row of month-old broad beans. Thick mops of hair covered their foreheads and damp matted their white underbellies where their winter coats hung long and dense. Kicki's fluffy grey ears twirled at her approach. He raised his head, pale bean roots protruding from his lips. Blinking sweetly, he nudged the dark brown cheek of his girlfriend, Cutie, before sucking the roots into his mouth and resuming his snuffle around the plants. A pair of innocent-looking equines with very naughty minds.

Muffy circled, her shoulders hunched, watching carefully for the turn of rump that foreshadowed a swift kick. No matter how Em tried to condition him, Kicki refused to soften his attitude. In his eyes, dogs were wolves with smaller teeth and that was that. Not a bad thing when it came to keeping strays off the property, but Em could have done without the vet bills from Muffy's injuries.

She whistled Muffy back and stalked towards them with thin lips, only for Kicki to bustle straight through the broccoli and early potatoes, dragging Cutie with him, and leaving squashed plants and hoof marks in their wake.

Em rolled her eyes and decided to leave them to it. When Kicki was in one of his 'you can't catch me' moods it was better to walk away. Besides, she could never begrudge his fun, not after all he and Cutie had suffered, and she still had the mystery of how they escaped their paddock to solve.

She headed out of the garden and into the open, pausing to take stock of the sky, until her gaze was drawn, like so often, upwards, to the majestic, ever-powerful presence of Rocking Horse Hill.

The volcano rose steeply almost a hundred metres from the ground, ending in rocky peaks that then plunged downward into a deep, flinty crater. It was one of the youngest in a chain of peaks that ran through western Victoria into South Australia, spattering the land like a broken string of misshapen pearls. Unlike most other volcanoes, which were spectacularly warped and eroded, Em's hill was an almost perfect trapezium, as if plucked from a child's drawing.

There was once a time when the Wallace family owned the crater itself, when they owned vast tracts of this windswept land – the forests and stone quarries, farms and industry, from Levenham, only twelve kilometres to the north, to Port Andrews in the south and points east and west. In those days Rocking Horse Hill was still known as Mount Stanislaus. Officially, it still was. But after the war, there had been a hard-fought debate to change the name, which had prompted the frustrated editor of the local *Levenham Leader* to dub it something so childish no one could argue against the original title. But the nickname had stuck. To outsiders the volcano was named after some obscure relative of Charlotte of Mecklenburg-Strelitz, King George III's wife. To locals it would always be Rocking Horse Hill.

For Em it would always mean home.

***

'Can you believe it? Digby engaged!' Em grinned at her two friends who, knowing how territorial Em could get when she was cooking, were perched in their usual positions on the opposite side of the breakfast bar. Teagan Bliss on Em's left, close to the glass sliding door, Jasmine Thomas on the right, nearest the fridge and wine supply, and closer to Em, a position she felt entitled to thanks to her 'older friend' status.

'Who'd have thought he could be such a sly dog,' said Teagan.

'All men can be sly dogs when it suits them,' said Jas, taking a swig from her glass. With no Saturday-morning shift at the building society to wake up for she was already deep into Friday-night party mode.

Em shot Teagan a look, warning her not to bite. Jas's long-term affair with a married man had been discussed enough, Teagan's disapproval voiced and noted, and Jas was hard enough on herself about it without Teagan taking swipes.

Teagan caught the look and took a sip of wine. 'So, what is she like?'

'Stunning. Long blonde hair, cheekbones like Angelina Jolie, sky-blue eyes.'

Jas rolled her eyes. 'In other words, utterly hateable.'

'Maybe, except she seems quite sweet and a bit shy, but that was probably more our fault. Everyone was so shocked and excited we kept throwing questions at her all at once. And then Mum started crying.'

'And your gran?' asked Teagan.

'Reserving judgement.'

Jas laughed. 'In other words, she thinks Felicity isn't good enough.'

'Well, she does come from Elizabeth.'

Teagan feigned a shock-horror gasp. 'Elizabeth!'

'Could have been worse.'

'Yes, it could have been Smithfield,' countered Jas with another of Adelaide's notorious suburbs.

'Or Salisbury.'

'Cut it out, you two,' said Em, trying not to laugh.

Jas raised her eyebrows. 'Bit rich coming from you, Miss Emily Wallace-Jones.'

Em pressed her palm against her chest. 'Unlike my grandmother, I reformed my ways and am no longer a snob.'

The girls grinned at one another. 'Much.'

'I'm not!'

'No,' said Teagan, pretending seriousness, 'of course you aren't.'

'Oh, shut up.'

Em sighed and returned to her pan, inhaling the winey fumes. No matter what anyone thought, she had reformed, although she had to admit to a slight wince when Felicity revealed where she grew up. But a birthplace shouldn't dictate someone's life, and it certainly didn't reflect a person's character. Experience had proved that more than once.

She studied the reduction and gave it a stir before peering through the oven door. A simple dish of *pommes boulangère*, lightly fragranced with rosemary, savory and thyme, occupied the bottom shelf. Above, three small racks of lamb sizzled, the outer layer of fat bubbling and browning. A few more minutes, and Em would take them out to rest while she finished whisking butter into the jus and steaming crunchy green beans.

Music floated from the stereo, the soft notes a counterpoint to the noise of the night. The weather bureau's promised storm front had arrived late afternoon, curdling up from the southwest, frigid and dangerous. Wind gusts splattered fat raindrops against the windows and branches from nearby trees scraped the walls. The front of the house was insulated from the worst by its thick blue dolomite and limestone walls, with only an occasional haunting roof moan or wind whistle to signal the wild conditions outside. In a flimsier house, winter could have easily swept its echoes into every corner, but even the newer brick and timber living area at the rear, with its big windows, open-plan design and stone floor, was as sturdy and insulated as the old structure, keeping the elements well cloaked. Winter might rage but it could never beat a stoked combustion stove, Em's homely decor and the cosy warmth of friends.

Tomorrow, according to the forecast, a change would come. God knows Em needed it. After a week of rain and high wind the yard was a mess of fallen branches, leaves and pine needles, with flattened plants, washed-out garden beds and soggy lawn patches. Kicki and Cutie were destroying the stables from boredom, pushing impatiently past Em in their race for outside the moment she opened the half-door each morning, with no pause for velvety donkey nuzzles or ear scratches.

Em returned to her jus. The stock, wine, pancetta and herbs had reduced to almost syrup. She turned off the gas, grabbed a mitt off the bench and opened the oven door. Delicious roast smells blasted out.

'God, that smells good,' said Jas, leaning over the breakfast bar to inspect the pan. 'Are they from Maloney's?'

'Horrigan's.'

'Ah.'

Em sensed her friends exchanging glances. Despite being the best butcher in town, she hadn't set foot in Maloney's for months. Although aware it was childish she couldn't help it. She'd thought her relationship with Trent was 'it'. Happily-ever-after fairytale land. Except it wasn't, and the realisation still smarted. But now, four months on, Em was uncertain if that was because she'd been tossed over for a hairdresser six years younger and far more fashionable and vivacious than her or because she'd really loved him. In dark moments, Em suspected the former, and found the realisation discomfiting.

With the lamb tucked in foil, she busied herself with the gravy, steadied for another dissection of the end of her relationship, but Teagan and Jas left her alone. So they should. Like Jasmine's affair with Mike Boland, they'd discussed it to pieces already.

Besides, there was Digby's engagement to discuss.

As Em finished her preparations, Jas and Teagan settled at their places around the massive ten-seater dining table. It had once graced Camrick's dining room, the dark, beeswaxed old timber with its dents and warps reflecting the warm light of the chandelier. Adrienne's modernisation scheme had almost seen it sold until Em stepped in and claimed it for Rocking Horse Hill. The table was far too big for her needs but she couldn't let it go. This was where she'd sat with Uncle James, drawing colourful crayon pictures of horses and hills on butcher's paper, where she'd learned to play canasta with nearly as much wile as him, the table where he'd patiently explained his sexuality to her when she'd innocently asked why he'd never married.

'So how did they meet?' asked Jas.

'A romantic bumping of trolleys in Woolworths. Well, not quite. Digby forgot to pack shaving cream and was trying to find the brand he uses when she accidentally rammed him.'

'Huh,' said Teagan. 'That old trick. She probably spotted him a mile off. Good-looking bloke, well dressed, probably reasonably well off. A bit of a ram and away you go. Except in Digby's case she hits the jackpot. Big time.'

Jas flopped her head to the side and raised her eyes. 'You are *such* a cynic.'

'And proud of it, too.' She refocused on Em. 'Will it be a church wedding?'

'I'd imagine so. I can't see Digby getting out of that.' With the exception of the early pioneers, all Wallace marriages were conducted in Levenham's Church of England, a late 1850s pink dolomite building that owed much of its impressively gabled construction and oversized spire to Wallace money.

'She might be Catholic.'

'She didn't strike me as the religious type, although she doesn't drink, so maybe she is.'

'Doesn't drink?' asked Jas, shuddering at the notion.

Teagan tilted her wine glass towards Em. 'Hardly a great match for a family of foodies like yours.'

'You never know, in time we might be able to show her the error of her ways.'

'Where will they live?'

Em made a face. 'Camrick, I suppose.'

'Not here?' asked Teagan.

A wash of fan-forced heat struck her cheeks as Em opened the oven door. She frowned as the idea of Digby and Felicity wanting Rocking Horse Hill took hold, and let it slide. Her brother wasn't one to renege on promises and, knowing how much she cherished the hill, Digby had sworn Em would have tenancy for as long as she wished, provided she maintained the property. Everyone knew when it came to Em that meant a lifetime.

Anyway, he'd always preferred town and Camrick. Plus Felicity was city born and bred. What would she want with an old farm far from fun and facilities?

'You know Dig. He's never been a fan of the hill.'

Jas nodded in agreement. 'And booting your sister out of the home she adores wouldn't make for happy Christmas dinners.'

'No.'

'Love does strange things to people,' warned Teagan. 'And what's going to happen when they decide to have kids? The stables make a great bachelor pad but they aren't exactly practical for someone starting a family. What woman would want to lug a pregnant belly up and down those stairs, let alone prams and bassinettes and all that washing.'

Teagan was right. Digby wouldn't tolerate it. He could move into Camrick, of course. Thanks to his inheritance it was, after all, his. But that would mean Granny B vacating her floor and finding other accommodation, or Adrienne relocating from the ground floor into the rooms opposite her mother's, neither of which Em could imagine happening. Besides, Uncle James had granted Granny B life tenancy and although she was fit she was still an elderly woman. It would be imprudent to shunt her out to the stables, or, God forbid, a nursing home. The family would never hear the end of it.

Which only left Rocking Horse Hill.

'I'm sure they'll sort something out,' said Em, hiding the twist of fear Teagan's warning had unleashed. 'It's not like Digby can't afford to buy a new place, and he did promise me the hill would always be mine.'

'Promises can be broken.'

'Tell me about it,' muttered Jas, before throwing warning looks at her friends. 'And before you ask, no, I don't want to talk about Mike and his shitty "word".'

Which, both Em and Teagan knew, was Jasmine's code for 'I want to discuss it desperately'. Exchanging a tiny smile, they let it slide. No point spoiling dinner with Mike. None of them had enough wine in their systems for that conversation.

Em carried the *pommes boulangère* to the table and placed the dish on a trivet alongside the beans for the girls to help themselves, and returned to the bench for their plates. The lamb racks stood with scraped rib bones upright, flesh pink and fragrant, the jus a rich puddle at their bases. Muffy raised her head, sniffing.

Em set down the plates and blew her a kiss. 'You can have the bones.'

'Best restaurant in Levenham,' said Teagan, smiling appreciatively at the contents of her plate.

Jas rubbed her palms together. 'Gorgeous, but you know me, I'm looking forward to dessert.'

'What are we having?'

'Chestnut bavarois with crème anglaise.' Em made a face. 'It had better be good. I had a hell of a time trying to source *marron* purée. Had to order it off the net along with a bunch of other ingredients I'll probably never use, just to make the cost of freight worthwhile.'

'The things you do for us,' said Jas, helping herself to a large scoop of potatoes. Unlike Teagan, who tended to eat with a birdlike fastidiousness that matched her sharp, heavily freckled features and feathery long copper hair, Jasmine's adoration of good food showed on her plate and well-rounded body. She wasn't fat or even overweight; she simply curved in all the right places. With her short dark curls, full-lipped mouth, clear pale skin and bouncy personality, men adored her. Frustratingly, the one man she adored back deserved castration. The bastard already had a wife, and children, but it was the false hope he kept giving Jas that made Em want to geld him. Three years of failed promises had worn gossamer thin, even, to Em's relief, for Jas.

They settled into a hearty discussion about the spring show season. The first event was still months away, but their horses all carried shaggy winter coats and fat grass bellies, and required considerable attention to bring to a competitive standard. With the three of them reducing costs by sharing transport, and with their jobs to work around, seasons required spreadsheet scheduling.

Only when Em was desperate would Adrienne man the shop, otherwise Em had to organise a relief assistant, an expense PaperPassion's profit margin could ill afford. Jas worked as a customer service specialist for a local building society and was often rostered for Saturday mornings. Though she coveted a different life, a hefty mortgage and damaging relationship had so far kept her stagnant. Teagan had to work around the demands of her parents' property, which in the last year or so, to everyone's great confusion, seemed to teeter constantly on the brink of forfeiture. The poor girl had been working herself ragged, trying to make machinery and fences in desperate need of replacement last a bit longer. Continually moving stock to different paddocks to preserve what little winter forage the Blisses had because they hadn't cut hay or renovated pastures since Teagan's brother left three years before.

A shared love of the land had brought Em and Teagan together in their teens, that feeling that their hearts were encased in a fist of soft soil, never to be released. To see her in despair over the farm she adored made Em ache with compassion.

Unfortunately, unlike show jumping, hacking offered little professional reward. This was a competition of aesthetics over athleticism, where the prettiest, most well-mannered and floaty-paced animal won. A win in the ring barely covered entry fees. The only way to make money was to on-sell the horses plucked off the racetrack or from under the knackers' nose and retrained, an enterprise Em gave up a few years ago. She didn't have time and she hated relinquishing animals she'd put so much work into and come to love.

Horse talk gave way to other topics. Worried about Teagan's lack of appetite, Em reached across to touch her arm. Only a month ago Teagan admitted to feeling like she was trapped at the bottom of a dark well with only a pinpoint of light far in the distance. Disturbed by the analogy, Em had tried on several occasions to get her to talk to a doctor, only to fail each time. Just going through a bad patch, Teagan assured Em. Everything would be fine once the farm turned around. Except now months had passed with no change.

'How are things at home?'

'The same.' Teagan smiled wanly. 'Dad's still hiding in his office, going over the books or whatever it is he does. Mum sits in the lounge, knitting and watching telly with this pinched look on her face.'

'And you?'

'Working my arse off. God, I hope this season's better than the last.' She fiddled with her cutlery and sighed. 'I sold the last of my cows this week. There's just not enough feed to keep them going through to the spring. I promised the sale money to Dad, to help out.' She bit her lip. 'But how can I when he hasn't paid me any wages for a month? I need money to live too.'

Jas slapped her palm on the table. 'Don't you dare give him that money. Not until he lets you look over the books.'

'I told you, he won't let me.'

'Then I think Jas is right,' said Em gently. 'You have to protect yourself in case it all goes under.'

Teagan shook her head. 'It can't go under. It can't. The farm's all I've worked for.'

'I know, but it's like me and the hill. No matter how I feel about the place, how much I love it and could never leave, the truth is it's not actually mine. It's Digby's, to do with as he chooses, just as the farm belongs to your parents, to do with as they want.'

'But your situation is hardly mine. For starters, Digby's loaded. All we seem to be doing is going broke. If things don't improve Mum and Dad won't have any control over anything anyway. It'll be the bank's call.'

'You need to see those books,' said Em. 'That farm is on some of the most productive land in the district. There's no way it should be going under.' She leaned closer. 'Promise me you won't give him that money until you see the books and find out where the hell all the cash is disappearing to.'

Teagan nodded but Em knew her well enough to know it meant little. When it came to the farm, Teagan was as bad as her with Rocking Horse Hill.

Sensing a change of tone was needed, Jas sat back with her hands over her belly. 'I always knew there was a good reason I had you as a friend. That lamb was amazing. As were the potatoes. If you weren't a girl, I'd marry you.'

'Just as well. I couldn't tolerate sharing a bed with someone who sleep-talks as much as you.'

'I can't help it. It's my vivid imagination. Speaking of which, how's that sexy Saxon going?' she asked, referring to the hero of *The Ballad of the White Horse*, King Alfred. When she'd seen a photograph of his statue at Winchester that Em had downloaded for research, complete with crown, shield and upraised sword, Jas had developed a hero-crush.

'Not bad. About a third of the way through the calligraphy.'

'But you only started it a month ago,' said Teagan. 'That's great progress.'

Em shrugged. 'There are only so many times I can clean the shelves and count stock. With the shop dead I've had plenty of time to work.'

She carried their plates to the sink and checked out the window. Enough light spilled out into the ebony night to expose the bent branches of the fruit trees lining this side of the yard and the flooded flower and berry fruit boxes that separated the orchard from the drive. Though the window was too small to capture more than the far, tapered end of the crater, she could sense its presence. Like a thrum deeper than the wind, as though the mountain was burrowing its ancient roots deeper into the earth as anchor against the assault.

Em stepped out of the way as Teagan arrived with the other dishes.

At the bench, Jas leaned over the desserts. 'They look amazing, as alw—'

A roaring crack of lightning ripped the air. Outside, the night exploded with phosphorescent light. The house shuddered, rattling the huge glass panes of the lounge. Em whirled back to the window and cupped her hands to the glass as another ear-splitting crash rent the sky, followed by more blinding white light. 'Oh, my God!'

'What is it?' asked Jas, scrambling to her side. 'Holy shit!'

Teagan peered between them. 'What?'

'It's one of the cypresses.' Em tried to assess the extent of the damage through the rain slick. 'Along the fence line. Looks like it's split.'

'What, like in half?'

'I think so. I can see exposed timber.' She let out a shaky breath.

'It's just a pine.'

'A pine planted nearly a hundred years ago as memorial to all the farm workers who died in the Great War.' She rubbed her face, forcing away the burn of rising tears.

'I'm sorry,' said Jas.

Em let her hand drop. Perhaps it wouldn't look so bad in the morning. At least the rain meant there was no risk of fire. 'I should check on the animals. Make sure they aren't frightened.' 'We'll come with you,' said Teagan.

'No point all of us getting wet.' Muffy had snuck into the kitchen to press her warm body against Em's leg. She stroked the dog's soft fur. 'You stay here and protect Jas and Teagan. I won't be long.'

'Then we can all sit around the fire, scoffing your dessert and drinking too much,' said Jas.

Teagan nodded. 'And planning your new sister-in-law-to-be's hen's night.'

'What if she's not a hen's night kind of girl?'

Jas grinned. 'Then we'll just have to turn her into one.'

Three

Granny B picked up a length of cypress branch, inspected the pale, ragged end and slung it away. Two splotches of colour seeped through her powdery makeup, giving her the over-rouged appearance of a porcelain doll. There was a stoop to her back, a slight sag in her shoulders, and her tread seemed to lack its usual purpose. Em understood. She'd felt the same yesterday, standing at the edge of the wreckage in the frigid Saturday dawn, her heart tight with sorrow as she surveyed the cypress.

It wasn't the tree so much. Trees grew and fell all the time – such was the cycle of life. It was the hole in the Avenue of Honour, the way the line of dense canopy abruptly faltered and opened to the sky, the shattered cypress's remains jutting into the rift like bleached and broken bones.

Granny B returned to Em's side and dug into the pocket of her Harris tweed coat, extracting a thin cigar and a beautifully etched rose-gold S. T. Dupont lighter, a thirty-fifth wedding anniversary present from Grandpa Philps. 'Who did you say this company was?'

'Argyle and Sons. They're based in Mortlake. Unfortunately they can't come for a few weeks.'

Em's gaze returned to the tree. Half of it had pitched onto the fence and across Stanislaus Road, dragging wire and old posts down with it. Em had used a tractor and chains to haul the worst of it to the verge but there was little she could do about the fence until the site was cleared. The remainder of the tree had caved inward, held from total collapse by the strength of its branches, dug into the dark soil like braced arms fighting the inevitable.

Muffy padded around the scattered needle clusters, bark strips and cones, snuffling and scratching. The air smelled glorious. A pure scent, strangely uplifting despite the sorrow of the tree's loss. Granny B flicked her lighter and pine gave way to fragrant tobacco. Em let the silence stand as her grandmother smoked and mourned.

Weak morning light coated the remaining trees, turning their outer canopy vivid green while their interiors remained shadowed. The rain had stopped at last. As predicted, Saturday had seen the wind swing to the south-west, driving the lumbering clouds eastwards. Now the sky shone with the sublime deep cold blue of a southern winter.

Em scanned the debris. She would have to keep some part of the tree, a cone or piece of timber, something, to touch and remember while she and future Wallaces waited for a replacement cypress to mature.

Every one of the half-dozen nurseries she'd phoned had no stocks of *Cupressus macrocarpa*. It was, she'd been told, a highly unfashionable tree and difficult to acquire. She'd be better off collecting seed and growing seedlings herself. For a while Em feared the gap was destined to be permanent. Finally, after extensive googling, she discovered a promising link to a specialist grower in Beaconhills, on Melbourne's far eastern side. A quick phone call and she had her prize, one that could even be delivered. At a price.

Her research had also led her to a business that harvested old cypress trees from farm sites and on-sold the timber to carpenters and woodworkers. For a single tree, collection would be expensive but Em felt it was the right way to proceed. The timber would have another life, and that seemed fitting somehow. As though the soldiers' memorial, and perhaps traces of Rocking Horse Hill, would live on elsewhere.

With a deep sigh Granny B flicked her half-finished cigar into the grass and ground it into the soil with the heel of her long leather boot. 'Your great-grandmother had names for all the trees.'

'After the soldiers?'

She nodded. 'This one was Second Lieutenant Stanley. I remember because he won the Military Medal at Polygon Wood only to be killed the next month at Broodseinde Ridge.'

'We'll replant. In the spring. Make it whole again.'

Her grandmother turned from the avenue to contemplate the crater. Em followed suit, grateful for the change of weather and the weak, though welcome, cast of sun. The day was sad enough without drizzle.

The ashy paths that once snaked to Rocking Horse Hill's summit were fading, overgrown with weed or hidden by an encroaching rash of plastic-collared seedlings, planted by a local Landcare group determined to rehabilitate the crater's eroded and denuded slopes. No matter how important their work, Em couldn't suppress her dismay at the sight of all the trees. They spoiled the hill's majesty; made it just another extinct volcano in a land dotted with many. Some of the best afternoons of her childhood were spent on those slopes: sliding from top to bottom on her bum, riding the hill like a giant, dirty slippery dip. Her mother exasperated by her wrecked jeans and inevitable scrapes, while her grandmother and uncle secretly encouraged the fun.

'Ugly, aren't they?' said Granny B, as though reading her mind.

'Just a bit, but they'll go. Eventually.'

What the crater would look like then, Em didn't know. Darker, she supposed. Perhaps a little mysterious, with the soft trees masking the hill's true stony nature. She smiled slightly. As a child Em had cultivated all sorts of romantic ideas about the hill, and spent countless days exploring its slopes and crags, imagining secret passages that led, Narnia-like, to parallel universes of mystical animals, kings and brave knights. But there never was and never would be anything mysterious or romantic about the volcano. Thousands of years ago the earth suffered indigestion and burped up molten rock and Rocking Horse Hill was the result. Even so, her heart continued to resist logic. Em loved the hill too intensely for pragmatism, and a person's sense of home wasn't something that could be rationalised or calculated. That connection belonged to the soul.

'Felicity seems keen to visit the farm,' said Granny B.

'Does she? That's great.'

Her grandmother gave a non-committal 'mmm' and bent to ruffle Muffy's ears.

'You don't agree?'

'I'm not sure I agree with the suddenness of all this. Your brother has never been one to make decisions in a hurry.'

'He's in love, Gran.'

'Apparently.'

'And she's beautiful.'

'Beauty alone does not make a marriage, Emily, as your mother will well attest.'

Although she'd never approved of Adrienne's choice of husband, Granny B didn't often refer to the breakdown of her daughter's marriage. For all his faults, Henry Jones was still Em's and Digby's father, even if they rarely saw him. A move to Sydney, remarriage and a new, young family kept him busy. And even Em understood how insular and exclusive the Wallaces, with their name, privilege and deep pride in their history, could feel to outsiders. A feeling she hoped Felicity would never experience.

'How is she settling in?'

'Why don't you come and see for yourself?' Done with the hill, Granny B snatched up a small cypress cone, filed it in her pocket and began marching towards Em's four-wheel-drive, her long coat flapping and Muffy chasing her heels.

***

Em knocked on the door of the old stables and waited. When there was no answer she glanced towards Granny B, who was still standing by the car, lacquered silver-white hair shiny in the rising sun. Her grandmother flicked her hand, indicating that Em should enter but Em had no intention of barging in. Once she would have knocked, called out and bounded up the stairs, but Felicity's arrival had changed things. For Digby, life now meant lazy Sunday sex, intimacy, indulgence, free of interruption from presumptuous sisters.

She stepped back and looked to the upper floor windows. Digby's lodgings consisted of a narrow downstairs entrance area, mainly used for coats, boots and other outdoorsy items, and a long open-plan first floor room that ran the entire length of the building, over what had once been stables but was now a five-car garage. The centre window was slightly ajar. Em moved beneath it, preparing to call up, but was halted by the electronic flourishes and sword clangs of Digby's favourite video game.

Em felt a surge of sympathy for Felicity. When in thrall her brother's world condensed to action and reflex, driven by sound and millions of pixels, which was fine for Digby but frustrating for anyone who wanted his attention. She retraced her steps and pushed the door open. Calling his name loudly, Em levered off her boots and padded up the stairs, continuing to announce herself as she went.

'Hang on,' said Digby, frantically pressing buttons.

Em watched in amusement as Digby carried on with the game. On the large flat television screen behind him, the Prince of Ulpherstone swayed at the edge of a precipice, a red-eyed green-and gold dragon roaring fire at his back.

She inspected the room while he continued to battle. The apartment remained pure bachelor pad: dark leather sofa and recliners, heavy square-cornered timber furniture, a coffee table with agricultural and horticultural journals in stacks. Discarded clothes littered the floor and bed of the far sleeping area, black and white striped doona forming a rumpled bank where it had been tossed back on rising. But unlike the kitchenette's normal state, the sink was empty of its usual pile of dishes, the dishwasher chugged quietly beneath the sink and there was a sweet scent to the air, like floral body wash or spray-on deodorant. A woman's smell.

The noise ceased. On the screen the dragon lay slain, the paused Prince's sword dripping with its blood.

'What are you doing in town?' asked Digby. Unlike his apartment, Digby appeared casually elegant in a pair of jeans and a checked shirt with the sleeves rolled midway up his forearms. Leather deck shoes encased his sockless feet. His jaw was unshaven and his dark hair, the same shade as Em's, stuck out at messy angles as though sex rubbed. Even dishevelled, his long lean Wallace frame and features kept him handsome. Once, he'd been too pretty, too poetic-looking, but age was at last beginning to sharpen his soft edges into masculinity.

'I came to see your fiancée, actually.'

'She's in the kitchen with Mum, getting a cooking lesson.' He scratched absently at his forearm. 'It's something she never really learned.'

Em blinked. 'What, at all?'

He shrugged, as if never learning to cook was perfectly normal. 'I don't think her mum had much interest in it.'

'Yeah, but —'

'Not every family's like ours, Em.'

'No,' said Em quickly, hearing the defensiveness in Digby's tone and realising how judgemental she must have sounded. 'Of course not. So why aren't you over with them?'

'I was but Mum ordered me out. She said I was distracting Flick and getting in the way.'

'Ah. Well, you know what us Wallace girls are like with our kitchens.' Em settled into a leather armchair. It'd been weeks since they'd last had a proper chat. 'Felicity's settling in okay, then?'

'Seems to be. Gran's being a bit stiff towards her, though.'

'Give her time. She's just worried about the suddenness of your engagement, that's all.'

He gazed towards the window, where the sky stretched clear and infinite. 'I reckon she thinks I'm being used, like with Cait.' Digby turned back to Em. 'I'm not. Felicity's nothing like Cait. She loves me. She had no idea who I was when we met. She'd never even heard of the Wallaces.' He looked down at the game console, smiling to himself. 'She was just this beautiful girl who wanted to talk to me.' He looked up again, still smiling. 'I've never met anyone like her, Em. Fragile but strong at the same time. I still can't believe she loves me. Not the name.' Voice cracking, he gestured towards Camrick. 'Not all this. Just me.'

To Em's discomfort, his words didn't fill her with pleasure in his happiness. Instead they brought envy of his joy, his fortune at finding someone. Digby's heart was bloated with love, his emotions fierce and magnificent. Something Em hadn't felt for a long time.

She swallowed her spiky feelings. 'It's good to see you happy, Dig.

Properly happy, I mean. It's been too long.'

'Yeah,' he said, suddenly sheepish, looking away and blinking rapidly.

Em let him recover for a moment while her own emotions settled. 'Gran says Felicity's keen to visit the farm. You'll have to bring her out one afternoon so we can climb the hill.'

'Maybe next weekend. We'll see.' A flush rose up his neck. 'I kind of want to keep her to myself for a bit, you know? Anyway, you'll only tell her things about me.'

'That's the plan.' Grinning, she rose. 'Come on. Let's go and annoy Mum.'

A delicious aroma swirled the moment they entered Camrick's hall. Savoury, meaty scents that put Em's tastebuds on alert. She smiled, wondering what her mother had made, knowing from the smell that it would be perfect for the cold day, and considered whether to hang around for lunch.

'Something smells good,' she called, heading for the kitchen, the hall's floorboards creaking comfortingly underfoot. As a child she used to fantasise it was the house talking, welcoming her inside. Uncle James humoured the idea, telling her the house had secrets it wanted to reveal; all she had to do was interpret its language. Em never did, but the idea still filled her with warmth.

In the kitchen, Adrienne's trusty pasta machine was clipped to one end of the granite bench. Felicity stood at the head, feeding in a thick sheet of dough while Adrienne worked the crank handle with one hand and supported the emerging thin sheet of pasta with the other. They were smiling, happy.

Like mother and daughter.

'Hello, darling,' said Adrienne. 'I'm teaching Felicity how to make pappardelle.'

'And duck ragù,' said Felicity, all trace of Tuesday's uncertainty gone. She glanced at Em, beautiful despite her flour-dusted cheeks. 'Doesn't it smell wonderful?'

'It does,' said Em, entering the kitchen on legs that felt like stilts.

'It's Digby's favourite,' continued Felicity in that same husky, almost smug voice. 'I've never had duck before. Mrs Wallace —'

Em's mother interjected. 'I've told you – it's Adrienne. You make me sound old.'

'*Adrienne*,' said Felicity, throwing a thankful look at her, 'used duck egg in the dough, too. I've never seen a yolk so yellow!'

'Yes,' said Em, lifting the lid on the pasta pot. A blast of steam heated her skin further. God, she was pathetic. So what if pasta making had always been their mother–daughter thing? That didn't mean Felicity couldn't enjoy it too. She was, after all, becoming a Wallace. There was nothing to be jealous of. Chastened, she turned back. Digby was already making a pest of himself, his arms around Felicity, nuzzling her neck. The look Adrienne gave the couple was more indulgent than remonstrative. 'It's because they're richer than chicken eggs. You wait, this will be the best pasta you've ever tasted.'

Felicity smiled and Em was struck by how delicate she was. Delicate bones, delicate hands – even her tiny nostrils flared delicately with each kiss Digby planted on her creamy skin. Her shoulders, though, were very straight, holding her simple white cotton shirt so it draped without wrinkles. The shirt was tucked into a faded pair of jeans that were several seasons old and did nothing to flatter her petite figure. They exposed a sliver of pale skin above the line of her white sport socks and cheap runners. Em wondered how long it would be before her mother took Felicity shopping. Perhaps they could do it together, a girls' trip to Adelaide, lunch at that new city restaurant Adrienne wanted to try.

'Adrienne said they came from your duck at Rocking Horse Hill.'

Em nodded. 'Her name's Chelsea. You'll have to come out to the farm and meet her.'

'What a lovely idea,' said Adrienne. 'Perhaps Digby and Felicity could make an afternoon of it. Stop for dinner afterwards.'

'Sure.' Remembering her earlier thoughts about the family and outsiders, she held Felicity's gaze, her tone sincere. 'I'd love to have you out. You're welcome any time.'

They all looked down as an insistent meow caught their attention. Peaches had crept in to sit at Felicity's feet, unnerving, pale Siamese eyes narrowed upwards, tail snaking.

Adrienne made a moue of disapproval and pushed a toe into the cat's side. 'Out with you now.' Peaches retaliated with an ankle swipe and one of those toothy hisses that again reinforced Em's preference for sweet-natured, obedient dogs.

'Oh, please don't,' said Felicity, scooping up Peaches. 'I love cats. I love all animals.' She lifted her face to Em's. 'Digby said you have all sorts at Rocking Horse Hill. Horses and donkeys and chickens. That must be wonderful.'

'It is. Mostly.'

Her mother raised her eyebrows.

Em gave a resigned sigh. 'Kicki keeps escaping. I can't figure out how he's doing it either.' She turned back to Felicity. 'Kicki's one of my donkeys.'

Mention of the donkeys triggered a lively discussion about Em's menagerie and other animals from the hill's history, including great-grandma Agnes's filthy-tempered Jersey milking cow, and a mischievous goat herd that was great for weed control but caused no end of strife. The stories flooded the kitchen with merriment, and left Camrick alive with the sound of family enjoying one another.

Finally liberating a loudly protesting Peaches from his fiancée, Digby dumped the cat outside while Felicity washed her hands and resumed her pasta duties. The jealousy Em felt on arrival faded as her mother demonstrated how to roll the dough to the right width, cut the pasta into rough but artful strips, and drape the golden threads over the multi-armed rotary drying rack that Em had bought Adrienne for Christmas several years before. Negativity was impossible to maintain while her brother perched on the stool alongside her, a dopey, lovesick expression on his face.

'You're staying for lunch?' asked Adrienne, when all the dough was rolled and cut. 'We'll have it now, if you like, so you can get back home.'

'Hard to pass up your ragù, Mum.'

The kitchen was so cosy that Em didn't want to leave, anyway. Her afternoon ride could wait a while longer. 'I'll call Gran down. What's she doing, anyway?'

'Smoking on her balcony, probably,' said Adrienne, before glancing at Digby and Felicity and mouthing, 'Sulking.'

Em frowned. Granny B wasn't the sort to sulk. Snap and snipe, yes, but not sulk. Em's eyes slid to Felicity, hoping the young girl didn't feel the snub, but she and Digby were too enraptured with one another to notice.

'I think she's a bit upset about the tree.'

'I'm perfectly fine,' interrupted a tetchy voice. 'Your mother made it clear I was quite unwelcome, so I took the hint and left her to it.'

Em hid a smile as Granny B sauntered in with a well-filled crystal tumbler, her eyes as glittery as the glass's cut surface. She paused to survey the scene before taking a large slug of Scotch.

'You were being disruptive.'

'I was not!'

Adrienne rolled her eyes. 'She was, you know.'

Em could imagine. Wallace women were all exceptional cooks who found leaving things be in the kitchen almost impossible.

Granny B sat at her place by the bench while Adrienne began to tidy, shooing Felicity away when she attempted to help.

'We might nick off for a shower,' said Digby, his mind clearly on more than showering.

Adrienne checked the clock. 'Make sure you're back by one.'

Three pairs of eyes watched them as Digby slung his arm around Felicity's waist and urged her out. They'd barely turned into the hall before Felicity was giggling.

Adrienne smiled. 'I can't recall the last time Digby was so happy.'

'Must be all that sex,' said Granny B.

Em nudged her. 'Jealous?'

'I am, rather. It's been quite some time.' She sighed. 'Sadly, all my male friends are past it and Levenham has a distinct shortage of suitable toy boys.' She slipped her granddaughter a sly look. 'Not for want of trying, mind.'

'Oh, Mum,' said Adrienne, turning her back and leaving Em and Granny B to grin at one another.

On Digby's and Felicity's return, Adrienne sent them to Uncle James's cellar for a bottle of Coonawarra cabernet to enjoy with lunch, an exercise that took far longer than it should have.

'Rabbits,' muttered Granny B in Em's ear, and once again Em experienced a twinge of envy at her brother's luck.

The ragù, as always, was divine; the duck-egg pasta rich and silky. Conversation floated from how comfortable Felicity was finding the stables, to how hard it was for an unskilled person to find work, drifting on to the disadvantage and crime levels of the area in which she grew up.

'You'll find Levenham rather dull in comparison,' said Granny B.

'Oh,' said Felicity, exchanging a secretive smile with Digby that caused his cheeks to redden, 'I doubt that.'

Digby cleared his throat and managed to drag his attention to his grandmother. 'There's plenty of crime here, Gran, if you look.'

'With much of it secreted away in the Wallace family vault,' said Adrienne before switching to address Felicity. 'You'd be surprised how many of Digby's ancestors were crooks.'

'Only Gilbert,' said Em. 'And he was never convicted.'

Bending closer to Felicity, Adrienne lowered her voice as though about to reveal a great conspiracy. 'Gilbert scammed the land office.'

'Manipulated the rules,' corrected Em.

'Cheated,' said Digby.

'Be careful with your criticism of Gilbert, Digby,' said Granny B. 'It's thanks to him you possess the wealth you do.'

Felicity reached out to grip Digby's hand. 'It must be wonderful to have such a rich family history.'

Em thought on that as she took a sip of wine. 'All families have a rich history. It's just that some are more colourful than others. That doesn't mean they're not special.'

'Mine sure isn't.'

Curious, Em cocked her head. 'How do you mean?'

Felicity shrugged. 'I never knew my grandparents. Mum was a ward of the state and Dad's parents died when he was young. He had a brother but he committed suicide when he was nineteen.'

'How sad,' said Adrienne.

'It was normal where I was from. I was lucky in one way. At least I knew my dad was my dad. Most of the kids I went to school with had no clue.'

Em was already aware of some of this from what Adrienne had told her, but to hear it from Felicity herself gave it a vividness she hadn't expected. It made her consider her own privileged upbringing, the closeness of her family. Even with Henry and the divorce, she and Digby knew their roots. She was a Wallace, with a history that stretched back to the district's settlement. She could trace it back further if she wanted – Uncle James loved genealogy and his records were stored in filing cabinets in one of the spare rooms on Granny B's floor. Felicity appeared to have nothing but her immediate family, who, from her tone, didn't appear to be close. How lonely that must feel.

'That's the past,' said Digby, rising to curl his palm around the back of her neck and stroke his thumb tenderly under her ear as he kissed her. 'Now you have us.'

The caress was gentle and heartfelt, the moment intimate with promise, her brother and his fiancée lost in a world that registered no one but them. Em looked away, feeling like an intruder, while her own desire to experience a love that intense again rose in a hot wave.

When she looked back, Felicity was smiling at her, the way a sister would, with understanding and sympathy. Em returned the smile. No, Felicity was nothing like Digby's gold-digging ex, Cait.

This girl wanted family.

And Em would make sure she had it.

***

Em sighed, carefully placed her pen down and recapped the ink bottle. Ruined parchment scattered PaperPassion's counter. No matter how hard she concentrated her hand refused to remain steady. As they had often since the day before, her thoughts drifted towards Digby and Felicity. Em rarely felt sorry for herself but since Felicity's arrival she'd become increasingly aware of the hollow that Trent's lost love had left, and wished that she, too, had someone to share her life with, whose protective strong hold forged an armour against loneliness.

Thanks to improved weather the street was busier than it had been in weeks, yet the space between customers felt infinite, and Mondays were commonly slow. She'd survived the morning, had even found it enjoyable. It had taken a good deal of experimentation but Em had finally managed to string PaperPassion's new stock up with fishing line, transforming this season's jewel-coloured notebooks into swooping birds and hovering butterflies. From the street, where the line couldn't be seen, her new window display appeared a life-filled terrarium. She'd draped off-cuts of satin dress linings in varying shades of green behind it, creating a bower of lushness. More satin sheathed the floor, the surface scattered with silk orchids and fern fronds. But it was the notebooks that made the window spectacular, glowing with the promise of tropical pleasure, a tease for those seeking warmth from winter.

Of everything she and her mother had in common, it was their artistic streak that dominated. Em channelled hers into her calligraphy, illuminations and gardening, Adrienne into cooking, fashion and home decorating. It was a good Wallace gene to inherit, and Em was proud of it.

With another sigh, she tucked the parchment into piles and stared out through the shop's glass door at the street. A woman halted to admire the display before glancing at her watch and moving on. Em checked her own watch. Hours remained, and caffeine would help her through the rest of the day. Giving the street a last scan for approaching customers, she headed into the storeroom.

The bell over PaperPassion's entrance door tinkled as she sugared her tea and added a drop of milk. Unconcerned, she took a sip. The stock was safe enough. It was probably someone she knew and PaperPassion wasn't exactly a shoplifter's paradise. Kids occasionally stole a fruit-scented eraser or coloured pencil but even that was rare, and the cost negligible. The worst shrinkage occurred from rough handling, when customers tossed notebooks back into racks without care, bending pages and denting covers.

With a welcoming smile on her face, she rattled apart the bead curtain and stepped back into the shop. A man stood with his back to her at the front shelves, flicking through a sky-blue B5-sized hardcover notebook. His hair was light brown and slightly too long, curling over the edge of his collar. A navy fleece jumper fitted snugly across his wide shoulders, before tapering to hug narrow hips. He wore light khaki cotton-drill trousers, the sort favoured by tradies, and though loose they couldn't hide the muscularity of his legs. His boots were brown suede and thick-soled. Framed against the artificially bright wall of stationary, he appeared earthy, solid and very, very familiar.

She checked his left hand. Three fingers, from the little to the middle, were missing, severed at the second knuckle.

Em placed her mug down behind the counter, her nerves sizzling. She knew that agonising boyhood injury. She knew those legs, those shoulders, that hair. She knew everything about this man and more.

Joshua Sinclair turned and smiled the same smile that had pierced her cool as a teenager. The smile that had made her first give him her heart, then her body, and let him preciously tend both until the day she'd snatched them back and broken two people in the process.

His eyes hadn't changed. The lids still tilted at the edges, giving him a thoughtful, almost sad, expression that Em had considered mysterious and deeply sexy back then. He had a way of holding her gaze with a toe-curling intensity, his molasses-coloured eyes not moving from hers. It was as if she possessed something he coveted but didn't know how to take.

For a heady moment, as his eyes widened in recognition, she felt that gaze again and her heart lifted with the hope that perhaps time had led to forgiveness or, at least, perspective. Then his smile died, and with it her dream.

'Emily.' He looked away, his mouth compressing, before staring straight back at her.

And everything in his stony expression revealed that no matter what emotions the years had softened, bitterness wasn't one of them.

Four

Karen had said PaperPassion was Em's shop. What Josh's youngest sister failed to reveal was that Em actually worked in it.

Emily Wallace-Jones, working in a shop. He'd laugh if he wasn't feeling like such a dick.

She stepped closer, all legs and haughty beauty, her pale hazel eyes revealing nothing, and held out her hand as though he were some kind of tradesman instead of the man she'd lost her virginity with. The fact that he *was* a tradesman made no difference. It was the gesture that told him all he needed to know.

'Josh, it's good to see you.'

Her voice held the same rich smoothness and articulation he'd once loved. Not affected, but every word given its proper due. He gave her hand a brief shake, resisting the urge to say, 'Is it?' Her grip was firm, her skin silky, and he was cursed with a flashing reminder of the first time she'd really touched him, lying face to face on one of Rocking Horse Hill's sun-warmed crags, her shy exploration an exquisite torment he wanted to last forever.

He tapped the book he'd chosen against the fist of his curled left hand, the habit of hiding his fingers ingrained even from people who knew him. The hiding was normal, the nervous tapping something else. An annoying something else.

'Filling in, are you?'

'No, this is where I work now.'

He scanned the shelves. 'Nice hobby.'

She crossed her arms and shifted her weight to one hip, the gesture both defiant and protective. 'It's not a hobby; it's my livelihood.'

Josh tapped the book again, the sound reverberating in the tense quiet. Her livelihood? What happened to living the life of landed gentry, like her mother?

Throwing him a look he couldn't interpret she stepped towards the shelves and spoke briskly. 'This is the new winter range. Beautiful covers. I take it you're after a notebook? For yourself or someone else?'

'It's for Mum.'

She stilled, her mouth softening. 'I heard about her illness. I'm sorry.'

He nodded. Though they came from vastly different backgrounds, Em had always liked his mum. He'd often discovered them chatting in the kitchen. The sight always left him feeling warm and hopeful, as if maybe they could fit each other's worlds. Time, though, had proved otherwise.

'She wants to keep a journal. For Karen and Sal's kids. Just in case . . .' He looked towards the street. He hated that 'just in case' thought. Just in case couldn't happen. Not to his mum.

A hand curled around his forearm. He looked down at Em's long fingers, with their blunt unpolished nails, and then at her, drawn to the sympathy in her eyes.

'She'll be all right.'

'Yeah.' He cleared his throat and held up the notebook. 'I'll take a couple of these.'

She smiled and shook her head. 'You want something more special than that for your mum.' Em searched for a moment, before plucking a glossy red-and-blue patterned notebook, then a green and yellow one from the shelves. She pointed to each in turn. 'Ruby and sapphire, emerald and citrine.'

Josh looked closer. The covers weren't patterned as he'd thought, but covered in photo image after photo image of faceted gemstones. Big, small, at angles. As she waved them they glinted, as though the jewels were real. His mum would love them.

'They're good. Thanks.'

'You're welcome. Would you like me to gift-wrap them? It's no trouble.' She paused before adding, 'No charge.'

That simple additional phrase set his jaw. 'They're fine as is.'

'Of course.' But to his irritation she took a length of wrapping paper the colour of weak tea and printed with rows of antique-looking type, and folded it around the centre of the books, like a wide belt. A dark-blue ribbon of paper raffia, the same colour as the shop's signage, followed. The knot arranged to her satisfaction, she handed him the package, shaking her head as he reached for his wallet. 'A gift.'

'I don't need your charity, Em.'

'It's not charity, nor am I doing this for you. It's for your mum.' She waggled the package. 'Take it.'

He hesitated then snatched the notebooks. He shouldn't give a rat's arse how she saw him, but he did. Still.

'Thanks.' He nodded, in a rush to get out of the shop, to escape these dumb feelings. 'I'll see you.'

He was almost at the door when she said his name. She stood near the counter, one hand curled on the top, the other awkwardly on her hip. He'd never known her to be awkward. Emily Wallace-Jones was all poise and elegance. Any lack of confidence or nerves she hid with Wallace aloofness and tight words. But the quiet, uncertain way she said his name held none of that. He faced her, waiting. The hand on her hip fell.

'Karen told me about your divorce. I'm sorry.'

He considered for a moment, wondering why she'd brought it up. 'Why should you be sorry? Sometimes stuff just doesn't work out.' He could tell that she'd caught his meaning. The 'like us' lingering unsaid.

'I heard you were going out with Trent Maloney. He's a good bloke.' And not the person he would have imagined for Em. Then again, she'd once shown herself partial to another bloke from the wrong side of town. Why not a butcher to go with the cabinetmaker?

'We're no longer together.'

'Right.'

She stepped away from the counter, stopping halfway across the shop floor, near a bin of rubbers and pencil sharpeners in garish fruit shapes and colours. She picked up a strawberry-shaped rubber and bent it back and forth. 'Can I say something?'

He shrugged.

'I also wanted to say I'm sorry. About what happened with us, I mean.'

'It was a long time ago, Em.'

'It was. But I still want you to know that I wish I hadn't done what I did. I've never had the chance to say it before.'

He looked back at the street, at the people hurrying from shop to shop, catching up on chores they'd let slide for drier days. Diagonally across from the shop, where Hubbard Lane joined McArthur Street, stood the limestone and pink dolomite Australian Arms Hotel, its iron-laced wraparound verandah protecting a pair of shivering smokers in the new outdoor area. It used to be a cosy pub, great for counter meals and a yarn with mates. He'd been away too long to know what it was like now but change never came fast in Levenham.

He looked back at Em, assessing her for a moment, assessing his own curiosity. A few minutes ago he thought he had her worked out; now he wasn't so sure.

'How about a drink tonight?' He nodded towards the pub. 'Across the road.'

'I can't, I'm sorry.'

He should have expected that. The skin of his cheeks itching, he placed his hand on the door handle, the stubs of his other fingers tight around the notebook parcel.

A step sounded behind him. 'But I'm free Wednesday night. How does six-ish sound?'

He took a careful breath before answering. 'Fine.'

'Great. I'll see you there.'

He nodded again and left, heart thumping, and with a stupid hopeful churn in his guts.

***

'They're beautiful,' said Michelle Sinclair, smiling at her son. 'Just what I wanted.' She eyed his face, suspicious and knowing at the same time. 'Did you choose them yourself?'

Josh resisted the urge to lie. 'Emily did.'

'Em? You saw her? How is she?'

'Good by the look of her.' He dragged over a chair and sat down. It felt strange talking beside his mother's daybed like this, as though she was a patient in a hospital. His sisters were used to it but he still flinched at the weirdness. Everything about this horrible illness made him flinch. His mother, the best of people, didn't deserve the ravage of cancer. She didn't deserve the shit chemo did to her either. At least now, thanks to the local hospital's expanded oncology services, she could rest at home with friends and family, surrounded by love instead of isolated in impersonal accommodation in Adelaide.

'Such a beautiful girl. Strange how she's never married.' His mother stroked the notebook covers. 'Still pining for you, perhaps.'

'Somehow, I don't think so.'

The catheter port, now permanently inserted above her left breast, an inch below her collarbone for ease of drug administration, shifted under her T-shirt as she reached out to him. 'I don't care what you say. She loved you.'

'Yeah, that's why she dumped me for that wanker Stephen Jacobs. So,' he said, keen to get off the topic, 'has Dad said anything to you?'

'Not yet.'

'Do you think it would help if I showed him the projections again?'

'Leave it a bit. You know what he's like. Your father's a cautious man.' She smiled gently. 'He has a lot on his plate right now.'

Josh looked at his hands. 'I couldn't have chosen worse timing.'

'No. It gives him something to think about besides me.' She returned her gaze to the garden, her longing palpable.

The house and garden were her passions. Theirs was an old-fashioned working-class family. Josh's mum had settled into the traditional role of housewife the day she married. They always had home-cooked meals, mostly made from home-grown or local produce shared between neighbours and friends. Chocolate crackles, honey joys, cakes and slices when they got home from school. Simple crumbles or fruit set in jelly for desserts. Homemade tomato sauce on sausage rolls to rival the best any bakery could make. She volunteered in the canteen, helped with cake stalls, supplied water and oranges during football and netball. Drove Josh and his sisters to sports events as far away as Adelaide, and once even as far as Whyalla. When their nan was still alive, his mum ran story time at the old people's home, reading local history and memoirs, enjoying the reminiscences as much as her audience.

She was a farmer's daughter who'd married a townie and created a warm and loving home and a family to be proud of. Watching his mum in this back room, an extension his father had built as a present to the woman he loved, her face wrinkled and pale with illness, made Josh's guts clench with the unfairness of life.

He wanted to stay. He wanted to get the hell out too.

'So, what needs to be done?' he said, referring to the garden.

Plenty by the look of it. Pruning for starters, definitely weeding. Stakes in the veggie garden needed to be removed and stored. The broccoli needed harvesting and, from the ragged appearance of the leaves, a good spray. The peas needed training. The rhubarb patch was thick with stalks. Perhaps he could cut some, ask Sal how to make a crumble, serve it as a surprise.

She turned back to him. 'Nothing that can't wait. You have your own work.'

Unable to help it, he glanced to the left, towards the garage, where his father's well-equipped home workshop was located.

'Go on.' She nudged him. 'I want to write in my notebooks, anyway. And I can't do that with you moping about like your father.' When he didn't move, she put on her best mum's voice. 'Workshop. Now.'

He grinned and kissed her cheek, then pointed to the phone. 'Call if you need anything.'

'I'll be fine.'

'I mean it.'

'All right.' She swatted him away, trying to sound annoyed, but there was no disguising the love in her voice. 'You're as bad as Tommy.'

Josh left her. He walked down the drive towards the green Colorbond garage, breathing in the crisp air. No one mentioned it, not even to each other, but a subtle, disturbing scent clung to his mum that no shower gel or deodorant or perfume seemed to cover. It wasn't bad so much as wrong. In Adelaide, when he'd visited after her breast surgery, he'd assumed it was the hospital's odour, but it had followed her home, to Levenham. It drifted through the back room, her bedroom, through the kitchen and lounge. He'd sensed it in Karen's and his dad's car, too, and each time he did, dread seemed to hollow his insides.

The chemo had to work. It just had to.

He slid the garage door right across to let in light and air. The building hadn't seen a car in years. Josh wasn't certain it ever had. Benches took up much of the available space. Some cleared for working, others with machinery bolted on top. Quality saws – table, circular, band and mitre – that his dad had collected over a lifetime, each saved for. Planers and routers, sanders and clamps, more than a home workshop could ever need. All perfectly maintained, poised for work, silent and waiting.

The walls were lined with shelves. Plastic jars with screws, nails and other woodworking paraphernalia aligned in orderly rows. At the rear of the shed, fixed against the wall, was the broad timber workbench that Josh had helped his dad make, that he'd once, foolishly, tried to complete on his own, determined to show his dad his competency in techniques he was far from mastering. The sight of it always made his hand curl. Already an eerie itch was developing in fingers that no longer existed.

He ran his good hand over the sanded surface of the almost-finished kitchen trolley. The timber came from his client's Adelaide Hills property; from a magnificent red gum sacrificed to make way for a vineyard. Josh suspected laws were flouted during the tree's removal, but that hadn't stopped his client. Fines could be paid, lawyers brought in to mitigate punishment. What did a landscape's heritage matter? The tree was doomed to be kitchen furniture for a multi-millionaire. All Josh could do was achieve some sort of justice by using his craftsmanship to transform that natural history into something admirable.

He'd taken the commission even though it felt like a desecration. If he wanted his business to grow, he couldn't afford to be sentimental. Romanticism was for the rich, not working-class blokes like him, trying to make a buck.

Which made him wonder again what the hell he was doing meeting Em for a drink.

Curiosity, that's all. And surprise. How long had it been? He was thirty-two now, which made her thirty. She was seventeen when they'd fallen in love – correction – *he'd* fallen in love. Thirteen years ago, a lifetime. And she'd never married.

He shook his head and wrapped a wad of super-fine sandpaper around a block. Like that made a difference.

But it did.

*****

She was waiting when he arrived at the Arms, in the quieter back bar, seated at a tucked-away corner table to the left of the old granite fireplace. She sat very formally, straight-backed, legs together and slightly edged to one side, hands clasped in her lap. Almost an anomaly in this relaxed space.

He glanced at his watch and saw he was early by a good ten minutes.

'Hey,' he said, curling his heavy coat over the back of the chair opposite. The rain had stayed away, but the wind was as bitter as it could get this time of year, howling across the flat land from the sea. The pub, like most places around the district, was well insulated and snug, the fire burning hard. A good place for a warming drink.

She looked up and smiled. 'Hi.'

Quiet ticked. He curled his damaged hand against the draped coat collar. 'What can I get you? White wine? Red wine?'

'Actually, I'd really appreciate a Guinness.'

He headed to the bar. Guinness, huh? Interesting. Not the drink he would have picked for her. Then he wouldn't have picked her going out with Trent Maloney, either. Or working in a shop. Or accepting his invitation for a drink. Yet here she was.

He didn't know the barmaid. She was young, with a nose ring, eyebrow bolt and a tattoo around her upper arm, but she knew how to pour a Guinness the proper way. He hadn't even realised there was a proper way until his honeymoon, when he and Bianca had laughed and shagged themselves to contented exhaustion around the UK and Ireland.

As he waited for the stout, he glanced around. Em had pulled out her phone, holding it below the line of the table, her movements suggesting she was tapping out a message. He looked away. She was probably sending updates to her mates. Jasmine, most likely, or Teagan, assuming she hadn't ditched them for someone better too.

He carried the Guinness back to the table and sat down, then immediately rose again to fetch coasters. To his relief, on his return, the phone was gone.

'Thanks.' She held up the glass. 'Cheers.'

'*Sláinte*,' he replied, making sure to use the proper Gaelic pronunciation.

She raised her eyebrows. 'You've been?'

'Yeah.'

'I'm jealous.' She looked away. 'I've never had the chance to travel.'

'You want to?'

'Yes.' Her brow furrowed, and he realised from the tiny wrinkles across her forehead that, like him, she was aging. Aging extremely well, but still aging. 'But then I think of the hill and all the animals. Mum and Gran and Digby.'

'How is Dig?'

'Foolish.' At his look she smiled. 'He's in love.'

'No need to explain further, then.'

'No. I spotted Karen walking past the shop the other day. Pregnancy suits her.'

'Yeah, she looks amazing. Sal keeps teasing her it won't last. Reckons that in a year Karen'll look as fagged out as she does.'

'I can imagine Sal saying that. She always loved to stir.'

They lapsed into silence. Cooking smells began to float in from the bistro, the scent of freshly fried chips and grilling steaks. New patrons began to move into the back bar, enjoying a drink in the cosy warmth before dinner.

Josh sorted through comments, anything to reignite the conversation.

Em ran a long finger up and down the condensation-soaked side of her glass. She looked up. 'I meant what I said about us. I made a mistake.'

'I could have told you that.' He took a mouthful of Guinness. 'But it was ages ago. Why even bring it up?'

She took her time answering, the hold of her gaze strong. 'Because it bothers me. It did then, believe it or not, and it does now. What I did was wrong.'

'And now you've said you're sorry.' He shrugged as if it didn't matter. But it did. He felt justified somehow. She'd been wrong. Good. And now she had to live with the guilt. Served her right for treating the man who'd loved her like a piece of worthless shit.

Her mouth parted then closed again. She stared beyond him to the pub with her chin raised slightly and her expression unreadable. He waited for her to say more, but as the quiet ticked by he realised that his bitterness had killed their fragile conversation and now they were stuck. Another minute passed. The stout remained high in their glasses.

Suddenly she touched her temple, frowning as she pressed her fingertips in hard. 'This was a dumb idea, wasn't it?'

'Seems like it.'

She pushed her chair back and rose, nodding towards the glass. 'Thanks, and I apologise for the waste. Please give your parents my regards. I hope Michelle beats the cancer. She's a wonderful woman.'

Josh watched her leave, admiring the swing of her hips, the confidence in her stride, the way she seemed different to the other patrons. Classier, somehow. Sexy.

He turned back to his drink, stared at the fire and brooded, his thoughts as dark as Em's leftover stout.

Five

Thursday dawned wet again. The wind had dropped, allowing the clouds to hang, bloated and grey, casting shadows on the damp soil. After an unsettled night, Em rose early to let the chooks and Chelsea out. The stubbornly broody hen she'd nicknamed Miss Buddha for her ability to sit in the same spot for hours warming non-existent eggs, squabbled and pecked as Em lifted her off her nest and carried her out of the coop. Muffy hung on her heels, her tail-wagging joy at a new day, lighting her gorgeous black eyes.

Em trudged out to check on Lod, Kicki and Cutie, hands deep in her pockets, breath pluming in the cold. The donkeys' escape remained an enigma, the only explanation that Em had somehow left the gate unlatched, despite her certainty she hadn't.

The day suited her mood, and not even the bunts and bustle of Kicki and Cutie cheered her. She stayed near their fence, absently fondling their tall ears and soft muzzles, while her mind tracked elsewhere.

It was twelve kilometres from Levenham to Rocking Horse Hill and last night Em had cursed her stupidity for every one of them. From the moment she recognised Josh in the shop she'd been flustered. The chance she'd longed for, had sometimes dreamed about, was hers to take. And she'd done so, giving the apology that had been aching inside her for years, trying to assuage the shame she'd carried since her teens, and admitted to no one except Jasmine and Teagan.

What had she hoped for? That he'd thank her for the revelation? How dumb could she get? Of course he wouldn't. If anything, he'd earned the right to his anger. She'd made her peace and now it was time to move on.

Except all she'd wanted to do was stare at Josh. At those treacle-coloured eyes. At the straight fringe that still flopped across his forehead and parted slightly on the right thanks to a mild cowlick that as a teenager she had thought so cute, but which now seemed edged with allure. At the closely cropped beard that chased around his jaw and across his top lip in a seductive stubble. At the utter jaw-clenching sexiness of him that seemed more powerful now in maturity than it had ever been in early adulthood.

Every gram of self control had gone into remaining aloof and unaffected, until her head began to throb with the effort. In the end it had seemed safer to leave him stranded with two barely touched pints of Guinness and contemplation in his turned-down gaze.

It was hard for her to imagine now but there was a time when she'd thought Josh wasn't good enough for her. That her Wallace genes made her different and special and above his love. Above his love. What a ridiculous idea. It was his love that had made her special, not her name, or privilege, but that most precious of human emotions.

A hot wash of shame coursed through her as she remembered the day she'd made up her mind to dump him. He'd been invited to Camrick for one of Uncle James's parties. The Jacobses were coming, along with other important families and players in the district. Stephen hadn't been backward with his interest and Em had been flattered. He was an attractive boy, Em's age, but with a farm lad's muscled development and his mother's sharp features. He was also a local footy star. Not in the border league, where Josh played, but in the main district competition, and there'd been gossip about scouts and recruitment to an Adelaide side.

Josh had arrived at Camrick in his chain-store clothes: neat, handsome and nervous. With Em at Rocking Horse Hill, with his friends, anywhere else, he had confidence. But at Camrick, surrounded by people who had likely never set foot on his side of town, with its public housing, disadvantage and poor reputation, he'd floundered. And Em, her insides buzzing with the looks Stephen Jacobs kept shooting her, had done nothing to help. All she'd done was compare and found Josh wanting.

Then she'd betrayed him in the worst possible way.

How immature she'd been. How selfish. And how cruel to the man whose only fault was to adore her.

Muffy bunted her leg, drawing Em back to reality. Her hands were stiff and stinging from the frigid gate top. She blew hot breath on her palms and rubbed them together, eyeing the congested sky before dropping her gaze to Rocking Horse Hill, the one perfect constant in her life. The place to which she'd always been faithful, which she loved unwaveringly. And it didn't notice or care. It just was.

Trust Mother Nature to smack her with irony.

Of course drinks with Josh turned into a farce. How could they have expected anything different?

She smiled down at Muffy. 'Probably just as well, hey, Muff-muff?'

Some things couldn't be set straight, even with heartfelt apologies. She'd cheated on Josh, humiliated him. It was a wonder he'd even given her the time of day, let alone asked her out for a drink.

Muffy waved her tail, her mouth open in what Em liked to kid herself was a canine grin, but was probably nothing of the sort. Her heart swelled a little.

Dog love. Uncomplicated and pure and more than enough for now.

But that didn't stop her thinking about Josh.

***

Despite reprimanding herself for it, Em spent the remainder of the week hoping every tinkle of the shop's bell would signal Josh's arrival. The new window display was proving worth the effort, attracting shoppers and compliments but, annoyingly, no Josh. By Friday afternoon she'd given up, convinced it was for the best anyway.

Distraction caused her penmanship to suffer further. G. K. Chesterton's rousing prose offered no respite and her calligraphy remained imperfect. She tried working on an illumination to begin the Harp of Alfred, but even that part of Chesterton's epic, with its chest-swelling declarations of defiance and bravery, failed to inspire her. When the shop was quiet, she procrastinated on the Internet, or listlessly made pencil sketches in the hope she could force her creativity into action.

Respite came in the form of her grandmother, heavily powdered and lacquered, and looking like a fifties haute couture model in a sable swing coat and cream wool knee-length pencil skirt.

'You need to be careful someone doesn't throw paint on you,' said Em, indicating the coat.

'It's vintage Chloé,' said Granny B, as if that made a difference.

'Still a dead animal.'

'Quite, as was last evening's steak.'

Em hid a smile. Her grandmother was one of a kind. 'How are preparations going?'

To celebrate Digby's engagement and welcome Felicity, Adrienne had decided to host a small drinks party at Camrick that evening. It had been a spur-of-the-moment idea, concocted over dinner on Tuesday night. Digby had attempted to talk her out of it, saying both he and Felicity wanted to keep things quiet, but Adrienne loved to entertain and the party was going ahead.

'Very well. Although your mother is doing too much, as usual.'

'Felicity's helping?'

'She is.'

Em stared at her sketchpad. The harps, swords and armour she'd drawn turned to scribbles as a surge of jealousy hit.

'Making herself quite invaluable, in fact.'

Em brushed aside her thoughts and studied her grandmother. 'Do I detect a hint of disapproval?'

Granny B gave an enigmatic smile. 'Just an observation. Now, are you going to offer me a cup of tea? Then you can tell me all about your little *tête-à-tête* at the Arms with a certain rather hunky ex-boyfriend.'

'How the hell —'

'I have my ways.' Abruptly her focus shifted to the door, her mouth curving. 'Ah, speaking of hunks.'

Em followed Granny B's gaze, her heart somersaulting as she recognised

Josh's outline against the glass. He pushed inside, the bell at last ringing for the customer she'd longed for.

'Granny B,' he said, grinning and striding over in work boots and a pair of blue drill pants, the collar of his matching shirt neatly folded over a woollen jumper the same syrup-brown as his eyes.

Granny B stretched out her hand and allowed Josh to shake it. 'Joshua. You're looking well, although rather in need of a shave. Nice to have you back in town. Must be a great comfort to your poor mother. How is she, by the way?'

'She's doing okay. Has her good days and bad.' He threw a sideways look at Em before returning to Granny B. 'You're looking pretty fit.'

'Indeed I am.' Granny B slid her gaze between Josh and Em, a sly smile curling her mouth. 'Emily was just about to make me a cup of tea. Perhaps you'd like to join us?'

'Sure. Sounds good.'

'I'll put the kettle on,' said Em, escaping through the storeroom's beaded curtain. Safe around the corner, she leaned back against the wall with her eyes closed, while her head cursed Granny B's presence and her heart thumped a nervous tattoo at Josh's.

She eavesdropped as she waited for the kettle. Talk of Josh's family, his sisters and dad, before Granny B moved on to his plans for the future, causing Em's body to still and her ears to sharpen.

'It all depends,' he said. 'I'm trying to convince Dad to go into partnership with me. Build custom furniture. I've developed a strong client base over the last five years – just working as a hobby mainly, doing favours, that sort of thing. But the last couple of years brought some good commissions. It's time to take it to the next level. I've been thinking about it for a while. Mum getting sick brought it all to a head.'

'And your father? Is he keen? I'd imagine he rather would be. Many fathers dream of working with their sons.'

'He's cautious. Thinking about it. He's been with Flanagan's for over thirty years now. It's hard to change.'

'I wish you all the best. Now, what are your plans for this evening?'

'Nothing much. Hanging around the footy club probably, talking tactics with the boys. We're playing Mount Pitt tomorrow. Grudge match of the season. God knows how I got conned into it. I haven't played for three years.'

'I'm sure you'll manage. But perhaps you could forgo the club for a drinks party at Camrick to celebrate Digby's engagement?'

Em tried not to groan. Surely her grandmother remembered the last time Josh was at Camrick? After all, she was the one who'd pinched Em's arm that night and ordered her to behave decently instead of acting like a trollop. A directive Em had ignored.

There was a long pause before Josh answered. 'Sure. What time?'

'Six, for six-thirty. Casual attire. Jeans will be fine.' Granny B's voice rose. 'For goodness' sake, Emily, are you picking those tea leaves?'

Em carried the tea out, addressing Granny B as she pushed through the curtain. 'I thought you had your hospital auxiliary meeting this afternoon.'

'Not until later. Besides, it's much more entertaining here.'

Em narrowed her eyes as Josh raised his hand to smother a smile. How nice. She was the butt of both their teasing now.

She handed a mug to each of them.

Josh blew on his tea and took a sip, eyeing her over the rim. 'You remembered.'

'Yes.' Aware of Granny B's oppressive scrutiny, she held his gaze but didn't comment further. She *had* remembered. She hadn't even had to think. The addition of milk and one sugar to his mug was as familiar as the straight black of Granny B's preference. She remembered a lot about him. His habit of running his shortened fingers through his hair, making his cowlick flare worse. The way he cocked his eyebrows when amused. Even his favourite football team.

'So what brings you into the shop, Joshua?'

'Mum's filled the notebooks Em gave her. I've come to get some more.'

'I should serve Josh,' Em said pointedly, tossing Granny B a 'Do you mind?' look that was promptly ignored.

'Indeed you should. Bad business not to.' Granny B pointed her chin towards the shelves. 'Rather nice, this collection. All those colours, and that display of yours is garnering quite a lot of comment. Even Barry McClintoff mentioned it to me.'

Josh raised his eyebrows at Em. 'Praise from the mayor. It must be good.'

'It's nice to add colour to the street,' she replied, keeping her voice mild. Stepping from behind the counter, she gestured to the shelves. 'Perhaps you'd like to choose the next books?'

He placed his mug down and followed her across the shop, stopping at the racks of jewel-covered notebooks, so near he broke the boundaries of her personal space.

He leaned closer. 'Your grandmother hasn't changed.'

'No, unfortunately. Now,' she said, plucking two notebooks from the shelves and holding them up. 'How about diamond and amethyst, and garnet and onyx?'

'Fine. And this time I'm paying.'

'If you want.'

She crossed the notebooks over each other and held them in front of her, before glancing again at Granny B. The old lady had moved behind the counter and made herself comfortable on Em's stool, sketchbook held up as she pretended to inspect drawings. Em wasn't fooled for a moment. Granny B had no interest in the sketches. Those ears were tuned in like a bat's.

'Look, about tonight,' Em said, deliberately turning away from the counter. 'You don't have to come.'

'I want to.'

Warmth began to channel through Em's insides. She glanced again at Granny B, who, frustrated by their quiet voices, had swivelled the seat around and was now making no effort to hide her interest.

'It'll give me a chance to catch up with Dig. Meet this fiancée of his.'

Her mood plummeted. 'Oh. Of course.'

Josh studied her face, his molasses gaze sweeping from eyes to mouth and back again. 'You thought I had another reason?'

'No. No, of course not.'

A lazy grin spread across his face, shooting Em's heart rate back into orbit.

Flustered, but determined not to show it, she waved the notebooks. 'Right. I'd better wrap these for you.'

He took them from her, his fingers gently brushing hers. 'No need. Just let me pay and I'll leave you to it.'

On their return to the counter, Granny B's shrewd gaze flicked from Em's hot face to Josh's amused countenance, taking in everything.

Em accepted Josh's money, careful not to meet his fingers. Her skin was still tingling where he'd touched her, her insides buzzing at the thought of this evening. The intent behind that slow, all-too-aware grin.

'You're leaving, Joshua? I'll follow you out.' Granny B turned to Em. 'Thank you for the tea.' She indicated the sketchbook. 'Not up to your usual standard. Must have something more interesting on your mind.' Leaving Em fuming, she linked her arm with Josh's and began to lead him away.

Josh cast a helpless look over his shoulder, before giving in to the inevitable.

'Now, Joshua, dear,' said Granny B as she strode to the door. 'Take some advice from a clever old lady and do something about that dreadful stubble. Our Emily – as I'm sure you know from experience – has rather delicate skin . . .'

The door closed, silencing Granny B.

Em watched them stroll away, then shrank onto her stool, buried her blazing face into her hands and prayed for rescue from her demanding, too-smart grandmother.

Six

Josh arrived at Camrick fifteen minutes late. His five-minute drop by the footy club had blown out, thanks to Gerrinton's captain and coach. Their nerves over the following day's grudge match saw them poring over match-ups and regaling anyone who'd listen with war stories about previous games.

Josh left them still fretting over players and positions. He'd have loved to stay, kicked back with a couple of light beers and talked footy all night. The clubrooms were small but cosy, the walls decked with gold-embossed honour boards and cabinets full of trophies. The musty mud smell only country football clubs seemed to possess was comforting and familiar. But he'd told Granny B he'd be at Digby's drinks party, and Josh wasn't the sort to not keep his word.

Or show cowardice.

He parked in front of the stables, next to an old tray-top farm ute, and regarded Camrick for a moment. He should hate the place but for some reason he didn't. It was just a big old house now and, thanks to his job, he'd been in bigger and better ones, from old-money estates to modern architect-designed piles. Mansions owned by people who'd done a hell of a lot more to earn their wealth than be born. And this time round he didn't have to impress anyone within its walls. His heart was safe.

Outside the comfort of the car, the wind sliced through his sports jacket. Josh tilted against the weather and made his way to the front porch. The heavy door swung open before he could raise his hand to the polished brass rapper.

Em stood with one hand on the door edge, the other hanging by her side, looking casually beautiful and leggy in long high-heeled brown boots over dark skinny jeans, and a soft angora jumper that all but invited him to stroke it. 'You made it.'

Her tone was too neutral to determine if she was happy about it or not.

'Thought I was going to chicken out?'

She touched her temple, held her fingers there for a second before scraping a lock of escaped hair behind her ear. The rest was knotted in an elegant bundle at the base of her neck, exposing her fine features. Unlike in the shop, she wore make-up. Her eyes were lined with smoky eye shadow and dark mascara that made her eyes look huge and gold-flecked under the soft light. 'I can't imagine you chickening out of anything.'

'It can happen. But not tonight.' He stepped inside and paused close to her, gaze sliding to her mouth and quickly back up again. 'Sorry I'm late. I made the mistake of dropping by the club and got held up.'

She gave nothing of what she was thinking away as she indicated for him to follow her. Josh scratched at his stubble as he watched her walk, her back held straight, wondering why he found her haughtiness so damn sexy. But he always had. It was like a drug. Except now it held even more allure because he had first-hand experience of the passion buried behind that controlled facade.

Em didn't take him to the front lounge as he'd expected, but to the big kitchen, where twenty or so guests stood crowded around a central workstation, holding drinks and canapés. Sound halted for a moment, heads turning towards him. Some nodding in acknowledgement, others frowning as they tried to place him.

Granny B stood with Barry McClintoff, a tumbler of something dark in her hand, which she raised in Josh's direction, her eyes twinkling in delight at his arrival. He recognised Teagan and Jas, who waved and grinned from the other side of the room. Adrienne, as stunning as ever, stood with an older man, talking to a couple who had their backs to the door, one tall, the other tiny and very blonde, wearing a long-sleeved navy dress made from some sort of expensive-looking material. At the halt in conversation, Digby looked over his shoulder. He grinned at Josh before bending his head to the blonde woman. She turned and smiled shyly, and Josh blinked.

'Jesus,' he said, forgetting who he was with. 'Lucky Digby.'

'I'm sure my brother would be first to agree with you.'

The dryness of Em's tone caught his attention. 'You don't like her?'

Her eyebrows raised in surprise. 'No. Not at all. I think she's very sweet. Come over and say hello.'

Josh followed, thinking he must have misheard, but he was sure he'd detected a hint of cattiness in Em's tone. His eyes slid towards her, considering. Something was going on behind that detached façade; he'd sensed it in the shop. Something deep and smouldering.

'Josh, I didn't know you were coming,' said Digby, shaking his hand. 'Good to see you.'

'And you.' Josh smiled. 'Congratulations. About time.'

'This is my fiancée, Felicity,' he said, putting his arm around her. 'Flick, this is Josh Sinclair, an old —' He glanced at his sister, frowning slightly.

'An old acquaintance of mine,' said Em, filling the awkward pause.

Josh held out his hand and she took it in a brief, weak press of soft flesh against calloused. 'Nice to meet you, Felicity.'

'And you.'

'So when's the big day?' he asked, resisting the urge to wipe his hand on his jeans to rid it of the wet fish handshake feeling.

'We haven't decided yet.' Digby tucked Felicity close. 'Soon, though. I'm not letting this one get away.'

'Would you like a drink?' asked Em. 'Beer? Wine? There's soft drink or juice if you prefer.'

'Beer would be fine, thanks.'

He watched her for a moment as she moved to the sink where bottles poked from an icy bath.

'So,' said Digby, 'you and Em are back together?'

'No. I just happened to call into the shop yesterday when your grandmother was there and she invited me.'

Digby shot a grimace towards his gran. 'She invited half the town. Still, good to see you again. It's been a while.' Digby reached behind him for his beer and took a mouthful. 'Are you still in Adelaide?'

'No, I'm home now, setting up my business here.'

'Ah, Joshua, you made it.' Granny B proffered a cheek for him to kiss. Amused, Josh obliged. 'Although I note you ignored my advice about shaving.'

Josh scraped his palm across his chin. 'Sorry.'

'No, you're not.' Granny B turned to Felicity. 'Are you enjoying yourself?'

'Yes, thanks.'

'You should mingle.'

'Flick's fine, Gran.'

Granny B's mouth puckered a fraction. She brought her sharp eyes towards Em, approaching with Josh's beer. 'Good to see you looking after your guest, Emily.'

'Your guest, if I recall,' said Em, handing over the bottle.

'So Joshua was. But one should take opportunities when they arise. Never wise to let an attractive man slip through one's fingers and our Joshua is very attractive indeed.'

The line of Em's jaw tightened. 'I should go and talk to Jas and Teagan.'

'I'll come and say hi too.' Josh threw a quick smile Digby and Felicity's way before winking at Granny B. The old lady laughed before stalking off to create mischief elsewhere.

'Josh!' Jasmine, as buoyant as he remembered, stood on tiptoe to plant a loud kiss on his cheek. 'Fancy seeing you here.'

He looked at Em. 'Em never said I was coming?'

'No.' She drew out the word teasingly. 'No, she didn't.'

'Hey, Josh,' said Teagan.

'Teagan, how's things?' Not great by the look of her. Her collarbones dug sharp lines through her silky T-shirt. She was still very attractive, though. Plenty of his mates had been keen on Teagan when he'd been with Em, although the only bloke Josh could recall her going out with was Lukey Martin, whose parents ran a dairy farm down Port Andrews way.

'Oh, you know.' She shrugged her thin shoulders. 'Busy on the farm. Not much time for anything else. And you? What are you up to these days?'

'Same as you – keeping busy. At the moment I'm trying to get a custom furniture business up and running.'

'What, here? In Levenham?'

'Yeah. Dad's letting me use his shed while I get sorted.' He took a slug of beer. 'Means I'm back living at home for a while.'

Jas gave him a cheeky poke. 'That must be fun.'

He picked at the stubby label. 'It's all right. Being there, I can help out a bit. Mum's a bit crook. Breast cancer.'

'I'm sorry,' said Jas, with genuine compassion. 'My aunt was diagnosed a few years ago. It's been a rough journey.'

'But she's okay now? She beat it?'

'Yes.' She smiled. 'That generation's pretty tough. Your mum will get through, too.'

Josh looked up and caught Em's eye. Throughout their conversation she'd said little, standing slightly apart from him in a way that reminded him of the last time he'd been at Camrick. Except this was nothing like that night. There was no contempt in her gaze, no disappointment, only sympathy.

Annoyed by the memory, Josh broke contact and pretended to scan the room. He'd made a complete dick of himself that night. Normally he possessed enough confidence to see him through any social situation, no matter how intimidating, but the night of James's party, with all the local who's who in attendance, he'd been sick with nerves. Not because of the venue or the people involved, but because he could feel Em slipping away from him.

He hadn't known why. He didn't understand what he'd done wrong. All he'd ever done was love her and yet she'd started getting secretive, shaking her head and saying 'nothing' whenever he asked what was up. He was scared enough as it was, but those 'nothings', with their lack of eye contact, sent him into panic.

That night had revealed exactly what was up or, rather, who. Stephen Jacobs. Even now, the thought of him made Josh's fists twitch involuntarily. He should have punched the fucker's lights out when he had the chance. Not that it would have done a scrap of good, but it would have given him some satisfaction.

He glanced at Em and found her studying him again.

'You don't have a drink,' he said.

'I'm fine. How's your beer? Would you like another?'

He shook his head. 'I have to drive and I have footy tomorrow.'

'Who are you playing for?' asked Jas.

'The mighty Gerrinton Giants.'

Teagan winced. 'You're up against Mount Pitt.'

'Ooh, the big grudge match,' said Jas, rubbing her hands together.

Like Josh didn't know that already. It was all he'd heard all week. 'Tell me about it.'

She tapped his stubby with a bitten-down fingernail. 'Definitely no more beers for you, then. Save them for tomorrow night when you'll need plenty to dull the pain.'

'Thanks, Jas. You really know how to give a bloke confidence.'

'You, needing confidence? That'd be a first. I remember when —'

'Would you excuse me?' said Em suddenly. 'I should hand around some canapés.'

But Jas wasn't having it. 'I'll do it. You talk to Josh. I'm sure you two have a lot to catch up on.'

'I'll help,' added Teagan, the pair grinning like naughty kids.

They darted off. Em briefly closed her eyes and took a deep breath before refocusing on Josh.

'So,' he said.

'So.'

He watched Teagan and Jas weave through the other guests with their plates. Most he didn't know. It'd been a long time since he'd lived in Levenham and he'd never run in the same circles as the Wallaces anyway. He caught Granny B's gaze and raised his beer towards her, she smiled foxily in return, before resuming her conversation with the mayor.

Felicity had moved to join Adrienne and the tall bloke Josh assumed was her partner now, Digby hovering protectively over his fiancée. Em's mum looked like he remembered – classy and extremely attractive, and intimidating because of it. She had to be well into her fifties but barely looked it. Alongside her, Felicity seemed to lack something that he couldn't pinpoint. Whatever it was, Em possessed it too. A certain air of . . . the only word he could think of was *quality*, but that made Em sound like a well-bred horse.

He returned his attention to her. 'Remember the last time I was here?'

Colour seeped across her cheeks but she kept her composure. 'Yes.'

'No Stephen Jacobs this time.'

'No.' Her chin remained high. 'He had something on.'

Josh's eyebrows cocked. 'So he was invited then?'

'His family was.'

Of course they were. The Jacobs were establishment, like the Wallaces.

'Caroline Jacobs is over there,' Em nodded towards a corner, 'if you want to talk to her.'

'I'd rather talk to you.'

Her mouth parted and again he had that sense of something smouldering beneath her coolness. She looked towards Adrienne. 'I should ask if Mum needs anything done.'

'I'll come with you. I haven't said hello to her yet.'

Adrienne welcomed Josh with delight, introducing him to her partner, Samuel, and checking he'd been properly introduced to Felicity before shoving a plate of canapés towards him. He took a tiny grape-topped tartlet, and then reached for another when his mouth exploded with juice and tangy goat's cheese.

'God, they're good.'

Adrienne smiled in appreciation. 'There are some rare roast beef and horseradish cream topped rosti around somewhere. Ah, Jasmine has them. Hopefully there'll still be some left when she returns.' She touched his arm. 'How is your mother?'

'Chemo's knocking her about a fair bit, but she's otherwise good.'

'Give her my regards, would you? And tell her that if there's anything I can do, anything she needs, I'll do my best to help.'

Josh's throat thickened at her kindness. 'Thanks. I will.'

A timer went off. Adrienne gave his arm another pat before excusing herself and heading off to retrieve another tray of food from the oven. Claiming an empty plate from the bench behind, Em followed.

Josh reached across to take another goat's cheese tart, hoping he didn't look greedy but not really caring if he did. Lunch had been hours ago and he needed food to soak up the beer.

'So you're from Adelaide, Felicity?' he asked, trying to make conversation.

She nodded, but didn't give up any information.

'From Elizabeth,' said Granny B, appearing at the edge of their diminished group. 'Isn't that right?'

'Elizabeth?' Josh regarded her with interest. 'My ex-wife was from the next suburb over, Smithfield, although we ended up buying a house at Golden Grove.'

'Oh,' said Felicity faintly. 'Right.'

It was like talking to a store mannequin, but Josh ploughed on. 'Bianca Sinclair? Although you might know her as Bianca Cameron.'

Felicity shook her head and, dismissing Josh with a tight smile, lifted her head towards Digby. 'I'll go help Em and Adrienne.'

Mother and daughter seemed fine to Josh. The tray was out from the oven and together they were arranging what looked like spring rolls onto a plate. He exchanged a glance with Granny B, who shrugged.

The spring rolls turned out to be filo cigars stuffed with Moroccan spiced lamb and pine nuts. Josh pinched two and added a couple of Adrienne's roast beef morsels to his stomach when Jas floated past. 'Need to keep my strength up for tomorrow,' he said to her.

She laughed. 'You'll need more beef than that to conquer Mount Pitt.'

He chatted to Digby a bit more and then Teagan and Jas, who kept him on his toes with questions about his failed marriage and plans for the future. For a while he wondered if Em had put them up to the interrogation, but using her friends had never been Em's style. This was just women looking out for one another.

She was watching him, though. He felt her scrutiny as sure as he felt the heat of the room. Perhaps she was comparing him to his younger self, when he'd stood awkwardly in clothes that had earned him proud praise from his mum, but which he was sure were unfashionable and ill tailored to the moneyed crowd looking at him.

Until that night, Em had never made him feel not good enough, but he'd sure as fuck felt it then.

'Thinking about the last time you were here?'

He turned to Granny B. 'How did you know?'

'I would consider it rather unusual if you didn't recall that night.' Granny B nodded Em's way. 'Fortunately, she's grown up since then.'

'We all have.'

'Yes. Rather nicely, in your case. Although you always were a good-looking boy.'

He leaned in close and lowered his voice to a tease. 'Granny B, are you flirting with me?'

She cocked her head and considered. 'Do you know, I think you'd rather like it if I was.'

'You bet I would.'

She laughed throatily. 'Oh, I do so like you, Joshua. It's good to have you back.'

And for the first time in weeks, Josh realised how happy he was to be home.

Although he'd planned not to linger, he stayed for another drink, hanging with Digby, a mate from Digby's work and Jas and Teagan. Both Em and Felicity kept their distance, preferring Adrienne's and Samuel's company to their group of twenty- and thirty-somethings.

Finally, when it was past time for him to go, he caught Em's eye and tilted his head towards the door. She came to escort him out, Jas and Teagan watching them leave with amused expressions, like this was the best entertainment they'd had in years.

The wind had died down, leaving a night lit by Camrick's warm glow. The gravel of the drive crunched underfoot, punctuating their lack of talk.

He leaned against the back of his ute and crossed his arms. 'Nice evening.'

'Yes.'

'Do you mind that I came?'

'No, not at all.'

'Then you're glad?'

She squinted at the sky. 'Digby would have appreciated it.'

'I didn't ask about Dig, Em. I asked about you.'

Again that hot pause, the deliberate regathering of self-possession that shot anticipation thrilling through his stomach. She shook her head. 'I have to go. Thanks for coming. Good luck with football tomorrow. Try not to get too hurt.'

As she brushed away he swung out his left arm, catching her hand in his. Startled, she pulled to a halt. Eyes wide and questioning, her body stiffly still, she held his gaze for several heartbeats before slowly dropping it to where their hands joined.

Realising what he'd done, Josh jerked his hand free and folded his tightly curled fingers against his thigh. 'Sorry.'

'For what?'

His lifted his fist and dropped it heavily. 'I forget what it's like for people.'

Her expression softened, causing something in his chest to swell. Not fizzy anticipation, something deeper. 'I never minded your touch, Josh. From either hand.'

With her words the thing in his chest ballooned, pressing against his ribs as though seeking escape. 'I want to see you again. Not here. Somewhere private. At the hill.'

'Josh . . .'

'Come on, Em. You feel it the same as I do.'

'We can't resurrect what we had.'

Josh considered for a moment, remembering. Their time together was unique, a coincidence of circumstance, intense mutual attraction and cheeky new-adult bravado that had somehow granted him the balls to lure the most unattainable girl in town to his side.

He smiled. When it came to her, he still had those balls. 'Yeah, we can.'

Seven

Given she hadn't touched a drink at all the previous night, Em couldn't even blame alcohol for what came out of her mouth in the yard at Camrick. Perhaps it was the moonlight, the memories his touch evoked, the way he'd kept his gaze locked on hers, causing excited tangles in her stomach, but somehow she'd asked Josh to dinner.

So much for making her peace and moving on.

Determined not to turn the evening into anything more than dinner between friends, Em forced herself to keep the menu basic. With only an afternoon to prepare, and with weekly chores around the farm still requiring her attention, she didn't have time for complicated stocks and sauces anyway. Mostly she didn't want to appear to be trying too hard. As she explained to Jas and Teagan, this was a casual affair, a simple get-to-know-you-again with an old boyfriend who was also once a very good friend. Not that they'd believed a word of it.

Probably because Em wasn't convinced she did either.

Stealing an early minute, she shut the shop a little before her usual lunchtime closing on Saturday, scanning the street as she locked up, hoping that none of the shoppers had PaperPassion on their lists. She needn't have worried. Other than a few rugged-up people hurrying for the pub, McArthur Street's Saturday hustle was already quieting as people drifted to sport and other activities. The weather remained dry, the wind light and Levenham locals were making the most of the respite.

On her way home she ducked into the supermarket for a tub of mascarpone, pancetta and, although it pained her to buy pre-packaged greens, a bag of baby rocket leaves. Her home-grown produce was usually bountiful thanks to the hill's fertile volcanic soil; now, assaulted by the weather and rampaging donkeys, it was scant. Even the chooks weren't laying well.

The afternoon dragged. Em tuned the radio to the football but the broadcast was for the district competition and there were few border league score updates. With so much to sort around the farm, Em had little time for the house anyway, ducking in only for drinks and loo breaks.

No matter how many times she told herself it was just dinner, the skip of her heart told her time spent with Josh could never be 'just' anything. Her nerves grew, upsetting Lod who shied and misbehaved as she trotted him around the perimeter of Rocking Horse Hill.

The chooks weren't much better when she came to lock them up, squabbling around the coop like puffed-up prison rioters, and refusing to settle. Chelsea zoomed for escape only to be foiled by Muffy, on point guard at the gate, and sent throttling in the opposite direction, her low-set bum waggling furiously.

After throwing hay to Kicki and Cutie, and filling Lod's manger with a half-bucket of mixed feed, the fading light forced Em back to the house. Inside, the combustion fire had pushed the worst of the cold into the corners. In an hour, it'd be toasty and comforting, perfect for a Saturday night in. She paused at the windows, intending to draw the curtains to help preserve heat, but the sight of Rocking Horse Hill stopped her. Earlier the sunset had painted the crest in orange; now moonlight cast it in silver and shadow, the stone edges luminous and magical. She left the curtains open, smiling and hugging herself as she padded in her socks to the bathroom.

Josh had mentioned going back. And there was no better time and place in the past than Rocking Horse Hill.

He arrived a few minutes past six-thirty, rapping on the front door and sending Muffy into a paroxysm of gruff barks. Em ordered her to shush and headed down the old passageway, flicking on light switches as she went, expectation bubbling inside, although expectation of what she had no idea.

She swung the heavy timber door open. Josh stood on the verandah in the dark, his body hunched against the arctic wind.

He grinned in relief as light flooded his face. 'Thank God. For a while I thought I had the wrong house.'

'Sorry, I should have told you to come round the back. No one ever uses this door.' She stood aside. 'Come in.'

Josh paused in front of her in the hallway, once again crossing the invisible border of her personal space, and for a breathy moment she though he was going to kiss her. Instead, he raised his hands. A wine bottle was gripped in each, one red, one white. Em quirked an eyebrow and pushed the door closed.

He laughed and shook his head. 'Don't read anything into it. I didn't know what we were eating or what you'd prefer.'

'So, did you win?'

'Lost by two points. Boys were a bit unhappy with the umpiring.' Josh shrugged. 'We had our chances, just didn't take them. I kicked a goal, though.'

'Hero, huh?'

'I wish. I played on some old bloke who hammered me.' Josh looked down as Muffy sniffed suspiciously around the cuff of his jeans. 'Hello.'

'This is Miss Muffet. Otherwise known as the phantom hairball horror.'

Josh crouched down, placed the bottles on the hall runner, and held out his fingers for Muffy to scent before stroking the dog's head. The afternoon outdoors had left her coat in knots and untidy spikes but Em hadn't had time to spruce her up. Josh didn't seem to mind, cooing nonsense to her as he petted. Finished, he rose and, noticing Em's expression, smiled. 'I miss having a dog. Bianca took ours.'

'I'm sorry,' said Em, not knowing what else to say.

'Doesn't matter. She loved the dog as much as I did.' His eyes took on a momentary downcast edge. 'Probably more.'

Em's mind filled with questions but she kept them to herself. Instead, she pointed down the hall. 'Come through.'

Bottles in hand, he followed, and she sensed him peering into darkened rooms behind her, no doubt as curious about her life as she was about his. At the entrance to the living area, he halted, frowning slightly as he scanned the room. 'This has changed.'

Em went to disagree and then realised that it had changed. Josh would have known the house when it was still her mother's domain. Adrienne favoured modern minimalism, with careful colour and fabric coordination, and no clutter. While most of the dark timber furniture from that time remained, beeswaxed to a comforting shine, the room now had an entirely different feel. Tartan wool rugs and colourful, mismatched cushions covered the impractical cream leather lounge. Row after row of books packed the built-in bookcases, fiction and non-fiction muddled together, polychrome spines forming a patchwork of colour. The remaining shelves were clustered with photo frames of various sizes and styles – the faces of all the people Em loved smiled out across the room. Other surfaces supported knickknacks, family heirlooms and other relics from Rocking Horse Hill's grand history, resurrected from storage and placed proudly on display. The effect was country, warm and literary, like a cosy library, and redolent with savoury cooking scents. Classical music crept softly from the stereo, adding to the bookish comfort.

'I could never keep it the way Mum had it,' said Em. 'Too much work.'

'And this isn't? Must take some dusting. I like it better, though. This has warmth.' Nodding to himself as he did, Josh gazed around again, before returning his focus to Em and smiling. 'Definitely more you.'

The comment flushed Em with pleasure.

He rested the wine on the dining table and headed for the windows, Muffy padding alongside. Em watched him, admiring his body from behind as she appraised his clothes and tried to assess how much effort he'd gone to.

He looked handsome, wonderfully so, and fit despite football fatigue. Neat camel jeans showed off his long legs. A classically cut charcoal blazer highlighted the width of his shoulders, a dark grey lambswool half-zip jumper hugging his chest beneath.

She'd opted for a similar look: jeans, short black leather boots, and a silky burgundy shirt with the sleeves folded up. Torn between looking good and kitchen practicality, Em had copied Friday night's form and knotted her hair into a loose bun, a style that exposed her neck and throat but reduced the risk of Josh discovering a hair in his food. Her make-up was subtle, enough to smooth her skin, give her hazel eyes a smoky sultriness and her lips a hint of gloss. The result was casual but quietly sexy.

Josh regarded her over his shoulder. 'You must love having this to yourself.'

'I do.'

He turned back and scanned the crater's outline against the night sky. She watched him, full of pride and pleasure, and struck by a sense of rightness, of something that should have been: Josh by the window, Muffy on her haunches nearby, Rocking Horse Hill filling the hollows of their lives.

Rich aromas drifted from the kitchen, reminding Em of her dinner preparations. She checked that the baking risotto had enough liquid and that the pumpkin was caramelising nicely, and closed the oven again.

When she straightened, Josh was leaning against the bar. 'Smells good.'

'Roast pumpkin, sage and pancetta risotto, courtesy of Jamie. Except I'm cheating and baking it instead.'

'Friend of yours?'

She laughed. 'Famous TV chef.'

'You know me, I just like eating food.' He contemplated her for a moment. 'You like cooking. I remember that. It's what you used to talk about with Mum. That and gardening.'

'Your mum was a great cook.'

'Still is.'

'I didn't mean —'

'I know you didn't. Now,' he said, indicating the bottles, 'a drink?'

Josh took his blazer off and settled at the bench with a glass of red wine as Em whisked vinaigrette ingredients together in a bowl. The rocket salad waited in the fridge, along with dessert. In keeping with the easy menu, earlier prepared ramekins of uncooked *moelleux au chocolat* lined the bottom shelf, with four spares to take to Jasmine's tomorrow as a treat. Twenty minutes in the oven, and she and Josh would enjoy gooey-centred chocolate puddings, a dessert disproportionately impressive to the effort it took to create.

The dining table was also kept simple, with a pair of plain white linen placemats arranged at right angles and set with Em's everyday cutlery, wine and water glasses. Only the silver napkin rings and heirloom linen napkins were special, satisfying Em's need for at least a little sense of occasion.

Keeping to safe topics, she chatted about the shop, show riding, Jas and Teagan, the upcoming season and how they'd all made a pact to volunteer for the show committee next year.

'Sounds like you keep yourself busy,' said Josh.

'I do, I guess.' Em stared across the room at the big windows. Rocking Horse Hill had disappeared against the reflection of light. 'I wish winter wasn't so long, though.'

'We all wish that.'

At the ring of the timer, she opened the oven door.

'Let me,' said Josh, sliding off his stool.

'I'm fine.' But Josh had already pushed up his sleeves and taken the mitts from her. She stood aside and let him work, aware of the way the sinews and muscles of his forearms moved under his skin. The way the light covering of hair held golden tints and seemed to shimmer in the kitchen glow.

He put the dishes on trivets and passed her back the mitts.

'Are you hungry?' she asked, removing the casserole lid.

'At the smell of that I am.'

She stirred the risotto and tasted it before sprinkling in more salt. 'I hope it's up to scratch.'

'It will be.'

She tipped in the small chunks of caramelised pumpkin, her stomach fluttering at his compliment and the certainty with which he'd said it.

'Why don't you sit at the table?' she said. 'I won't be a minute.'

He took the long side seat, leaving Em the place at the head of the table. Trent had always automatically sat at the head of the table, as if this was his house instead of hers. At the time she hadn't really noticed or been bothered, but the difference in Josh's attitude struck her strongly, and deepened feelings for him that were already too unruly.

She used her favourite wide-brimmed dishes, the cheffy ones she'd bought on impulse off the Internet one night after seeing them on a cooking show. The risotto, with its autumnal colours, creamy rice grains and indulgent swirl of rich mascarpone, was shown off to perfection.

Josh inhaled appreciatively, before taking the salad servers and heaping two serves onto his side plate. Except for the occasional murmur from Josh, they ate with little conversation. Several times, Em caught herself staring at his mouth, his half-smile as he ate, as if each forkful gave him some exquisite secret pleasure.

'That,' he said, placing his cutlery carefully into his clean bowl, 'was amazing.'

'It's a good recipe.'

She reached for his plate but he pressed his hand over hers. The flush that had been rising in her cheeks flared higher.

'I'll do it,' he said.

'Who's the guest here?'

'Doesn't mean I can't help.'

'You're fine, Josh. Just sit. I'll sort it out.'

She cleared the table, catching his eye often, wondering what he was thinking. They'd started their re-acquaintance badly – her snapping at him in the shop, walking out on him in the pub, avoiding him at Camrick. And now here he was in her house, enjoying her cooking and watching her with an expression that seemed to promise more than she was sure she was ready for.

Em's body felt light from the wine as she settled back at the table. Outside, the wind rocketed through the trees and under the eaves, tugging at the house. But she and Josh remained cocooned, secure in comfort and intimacy.

He held up his glass and, when Em lifted hers, leaned forward to clink the edges together. His eyes caressed hers, raising Em's heartbeat.

'To old friends.'

She tilted her head, overtaken with recklessness. 'Friends?'

'Lovers, then.'

She drew her glass away, her eyes locked on his. The CD stopped, leaving a tension-rippled quiet.

'Tonight's not going how I expected,' he said.

'What did you expect?'

He placed his glass down and looked into the wine for a moment. 'I thought it'd be harder. I thought you'd want talk about Bianca. Ask what went wrong. Check I haven't turned into some hate-filled divorcee.'

'It's not your nature to hate, Josh.'

'I could have changed.'

'Not like that.' She frowned. 'Did you want to talk about her?'

'No.'

'You can, if you want.'

'Do you want to talk about Trent?'

'No.'

He shrugged as if that explained it all.

She rose to change the CD and check on the puddings, grateful for the chance to collect herself. He was right. The night wasn't going as either of them expected. It was moving too fast, tension rising in the fudge-scented air. This was meant to be a reconciliation of sorts, yet Em felt restless with desire and she wished she'd waited longer before putting the moelleux in the oven. Her hunger lay elsewhere, in the hankering need to push Josh's chair away from the table, settle astride his sexy hips and kiss him furiously until he lifted her up and carried her down the hall to her bed.

Except there'd be no sex tonight. She wasn't that kind of woman, and these feelings were only the residue of something sweet but lost. If they were to have something again it wouldn't be the same. Thirteen years ago they had no cares, only the selfishness of their desire and the rawness of their need. This time, it would be friendship and mutual respect that led them into a relationship, not base lust.

Assuming respect was still possible after what she'd done.

Dessert was as big a hit with Josh as the main course. He settled back to regard her with a lazy, satisfied smile. 'If you set out to impress me, I'm impressed.'

Em's desire soared hill-high. She smothered it with domesticity. Figuring that he wouldn't be easily fobbed off, she allowed him to help with the dishes, and was glad she did. The practical chore took the edge off, and let them talk about developments in the town and local gossip. By the time the last dish was stowed and the benches were wiped, they were back to easy friendship.

Josh glanced at his watch. 'I suppose I should get home. It's been a big day.'

'You sure you don't want coffee?'

'Thanks, but no.' Josh wandered towards the sliding door, carrying his jacket, Muffy trailing behind. At the glass he stopped and gave the dog a stern look. 'You look after your mistress now.' To Em's astonishment, Muffy pressed her shoulder into Josh's leg, a sign of affection Em had always considered exclusively hers. Josh ruffled Muffy's ears before turning to Em. 'Thanks for tonight. It was great.'

'You're welcome.'

They stared at one another. The CD finished. Wind threaded through the roof and brushed against the house.

'So.'

'So.'

The temperature rose.

He leaned forward to kiss her cheek but the kiss lingered. The tiny hairs on her skin stirred against his breath. She could feel his swallow of hesitancy, then his long exhale as he made his decision. Another kiss: soft, fluttery. Heat swept her body, scattering it with delicious prickles.

Em closed her eyes against the pull of yearning. 'Josh . . .'

His lips crept in a series of butterfly touches towards her mouth, leaving little puckers of ecstasy in their wake, the chasing skim of his stubble shooting thrills down her back. 'I know.'

'It's too soon.'

'Yeah.'

'Then . . .'

And suddenly she didn't care. It was simply him, back where she needed him.

He dropped his jacket and cupped her face, scanning her expression. His eyes hooded when he recognised her desire, then his mouth was on hers and her mind turned frantic with the need for more.

Only when Muffy tried to follow them into the bedroom, wide-eyed with curiosity, did Em speak again, ordering the dog back to her box. Head lowered and hunch-shouldered, Muffy skulked back down the hall, the scratch of her claws like sulky tickings-off until they finally faded to quiet.

Leaving Em and Josh alone and breathless in the night.

Eight

The bed rocked, rousing Josh from his half-doze. He reached out a hand, fingers catching a patch of silky skin before it slid away.

'Come back,' he said, leaning across to slip his arm around Em's waist. Cold seeped in under the sheets where they'd rumpled down as she'd twisted out.

She smiled and brushed his fringe from his face. 'I have to let Muffy out. She's desperate.'

As she spoke another forlorn whimper broke the silence. Josh sat up as Em snatched a thick jumper from the leather armchair tucked against the wall, and tugged it over her head. Muffy sat miserably in the doorway, her front paws moving up and down as though on hot asphalt, haunches tucked beneath her and her fluffy tail between her legs. He threw her an amused look only for it to stall as Em bent over to retrieve her jeans from the floor.

Her bum curved in two pale globes, wide at the hips before tapering upwards to her slim waist. Long, slender legs gave the impression of athleticism, the muscle tone strong enough for definition without affecting her soft feminine lines. For an intoxicating moment, his mind was caught by the gap between her upper thighs, the way the flesh almost, but not quite, met. Josh's groin stirred with the thought of what lay above that point.

'Don't be long,' he said.

Em's eyes were lit with amusement. 'Long enough to let my poor dog out, and the chooks and Chelsea.'

'And then?'

She knelt on the bed, her loose hair swinging as she leaned close. 'You can warm me up again.' And with a light kiss she was gone, a relieved Muffy scampering in her wake.

Josh lay back, his erection pulsing. He listened for her outside, but caught only birdsong and a distant whinny. It was wonderfully soporific and if it wasn't for his desire he'd doze again, but he wanted her – badly. Last night had been good, better than good, but a little too sudden, too frantic and desperate. Almost as though it wasn't about them but some pent-up force that needed satiating. This morning would be different. This morning would be lazy and sexy and indulgent.

If only she'd hurry up and come back.

He studied the room as dawn spread and stole into the corners. The drapes were undrawn and only a flimsy layer of gauze diffused the rising light. Her room was as elegant and classic as she was. Like the queen-sized sleigh bed, the rest of the furniture was plain dark timber – American walnut, he guessed – and lustrous with polish. A five-high stack of books occupied one corner of the left-hand bedside table. He scanned the spines, marvelling at the variety: a poultry management book, a cookbook on French provincial food, a fantasy novel that he'd read himself, a hardcover about the *Book of Kells* and, on top, a brick-sized historical novel.

The doona cover was cream damask, matching the walls. An unusual lightshade puffed out above him like a taffeta skirt, reminding Josh of his sister Karen's debut dress, the bodice of which his mum had sewed hundreds of tiny pearls to, nearly sending herself blind. On the tallboy opposite the bed stood a line of silver frames. He was too far away to identify the subjects. A couple were obviously of horses, the rest, people. Family, perhaps friends, he guessed, while a jealous voice inside him hoped that was where her love had stopped.

He frowned at the door. Surely it didn't take that long to let out a dog and a few chooks, but he could hear no sound of her return and she'd been gone at least ten minutes, perhaps more. His erection had faded, the bed cooling with his restless movement and without her to warm it.

Josh called her name and listened. Something in the house creaked but her voice didn't come.

Muttering an oath, he slid out of bed and pulled on his jeans before padding out into the living area. The air was warmer here, fed by the smouldering combustion stove. Past the floor-to-ceiling windows, the tip of Rocking Horse Hill was lit with a fiery sunrise. The weatherman had got it right. It was going to be one of those brilliant, hope-filled days, where everything was washed in light and the dullness of winter seemed far away.

Enjoying it could wait. Right now all he wanted was to find Em and drag her back to bed.

He crossed to the glass door and slid it open, wincing as the gelid dawn draft struck his bare chest and feet. Gingerly, he stepped out onto the porch and called her name again. Only a magpie warbled a reply. He scanned the garden and beyond, towards the low slopes of the crater and its grim scar, worry churning his insides.

Ignoring the rapidly growing pain in his feet, he stepped off the porch and followed a mossy brick path towards the rear of the yard, where he guessed the chooks were housed. The henhouse door stood open, with half-a-dozen chooks and a weird-looking white duck exploring nearby, but no Em or Muffy.

'Em, come on. It's freezing.'

He rubbed his arms, then followed another icy path to the edge of the garden where it met a double-bayed carport. An older-model SUV occupied one side, an aluminium float the other. He circled past, out into the open. An unoccupied besser-brick stable block and yards faced the north. Past it stretched a long, narrow paddock, which extended to the base of Rocking Horse Hill.

Josh inspected the crater, wondering if after last night she'd needed some sort of communion with the place. Bit of a weird, hippie thing to do, but she'd certainly felt strongly enough about Rocking Horse Hill in the past. It spoke to her, she'd once cautiously admitted, assessing his expression for laughter, through tiny vibrations no one else could feel. At the time he'd been too in love and struck by the shy honesty of her admission to scoff, but now he wondered.

But that was a long time ago. She was a mature, self-possessed, intelligent woman now. He could no more imagine her communing with Rocking Horse Hill than he could himself. Or could he? He'd seen her bookshelves. All those romance and fantasy novels, the books on mediaeval manuscripts and art. Her desk was covered in sketches of sword-wielding kings and mythical creatures, and a sheet of beautifully inked poetry that spoke of gods and ancient Wessex kings.

The walls featured photographs of Rocking Horse Hill in dramatic light and backdrops, hung like icons in a room that, when he thought about it, was almost a temple to the crater. Em's love for the place ran soul-deep, had done since childhood. And he hardly knew her now. How the fuck was he supposed to know what she thought these days?

He scraped his hand through his hair and turned round, then continued past the carport to where the driveway bent back beyond the house to the road. His feet throbbed with cold, but worry stopped him from heading back inside.

His Hilux was parked to the side of the drive, inside the still-latched gate, near the front of the house. Josh stopped at the passenger door and scanned the tree line, saddened to see one of the old cypresses had taken a hit. Finding no sign of Em, he stepped to the back of the ute and checked the front garden. Again nothing. He swore softly, just to make a noise. The enduring quiet was beginning to give him the creeps.

Turning back, he noticed the road paddock gate was swung half-open. A rugged horse stood in the far corner of the adjacent paddock, ears pricked and head high, watching something further down the road. Growing alarm swept away the chill. He threaded through the fence and, keeping to the soft pine straw, jogged to the edge of the gravel, eyes narrowed as he peered into the distance. Stanislaus Road stretched gloomily as it chased the volcano base, heavily shadowed by the line of cypresses, brightened only by an occasional shaft of orange light filtering through the thick canopy.

Josh opened his mouth to yell her name again but stopped as a dog cantered around the corner. A figure emerged behind, along with two shorter animals. His breath billowed steam into the frigid air.

Relief made him aware of the cold again: the numbness of his feet, the trembling of his body. He crossed his arms, hopping from foot to foot, as he waited for Em to approach. The two donkeys she was ushering along the road slowed her progress. One was small and brown, the other larger, grey, and with a dark crucifix across its shoulders. Though her hands were gripped in their manes, and she was talking them forward, the donkeys went at their own pace. When one stopped the other halted, only moving again after a hefty push on the rump. By the time Em reached him her expression was mutinous.

'What happened?' He moved to grab the mane of the grey donkey.

'I don't know. The gate was open and Kicki and Cutie were gone. They weren't anywhere on the farm so I checked the road. They were nearly at Peter Harlow's. Must've been out all night.' She shook her head. 'I don't know how it could have happened. The gate was secure when I fed them last night.'

'Maybe they unlocked it?'

'It's a hook and eye. How could they have done that?'

Josh shrugged. 'Could've been kids.'

'Here?'

'We used to play around here, remember?'

Her frown turned into a smile as she caught his meaning. 'We did. Quite a lot.' The smile faded. 'But we never opened gates for the fun of it.'

'Town kids, maybe. Wanting to play with the donkeys.'

She wrapped her arm around her donkey and squeezed. 'I hope not. These two have been through enough without being terrorised in the night.' She gave the donkey another cuddle. 'They're rescue animals. Poor things were found in a paddock near Murray Bridge. The owners bought them as glorified lawnmowers and then forgot about them. By the time the rescue people were alerted they were skin and bone. Hooves so long they curled up, lice everywhere and stomachs full of worms. So depressed they wouldn't respond to the carers. They just stood in corners with their heads down. It must have been heartbreaking.'

Her voice cracked and Josh wished he could hold her, but when she carried on, her voice had regained its strength.

'I've donated a bit of money to the shelter over the years, and even helped with a few local cases, so when I heard they were looking for homes for these two, I volunteered. I'm so glad I did. They're the sweetest things.' The donkeys' big ears swivelled as if they sensed the deep affection in her tone. She tousled her donkey's forelock. 'This one's Cutie, short for CuteArse, and that one's Kicki, short for KickArse.'

'CuteArse and KickArse?' He laughed as she pulled a face. 'Okay, so I'm guessing that wasn't your idea.'

'*I* wanted to call them Merry and Pippin, after Meriadoc Brandybuck and Peregrin Took in *Lord of the Rings*, but Jas said she'd call me a pretentious snotnose for life if I did, and insisted I name them KickArse and CuteArse. She wanted to call Cutie BadArse but I had to draw the line somewhere. Kicki's name at least suits.' At Josh's look she explained. 'He used to kick when he was first rescued. Poor thing didn't mean it. He was frightened. It took a lot of work to cure him of the habit, but we made it in the end. Cutie here has always been a sweetheart.'

She gave the donkey another hug and then muttered under her breath as the animal halted and turned to sniff something on the side of the road. Josh found himself dragged alongside as Kicki followed suit.

After much cajoling, and a great deal of swearing on Josh's part, they escorted the donkeys through the gate, where they happily shuffled off into their paddock without further urging. Leaving Em to lock up, Josh hurried on deadened feet back to the house.

He was stretched out on the rug, his feet as close to the fire as he could stand, by the time she returned.

'I'm sorry. I should have come back and warned you I'd be a while, but I was so worried I didn't think.'

'No harm done.' He propped on his elbows, watching his feet. The ache felt bone-deep and he sensed a bruise developing on one heel. An experimental toe-curl resulted in a shocking pain through the knuckles of his toes. 'At least I don't think there is.'

Em sat down, cradled both his feet in her lap and began to rub. 'This might help.'

Josh flopped back, trying not to grimace as the increased circulation made his feet throb even more.

'I wish I knew how they got out,' she said. 'That's the second time now. I can't believe it was kids. It had to have been me. I was distracted and forgot to lock the gate.' She slid him a sideways look. 'After all, I did have something to get distracted about.'

'I'm distracting, huh?'

'Just a little.'

'A little?'

'Well, maybe more than a little.'

He hoisted himself up to drag her, laughing, back onto his chest before snaking his hands inside her jumper. 'Now,' he said, his erection growing as she wriggled over him, 'why not let me show you just how distracting I can be?'

***

Tiredness infected Josh's limbs as he pushed through the back door of his parents' house. His feet ached from the morning's adventure, yesterday's football and the impact of long-studded football boots. He had bruises in places he didn't want to think about and a pulled muscle in his shoulder that was making itself known, but his mood was high.

His mum was up and in the kitchen, stirring soup at the stove. She looked better today, with none of the greasy pallor of nausea the chemo normally left, and a smile that seemed genuine instead of forced. An open notebook and pen lay on the table, a glass of ginger ale alongside. The air smelled of bacon bones, buttery toast and love. He kissed her cheek and peered into the pot, inhaling deeply. He'd missed the aromas of his mum's cooking. With them both working long hours, he and Bianca had tended to buy ready meals and pre-made sauces. It diminished their home somehow, starving it of the warmth his parents' had. He couldn't shed the feeling that it might have starved his and Bianca's hearts too.

'Pea and ham soup,' she said. 'Would you like some?'

Josh shook his head. He'd eaten at Em's: poached eggs, bacon, and fritters made from potato and corn. And sweet extras. Lots of sweet, sexy extras. 'Maybe later. What about you? Have you eaten?'

'I had a bit of toast.' She took his left hand, cupping her palm around his stumps as though they were normal fingers. The action reminded him of Em. His missing digits had never bothered her either. His ex-wife was okay about it too, but lacked the same complete acceptance as Em and his mum. Bianca's mouth always twitched that tiny fraction when she sensed the stumps on her bare skin, the tic leaving him with a hollow sadness and strange sense of shame.

'Sore after footy?' his mum asked.

'Actually I'm pretty good, considering. How about you? Good morning?'

'Oh, not too bad.' She glanced towards her notebook. 'I've been writing for most of it.'

'Don't wear yourself out. You're meant to be resting.'

She touched her other hand to his cheek and gazed at him lovingly. 'You're a good boy.'

'Not always.'

'No.' Her smile turned sly. 'You didn't come home last night. Was she nice?'

Laughing, he slipped his hand free of hers. 'Come on, Mum. You know a gentleman never tells. Dad in the shed, is he?'

'Where else?'

'You need anything?' When she shook her head he strode towards the door. 'Ring if you need us.'

'Yes, yes.' She flapped a hand at him, then, when he was almost out, added, 'Give my love to Em when you call her.'

He halted and stared at her. 'How —'

'Mothers have their ways.'

He wanted to press her but the glint in his mum's eyes, so rare lately, kept him quiet. Let her have her fun. She deserved it, and if the pleasure on her face was anything to go by, the development made her happy. For all of them right now, that's what counted.

He found his dad at the back of the workshop, crouched at the timber Josh had laid out on an old blanket. Tom smoothed his hand over the rich red jarrah, feeling it the way Josh did, with one ear canted, as though the rings and marks of the old tree still whispered.

'Good quality,' his dad said, straightening.

'It's for a blanket box. Should look good when it's done and polished.'

Tom nodded in agreement before regarding his son with eyes even more heavily drooped than Josh's own. The tilt was worse these days, dragged down by his wife's diagnosis, interrupted sleep and the creep of age. Age that seemed to have accelerated dangerously this last month and hooked its claws into every part of his body. Like Josh, Tom was a large man, fit and muscled from work. He always stood straight-backed, kept his step deliberate and his conversation laconic, but now he seemed weighted with weariness.

'Good night?'

'Not bad. You up to giving me a hand? I've got some timber in the ute.'

Tom nodded and followed Josh out to the Hilux. Josh pulled back the tonneau cover and showed his dad the thick cypress log.

'From Rocking Horse Hill,' he said. No point hiding what Mum had already worked out. 'One of Em's cypresses was struck by lightning.'

Tom traced his palm over the bark and axe-hewn end. The log was about two and a half metres in length and four hundred millimetres in diameter, cut, with sweaty effort, from one of the thick lower branches by Josh that morning. 'What do you plan to make with it?'

'No idea.'

His dad regarded him thoughtfully. 'Not a commission, then?'

'No.'

Josh didn't elaborate. He didn't want either of his parents reading too much into his relationship with Em. Technically, they didn't even have one. One night and morning of sex didn't mean the same as when they were younger, when sleeping together held so much meaning and power. Now they were simply two consenting adults enjoying themselves without the clumsiness of inexperience.

Other than a promise to craft something from the log, he'd left Em with no set plans to meet again, just a kiss that lingered as he rested his back against the door of his car, her hips against his groin, legs nested between his and her arms linked around his neck. He kept toying with the belt loop on the back of her jeans, hooking his thumbs through and withdrawing them, not wanting to leave.

It'd been easy until that point, but the moment Em had walked with him to the car something restless had settled inside Josh, an anxiety that this might be the end. He hunted for a concrete reason to return, something that didn't look like he was using her for his own gratification, and settled on the cypress. It bothered her. He could tell from how often she looked at it.

First he offered to help clear the timber, only to discover she'd already made arrangements. So he suggested crafting something from a piece of scrap, and she'd accepted, telling him how much her grandmother would like that.

Except whatever he made wouldn't be for her grandmother.

He and Tom carried the log inside the shed, laying it on a sheet of cardboard near the roller door and standing back to regard the barked surface.

'You and Em together again?' asked his dad after a while.

Josh shrugged. 'Bit early to tell.'

'Mum'll be pleased.'

'Yeah.' He tilted his head, mind still on the log. 'I suppose I could carve something. Never really done anything like that before, though.'

Tom pursed his mouth as he considered. 'Table, perhaps. Marquetry top.'

'Maybe.' The late night, early morning and rigours of football were wearing him down. 'I'll need to think about it more.' At the front of the shed he ran his hand over the kitchen trolley. The chopping-board insert was propped against the wall, the timber pale and in need of oil. Tomorrow, he would begin the labour-intensive task of polishing the frame. 'Mum looks a bit better today.'

'She does,' said Tom. 'Still writing in those books too much. Can't stop her, though.'

'No.' Assessing the time as right, Josh took a breath. 'So, have you given any more thought to my proposal?'

His dad squinted at a dovetail corner join, running his thumb over the tightly paired timbers. 'Your mother and I are very proud of you, you know.' He looked up, love in his weary eyes, and moved around the trolley, fingers that had seen a thousand cuts and splinters tracing the edge. 'You're a good craftsman, with a good eye for detail. The quality's there. The demand too, by the look of things.'

Josh's heart sank as he realised where this was going. 'But?'

'It's not a business for two.'

'With two of us working it will be. The only reason I'm not producing more is because I can't. Not on my own.' He stepped towards his dad. 'With both of us we could double output. Start to display some products. The website's already getting hits and enquiries. A bit of publicity and this could really take off.'

'I'm sorry, son.'

'Dad, please.'

'No. Not now.'

'Then when?'

'Maybe when your mother's better.' He looked away. 'Right now what this family needs most is security. I'm not about to risk that by leaving a job that's put food on the table and a roof over our heads for more than thirty years.'

Protest was pointless. The old man knew what he stood for, what was needed in his world, and what he could provide. Most of all, he loved his wife. Josh's arguments wouldn't stand a chance.

'Okay. We'll talk again when Mum's better.'

Tom's chin suddenly dropped. For a long while he remained silent. Josh watched him, not liking this at all. The same anxiety that had struck when kissing Em goodbye that morning was creeping around his insides. Finally, his dad looked up. 'She might not get better.'

'Of course she will. The doctors said she has a great chance.' He stared at his father's watery eyes in horror. 'Dad?'

'She does, but only if she has a mastectomy.'

Josh's jaw tightened as he took that in. A mastectomy. The cancer must be worse than she'd let on. 'So when's the operation?'

His father regarded him like a man lost. 'She's refusing to have it.'

'What?' Breathing hard, Josh leaned on the trolley. His mum refusing treatment that could save her life? What the hell was she thinking? And why wasn't his dad doing anything about it?

'Dad?'

Tom took a few shaky steps to a sawhorse and sagged down on it. 'I've tried to convince her. She won't listen.'

'What about Karen and Sally? Have they tried?'

'They don't know. Michelle made me keep it from them. She made me keep it from all of you, but it's not right, whatever she says.' He shook his head. 'She keeps telling me that the choice is hers to make.'

'But she could die!'

'You think I don't know that? You think I'm not trying everything I can to make her see sense?'

'But why?'

'She's scared about not being a woman or something. I don't know. It's all bloody stupid to me. I don't care if she has no breasts. I just want her with me.'

His dad began to cry in earnest. The sound was like nothing Josh had ever heard, as if it had been dragged up from somewhere so deep the human edges had scraped away, leaving nothing but pure animal pain.

Josh moved to comfort him but Tom jerked to his feet and, with his palm held up, stumbled to the end of the shed. His own mind scrambling to understand what he'd just been told, Josh let him be.

The notebooks. The fucking notebooks. He should have realised. She'd been scribbling in them nonstop since he'd bought them. But the urgency wasn't because she had nothing else to do; she was racing her cancer. Which could only mean one thing.

His mum believed she was going to die.

After several minutes, his dad pulled a hanky from his pocket and blew his nose, before heading back to Josh. His eyes were rheumy, sad and shame-filled, his voice hoarse. 'Sorry, son. Lost it a bit.'

'You don't have to be sorry, Dad. You love her. We all love her.'

'I don't know what to do.'

'I do. We deal with this as a family, the way we've always done. That means telling Karen and Sal.'

'Mum won't like it.'

'Too bad.' Josh gripped his dad's shoulder and squeezed, trying to smile encouragement. 'Mum can get away with a lot of things, but dying isn't one of them. Hang in there. We'll have her sorted out before you know it.'

Tom regarded him hopefully, and Josh wasn't sure what upset him most – his father's tears or his look of uncertainty, as if Tom's world was collapsing and only Josh could save it. 'You sure?'

'Course I am.'

But inside Josh knew that when it came to his mother, nothing was sure at all.

Nine

Jasmine's voice carried sharply over the sea breeze. She twisted in the saddle, gaping at Em, and pulled her grey show horse, Ox, to an abrupt halt. 'You *slept* with him?'

Em winced at her friend's incredulous tone. It was just sex. Hardly new or innovative, and not something she hadn't done before. Or with Josh. She eased Lod back to a walk and turned him to face Jas.

Teagan manoeuvred Astra alongside, the filly protesting at the change of pace with her usual skittery dance and extravagant neck arching. As a horse recently off the track, Astra still believed there were only two speeds: stop and go. But she was the prettiest horse any of them had seen in years and Em could understand why Teagan persevered.

Rose-pink spots sat high on Jasmine's cheeks, whether from wind blush or shock, Em couldn't be certain. The sight of them shot irritation down her spine. Jas didn't hold an exclusive license for bedroom fun.

Em couldn't prevent the sulkiness in her voice. 'Aren't I allowed to?'

'No!'

'Jas, don't be ridiculous,' said Teagan.

Jas blinked and her voice dropped back to normal. 'I mean, yes, of course you're allowed but, Em, this is *you* we're talking about. Since when do you sleep with someone on the first night?'

Em slid her palm down Lod's shaggy neck. Time for the clippers. Any further delay and his coat would be too short to look its best at the first show.

Perhaps she, Jas and Teagan could make a day of it, at the hill.

'Well?'

'It was just sex.'

Jas held her eyes heavenward. 'With Josh Love-Of-Your-Life Sinclair. And on the first night!'

'Who could blame her,' said Teagan. 'You saw him Friday night at Camrick. The bloke's grown into a complete babe.'

Josh had always been a complete babe, but Em didn't need to add that to the conversation. 'Since when did you become so judgemental? You've had sex on plenty of first nights. Mike, for starters, and how could any of us ever forget Rory Davidson?' Em feigned an exaggerated shudder, which at last earned her a throaty laugh.

'You're never going to let me live that down, are you?'

'Never.'

'With good reason,' added Teagan. 'God, he was *awful*! Those zits.'

'That penis,' countered Jas.

More laughter followed. They urged the horses back into a walk, keeping to the wet sand, where the footing was firmer. The wild weather from the previous week had cast high drifts of seaweed further up the beach. The air was rich with its iodine smell and noisy with seagulls picking at scraps caught up in the weed tangle. Fish, crustaceans and molluscs brought up from deeper water to slowly die. Here and there a fluoro orange float added brightness as well as sadness to the decaying browns. Each year the mess seemed to get worse; the selfishness of humans captured like abstract art in the masses of marine rope, plastic rubbish and fishing line.

'So,' said Jas, 'how was it?'

'How was what?'

'Don't play cute. We're your best friends.'

'The same.' Em looked towards the sea. A rippling white line stretched across the water where the swell hit one of the coastline's many distant reefs and formed a bank of ocean breakers. She smiled at the crashing wave inference, thinking of Josh's skilful touch. 'Better.'

'Better? From the man you once described as the ultimate bed-mate?' Jas flicked her dark curls. None of them wore helmets. The day was too fine, the air too enticing. 'Bloody hell.'

Teagan speared her with an envious look.

Em said nothing. What was there to say? They'd had amazing sex. Sex she'd enjoyed every delicious second of, that made her feel womanly and desirable and alive. Sex she wanted to repeat. Soon.

She wondered what he was doing, if he would be free tonight. She could cook something simple, an omelette with *fines herbes*, all fresh-picked from the garden, with perhaps a sprinkle of parmigiano, and a dressed salad. They could share a bottle of rosé or pinot noir, and relax afterwards on the lounge. Then later, when their slow caresses signalled a change in mood, Em could lead him to bed where she'd rub his sore body with warm vanilla-scented oil until they were both slippery with excitement.

'Oh, you are so gone.'

'What?' said Em, jerking around to blink at Jas.

'You should see your face. Last time you looked like that you were seventeen.'

'You never looked like that with Trent, that's for sure,' said Teagan.

Em twisted her fingers through Lod's mane, her cheeks hot. 'I had a good night, that's all.'

'A very good night. So what's next with the sexpot?'

'I don't know. Nothing, I suppose.'

'Nothing!'

'Bullshit.'

Em released an exasperated sigh. 'It was just sex.'

'You mean sex for old-time's sake?' asked Jas. 'Like Daniella Foltz's high-school reunion one-night stand with Wade Quinn?'

'No!'

'Good. Because we all know how badly *that* ended.'

Teagan's snort of laughter had Astra shooting off on another of her skittery fits. Given how thin Teagan was these days it was a wonder she had the strength to control the horse at all.

'Daniella and Wade were married,' said Em. 'Josh and I are completely unattached.'

'So, just your run-of-the-mill, wham-bam-thank-you-ma'am, means-nothing one-night stand, then?'

Em narrowed her eyes, but Jas only laughed. Her friend was enjoying this enormously. Fortunately Teagan was too occupied with Astra to keep digging the boot in.

'Poor, innocent Emily,' teased Jas, 'why do you lie to yourself so?'

'I'm being realistic.'

'Realistic? Oh, come on. This isn't just a one-nighter with your average hot bloke. This is a one-nighter with Josh Sinclair, and you know there's only one place that can lead. Oh, yes. Sex with Josh Sinclair can only have repercussions. Serious repercussions. Repercussions like' – she slapped her hand to her heart and gasped theatrically – 'love!'

'Jas, darling, I love you dearly.' Em held up a hand and began ticking off counterarguments. 'But his mum's sick. He's been through a divorce that's left God knows what scars. And he's only just come home. He's not interested in anything more than a bit of fun.' Except that was a white lie. The way he'd looked at her in the drive at Camrick conveyed something very different, as did his farewell that morning. The way he'd held her, gently trapped between his legs, arms around her waist, continuing to kiss and nuzzle long after he should have gone. Em had been just as bad, not wanting the magic to end, letting the day rise and warm over them when she should have been organising Lod for their trip to Admella Beach.

For some reason she didn't want to tell her friends about those intimate moments. As ridiculous as the feeling was, Em harboured a superstitious fear that she might have read too much into Josh's expression and caresses. Her hopes were fragile, like the bubbles left with each wash of the tide. This could be nothing. This could be everything. Examining it wouldn't change Josh's feelings, or his plans. She had to let it flow.

'I think you're wrong,' said Jas, contemplative now. 'A man like Josh doesn't play games. And when you think about it, the attraction must still be pretty intense for him to accept an invitation to Camrick, especially given what happened there. And after. He has every right to hate you, but he doesn't. Instead he gives you last night.'

They rode on. The horses plodding contentedly as seagulls flapped and bickered, and the ocean kept up its soothing swish.

Em noticed Jasmine's mouth turning down as her thoughts channelled inwards. 'How are things with Mike?'

'The same. He feeds me the usual promises and I believe them.' Jas bit her lip and Em immediately wished she hadn't brought the subject up. 'I'm so tired of this, Em. Everything to do with it – the lies, the loneliness, the way I hate myself.'

'So stop,' said Teagan, although gently this time. The pain in Jasmine's voice was too acute for stone throwing.

Jasmine's eyes filled. 'I wish I could.'

Em experienced a surge of loathing for Mike and his selfish heart. All that hurt for the sake of willing sex and the pathetic thrill of adultery. The man deserved nothing, certainly not this beautiful, big-hearted woman.

'I love him as much as I hate him. Every time I see him I say this is going to be the last. And then he touches me and it's like I'm possessed.'

Em reached across to rest her hand on Jasmine's back. As though sensing his mistress's distress, Ox tossed his head but stayed steady alongside Lod, his black-tipped silvery ears twitching. 'You have to find the strength. You can't keep going like this.'

'No man is worth this sort of pain, Jas,' said Teagan.

'I know.' Jas dragged the sleeve of her polar fleece across her eyes and sniffed loudly. 'God, I don't know what I'd do without you two.'

'Oh, I think you'd cope all right.' Jas was as tough as they came. Except when it came to the man who knew how to manipulate every cell in her body.

Jas remained serious, her focus on Em. 'You know, you've never once condemned me for this. Teagan's always made her disapproval known, but you've never blamed me.'

'None of us are pure, Jas. Me especially.'

'Not after last night, anyway.'

Em laughed, relieved to hear humour return to her friend's voice. 'Definitely not after last night. Come on, let's clear these boys' pipes out.'

She urged Lod into canter and leaned forward, setting her weight on her knees as she let the horse have his head. Wind rushed past her ears, Lod's hooves making wet thumps against the dense sand, Ox's and Astra's adding to the beat. She steered him into the water, where the beach sloped gently and the tide surged in broad shallow sweeps. The horse powered on, flicking up water that hung like glittering diamonds in the winter sun.

And suddenly Em was free of everything. Of the intense, uncertain feelings that last night unleashed. The world was salty and scented and brilliant, and she was galloping on the very edge of it. Elated, excited and brave.

***

'Your mother is in the kitchen with Felicity,' said Granny B in her most cut-glass voice, a sure indication of her temper. 'Poring over carpet samples, every one of them in that God-awful curdled cream colour to which, for some unfathomable reason, she's taken a fancy. Wholly impractical, and bound to make Camrick look like a consulting room. Damned shame to cover those floorboards.'

Em thought it was too, but if her mother possessed anything it was good taste. Whatever carpet she chose, the hall and stairs would look designer-perfect. 'The runner was pretty worn, Gran.'

'Rubbish. A few threads missing, that's all.' She sighed. With the Persian runner pulled up, the hall appeared gloomier than usual, a vast expanse of dark polished timber and shadowy corners. 'I'm going to miss these floorboards. Creak like an old ship, they do. Always made it easy to determine if a burglar was in the house. They'll be able to prance around pinching silver all they please once that carpet goes down.' She and Em walked to the kitchen. 'Still, that's your mother's problem.'

Adrienne looked up from her booklet as they came in. 'It is, which is why I can't fathom why you insist on carrying on about it.' She smiled at Em. 'Hello, darling.'

Em greeted her with a kiss and a quick hug, and a smile and hello for Felicity. The kitchen smelled as it usually did on a Tuesday evening, aromatic with good cooking and homeliness. Tonight, the air was savoury with vegetables and herbs, and a touch humid thanks to a steaming stockpot on the stove.

'Minestrone?' she guessed, although it wasn't a difficult one. Her mum's minestrone was a family winter favourite, and tonight was cold, the southern breeze bone-chilling.

'All Felicity's work.' Adrienne smiled at her future daughter-in-law, and reached across to squeeze her hand. 'She's proving quite the talented cook. And I've attempted another batch of sourdough.' Releasing Felicity, she threw Em an apologetic look. 'I know I said I wouldn't but I simply can't stand the thought that it's beaten me.'

Adrienne's battle to make the perfect sourdough loaf had been waged for a few years now, ever since Samuel escorted her to France on holiday. Em's mother made perfectly serviceable bread, delicious bread, in fact, with a lovely tang, chewy texture and crisp outer crust. But it was never the same as the loaves she'd enjoyed in Paris, and so the fight continued. Em suspected it would never end.

Perhaps if Adrienne had kept Camrick's old combustion stove she might have stood a chance but that went after Uncle James's death, when Adrienne moved from Rocking Horse Hill into town and embarked on yet another of her modernisation missions. Although stunning, its sleek stainless-steel replacement seemed to lack that certain something, as if its efficiency starved the bread of soul.

'I'm sure you'll win in the end. So where's Dig?'

'Held up at some irrigation forum FirstAg is running. He shouldn't be too far away.'

Em pulled out a stool and sat opposite her mother at the large granite-topped workstation. Samples of cream carpet were scattered across the surface. Each was plush and expensive-looking, but with differing piles and textures. Em scraped her palm over the surface of one piece. It changed shade the way shot taffeta did when it shimmied against the light. 'This is nice.'

Shooting Em a mutinous look, Granny B harrumphed and stalked from the room, leaving mother and daughter to share a smile.

'Mother's not taking it well.'

'You know Gran, she's not one for change.'

'No,' said Adrienne. 'But change is part of life.' She passed her sample on to Felicity. 'What do you think?'

Felicity threw up her hands. 'You're asking the wrong person. I can barely coordinate my clothes.'

'Sure,' teased Em. 'That's why you're looking as stunning as Mum tonight.'

Both women wore their hair piled up in messy but flattering buns, loose wisps curling becomingly around their foreheads and cheeks, the style exposing the creamy skin of their necks. They both wore cotton shirts with the sleeves rolled up to reveal the fine bones of their forearms; Adrienne's shirt a rich autumn orange-brown that brightened her face, Felicity's a cobalt blue that matched her pale colouring and highlighted her eyes. A stylised horse logo was embroidered on one of the chest pockets, an expensive brand that Em recognised as one of her mother's favourites.

'That colour suits you,' she said. 'Matches your eyes.'

'Thanks.' Felicity brushed her palm down the sleeve of her shirt. 'I've never had clothes of this quality before. They feel so different.'

'Best get used to it,' said Adrienne. 'You're a Wallace now. A lot of things will be different.'

Em regarded her carpet sample. Perhaps when they had a moment alone she should chat to her mother about getting ahead of herself. It was wonderful Digby was engaged but he'd been in that situation before, with Cait. And what a mess that had turned into, leaving Digby emotionally burned and Em worried that he'd end up rattling around Camrick alone, a man who possessed everything he could want except love.

'You look tired,' said Adrienne.

Self-consciously, Em touched the puffy flesh under her eyes. 'It's nothing. A bad night's sleep.'

Her mother pushed the booklet aside and leaned forward. 'Everything okay?'

For a brief moment Em considered telling her about Josh, then changed her mind. She was being silly. Two nights without hearing from him meant nothing.

Except a disappointed ache in her chest that refused to ease.

She dropped her hand and chose another sample. 'Everything's fine.'

Adrienne regarded Em for a moment longer, before selecting a sample herself. 'I was thinking of this one. The colour's called raffia.' She ran her palm over the surface as Em had done and passed it across. 'It's a bit shaggier than I wanted but I can't help liking the way it feels.'

The carpet did feel lush. It would be delicious to walk on, and quiet. As for practicality, Em wasn't so sure. 'It's nice.'

'It's also the most expensive.'

'Now why doesn't that surprise me?'

Adrienne laughed. Her expensive taste was a family joke. But that taste also made her one of the most stylish women Em knew. It was something in the way she held herself. The way her shirts hung neatly and always tucked, her trousers unwrinkled. Her jewellery always golden, with no hint of tarnish, her diamonds fiery with refracted light. Even when windblown her hair was lovely in its messy dishevelment.

Em had once heard someone describe it as old-money beauty, as if such a look could only be bought. But it was far more than that. Adrienne's appearance was borne from attention to detail, and a grace and charm that came from within.

Felicity rose to check on dinner. Em followed her to the stove, grabbing a teaspoon from the drawer as she passed. She dipped it into the simmering soup and brought it to her mouth, blowing a few times before tasting.

The mix of vegetables, herbs and pulses was delicious and comforting. 'Perfect.'

'I can't take the credit. It's your mum's recipe. I just chopped and stirred.'

'There's more to it than chopping and stirring,' said Adrienne, joining them to dip her own spoon in. 'Cooking takes passion.' She blew and tasted. 'Couldn't have done better myself. It'll be even nicer in the summer, when Em has tomatoes.'

'Assuming I can keep Kicki and Cutie out of the garden. Speaking of which,' she said, addressing Felicity, 'when's that fiancé of yours going to bring you out to the hill?'

'How about this Saturday?' asked a deep voice behind them.

Felicity dumped the pot lid on the sink and flung herself at Digby.

Adrienne and Em looked on in amusement as the pair kissed as though they'd been apart for months instead of hours.

Em couldn't recall the last time she'd seen her brother so confident. In a few weeks, Felicity had restored what Cait had sucked away. Their love radiated heat through the kitchen, making Em acutely aware of how uncertain her relationship with Josh was. They'd had a one-night stand, caved into their attraction. They had fun and great sex, but that was no guarantee of anything deeper as Josh's lack of contact had proven.

She swapped her teaspoon for a wooden one and gave the pot an unnecessary stir. What did she expect? She'd cheated on him, humiliated him. Impossible things to forget. Perhaps impossible to forgive, too.

'Is Saturday okay?' said Digby. 'We could stay for dinner. I'll pick out something decent from the cellar for you.'

'You and Josh, and Digby and Felicity,' said Adrienne.

Em made a noise that committed her to nothing.

'Good that you and Josh are getting back together,' said Digby, not registering his sister's response. 'He's a good bloke.'

'We're not.' Em caught his raised eyebrows and backtracked. She didn't want her family speculating about something she understood little herself. 'It's early days. Anyway, about Saturday. I have the shop in the morning and a few chores to do, then I want to take Lod for a ride, but any time after that would be fine, say about three? That should give you enough time to look around and climb the crater while there's still light.' She clapped her hands, eager to move off the topic in case someone brought Josh up again. 'Right, who's up for a pre-dinner drink?'

Digby raided the fridge for a beer and wine for his mother and Em. Felicity filled the kettle for tea and turned it on before moving back to Digby's side.

'I'll sort it,' said Em, when the water had boiled. She listened to their chatter as the tea brewed, thinking how much Felicity had changed since her arrival. The shyness had disappeared completely, along with the little girl ponytails and daggy clothes. Even her speech was changing, the way she enunciated her words. Not Granny B posh, but with a subtle affectation.

Em carried the tea over. 'Careful, it's hot.'

'Yes.' A strange enigmatic smile flitted across Felicity's face and then died. 'Scalds can be very painful.'

Em frowned. The statement was innocent enough, a simple observation, but that expression? That was very odd. Almost triumphant.

Felicity caught her puzzlement. 'I worked in a kitchen once.'

'Oh.' Now Em was even more confused. 'But I thought you couldn't cook.'

Felicity's eyes widened with an emotion that seemed akin to panic. 'I —'

'It was an industrial place,' said Digby, cupping her shoulders. 'Not exactly cooking.' He held Felicity's gaze, the pair exchanging a secret message. 'More like throwing mixes into vats, wasn't it, Flick?'

'Yes. Yes, more like that.' She took a quick sip of tea that must have burned but caused no reaction. 'You look very nice tonight, Em. I like your jacket.'

'Thanks,' said Em, bemused by the sudden change of topic and the weirdness of the conversation. It was as though she'd stumbled into the centre of some private joke, except this one didn't seem remotely funny. 'I bought it from Campbells. They're our local country outfitter. Been in business nearly a hundred years. You should get Mum to take you there one day.'

'We'll go tomorrow,' said Adrienne. 'You'll need boots for the farm.'

'The farm!' Felicity was suddenly all joy. 'I can't wait for Saturday. It's going to be such fun.'

'Yes,' said Granny B from the doorway. But her eyes were on Em instead of Felicity, and filled with something Em couldn't interpret. 'I'm sure it will be.'

Em blinked and reached for her glass of wine. Whatever peculiar disorder had infected her family, she wasn't in the mood for it. She had more than enough worries in her life right now without playing nurse. The most nagging of which possessed hands capable of moulding female flesh into something exquisite as easily as he did with wood, yet for some reason lacked the dexterity to dial a simple phone number.

Ten

'Sit down, Karen,' said Josh, but his sister continued her march, the fabric of her red T-shirt stretched tight over her wonderfully round, seven-months-pregnant belly.

'I bloody won't sit down!'

Across the table, Sally smiled wryly. Since Karen had heard the news about their mum she'd been in a state, pacing the narrow space between the window and Sally's dining table, sleek brunette bob whipping with each about-turn, lasering her narrowed eyes between her two siblings as if this was their fault.

Josh had already faced remonstrations from them for keeping the news to himself for almost three days. Aware their anger came only from distress and guilt, Josh had let it slide. He'd contacted them both Sunday afternoon, wanting to arrange a meeting, but between Karen's busy life and Sally's frantic one with Cameron and the boys, scheduling hadn't been easy. Wednesday was the earliest they were all free.

He could have pressed harder, revealed the urgency of the matter, but Josh wanted to make his own gentle approaches to his mum. His failure had left him no choice but to divulge what his mum hadn't wanted them to know.

Karen slapped her palms against the Tasmanian blackwood table, a beautifully crafted wedding present for Sally and Cam from their dad, now bearing the blemishes of much use. 'What the *fuck* is she thinking?'

'Hey!' Sally jerked her head towards the lounge. Though the glass double doors were closed, the room wasn't soundproof. Comic Loony Tunes music filtered through, occasional spills of canned laughter mocking the pressure-cooker atmosphere of the dining room. Normally Sally hated using the television as a babysitter for Jack and Cooper, but this was an emergency. That she even raised her voice revealed how tense this had made them.

Josh went to pick up his cup of coffee and put it back down again. A slick had formed on the surface where the milk had cooled. They'd all forgotten their drinks the moment he explained, as calmly as he could, the events of the previous few days – his father's revelation and tears, his own clumsy attempt to talk to his mum, the sense of hurt and betrayal he'd recognised in her face and, worse, her determination.

'Sit down, Karen,' he said, and this time Josh made it an order.

Finally she huffed and sat. Placing her hand on the shelf of her belly, she turned towards the window and the raw day beyond, her eyes filming with held-back tears. 'Why can't she see that a breast means nothing compared to how much we love her?'

Josh dropped his head. He'd wondered that himself a thousand times and still had no answer. 'I don't know.'

'Do you think she's worried about how Dad will feel about her afterwards?' said Sally. 'Sexually, I mean.' She glanced from Karen to Josh and back again. Where Karen was all planes and corners, Sally was curves and cloudy-haired softness. Both were attractive, like their mother, but in opposite, individual ways. Personality-wise, Sally tended to be the calmer, more sensible of the two and Josh listened carefully as she explained. 'You know what men are like with breasts.'

Karen regarded her own chest. 'As if I need reminding. Davey loves mine at the moment. Reckons they're huge.'

'You wait until you start breastfeeding and he clocks the size of your nipples. He won't be able to leave them alone.'

'Won't they be too sore?' asked Karen, frowning.

Sally shrugged. 'Depends.'

Josh shifted, trying to look unaffected by the conversation when the whole thing made him want to clap his hands over his ears and say la-la-la, loudly. He didn't mind a good nipple himself. As long as they weren't his sisters'.

Sally caught his discomfort. 'Sorry. Girl talk.'

'Bit off topic, too.'

'It's not, though,' said Karen. 'What if it's all to do with her sense of womanhood. How do we counteract that?'

Sally's gaze shifted towards the glass doors, her heart-shaped face edged with anguish. 'Show her all that she has to live for.'

Josh ran his forefinger over one of the table's blemishes; the curve of the dent was suggestive of a spoon banged by a child. He'd tried the grandchildren angle too. It had been one of his first parries. But it hadn't worked. Michelle's expression had twisted at the mention of Cooper and Jack, even more so at the mention of Karen's unborn baby, but her mind wasn't changed.

His inability to fathom why was costing him sleep and sanity. For his dad it must be even worse, especially if, as Karen suggested, Michelle was holding back on the operation for him.

'But she's not dying, is she?' countered Karen. 'The surgery's precautionary, isn't it? I don't know about you but I don't want to go in there treating her like she's already on death's door.'

'They didn't get all the cells, Karen. The surgical margins weren't clear, which is as good as saying it's still there. And don't forget she's HER2-positive,' said Sally, reminding Karen of the result they'd all feared hearing after the first biopsy. HER2-positive cancers tended to be more aggressive thanks to a gene mutation in the cells, leading to a tough, protracted fight. 'How long before it spreads again? It's probably on the move now. And the longer it remains untreated the higher the risk of it developing into secondary cancer.'

Secondary cancer meant surviving with the disease, not combating it. It meant their mum's liver, bones, everything, was at risk. It meant their mum's life. And in a close family like theirs, it meant their lives were snared too.

'So what do we do?' asked Sally, looking at Josh.

Josh scraped his palm down his tired face. 'We talk to her. *Gently.* We don't want Mum feeling like she's under siege, from us or anyone. So this stays in the family.' He looked hard at his sisters, neither of whom seemed impressed by the idea.

'But her friends. Margie. Dale.'

'No, Josh's right,' Sally said reluctantly. 'Once this gets out we'll have everyone on the doorstep.'

'Gang up and she'll only dig her heels in more. Remember the episode with the apricot tree?'

Karen rolled her eyes at the memory. The tree was infected with a soil-borne fungus and needed to come down. 'Over my dead body!' their mum had said. No amount of argument could convince her, not from Dad, the tree surgeon, or Digby Wallace-Jones, who'd been called in to consult as a favour to Josh. The apricot tree was part of the orchard Michelle planted after she and Tom married. The first tree in their first and only house. A tree with meaning, she claimed. And so it remained, barely producing fruit, losing limbs as each affected branch was removed, for three more years. Time in which the original could have been cut down, burned, the soil treated and a new tree planted on resistant rootstock, almost ready for its first crop. Eventually the inevitable happened. The tree couldn't respond any further to her loving attention and died. The space where it existed still remained. A tribute, although to what no one was really sure.

Karen crossed her arms. 'What about Dad?'

'His job is to keep doing what he's doing. Telling her he loves her no matter what.'

'I'll talk to the hospital,' said Sally. 'Get the number of that counsellor they talked about. Maybe check out the library too. There'll be books on this sort of thing.'

'I'll check out the Internet,' said Karen. 'There's probably a stack of blogs and forums on the topic. Josh?'

Josh looked at his hands, at the spaces where his fingers should have been, remembering the day his dad discovered him collapsed in the workshop, moaning and faint as blood spread over the concrete. The speed with which he'd acted, stripping off his shirt and binding his son's hand and arm before carrying him into the house and calling triple-0. How he'd cradled Josh as they waited, promising him it would be all right. How there was no need to be frightened, Dad was there. Dad would always be there.

He blinked at the sting in his eyes and pushed back his chair. 'I've said my bit. I'm not going to push it any more unless you need me to. But the best weapon we have is Dad, and right now he's not coping, no matter what show he puts on. My priority is to take care of him.'

And repay a little of what he owed.

***

Plate of toasted crumpets and tea in hand, Josh settled down at kitchen table's far end, where early sunshine warmed the seat and lit the front page of the local paper that his dad had left behind.

He took a bite of honeyed crumpet, eyeing his mum as he chewed. She looked better this morning. Though her face lacked its pre-diagnosis brightness, she didn't wince as much when she moved. It was the lymph gland removal that seemed the most painful. The way she had to keep her arm out and away from the healing wound. Josh tried not to think about what it would be like if she had her entire breast removed. The pain, both physical and psychological.

Yesterday, as he'd driven from Sally's, he'd tried to consider the loss from her perspective, and could only come up with the comparison that it'd be like losing a testicle. The thought had left him wiping sweat from his palms onto his jeans and shifting uncomfortably, but rallied at least some sympathy for her feelings. Sympathy but not understanding, and definitely not acceptance.

She'd been perky since his sisters began their Saving Mum From Herself campaign the afternoon before, as if the confrontation had flicked a combative switch inside her mind. His mum had always hated being patronised, and any mention of stupidity left her mutinous. It came, she'd once explained, from being looked upon a certain way simply because she'd chosen to be a stay-at-home mum. As far as Michelle was concerned, her career was the most important in existence. More important than a doctor or politician or any other profession. She, and women like her, nurtured the future. They moulded the growing minds of the next generation. Just because that involved cleaning up vomit and poo, reading picture books and crafting spaceships from toilet rolls, didn't make her unintelligent or without worth. Far from it.

Josh hadn't been there for yesterday's discussion, but it didn't take a genius to work out that his sisters' approach had failed. The irony was that defiance appeared to have done her wonders.

He indicated the notebook lying open at the opposite end of the table, both pages blank. 'Run out of wisdom?'

She smiled as she sponged toast crumbs from the bench into her hand. 'Mothers never run out of wisdom.'

He smiled back, on her side. 'I wouldn't go saying that to Sally or Karen right now. You're liable to cop it.'

Michelle picked up her cup of tea, leaning against the bench as she sipped. Light streamed behind her, leaving her front shadowed and her hair a gauzy halo of white-gold. 'Good thing I can give as good as I get, then.'

'They're only doing it because they love you. We all are.'

His words brought her across the room. Josh sat back and let her cup his cheek. Her gaze was soft and understanding. 'I know. But this is my battle, not yours.'

Josh couldn't hold onto his calm. He couldn't keep up the pretence of understanding, not when he wanted to shake her and bawl into her chest like he was a kid. 'No, it's not. It's all our battle. When something happens to one of us it happens to all of us. You taught us that.'

For a moment he thought he'd made it through to her. Her gaze flitted to the china cabinet behind him, towards its mismatched cluster of photo frames and old and new family snapshots, before losing focus as she drifted somewhere beyond. Then her eyes cleared and she shook her head. 'Not this time, my sweet. Not this time. Now,' she said, sliding her hand from his cheek and reaching for her tea, 'why aren't you out in the shed creating something beautiful?'

'I wanted to talk to you.' At her expression he hurried on. 'Not about that. About Dad. About the business.'

'What about it?'

'He won't leave Flanagan's, Mum. I think there's something worrying him. Something about me.' That wasn't quite the truth. His dad had inferred no such thing but he couldn't say it was her holding Tom back. His mum needed strength, not guilt.

'Like what?'

Josh tried to form words around a thought he wasn't sure about. The idea had only arrived that morning. 'We've never really worked together before. Not commercially. We've made plenty of stuff but that was always for things around the house or gifts, like Sally's table.'

'You think he's worried you mightn't get on?'

'I don't know. It's a possibility, though. I was thinking I could approach Flanagan's, ask Brendon if I could work for them for a while. With Dad.'

'But what about your business, your commissions?'

He shrugged. 'I could do them at night.'

'No.' She shook her head. 'No, I won't have it.'

'Mum.'

She held up her palm. 'I'm serious, Josh. I won't have it. You've already sacrificed enough, leaving your job to come back here. I'm not having you sacrifice your dream as well.'

'I won't be sacrificing my dream. The idea is to make it come true.'

'By wasting your days at Flanagan's? I don't think so. The sooner you build your business the sooner we can get your father working with you. Now,' she said, in a voice that conveyed she wanted no more of this talk, 'tell me what's happening with Em.'

He blinked at the change of subject, opened his mouth and then shut it.

Michelle's gaze sharpened. 'Don't tell me you haven't called her?'

Hot shame crept across Josh's skin. He concentrated on his crumpets, on the honey and butter smears, anything to avoid his mother's disappointed stare. He'd meant to call Em. He had great plans after Saturday night but they all disappeared the moment he saw his dad cry, when his chest became thick and heavy with fear. Even when he'd driven past the shop, Em's window display shining brightly, he'd meant to call in and say hi, ask how she was, what she thought about seeing him again, but his mind wasn't in the right place. This wasn't the time. She didn't want the burden of all his worries.

Deep inside, he knew the truth was more selfish. Those hours with her had reignited buried feelings, the intense, vulnerable ones that exposed him to hurt. Far more than he'd anticipated when he'd grabbed her hand at

Camrick. That had been more about being walked away from than anything else. He'd let her do it the last time he'd been at Camrick and he was stuffed if he'd let her repeat the act. Ego played a part too, whether he could win her over again. He'd won her over, all right. Bodily, anyway. But her heart?

He wanted her in his life, no question. But needing her the way he once had? Leaving himself wide open to another bout of the worst pain he'd ever felt? That left him shit-scared.

'Oh, Josh.' His mum's dismay made him squirm. 'I thought we brought you up better than that. What must she be thinking? And you were so happy on Sunday.'

'I'll call her, I promise.' At her raised eyebrows he sighed. 'I will.' Tomorrow, when he'd thought about how to explain why he hadn't called without giving anything away about his mum.

'Go and see her.' She snatched his hand and squeezed hard. 'This morning, Joshy.'

Joshy. His mother hadn't called him that in years. It was her manipulative name, the one she used when she wanted to get her own way. The one he could no more resist now than when he was ten.

He let out a long breath. 'All right. But only for you.'

'Oh,' said his mum, smiling slyly, 'I think this might be for you, too. You might be able to fool yourself' – she patted his hand – 'but you'll never fool your old mum.'

***

Josh paused at the edge of PaperPassion's window, peering down the thin space between the display and the wall. Em was behind the counter, a pencil clenched between her teeth.

He eased away from the window and eyed the street. Levenham was quiet, relaxing in that sleepy morning period after the school drop. Soon the footpath would be busy again with mothers and children and the bustle of business. Perhaps the shop would have customers.

A tray-top Toyota cruised by, the kelpie on the back with its head to the wind, watching the footpath and road with clever, curious eyes. Further on, where the road widened to form a small island around the town's central cenotaph, council workers in fluoro-green shirts weeded flowerbeds. A woman called out, waving to a friend on the opposite footpath before crossing the road. Small-town life going on. The tug of all he'd once thought he wanted.

He turned back to the door and started. Em stood behind the glass, watching him, her expression cool. Only the way she fiddled with the leather band of her watch gave any indication of her mood.

He walked to the door, Em retreating a few steps as he pushed it open. 'Hey.'

'Hey, yourself.'

He kept his hands tucked in his pockets as he tried to think of something to say. Sorry didn't seem right.

'Has your mum run out of notebooks again?' She sounded clipped, businesslike.

'No.'

When he didn't continue she tilted her head to one side, waiting.

'Look, Em, about Saturday night.'

'It doesn't matter. We're not kids any more. We had a nice time.' Her gaze slid away. 'It didn't mean anything.'

'It did for me.'

She stared at him and Josh noticed the heaviness under her eyes, the slight reddening of the lower lids. Not from tears but from extreme tiredness. He hoped like hell he wasn't the cause.

'The last week's been a bit hard at home. I've been meaning to call but there's been stuff going on.'

'Not your mum? Is she all right?'

He slid his hand over his head. He'd already said too much.

'Josh?'

'Mum's . . .' He sighed and shook his head. 'It's nothing. A bit of a family argument, that's all.'

She studied him. 'Are you sure?'

'Yeah.' Josh shoved his hand back into his pocket. While Em wasn't being openly hostile, she wasn't exactly welcoming. Josh supposed he deserved it, given his lack of manners. 'How about you? Are you okay?'

'I'm fine, why?'

'You look a bit tired.'

'I didn't get much sleep last night.'

He wanted to ask if it had anything to do with him but couldn't bring himself to.

'I was about to boil the kettle.'

'Is that an invitation for a cuppa?'

That earned him a smile. 'It is.'

He followed Em to the back of the shop. Behind the counter, her sketchbook sat open, discarded papers either side, the pencil she'd held between her teeth on top. He glanced at the drawing and recognised the Uffington White Horse, a famous prehistoric chalk figure carved into a hill in Oxfordshire. He'd climbed to the top with Bianca, saw the place where legend told St George slayed his dragon, and walked the iron-age hill fort alongside. Afterwards, they'd checked in early to their thatched holiday cottage and spent the night playing honeymooners. But at the top of that hill, as he studied the exposed chalk, there'd been a second, a heartbeat, when he'd thought of Em, the girl who'd loved horses and hills. The girl who'd cast him aside.

He stepped behind the bead curtain. The back room was dimmer than the bright shop, lit by a single naked bulb. Steel shelves along one wall held more of the jewel-covered notebooks. He looked away, reminded of his mother's books and their potential purpose. If it weren't for how they'd brought him to Em he wished he'd never set eyes on the bastard things.

Em was leaning against the bench, arms crossed, one hand at her mouth, watching the kettle. She'd left her hair long, and it fell in soft waves around her face. His heart contracted at the same moment he warned himself to be careful.

'I saw your sketch,' he said. 'What's it for?'

'The book I'm working on. G. K. Chesterton's *The Ballad of the White Horse*. An epic poem. Do you know it?'

Josh shook his head, amused she thought he would. He'd read the signs at the site, explaining about the White Horse, but not poetry. Neither could he remember Bianca reading anything like that. She was like him, working class, simply educated. Not dumb – far from it – but theirs was different world.

'I want it to open the first poem, "The Vision of the King". "Before the gods that made the gods had seen their sunrise pass, the White Horse of the White Horse Vale was cut out of the grass."' She smiled. 'It's a wonderful poem. Very English. Very romantic.'

'Perhaps I should read it.'

'I doubt it'd be your thing.'

'Why? Too romantic for a bloke?'

She stiffened. 'Perhaps.'

Josh curled his fists to stop himself from reaching out for her. The way she was acting he wasn't sure what her response would be if he did. 'I'm sorry. For not calling. I should have.'

'It doesn't matter.'

'Yeah, it does.' He smiled slightly. 'Mum gave me a telling off when she worked it out.'

'Is that why you're here, now? Because she made you?'

'No, I'm here because I want to be.'

She nodded but he couldn't tell if it was cool or warm. That he'd hurt her was obvious. The woman from Saturday night was somewhere untouchable, leaving a shell of Wallace aloofness in her place. Shame burned in him again. Regardless of what was happening at home, he should have called. He was a better man than that.

She stared at the kettle, her arms still crossed. Its rattle filled the room. She hadn't prepared mugs. Perhaps she wanted him to leave.

Perhaps he should.

'You're angry with me.'

She looked up. 'No.' Her expression softened. 'It's not you. I really didn't get much sleep last night.'

'What's up?'

'Two donkeys, that's what.' She grimaced. 'Two o'clock in the morning and Muffy starts barking the roof off. I race out of bed thinking it's burglars only to discover Kicki and Cutie on the back verandah destroying every last one of my spring seedling trays. When I opened the door they took off down the stairs and went rampaging through the garden.' She rubbed her hand across her forehead and swept some hair back. 'It took me nearly an hour to catch them and by the time I'd finished I was too hyped to go back to sleep.'

'Do you know how they got out?'

'That's the frustrating thing. I've no idea.'

The kettle clicked off but instead of sorting out their drinks she lifted a curled finger to her mouth and pressed it for a moment before regarding him with tired, stressed eyes. 'What if they get out and get hurt? Hit by a car or fall or something? I'm supposed to be keeping them safe and they've been through so much.'

Protectiveness stirred Josh into action. 'Come here,' he said, turning her into his arms and letting her press her forehead into his shoulder. He rested his cheek against hers and stroked her back. 'They'll be okay. They're tough. Animals clever enough to escape their paddock are too clever to get into strife.'

'God, I hope you're right.'

Josh expected her to move away but she stayed. The feel of her in his arms, knowing the simple act was giving her comfort, kept his hold steady.

'I don't know what I was trying prove by sleeping with you,' she said after a while.

He pulled back to regard her. 'I'm not sure it had anything to do with proving anything. We both wanted it. Didn't we?'

She sighed and he caught a hint of smile. 'Yes.'

'Good.' His own smile broadened. For the first time since his arrival, he felt grounded. Time to lighten the mood. 'So does that mean we can do it again?'

Her laugh spilled. 'Maybe. If you behave.'

'Behave? Like this?' In a flash his hands were sliding up the inside of her shirt, caressing her stomach. He pressed against her, his hand cupping the hollow of her back, and nuzzled her neck. Her skin came alive at his touch. Desire uncoiled within him, twisting deeper feelings with it.

What started as a joke became serious. His mouth trailed her throat, hungry for her lips. She kissed him hard, needily, like nothing else existed bar him. Her palm curved around the back of his neck, drawing him down so her mouth could trace away from his and along his jawline towards his earlobe, taking nips that jolted him with tiny electric shocks. Her rapid breath brushed his ear as her fingers slid over his bulging pants.

'Jesus, Em.' They were in the shop, protected from sight by a dangle of colourful beads. And she was doing this.

She pulled away. A band of colour streaked each cheek. Her eyes were wide, her lips parted and full. Everything about her triggered his hunger for more, to sweep the bench clear and hoist her up to slide between her thighs.

She frowned as though breaking a trance and then smiled in a way that made his heart falter. 'I think the kettle's gone cold.'

'Unlike us.' But he understood the moment had passed. He slipped his hand from her shirt and pressed his forehead to hers. 'What are we doing?'

'Reliving our youth, I suspect.'

'I had fun in my youth.'

Her eyes glittered as though she'd read the memories in his mind, the ones involving hidden rock shelfs at Rocking Horse Hill, of lazy summer days and adventures like no other. 'So did I.'

'Can I see you tonight?'

She nodded. 'Dinner?'

'No, just sex will do.' He grinned at her raised eyebrows. 'Best cure for worries there is.'

She laughed. 'Is that right?'

The turnaround in her mood made him want to whoop. Instead he kissed her. 'You bet.'

'Good, because this is one theory I could do with being proven.'

'About seven?'

'Sounds good.'

He planned for it to be.

Eleven

Em rolled onto her side and stared at Josh. He lay on his back, one hand on his chest, the other by his side, breathing steadily. Despite the cold, he'd pushed the quilt down to under his ribs. Moonlight caught his bare chest, silvering his skin and casting the curled tips of his light brown hair in shiny nickel. His body rose and fell with each breath, his lips slightly open. She smiled, feeling like she could watch him for hours, but the neat contours of his profile had roused something in the creative hollows of her mind. An idea that niggled and nudged the longer she studied him, until its prods became impossible to ignore.

She kissed the point of his shoulder and slid carefully out of bed. Scooping up her knickers, she padded to the door, turning back to feast once more on his quiet form.

She hadn't believed him in the shop that sex would cure her tiredness and worries, but it had. Temporarily, anyway.

Em pressed her cheek against the cool timber of the door, thankful for the respite he'd granted. They'd never had the delight of a night together in their youth, yet she was strangely glad. Em wasn't sure her younger self would have appreciated the simple peace of it. Josh asleep in her bed filled her with contentment, as if the house had at last been made entire. As if perhaps her life had too.

She shook her head and left. Darkness had given flesh to fantasy. Time to channel it where it belonged.

Though the fire burned low, night had yet to pull all the warmth from the living area. Muffy rose from her basket, sinking again when Em bent to shush and soothe her. Through the big windows the waxing moon hung over the hill, bright enough for Em to see without turning on the main lights.

She paused in front of the fire to tug on her underpants, smiling as Muffy watched with her fluffy eyebrows lowered. A bit of nudity was nothing compared to what the dog had been exposed to earlier, when Em and Josh had entertained themselves against the dining room table, and elsewhere.

From the moment he'd appeared at the back door, casually sexy in jeans and a faded rugby jumper, smelling soapy and clean after football training, she'd turned molten. Her blood had pulsed heavily under his intense gaze, his channelled, need-filled focus heating her inside, drawing her desire. His touch ignited her skin until she couldn't stop her own hands from exploring his body, rousing Josh as he did her. It had been the same when they were younger and found privacy; their primitive need making it imperative their bodies join.

At least now they had comfort and no fear of discovery. No matter how careful Josh had been, lovemaking in the secret crevices of Rocking Horse Hill left scrapes and scratches. Every one of them had been worth it: ritual marks to be treated with pride.

The only mark he left now was on the inside. An ache of longing that grew with each encounter. Josh Sinclair had always been an easy man to love, and her ability to love him now wasn't in doubt. Not in her mind. His was another matter. What he was thinking, beyond lust, she had no idea. After all, it was Em who'd cheated all those years ago. Sexual attraction was one thing, affection another, but trust was something else entirely.

Em snapped on her desk lamp. Its reflection on the windows cut back the night and the changing shapes and shadows of the garden. She sat down, flipping over pages in her sketchbook until she came to the drawing she sought. The design was painfully earned: the result of more than twenty drafts. Em wasn't a naturally gifted artist. A honed technique gave the illusion of it, but each illustration in her handmade books was the result of tenacious work.

She regarded the picture grimly, now understanding its flaws. The basics were right – a man in the foreground, cloaked and crowned, head held regally in profile as he regarded something in the distance. A hill rose behind him under a sunlit sky, its surface scarred by the outline of a stylised horse. Now she could see it was his profile that was wrong.

The illumination would take an entire page, prefacing "The Vision of the King", and leading the reader into Alfred's world of bravery and battle. Chesterton's poetry wasn't easy for the modern reader and she wanted whoever bought the final book to use it, feeling the story as she did. That required a hero the reader would love.

Picking up a soft pencil, Em began to sketch while the night drifted on and the fire burned its way to ashes.

A sound, some time later, made her look up. Josh stood in the doorway, wearing only snug-fitting trunks that emphasised his narrow hips and strong legs. Slumber hooded his eyes. His beard was heavier, not by much, but enough to give his good looks a dark, smouldering edge. Muffy sat at his feet, head tilted as though waiting instruction.

Time had seen Josh's body fill out from his early twenties. His chest was wider, his shoulders broader. Hair dusted his chest in a delicious swathe, forming a T that crossed his pectoral muscles before dipping downward in a thin masculine trail. Boyhood no longer existed in that body. He was all man.

Several months prior to her relationship with Trent, Em had briefly dated a doctor, a locum Samuel had introduced her to. She'd slept with him more out of loneliness than desire and regretted it almost immediately. He was fit, with minimal body fat and sinewy muscles. But she'd found herself not turned off so much as wanting. Wanting a man whose body was formed by work instead of slavish routine and vanity.

A man like Josh had become.

She glanced down at her drawing. Chesterton's king stared back at her with eyes the same shape as Josh's. He dominated the foreground, a mesmerising, armoured warrior with a cape draped across his shoulders, the cloth fixed in place with a clasp containing the ancestral jewel he was destined to cast at the feet of his vision of the Blessed Virgin.

It was perfect now, as she'd known it would be from the moment she woke to watch Josh.

Smiling sleepily, Josh crossed the room, Muffy trailing behind. He stopped behind Em's chair and leaned forward to place his hands on the desk edges and press his warm chest against her upper back. His breath caressed her neck as he chased the contours with delicate kisses.

'Inspired?'

'A little.'

He stopped his nuzzling and leaned his chin on the top of her head. 'Is this your king?'

'Alfred of Wessex. He fights a great battle against Danish invaders and, despite all odds, wins.'

She felt his pause and inhaled breath and waited. To her relief he sounded more puzzled than annoyed.

'He looks a bit like me.'

'It's the eyes.'

He shifted, nuzzling her again. His smile felt delicious against her skin. 'So you've modelled your brave king on me, huh?'

'Don't get a big head.'

'I'm getting a big something else.'

She laughed and twisted around. 'You're completely oversexed.'

His eyes glimmered in the glow of the lamp. 'And that's a bad thing?'

The look sent wings flapping deep in her belly. Em used the end of her pencil to trace a line down his chest until it lingered at the top of his trunks. 'Did I say that?'

Josh caught her hand and lifted it to his mouth, gaze locked on hers as he kissed the point of each knuckle. He slipped the pencil free, and placed it on the desk before sliding his hands under her arms and lifting her gently up.

He kissed her, leading her away from the light to the edge of the lounge, until she stood near the window. 'Stay there,' he whispered, and went to flick off the lamp.

Soft moonlight took over the darkness. Josh moved back to gaze at her with an expression she couldn't fathom. Goosebumps began to speckle her skin, tightening her nipples. His mouth parted a fraction. He lifted his eyes to hers as though seeking permission. Em smiled, insides fizzing when he smiled back and came to her, his body warm and strong, his caresses tender. For a thudding heartbeat, before her eyes closed and her body shuddered under his touch, she looked past his shoulder. The land rose behind, trees swaying in the night, while beneath its gaze a man stood, worshipping.

***

To Em's bemusement, Felicity took to Rocking Horse Hill with spontaneous joy. She had no fear of any of the animals. She cooed at the chickens, clucked and laughed at Chelsea, as the duck, shocked by the attention, zoomed away with her low bum waggling, quacking hoarsely in complaint. Ever the gentleman, Lod behaved impeccably, blowing warm breaths into her ear, allowing himself to be fondled and scratched, and taking delicate bites from the apple Felicity presented to him. But it was Kicki and Cutie who enchanted her most.

Felicity put Jas to shame with her indulgent cuddles. She stroked their long ears, caressed their fuzzy faces, traced the soft lines of their muzzles and marvelled at their tiny hooves. She thought the legend of the dark crucifix across Kicki's shoulders and spine was amazing and special. Knowing a donkey fan ripe for exploitation when he saw one, Kicki responded to her with ecstasy, bunting her whenever she transferred her affections to his smaller girlfriend, and forcing Felicity to stand between them, her left hand scratching Cutie's tufted brown mane, her right rubbing Kicki's forehead, the jack's eyes almost rolling back into his head with happiness.

Digby couldn't tear his gaze from Felicity, who, with the exception of her new Akubra hat and what appeared to be Adrienne's favourite amber-and-gold earrings, was kitted out in R.M. Williams from head to leather-covered toe. Once she'd recovered from her annoyance over Felicity's reckless wearing of Adrienne's jewellery, Em took pleasure in her reaction too. There was something delightfully childlike about it that made Em wonder if Felicity had anything to do with animals when she was growing up.

'No,' said Felicity when Em asked. 'Well, not really. Dad had a dog but he wasn't really a pet.' She crouched to stroke Muffy, her tone wistful. 'I wanted a dog of my own but was never allowed.'

The afternoon fell into relaxed enjoyment. Coffee and cake in the warm fug of Rocking Horse Hill's kitchen followed by another wander around the paddocks trailed by Muffy, Kicki and Cutie, who Em had kept loose at her guest's request and because they broke into loud, plaintive brays the moment Felicity left their paddock.

'I can't believe you own this as well as Camrick,' said Felicity to Digby before turning to regard the crater and addressing Em. 'It's beautiful, isn't it? Perfect, almost like a cartoon volcano.'

'I think that's why I've always loved it so much. It has this magic about it, the way it rises from the land like something in a fairy story.' Em laughed. 'The hill turns me into a terrible romantic.'

Felicity reached out to squeeze her hand. 'I can understand why.'

Surprised and honoured by the touch, she smiled back.

'Em knows everything there is to know about the hill,' said Digby as they headed towards it.

Em didn't need another prod to launch into a passionate description of the history of her home and the area, and Felicity listened, rapt, taking in every word. Succumbing to the spell of the hill.

'Can we climb it? Watch the sunset?'

Em threw a questioning look at Digby, expecting him to say no. Not being great with heights, he'd never had the same enthusiasm for climbing the crater as Em.

'Sure,' he said and glanced at Em. 'You want to come too?'

She hesitated, eyeing her watch. Josh wasn't due until after football and the usual beers, war stories and presentations back at the Gerrinton clubhouse. When she'd phoned to invite him to dinner, he promised to try and get away early but was unlikely to arrive before six-thirty. With the perfect winter day and the sky a magical clear blue, the view would be magnificent. But it was one for lovers. An intimate experience for two, not three.

'You don't need me. Dig can take you. You remember the quarry path, don't you?'

At the mention of the quarry, Digby's fingers went to his bottom lip. 'I haven't climbed it in years.' An edge of pleading entered his voice. 'Might be safer if you led the way.'

'Sure,' said Em, immediately understanding. Some fears, especially those from childhood, weren't so easy to conquer, and Digby didn't want to appear a wimp in front of Felicity.

They climbed the hill paddock, donkeys in tow. Em dithered over whether to order Muffy home but decided that she might need the company.

Technically, Em didn't have permission to cross out of her property. The land was under rehabilitation. For those wishing to climb the hill a tourist trail existed but to reach it they would have to walk half a kilometre around Stanislaus Road, and Em resented being told what to do on land that the government had compulsorily acquired from Grandpa Philps in the eighties. He, Granny B and Uncle James tried to fight it but even that formidable combination was no match for a government, high on the environmental vote and claiming that the quarry proved the Wallace's inability to sustainably manage the site. That it was Grandpa Philps who'd closed the quarry voluntarily for environmental reasons made no difference.

Two-thirds of the way up the slope, Em paused where a weathered timber stile crossed the fence. When she'd been ordered by letter to remove it, she'd responded that whatever structure existed on the farm's property was the landowner's responsibility. If State Heritage wished to remove their side of the stile, they could. Em's side, though, would stay exactly as it was. Bureaucracy didn't let Em down. Letters came and went but the stile remained.

A few feet past the fence, out of greedy donkey reach, the grass grew tall and rank. Em shook her head as she spied a new blackberry outbreak among the dense clumps of phalaris and fescue. It was all very well planting trees, but if the weeds weren't controlled the effort was wasted. The volunteers who were given charge of the hill refused to spray, and inevitably the weeds remained rampant. Around the crater's southern side, near the car park, one of the smaller collapsed vents was almost full of blackberry. In the past the Wallaces had kept the weed under control through spraying and occasionally releasing goats onto the slopes. Now, both techniques were anathema. And so the hill was being overtaken.

She led them further on the old path, not yet fully colonised by grass and weeds. As they walked, Em pointed out her neighbour, Malcolm Fuchs, property, explaining to Felicity the centre pivot irrigation system and the crops and pastures Malcolm grew.

Fifty metres after they left the fence, Em reached the northern edge of the quarry, where green growth gave way to black soil and grey basalt. It was as though a giant creature had taken a painful bite out of the side of the hill. Below, the old works formed a vast gravel plain.

Erosion now brought the quarry edge much closer to the path than it had been in Em's childhood, when no one had minded her climbing the hill. Digby kept to the extreme left, almost veering off into the weed in an attempt to keep as far from the quarry as he could. As with the animals, Felicity seemed to have no fear of anything, moving dangerously close to the edge and peering over to inspect the former blast line.

'Come back, Flick. You're too close.'

Em agreed. 'You need to be careful. The ground's not that stable.'

'You'd think they'd fence it off.'

'There are plans to but there's no budget for it.' Em grinned. 'And we're not meant to be here anyway.'

Felicity eyed her with amusement. 'You never struck me as a rule breaker.'

'I'm not normally.'

'It's the hill,' said Digby. 'It has this power over her.'

Felicity laughed. 'There I was thinking it was my bad influence.'

'You're not bad; you're beautiful.' Digby pulled her towards him and kissed her. 'And I. Love. You.'

'Are you done?' said Em, crossing her arms and pretending exasperation.

Felicity broke away. She sucked in a deep breath and stared out over the countryside before focusing back on the house, now far below. 'I can't blame you, Em. I'd break rules for this too.'

Em began to move on. 'Come on, you two. Or you'll miss the sunset.'

From the quarry the trail turned upward and the going became harder.

Em could hear Digby's huffs behind her. Her brother had obviously been spending far too long with his PlayStation. Or too much time in bed with his fiancée.

Towards the top of the crater, the path veered sideways before meeting a sheer rocky slope. Eroded holes gave them foot-holds and Em emerged at the crest, near one of the timber platforms built to make the path around the crater-top less dangerous for tourists. She grabbed the rail and hauled herself up, moving quickly out of the way to leave space for Felicity and Digby.

They leaned on the rail, squinting into the falling sun. Below them, the quarry turned a thousand different colours as the light hit the workings and dregs of blasted rock. The rusted old silos and conveyor belts looked alien in the glow. The white shell of abandoned diesel bowser a forlorn sentry.

Em pointed to the south. 'See that tower? That's Port Andrews' water tower.' She crinkled her nose. 'I should have brought the binoculars. With it being so clear you'd be able to see the lighthouse.'

'Maybe next time.' Felicity gazed back towards the west. The main road to the south left a black dividing slick, like a crayon mark across the green. From it, Bradley Road ran at right angles, extending east and west, its western run characterised by a sudden incongruous loop. Felicity frowned at the bend. 'That's odd. Why does the road do that?'

'To avoid a sinkhole. You should get Dig to take you there. It's very pretty.'

'Creepy, you mean,' said Digby.

'Don't be such a sook.' Em grinned at Felicity and pressed her shoulder companionably against hers. 'Digby never did like sinkholes. I'll admit that one is poorly named, but I promise you it's lovely. You can swim in it in the summer.'

'What's it called?'

'Devil's Dungeon.'

'Good name for it too,' muttered Digby, causing Em and Felicity to smile.

'There used to be a lake here as well.' Em stepped off the board to the rocky edge of the crater. 'But it dried up in the seventies.' She pointed east, to the landscape beyond the rim of Rocking Horse Hill which, like the western view, was dominated by centre pivots and lush pasture land before finally merging into thick pine forest. 'Between irrigation and drains the water table has dropped significantly over the years.'

'Can you go down into the crater?'

'Yes.' Em glanced at her watch. 'No time now, though, and the truth is there isn't that much to see.' The feeling, though, standing in the centre, looking up at those skyscraper walls, was something else. And there'd be other days. She indicated the tourist path. 'If you follow the path to that next platform, you can see right over the farm.'

'Does that bother you? Being looked down on?'

'Not even a little bit. It's not like I run around the garden nude or anything. And there are plenty of trees to screen things. Anyway, what does a little lost privacy matter when you're surrounded by all of this?' She swept her hand around her. 'The hill's worth it.' She dropped her arm and breathed in a lungful of crisp air. 'The hill's worth everything.'

She let Digby and Felicity go, calling to Muffy as she took the eastward path. The terrain was rockier this way, the drop to the crater floor sheerer, and there had been some talk about blocking access. No one had fallen yet, but it was bound to happen.

Further along she dropped off the path, ordering Muffy to stay put. Although the slope was steep, there were enough footholds. Out of the sun, on this shadowed side, the cold immediately cut into her jacket. She paused to zip up the front of her coat before resuming her climb. Several metres along, Em stepped up to a hidden ledge. A quirk in the ancient rock flow had left an overhang, concealing the ledge from the path above. The curve of the volcano meant the space was out of sight from the main path.

She sat on the edge, her legs dangling over a precipice that plunged straight into one of the hill's collapsed side vents. It was here she and Josh used to sit, basking in the morning sun, talking about the world. Where she'd smiled at his hopes and dreams and then come to the conclusion that they were too little for someone of her name.

She glanced to her side. Even now, after all this time, the crudely carved heart remained. She traced her fingers over the letters within: EWJ L JS. At the time they'd thought the whole thing childish. Carving a love heart with your initials inside was something a thirteen-year-old would do, but that hadn't stopped them doing it. It was their mark on their special place. Permanent, like Josh had thought their love was.

Em stared at the dimming sky and wondered if perhaps it could be again.

***

Em observed Josh from behind the kitchen bench as she set out plates. Beer in hand, he stood relaxed in front of the fire, chatting to Digby and Felicity as they leaned into one another on the couch. She wished she hadn't been so cavalier in ordering her guests away from the kitchen. Her afternoon with Dig and Felicity, their love bright-hot, had left Em feeling uncharacteristically needy for Josh's company.

His football game had left its mark. His cheekbone was bruised where an opponent had misjudged a punch at the ball and caught his face instead. The deepening colour gave him the air of a warrior returned from battle, weary but sexy in his ruggedness, and Em tried to lock the image in her mind for future use.

Em wasn't sure what she'd expected of Josh's reaction to Felicity, but for some reason he didn't seem to be warming to her. She was pink-cheeked and happy from the afternoon, a woman to be entranced by, but Josh had shown only politeness. Felicity demonstrated equal disinterest, leaving Em wondering if they'd somehow crossed paths before Levenham.

As though sensing her scrutiny, Josh looked up and smiled, holding Em's gaze in a way that made her stomach flip. He closed the distance between them.

'You okay?'

'Of course.'

He studied her face. 'You looked a bit funny for a second.'

She felt a bit funny too. The memory of how he used to look at her, when they were young and he'd loved her with all the commitment of a man who had his future mapped and locked, tickled her mind, demanding attention. She wanted to compare expressions, contemplate what it meant, but she had dinner to cook and a night with Josh ahead. Contemplation could wait.

'I'm fine.'

He glanced across at the stove. 'Are you sure there's nothing I can do?'

'The kitchen isn't really big enough for two.'

A smile tilted his mouth. 'Yeah, but I like things cosy.'

That smile, so full of promise for later, made her stomach flip again. Flustered, Em checked her white wine reduction. She'd managed to score some local whiting from the fishmonger and decided to serve it with a simple *beurre blanc*, sautéed new potatoes and salad. Light food to match the evening's mood.

By the time she looked up his attention had drifted back to Felicity. Although his expression wasn't unfriendly, it wasn't favourable either. If anything, it was perplexed, and it gave Em an unpleasant flutter of panic.

'Have you and Felicity met before?' she asked, trying to make the question nonchalant.

'No.' He turned to face her, his expression back to normal. 'I thought she might have known Bianca, though, given where she grew up, but apparently she doesn't.'

'Adelaide's a big city.'

'Has she talked much about her life there?'

'Not really. I get the impression things were pretty tough.' She frowned at him. 'You don't like her?'

'I don't really have an opinion. She seems nice enough and Digby's obviously nuts about her.'

'He's that all right.' She glanced across to where Digby was talking Felicity through Em's collection of family photographs. 'I'm just glad to see him so happy.'

Josh stayed by the bench, watching her as she prepared the salad, talking about the football match, how he was thinking next year he might put his hand up to coach a kids' side.

'You're really set on staying, then?'

He gave her a puzzled look. 'Yeah. Why? Did you think I wasn't?'

'I didn't know for certain, that's all. I thought maybe when your mum's better you'd want to go back to Adelaide.'

'No. I'm here to stay.' He held her gaze. 'Nothing's going to drive me away this time.'

Em ducked her head, thinking of the ledge and the initials they'd carved there.

He slid around the bench to stand by her side at the stove and wrapped an arm around her waist. 'Hey,' he said, kissing her temple. 'It's okay. What happened happened. Things are different now.'

'Are they?'

He pulled back to frown at her. 'What does that mean?'

'I don't know. Nothing. It means nothing.' She closed her eyes briefly, wishing she could shed the uncertainty that he'd ever forgive the past. 'Sorry.'

'No worries. You've had a long day.'

'So have you.' She tugged at the front of his shirt to prove the mood had passed. 'Footy star.'

That brought on a laugh. 'Two goals doesn't make me a star, not when we lost by five.'

Despite her protests he stayed in the kitchen, using the limited space as an excuse to touch her, playing it all as a game. A game that continued throughout dinner as he sat alongside her, stealing hand squeezes under the table. Promising more to come.

Conversation rambled, from the local football competition, to Digby's work, to Josh's business plans and Em's calligraphy hobby. Several times Josh attempted to draw Felicity out about her family and where she grew up, but her answers tended to be vague and immediately followed with another question or comment about the hill, or the Wallace family. Em sensed Felicity's need to let that part of her life go, and she murmured for Josh to drop the topic.

At ten, Em and Josh escorted Felicity and Digby out onto the porch. The wind had stayed light but a clear sky had caused the temperature to plummet. Em hugged herself as the cold crept under her shirt and seeped up from the timber deck, through her socks.

To Em's surprise Felicity kissed her, standing on tiptoe to lightly peck her cheek.

'Thank you. I had the best day,' she said. 'The best.'

'Come on, Flick. It's freezing and Em and Josh want to go to bed. There'll be other times.'

She looked eagerly at Em. 'Will there?'

'Of course. You're welcome any time.'

Felicity's face turned radiant. Happy now she had her guarantee, she took Digby's hand and followed him to the edge of the porch. Suddenly, she halted and lifted her face to the hill, its dark outline rising into the spangled sky like a giant stone temple. Moonlight glinted off her hair and luminous skin, and cast sparks off the dangling gems of Adrienne's earrings. She kept staring, her lips parted slightly as though she'd just experienced a moment of rapture. Then she smiled broadly at Digby, skipped down the stairs and disappeared into the night.

Leaving Em in the chill, staring at the hill, speculating about what she'd seen.

Twelve

'Hey,' said Josh, holding his phone with his right hand and twirling a brass screw between the thumb and undamaged index finger of his left. Despite the sun streaming through the shed window, the metal was still cold from the night. 'It's me.'

Bianca's voice came back full of warm surprise. 'Josh. I didn't expect to hear from you. How's tricks? More importantly, how's your mum?'

He relaxed a bit. They'd had their moments, especially towards the end, and it always came as a relief to discover her affection for his family remained intact. News of Michelle's cancer had upset her deeply, and Bianca had immediately offered assistance and a place to stay in Adelaide if any of them needed.

'Not great but we're getting there.'

'It must be hard seeing her sick. She was always so active.'

'Yeah.' He swallowed and forced his tone brighter. 'But she's tough. She'll beat it. Anyway, the reason I called is because I'm trying to chase a bit of info about someone, and I thought you could help.'

'Sure. Who is it?'

'Felicity Townsend. She's from Elizabeth, or so she says. She's a couple of years younger than you but I thought you might have come across her, maybe in school.'

Bianca repeated the name twice, the second time faltering before she finished. 'Oh, God, Josh, please don't tell me you're involved with her.'

'Not me. A mate. So what's the story?'

'If it's the same Felicity Townsend, then she comes from a pretty notorious family. Involved in amphetamines, I think, drugs anyway. The dad went to jail for shooting someone. I remember her older brother Brett bragging about it. This was in primary school, mind. Thought it made him look tough which was stupid when half the school had a family member in jail, but he never was the brightest spark. I'm not even sure he made it to high school. He didn't make it to mine, that's for sure. I think I read about him being involved in an armed robbery a while back.'

'And Felicity?'

'Nothing that I can recall. Oh, hang on.' Josh could hear her tapping something as she thought. 'Nope, sorry. I'm sure there was something but after we moved I never bothered paying much attention.'

'That's okay, you've told me enough anyway.'

'Does he know, your friend?'

'That she comes from a dodgy family? I think so.'

'So what's she done to attract your interest, then?'

'Not a thing. It's just this gut feeling I can't get rid of.' He let out a breath and dumped the screw. 'I'm probably worrying about nothing.'

Except he wasn't. Felicity might be stunning to look at but she set his teeth on edge. Not that he could pinpoint any particular reason why. On the surface she seemed pleasant enough, and she made all the right moves with Digby, but trust her? Not a chance. Not after he'd watched her move around Em's house, touching her photos and books in that weirdly covetous way. Even Muffy wasn't exempt from her over-attention. And the way she'd studied Em when she thought no one was looking was even creepier.

Digby was so love-drunk he'd be lucky to realise his own arse was on fire, but Em's lack of awareness worried him. It was almost as though she deliberately didn't want to see.

He grimaced and refocused on his ex-wife. 'Thanks, Bianca. You take care, okay?'

'You too.' She paused. 'Josh?'

His gut tightened. He knew what was coming. He'd been expecting it for a while but the idea of someone else succeeding where he'd failed still hurt. 'Yeah?'

'I've met someone. It's pretty serious.'

Josh made sure to keep his voice steady. 'That's good, Bianca. Really good. I'm glad.'

'Thanks,' she said, a smile in her voice. 'And you? Are you seeing anyone?'

Josh picked up the screw again and twisted it around his fingers, feeling the sharp edges of the thread. 'Sort of.'

'Sort of?'

'I've had a couple of dinners with Emily.'

There was a heavy hush before she spoke again. 'Your old girlfriend?'

'Yeah.'

Michelle had never purged the Sinclair family photos of Em, believing that just because she and Josh had broken up didn't mean the relationship never existed, and so they'd remained in the albums. Em and him laughing at the camera, Josh's feelings for her flying like the world's biggest banner. Bianca had seen them, asked questions, and Josh had sensed her considering expression as Michelle explained Em's place in his past while Josh sat with his jaw clenched, avoiding eye contact.

Another pause. 'Well, I hope it works out this time. Look, I have to go. It was nice to hear from you. Give your folks my love, okay?'

Josh hung up and stared out through the filmy window at the bright day, thinking of Bianca, then Felicity before his mind drifted back to Em.

Last night, after he'd dragged her inside out of the cold, he'd stood her near the fire, brushing loose hair from her face, lightly caressing the skin below her ear. She'd shivered a little, a slight tremble he wasn't sure was from cold or anticipation. From the heat of her gaze he figured the latter but teased anyway. 'Cold?'

She'd smiled knowingly. 'A little.'

'Want me to warm you up?'

Her mouth tilted higher and she leaned closer, voice low. 'And how do you propose to do that?'

Josh threw her one of his lazy smiles, gratified when her eyes widened in response. In all these years, her reaction to his come-ons hadn't changed. The way her lips slowly peeled apart, full and luscious; the way a pulse in her throat fluttered and her chest rose that little bit higher, told him more than any words. A million bucks had nothing on the feeling of triumph that came with her reaction. He could watch it forever.

He slipped his hand into hers. 'Follow me and let me show you.'

And he had.

No, there was no 'sort of' about him and Em. This was real. Despite all self-warning, Josh had fallen.

And he was going down hard.

***

Karen leaned back in her recliner and curved her hand over her protruding belly. 'So how's it going with Em?'

Josh glanced at his mum, who feigned innocence, while Sal grinned at his discomfort.

Karen boggled her eyes at him. 'What? Did you expect us to pretend that we didn't know?'

'Em's going okay,' he said with a patience that came from having endured sisterly interrogations before.

'That's not exactly what she asked,' said Sally.

Josh stood and crossed to the window, looking out at Karen's front lawn with his thumbs looped in his pockets. Sal's two boys were playing kick-to-kick with his dad and brothers-in-law, Karen's golden retriever bouncing between them, pink tongue flapping, curls golden in the winter sun. Josh should have stayed out there with them, in safety, but he'd wanted to check on Mum. This latest dose of chemo had knocked her about badly, but she'd insisted on joining them for lunch, even if nausea meant she couldn't eat much. He guessed it was a show of defiance and strength against their demands, as if she wasn't really dying at all.

Dying. Jesus, he hated that thought. It made him angry and hurt and every which way confused. He knew it was insane, but he couldn't help the idea that if Bianca had stopped loving him, maybe his mum had too. As for Em, she'd proven that once before also . . .

Josh glanced at his mum. Michelle wore a scarf now to cover her hair loss. She'd put on weight, which he hadn't expected, causing her face to appear bloated and her belly more rounded, but her stubborn streak remained intact as ever, immune to chemicals, immune to her family and its fear.

Immune to him.

'Well?' asked Karen.

'Well what?' He tossed her one of his looks, the one from childhood that warned of Chinese burns and other tortures.

'Em, you twit,' said Sally.

He let out a sigh and turned around. 'We're seeing each other. Nothing else to report.'

'Seeing each other properly? Or just seeing each other?'

'What's the difference?'

The two sisters shared a roll of the eyes. Shouts of laughter filtered in through the window, followed by a series of loud barks. More than ever Josh wished he'd stayed out with the other males.

Karen stared at him as though his IQ had dropped to imbecile level. 'A lot.'

He sighed. 'It's not serious, if that's what you want to know.'

Sally regarded him. She'd always been the sharpest when it came to his sisters. 'But you want it to be.'

He shrugged. 'Maybe.'

'Oh, don't lie, Josh. You've always loved her.'

'Not always. I was married, remember?'

Karen waved a hand. 'Other than when you were with Bianca.'

'She's right,' said Sally. 'First loves always leave their mark.'

'Funny, I thought my first love was Mandy Glenson,' he said, referring to the girl he'd been mad for when he was twelve.

'Childhood crushes don't count.'

Could have fooled him. He'd been nuts about Mandy. Until she went off with Ed Palfreyman. He raked his hand through his hair. Christ, another one. Now that he looked back, he'd been ditched a fair few times.

'And she was a skank,' said Karen, earning an admonishing look from her mother. 'Well, she was!'

'Not in Emily's class, that's for sure,' said Sally.

Josh had to agree on that point. But then no one was in Em's class. She stood on her own pedestal. Perhaps she stood too high for the likes of him.

He scowled at the idea. This lack of confidence was stupid. She wasn't any better than anyone else. Nor did she act as though she was. Not the mature Em he knew now. Sure, she could be aloof and unreadable, but there were times, like the previous night, when she touched him with a neediness that went beyond arousal. That spoke of vulnerability and the desire for something deeper, more intimate, like what he used to believe they had. Maybe he was reading too much into it, creating reality from wishes, but he didn't think so.

Perhaps it was about time he turned this 'seeing each other' into Karen's 'seeing each other properly'. Asked Em out on a date or something. A proper dinner. Something different to food and sex at Rocking Horse Hill, which was all their present relationship seemed to amount to. She deserved more than that.

And Josh sure as hell wanted it.

He turned back to the window but the boys and men were trailing inside. Josh raised a hand to his dad, who smiled back. Time with the grandkids always perked him up.

The boys erupted into the room, throwing themselves on Sally, who protested but hugged them anyway and grinned at her husband over their heads. Crouching by the recliner, his hand on the mound containing his unborn child, Davey kissed Karen. She complained about his cold lips but her eyes showed nothing but happiness. Josh's dad crossed to Michelle and stroked her cheek, murmuring quiet words. She took his hand and clutched it, before turning it over to kiss his palm.

Josh felt a sudden sear of loneliness. Once, he and Bianca would have added their own love to the room, but they'd forgotten that marriages took effort. Their love had slipped away without either seeming to notice, eroded by work and fatigue, a mortgage and, most damaging of all, indifference, until the hollow became too huge to ignore.

He hadn't tried hard enough.

Not a mistake he was about to make again.

Laughter dragged him from his thoughts. Sally was rising, the boys grasping at her arms as they tried to hold her back, squealing about not wanting to leave, about more footy with Grandpa, Uncle Dave and Uncle Josh. When Sally ignored them, they fell to the floor and grabbed her legs, forcing her to drag them along like human shackles.

Sharing a look with Cameron, Josh picked up a squirming Jack while Cam took care of Cooper. The boy whooped in delight as he hoisted him over his shoulder in a fireman's lift, backed him up to his grandmother and bent his knees to lower Jack down for a kiss.

'Say goodbye to Grandma.'

Wet, lip-smacking noises ensued as Jack enthusiastically kissed his grandmother goodbye. Michelle ordered him to be good, before the pair broke into several proclamations of how much they loved one another.

He and Cam carried the boys to the car and strapped them in.

'You heard the latest plan?' Cam asked.

'No.' Though he'd tried a couple of times, Josh hadn't been able to get Karen and Sally alone. Between lunch and the kids and Michelle's flapping ears, it had been too hard.

'Sal's found some woman from Adelaide who's had a double mastectomy and reconstruction. Came down and talked at some support group she sat in on. Lifted her top up and showed off her new boobs. Sal reckons if it weren't for the scars you wouldn't know. So now Karen wants to work out a way to get her back to talk to Michelle.'

Josh looked to the front door and stairs, where his mum was making her way carefully down, with Tom's support. 'Worth a try.'

'Yeah.' Cam held Josh's gaze. 'I know she's not my mum, but I love her like one. With my olds in Melbourne, the boys need at least one grandma close. We can't let her get away with this. It's not right.'

Josh put his hand on his brother-in-law's shoulder and gave a gentle shake of reassurance. 'We won't. I promise.'

They'd save her, whether Michelle wanted it or not.

Thirteen

Josh slowed as Bradley Road hooked around the crumbling remains of a lava vent to join Stanislaus Road. Falling dusk cast the contorted spire of stone in gold and black, its outline stark against the backdrop of Em's cypresses and the imposing slopes of Rocking Horse Hill. He decelerated further for the T-intersection and turned left carefully, alert for potholes and places where the road's soft edges may have given way.

After the weekend's warmth, a massive front had swept in Sunday night and dumped unprecedented levels of rain over the next few days on an area conditioned to heavy winter falls. It fell in great swathes, rushed offshore by a south-westerly that brought with it the icy edge of Antarctica.

Many of the district's rural roads were washed out. Water lay in side gutters and in great ponds across the flat lands to the north. To the south, on Em's side of town, the ground was woven with endless eroded limestone channels, caverns and sinkholes hidden beneath the sodden soil. There the impact was less visible. But the landscape still appeared to droop when the sun finally reappeared Friday afternoon, albeit weakly.

The rain on his dad's shed had been deafening at times. Josh was used to loud machinery, but this was endless. After the first day he'd taken to wearing his protective earmuffs even when the machinery was idle.

He turned into Em's drive and spotted her in one of the paddocks that ran along the base of the hill, cantering helmetless on Lod in the fading light. She waved but made no move to ride towards him. Josh alighted, crouching to greet Muffy who trotted from the paddock to say hello, her paws and muzzle coated in mud.

Josh headed past the stables for a closer look at Em. He used to love watching her ride. There was something deeply erotic about her straight back and long slim legs, the way she controlled those big horses without effort. The first time he travelled to a show to watch her compete, he'd spent most of the day with a hard-on. She appeared like a schoolboy's wet dream: long shiny black leather boots, a tightly cut coat that showed off her slim waist and emphasised her hips and shoulders, some sort of cravat thing around her throat, and her dark hair knotted in a tight bun at the base of her neck. The effect was austere, upper-class beauty. Untouchable. His.

He regarded her now. Different and yet the same. She still rode with that same fluidity, as if she and the horse were dancing to some tune he couldn't hear. Her ponytail bounced with each beat of Lod's elegant canter. Her chin was raised, her shoulders back, hands soft in front, and those long legs that had wrapped around him the previous weekend, guiding Lod with subtle movement.

Arousal tugged, like before. Only this time, he had no true idea where he fitted in her life. All he knew was that he wanted her in his.

She wheeled Lod around and cantered towards him, reining to a walk a few metres away, the horse tossing his head, nostrils blowing from effort.

'First time I've been able to ride all week.'

'Doesn't show. He looks good.'

'He looks fat is what he looks.'

Josh stroked Lod's forehead, smiling as the horse's eyes closed and he pressed into Josh's hand in anticipation of a head rub.

'It's getting dark,' she said. 'I'll be a while sorting Lod out yet. Why don't you wait inside?'

'I can handle a bit of cold.'

She slid off the horse, Josh admiring the firmness of her rear as she ran the saddle's stirrups up their leathers. She wore brown suede gaiters over navy jodhpurs. The fabric curved with the line of her body and the jodhpurs' brown leather insert, shiny from wear, arced from her inner thighs upwards over the taut globes of her bum. A fitted red fleece jacket complemented a get-up that seemed designed not only for riding comfort, but to amplify her sexiness and his arousal.

'Nice outfit.'

She threw him an amused, sideways look, signalling she remembered the agony she'd once caused him, causing his heart to skip. 'Nice to see some things haven't changed.'

'What can I say?' he said with a shrug. 'I like you in breeches.' He broke into a grin. 'I don't mind you out of them either.'

She laughed, the sound warm in the rapidly cooling air, and headed towards the stables, her fingers tangled deep in Lod's mane.

Josh strode alongside. 'How was the shop today?'

'Not too bad. I've been busy ordering Father's Day stock. Pen sets and the like.'

He frowned. 'I didn't think you stocked much in that way.'

'Not a lot. Novelty pens for kids, mainly, but the people who supplied the notebooks – the ones you bought for your mum – have brought out a range. They're beautiful too. Lacquered in the same jewel colours, some with etching on the barrels, and great quality nibs and ballpoints. I ordered one of the gold and sapphire ones as a present for Samuel.'

'For Father's Day?' said Josh, surprised. He didn't think Em's relationship with Samuel was that close. On the few occasions she'd mentioned her mother's boyfriend it had been more with respect than affection.

'Yes. He's been good to Mum. And Felicity, making her feel welcome.'

The mention of Felicity made Josh's mouth thin. He glanced at Em, wondering if he should mention his chat with Bianca, but she was staring at the hill with a pensive look on her face and ex-wives didn't make for good conversation, no matter how amicable the parting.

While Em finished with Lod, Josh wandered off to muck around with Kicki and Cutie, the donkeys bunting him for more each time he tried to leave their paddock.

'All my animals are turning into sooks,' said Em, coming to join him and kissing Cutie on her delicate nose. 'Muffy's the worst, but these two aren't much better.'

'Spring's coming. Everyone's looking for affection.'

She smiled. 'Hence why you're here.'

Josh focused on Kicki, unable to smile back. He wasn't here just for sex. He was here for her, and the way she made him feel.

Maybe at the start his motives had been different. He'd been as attracted to her as when he was younger, perhaps even more so. Em was beautiful, classy, intelligent, sensual. She was also a challenge that he'd taken up without thinking. This was the girl who'd humiliated him, who'd left him confused and wracked with doubt. He'd thought he'd be able to control his emotions but there was no way to stopper his memories from their time together. Not the shame and confusion of the end, but the good stuff. The more time he spent with her, the more the old emotions and old dreams were roused until they were resurrected in full. Leaving him more vulnerable than ever.

'There's your cooking too,' he said, trying to keep up a joke that held no humour.

'I should have guessed your stomach would come into it somewhere.'

They headed towards the gate, trailing donkeys.

She fixed the latch and waggled a finger at Kicki. 'Don't even think about escaping tonight. I mean it. Once more and I'll padlock you in.'

The donkeys swung their heads toward one another, as though sharing a joke, before blinking innocently back at Em, who raised her eyes and let out a long sigh. 'No one ever listens to me.'

Josh took her hand. 'I do.'

Her smile beat the sunset for beauty.

'Poor Chelsea,' said Em as the wobbling white duck shot across the garden path and streaked toward the veggie patch, squabbling madly. 'She still hasn't recovered from Felicity's visit.'

'Why Chelsea?' said Josh, unwilling to let more talk of Felicity spoil the moment. 'Seems an odd name for a duck.'

She shrugged. 'I don't know. She just looked like a Chelsea.'

'Right.'

Em eyed him sideways. 'If I recall, you once had a dog called Rufus.'

'He was a red kelpie. What else could he be called?'

The house was snug with the fire when they ventured inside. Em went to the bathroom to wash her hands, and Josh sidled over to her desk, curious about her progress on her White Horse book and her picture of the king.

He scanned the scattered pages, his frown deepening when he didn't find the drawing. The only pages he could see were covered in faint pencil lines and inked with large, flourished capitals, some in ornate boxes, others surrounded with organic swirls.

His fingers hovered over the desk, the urge to dig strong. He glanced at the hall door and let his hand drop. Any second Em would walk back in and Josh wasn't about to let himself be discovered riffling through her things. He turned to the window and stared at the shadow-filled garden.

As she worked on dinner, he watched her in the window's reflection, trying to settle his temper, but the missing king had upset him more than he thought possible. That and the comment about him being here just for a shag.

Still stewing, he sank into the sofa. Em was all the good things in him and also all the worst, and tonight it seemed the worst wanted out.

'Did you want some music?' she asked.

'If you want.' He hadn't intended to be so terse, but his mind was still on the absent picture and all the other signals revealing his place in her life.

'That's not what I asked, Josh.'

He glanced over. She stood in the kitchen with a cleaver in one hand, a raw chicken on the board in front of her, and a shuttered expression on her face.

'Sorry,' he said, standing and heading towards her CD collection. 'Mind elsewhere.'

'Your mum?'

He nodded and then hated himself for the lie. He flicked through her shelves, not paying much attention to the titles. It bemused him, the way she lived an almost old-fashioned life. No iPod dock, no enormous flat-screen TV. A laptop that he'd never seen opened. A no-frills mobile phone that seemed to spend more time on the bench than in her pocket. Just loads of books, CDs and photographs, and a desk filled with ink pens and paintbrushes. Items that told stories and took time to appreciate. The opposite of his life with Bianca, where distraction was everywhere.

Em's home was designed for communication, a place for love to grow. A place he could see himself living, with her.

The thought pulled him up. Jesus, he was in a bad way. He snapped out a CD and loaded it.

The dark opening of the Foo Fighters' *Down in the Park* thudded through the room, causing both Muffy and Em to look up.

'Interesting choice.'

He wandered over. 'More interesting that you own the CD. I wouldn't have thought the Foo Fighters were your thing.'

'You'd be surprised.' She returned to her chook dissection. 'Actually, I have a feeling it's Trent's. He never liked what I had and used to bring his own.'

'Nice of him.'

'Not really. Although it took me a while to see that.'

Josh leaned against the bench and wished he had a beer. No bloke wanted to hear about a girlfriend's exes, yet there were things he wanted to know. Whether she'd loved any of them. Or whether they were all stopgaps until someone more suited to the Wallace name came along.

'Must've hurt, breaking up.'

She tugged on a chicken wingtip, raised the cleaver and brought it down, separating the tip from the wing in one easy movement. The meaty part of the wing went into a bowl, the tip into her compost bucket. 'All break-ups hurt.'

Didn't he know it. 'Some more than others.'

'What makes you say that?'

'The way you just attacked that chook.'

She held his gaze for a moment before dropping it back to the chicken and expertly separating the legs from the body. 'He left me for a 24-year-old hairdresser, if you must know and, yes, it hurt.'

'Pride or feelings?'

'What does it matter? It's over. That's all that counts.' She tilted her head. 'Or have you heard something to the contrary?'

'I haven't heard anything. I wanted to hear it from you.'

'Why?'

Why indeed. Who knew? He certainly bloody didn't. All he had was this fear in his gut that he was as disposable as the bloke who'd been before him. 'No reason. Just curious.'

Her mouth tightened like she didn't believe him. He couldn't blame her. He didn't believe it himself.

The sudden craving to take her to bed, to lay claim to the only part he was certain he had of her – her passion – hooked through Josh's body. He scratched at his stubble, contemplating the idea. The cleaver rose and fell, its blade whacking through flesh and bone before ending in a savage thunk against the board. He dropped his hand. Perhaps later, when her mood was better.

'There's wine in the fridge if you want,' she said. 'I forgot to buy beer, sorry.'

'That's okay. I should have brought some myself and you've been catering for me too much as it is.' He leaned on his elbows, looking up at her. 'I've been thinking . . . Tomorrow night. How about coming out with me, on a proper date?'

'A proper date?'

'Yeah.' He smiled. 'Like normal people. You could come with me to footy, hang around for a few drinks afterwards, then we'll head back into town to the Arms. Have dinner, some wine. Catch a taxi back here after.'

'I'm sorry, but I can't. Felicity's coming out tomorrow.'

Josh couldn't stop the bitterness infecting his voice. 'And I guess you couldn't possibly stand up your brother's precious fiancée for me.'

She put down the cleaver with deliberate slowness. 'Okay, what's up?'

He closed his eyes briefly, wishing he hadn't started any of this. Wishing he'd stopped home where it was safe. Wishing he wasn't such a frigging coward and could ask how she felt. 'Nothing. It's nothing. Just me being a dick.'

'I thought you said you liked her.'

'I don't know her enough to like or dislike. And this isn't about her anyway.'

Em looked at the cleaver blade and bit her bottom lip. 'Then what is it about?'

He wanted to say 'us'. He wanted to tell her how scared he was, but he couldn't manage any of it. 'Nothing. Forget I said anything.'

Her voice quietened. 'You never used to be like this. Before.' She took a shuddery breath. 'Before I did what I did.'

That was because before he had certainty. He believed. In her, in them, in a future.

'It's what I did, isn't it? Back then.'

'No.' He moved around the bench and wrapped his arms around her stiff body. 'No. It's not you. It's not anything. It's just me being stupid.'

She kept her face pressed against his shoulder while her arms remained by her side. He stroked her spine, wishing her hands weren't chicken-coated and she could hold him properly. The shuddery swell of her back as she breathed in made him wonder if she felt as vulnerable as he did. Why else bring up what she'd done like that?

'Em?'

She looked up.

'Come to footy with me tomorrow.'

Her gaze softened. 'You mean like I used to?'

Josh's breath caught. Like she used to when she was his girl. When she'd stand on the sidelines cheering him on, making him proud. Making him play better. Making him feel like he could do anything as long as she loved him. 'Like that.'

She smiled her apology. 'I really can't. I promised Felicity her first riding lesson. She's so excited, I can't let her down. I'm sorry. Another time?'

'Sure. Another time.'

His disappointment ached. He glanced towards her desk, remembering once more the night she'd made him her king. The night he'd held her in the moonlight, marvelling at the exquisiteness of her, at his luck in finding her again. Knowing even then that he couldn't let her go a second time, that this time he'd fight. Whichever way he could.

Wearing a plastered smile, he led her to the sink and turned on the hot water.

'What are you doing?'

'Washing your hands.'

'What for?' She glanced back at her half-dismembered chook. 'I haven't finished preparing dinner.'

'Forget dinner,' he said. 'I have better ideas.'

Fourteen

'I think I hate her,' said Jas. 'It's unfair enough that she's beautiful, but to look so bloody good on a horse as well?' She shook her head in mock disgust. 'There is no God.'

Em smiled and continued to observe Lod as he picked his way around a worn, circular track. Upon Jasmine's arrival, confident that Felicity was in no danger of falling off or mistreating her mount, Em had left Digby in charge of the long lunge rein attached to Lod's bridle. They were in the paddock next to the stables, on the stretch of flat ground that Em had laser-levelled a few years earlier, and where she did most of her training. When she'd learned that Felicity would be coming out that afternoon for a riding lesson, and with Rocking Horse Hill only a short detour from her way home, Jas couldn't resist calling in for a chat and sticky-beak.

Felicity sat in the saddle, wearing a new black velvet-covered helmet, her cheeks blossoming with cold and pleasure, not in the slightest afraid. Not that she needed to be. Lod had been the perfect gentleman from the moment she mounted, and though Digby had never been much of a horse enthusiast, he knew enough of Lod's temperament not to fret and risk infecting Felicity with his nerves.

For someone who'd never been on a horse before, Felicity showed remarkable poise. Her body possessed an innate suppleness and, unlike many learners, she didn't rely on the reins for balance. Instead, she seemed to find a natural centredness that allowed her to sit with ease in the saddle.

Perhaps it was the stylish new riding attire she wore that made her look so competent: the fashionable check breeches with a black, full-seat suede insert; the tall leather riding boots; the parka shaped like a hunting coat that narrowed her waist and accentuated her straight shoulders; the matching black nappa leather gloves. Clothing that expensive and well cut would make anyone look good.

Jas lifted her face to the sky as a cloud scudded past and revealed a sudden streak of sun. 'At least I can feel smug that she'll have sore thighs by the end.'

The weather still hadn't cleared completely and the forecast predicted more chilling wind and rain squalls. Em hankered for spring. Her garden and paddocks were saturated and bedraggled, and she worried for the buds on the stone fruit trees. The chooks ran about with their feathers ruffled, clucking in discontent. Though she'd moved them to the most sheltered paddock, Kicki and Cutie had spent the week standing forlornly with their rumps to the wind, looking as dejected as Em felt. Only Chelsea seemed to be enjoying herself, zooming around the garden, plucking slugs and half-drowned snails, and snorkelling her orange beak through puddles.

Em had never minded winter. Winter meant fires and comfort food, a time for nesting, but this winter seemed to drag. She wanted spring, sunshine, happiness. The chance to trot Lod around the crater after work and watch the sunset paint the slopes, to take her calligraphy outside and work in proper light, to hold family picnics and barbecues in the yard like they had when Adrienne and Digby lived at the hill. Watch her ruined garden bloom and abound with produce.

She rested against the fence's top rail and closed her eyes, lifting her face to the sun as Jas had.

'Have you heard from Teagan this week?' Jas asked.

'No. Have you?'

'Not a peep.'

'I rang and left a message on her mobile but she hasn't called back.' Em opened her eyes and frowned. 'Come to think of it, that was Tuesday when I rang. That's not like her. I'll call her again.'

'Do you think she gave her dad that money?'

'I hope not. I hate the way he uses her. She should leave, find a job managing a property where they at least pay her for her work.'

'She can't. She loves the place. It'd be like telling you to leave here.'

'I know.' She turned back to listen to Digby and Felicity. Digby's voice was filled with pride, his fiancée's bright with delight.

'I wish I could do this every day,' Felicity was saying.

'You'll be able to when I buy you a horse.'

Excitement turned Felicity's voice even huskier. 'You'll buy me a horse?'

'Sure. Em will know where to get a good one. You can keep it here. Come out and ride whenever you want.'

Em pursed her lips and tried to remember that it was by Digby's grace that she lived without charge at the hill. If he wanted to keep a horse here, she was in no position to argue.

'They're taking a few liberties, don't you think?' said Jas.

'A bit, but depending on how today went I was going to offer to find Felicity a horse anyway.'

'But for Digby to say she can come out whenever she likes . . .'

Em shrugged.

Jas ducked her head to make eye contact. 'Em, this is your home.'

'And Digby knows that.'

Jas watched her closely and Em knew she wanted to pursue the topic further. Ignoring her own doubts, she injected her voice with confidence. 'It's fine, honestly.'

'If you're sure.'

She wasn't, but nor did she feel up to revealing how trapped and insecure all this made her feel. And Digby could hardly renege on his promise. All the family knew about it. Plus he was her brother. She had to believe he'd keep his word. Rocking Horse Hill would be her home for as long as she wished. Besides, Felicity, too, was well aware of how Em felt about the place. Digby had the stables, Camrick. Money. He didn't need the hill. He didn't even like the farm that much.

A throaty burst of laughter had Em regarding them again. While she might harbour some worries, one thing wasn't in question: Felicity made

Digby happy. That ugly business with Cait had battered his self-esteem. Now he walked with a swagger, almost like his dad, and he smiled more. Even the way he dressed showed more confidence. Today he looked like a typical rural bloke in a pair of well-fitting moleskin jeans and a blue-and-white striped shirt, an unzipped quilted vest over the top with leather patches over the shoulders.

He and Felicity looked like wealthy landed gentry, which, Em supposed, they were.

'She's done wonders for Digby.'

'Must be all the testosterone swirling through his system from all that sex. He'd have balls the size of a bull elephant's by now.' As Em made a face, Jas nudged her. 'Sex isn't reserved exclusively for you, you know. Just because you've been going at it hammer and tongs with the sexpot.'

At the mention of Josh, Em's contentment disappeared.

'I don't know how much longer that's going to last.' She smothered a stupid urge to cry. She'd been trying to put Josh's strange behaviour out of her mind, but now her anxiety was back in full. 'I think he's going off me.'

'Bullshit.' Jas studied her, her expression softening when she saw that Em was serious. 'Oh, Em, what makes you think that?'

'The way he's behaving?'

'Like how?'

'I don't know. He keeps going quiet, as if he's mulling over something. And I keep catching him watching me. It's like he wants to tell me it's over but doesn't know how.' She sighed. 'He wanted me to go to the footy with him today but I said I couldn't because Felicity was coming out. Then he made this snarky comment about it, and when I challenged him he just dragged me off to bed.'

'Sounds a bit cave man.'

'But that's the thing. It wasn't. Far from it.' Her throat thickened and she bit her lip. Despite Josh's tenderness, everything about last night made her feel sad. Even her bones felt heavy. 'I think he still blames me for hurting him so badly. He says he doesn't, but . . .'

'You're reading too much into it. He's distracted by stuff at home. It's a tough time. Anyway,' said Jas, grinning, 'how could he possibly go off you? You're the biggest chicky babe around.'

'After you, you mean,' said Em, trying to lighten things up. Jas was probably right. She *was* reading too much into things. The same as with Digby and the hill. And Josh's mum was terribly ill.

'Naturally. But I thought that went without saying.' Jas straightened. 'I'd better get home and work Oxy. Poor old thing's so fat he has cellulite on his bum.' She screwed up her nose. 'Like owner like horse, I suppose.'

'You don't have cellulite.'

'I do. Mike pointed it out the other day.' She darted a glance at Em. 'Don't say it.'

'I wasn't going to say anything.'

'You never do but that doesn't mean you don't think it.'

'You need a man who loves you, not one who points out your imperfections.'

Jas swung up her palms. 'I know, I know.'

'Then please end it. I worry about you.'

'I'll be okay. Anyway, it's Teagan you should be most worried about.'

Em agreed. In time Jas would sort herself out. Teagan she wasn't so sure about. 'I'll call her. See if I can con her into another girls' night. We'll ask Felicity along too, make it a big one.'

Em caught Jas's flicker of consternation at the mention of Felicity and experienced a surge of irritation. This was her brother's fiancée, her sister-in-law to be – of course she was going to include her.

Em hugged her goodbye anyway. Jas was her oldest friend; she wasn't about to argue with her over something as stupid as this.

*****

Fine days meant cold nights and when Digby and Felicity had finally left, happy and elated and talking shows and other horsey futures, Em had knuckled down to cooking, a task that usually left her soothed and settled.

With music on the stereo and the fire spreading warmth, she'd relaxed, convinced everything would work out with her and Josh. He would arrive soon. They'd open a bottle of wine, talk. And maybe she'd find the courage to ask him again where they were headed, how he felt. Maybe she might even hint at her own feelings. How they'd grown into something important, something she didn't want to let go.

Around seven, the southerly that had been soft all day strengthened: a strong-armed wind that pried at the roof and yanked at the garden. Em ducked outside to check on the animals. She lingered in the cold for longer than necessary, hoping to spy the headlights of Josh's ute on Bradley Road, but the only light was a waning moon and the distant glow of Levenham.

At eight she pulled the casserole from the oven and set it on a cork mat. The simple wholemeal soda bread she'd made earlier had long cooled.

Josh hadn't promised anything. He'd left her early that morning with a simple kiss, citing chores to run and a need to spend some time with his mum before footy. Em had hovered at the edge of the orchard path, wanting to call him back, to say something, to hold him in a way he couldn't mistake, but was too afraid of her neediness. Only when he'd stepped into the car and sat for a few moments, staring at her through the windscreen, had she experienced that same lurching sensation of the night before, that he wanted to say something important to her. Then he'd started the engine, saluting as he headed out the gate.

Stupidly, she'd assumed he'd come back.

'You know what assuming does, hey Muff-Muff,' she said, leaving the kitchen to crouch by the dog's basket. She stroked the collie's soft fur. 'It makes an ass out of you and me.' She kissed Muffy's forehead and glanced around. Nothing to do except fill in the night with work.

Her glass of cabernet shone deep maroon and Em thought how perfect the colour would be for King Alfred's cape: dramatic and predictive of the bloodshed to come. She pulled the sketch from her desk drawer, intending to make a note, but the sight of Josh's face had her setting the paper aside, her heart ballooning with feeling. Love she knew she was losing. That she never really had.

She sipped her wine, resisting the urge to take a bigger gulp. Em needed a steady hand for gilding and she wanted this book to be perfect. No matter what happened between them, *The Ballad of the White Horse* now belonged to Josh. Her way of saying sorry for the strong heart she once broke.

Em cleared the desk and laid out the piece of parchment upon which she'd already completed the first page of script. At the top left, a box had been left clear. Pencilled inside was a drawing of the white horse. She'd toyed with painting the background green, to represent grass, but had instead decided to emboss it in gold. Around the edges of the illumination, and extending down and across the page as marginalia, vines would ramble, animals would peek and birds would wing, bringing the scene and lettering to life.

Ignoring the grumbles of the wind-wracked house, she concentrated on her task, soon finding herself soothed by the precise layering of glue that formed an essential underlay to the gilded surface.

She was peering closely at her work, using her pen nib to draw the gesso into a corner when three loud bangs sounded on the door. Her pen slipped. She swore and jerked back, bumping the desk with her knees and almost toppling her empty wine glass.

Muffy scrabbled out of her basket and ran, barking loudly, to the door. Em glanced across the room at the kitchen clock and rose, her heart thumping, momentarily fearing for her family. It was after ten, a Saturday night. A bad time for bad news. Then she registered Muffy wagging her tail and realised that whoever was there knew her. Besides, the police would come to the front door.

Josh. It had to be.

He was hunched against the cold, with only a thin long-sleeved shirt and jeans as protection. She paused, taking a moment to assess him, seeking too-bright eyes, the poor balance of someone who'd drunk too much.

Deciding he appeared sober enough, she slid open the door and leaned against the frame, arms crossed. 'Good evening.'

'Hey.' When she didn't move he glanced behind her, eyes narrowing in a way she wasn't sure she liked. 'Can I come in?'

She stepped aside, watching him as he crouched to greet Muffy, noting how he kept looking around the room. She slid the door closed but didn't move from it, her arms tight under her breasts. Though Em knew it was unfair, her worry and hurt had turned to anger.

He glanced at the bench, where the pot, bread, crockery and cutlery still lay. His mouth thinned. 'You cooked.'

'Yes.'

'For me.'

Em said nothing.

'And now you're pissed off.'

'We didn't make any plans,' she said, raising her chin and attempting to cover her hurt with nonchalance.

'No, we didn't. We never make plans.'

'What's that supposed to mean?'

This time, it was Josh's turn to say nothing, which somehow made it worse. She walked away from him, crossing the room to hide her work in the narrow top draw of the desk and cover the remaining *Ballad* work in practice sheets. Once again, the picture of the king stalled her. She held it, the paper inexplicably shaking. What was going on with her? Where was her Wallace cool? She knew what he was here for. Football, a laugh and a few beers with the boys and now he was here for sex. And the stupidity of it was that she would let him, because she wanted him. She'd always wanted him; even when she made the cruellest decision of her life, she'd known she didn't mean it.

Em let the paper fall and looked up. He was watching her, Muffy pressed against his leg, his hands shoved in his pockets.

'Did you win?'

'Yes, much to everyone's shock.'

Em nodded and scratched around a few more papers.

'How did it go with Felicity?'

'She's a natural. Digby's going to buy her a horse. We'll be able to go riding together.' Those molasses eyes didn't move from hers. What did he see? What did those ever-so-slightly pursed lips mean? She remained behind the desk, needing to keep a space between them. 'Have you had dinner?'

'Steak at the club.' He frowned and pulled his hands free. 'Look, Em, I think we need to talk.'

'No.'

He stared.

'Have a drink.' She picked up her wine glass and headed for the kitchen. 'It's nice wine. A cab sav from the Coonawarra. Won the Jimmy Watson Trophy several years back. Mum knows the winemaker and he says it's the best wine he's ever made. You should try —'

He caught her hand as she rushed past, his half-fingers closing around hers, pulling her to a halt as he had outside Camrick. And, as before, her heart tumbled with the same shock and excitement at the resoluteness of his grip. The difference this time being that he didn't let go.

'Come here.'

He tugged lightly. Em followed until she stood between his parted legs, their hips touching, his hands falling to hook loosely around her waist, trapping her, but in a nice way. He pressed his forehead against hers and she could smell the faint scent of beer on his breath.

'I'm sorry,' he whispered.

'You don't have anything to be sorry for.'

'I don't?'

'I just assumed.'

'I was going to come and then . . .' He shook his head. 'It doesn't matter.'

'It does.' She breathed in. 'To me.'

He was watching her in that intense way, like he was trying to see inside her. 'Does it?'

'You know it does.'

Their gazes locked and then his mouth was on hers and she was soaring.

Em didn't care why he'd stayed away. She didn't care if he wanted to end things. Here, now, he was hers. And maybe, just maybe, she could convince him that he didn't really want to let go.

As she floated on hope, Muffy slid on quiet paws to her basket.

Fifteen

Josh held up the blanket for Em and let it drop around her, smiling as she wriggled her cold skin against him. He'd offered to help sort the animals but she'd ordered him to stay and keep the bed warm. A chore he'd dutifully done, even if he was now suffering for it.

He curled his arm around her and kissed her hair. 'Your feet are freezing.'

'Sorry.' She twined them further with his, her toes like ice cubes against the tops of his feet.

'No, you're not.' He kissed her hair again, and rested his cheek against the silky strands. She had beautiful hair, richly coloured and soft. Her skin was the same. Finely textured, his fingers gliding over it like satin. Josh had worried his fingers were too rough, too abraded by timber and the scars left from countless splinters and cuts, but Em had assured him they were perfect. A real man's fingers, she'd called them.

She wormed her way further into his hold, seeking body heat. 'What are you up to today?'

'Not much.' He stroked the velvety curve of her shoulder. 'Sally's later. I promised to teach the boys the finer arts of footy in exchange for roast lamb and sticky date pudding, although with this weather I guess I'll be stuck with Matchbox car races instead.'

'I hope you let them win.'

'What sort of uncle do you think I am? Of course I don't let them win.'

She laughed and shifted to rest her upper body across his chest, and placed her chin on her folded hands. He felt himself rouse at the touch of her. 'Must be nice to have nephews to play with.'

'They're great. Though they can be little shits sometimes, too.' He reached for a coil of her hair, twined it around his finger and let go. As it unwound, the strands took on different highlights, before springing back to curl gently around her face. 'The way Digby's going he'll be producing some for you soon.'

'I hope so, although I hope they get married first.'

Josh regarded her with surprise. 'Bit of an old-fashioned attitude.'

She laughed. 'It's not me. I don't care what they do, but could you imagine Gran's response to an illegitimate great-grandchild? We'd never hear the end of it.'

'The Wallaces must have had a few in their time, surely.'

'They have, although it was easier to ignore them in the past. Gilbert was reported to have had at least five illegitimate offspring, two of them Aboriginal.'

'Charmer.'

'He was an unprincipled pig of a man from what I can gather.'

'Times were different then. What's that saying? The past is a different country?'

'"The past is a foreign country: they do things differently there." It's the opening line of *The Go-Between* by L.P. Hartley.' Suddenly Em's smile dipped. Swapping her chin for her cheek she closed her eyes and continued, face turned away. 'It's about childhood innocence and social hierarchy, friendship and betrayal, and how past actions can affect entire lives.'

She fell quiet. Josh frowned down at her head, wondering what the hell he'd done to cause this change in mood. He stroked her back and waited until he could stand it no more.

'Hey.' He set his hands under her arms to tug her further up his chest. 'What's up?'

'Nothing.'

'Don't tell me nothing, Em. Not after last night.'

Not after she'd said he'd mattered.

She remained quiet for a long while and he could feel her thinking. Finally, she spoke. 'How fit are you feeling this morning?'

He studied her face, trying to work out where the hell this was going. 'Fit enough. Why?'

'I want you to climb the hill with me.'

***

'We'll have to walk round,' said Em, resting her hiking boot on the back verandah rail and lacing it tight. 'There's been a slip at the quarry. Heritage have made it strictly off limits.'

'That never used to stop you.'

'For once I think they're right. The edges were looking unstable when I took Dig and Felicity up the hill. It's bound to be worse after all the rain.'

Josh scanned the sky as they walked. The wind remained up, keeping the cloud layer moving and with it the threat of rain. They wore raincoats in case. Em had given Josh a worn three-quarter-length oilskin from the farm's collection of spares. In one of the pockets he'd discovered a few tattered Minties that seemed, from their hardness, to have been there for years. They probably had, Em told him, given the lollies most likely belonged to her late Uncle James.

The tourist car park was empty, the rubber and chain swings of the attached small children's playground limp. Em dodged puddles as she headed for the gravel track that wound back and forth across the south face of the crater in a series of steps and steep inclines. Josh followed close as she began the climb, primed to steady her if she stumbled or slipped. The track was in a poor state, eroded with deep gullies and washed-out steps. Stony avalanches had left trails down the outer sides, flattening bracken and grass.

'I'll have to keep a check on the paper for working bees,' she said, her breath shortened from the ascent. 'They'll need all the help they can get with this damage.'

'Let me know. I can lend a hand if I'm free.'

As they climbed, the lowest clouds began to burn away, and sunshine and bright blue sky filled the rapidly expanding spaces. The remaining clouds were heavy, with dark grey bellies, but drifted fast, casting strange shadows that made the rock face above them flicker from dark to light, as though the crater throbbed with life.

Despite the cold, Josh arrived at the peak with his forehead speckled with sweat. His thighs, still sore from football, groaned from the effort. Em's skin shone with good health and exertion, her cheeks a becoming pink that triggered visions of how she looked in bed. Rocking Horse Hill had always excited her. It had once excited him too, although differently. The hill meant being alone with her. For Em it was something more visceral.

He was curious as to why they were here. Curious, and a little apprehensive. He thought they'd reached an understanding last night. Now he wasn't so sure.

Momentous things had happened on the hill. Here they'd touched, kissed. Here he'd looked into her hazel eyes, swallowed hard, and said, 'I love you'. They'd made love on their special rock ledge, defined their future life. Drafted plans.

He'd lost her here too.

Josh turned to the south and watched a herd of Friesian dairy cows lumber down a lane towards their day paddock, remembering. Full of hurt, he'd driven to Rocking Horse Hill, desperate to learn it wasn't true. That what he'd heard was a lie. Adrienne had directed him up the crater, where she said Em had been most of the day. He'd sprinted up the hill paddock, circled the edge of the quarry, scrambled up the rock face, and found Em sitting at the top, legs tucked up to her chest with her arms locked around them. She turned, her eyes red, her cheeks messy with tears. Then she'd lifted her chin at his approach, her expression taking on that haughty coldness he thought he'd broken past forever, and he knew.

He'd wanted to fall to his knees. Roar. Do something, anything to block her out. Instead, he placed his hands on his hips, legs apart to brace himself, and invited catastrophe in. She'd hesitated then nodded once in answer to his question and turned away to refocus on the farm. Josh had stared for a long time, brain whirling, wanting to bellow at her, wanting to cry, wanting to know what the fuck he'd done wrong. Wanting, most of all, to know *why*.

But there was no point. That night at Camrick had provided a glimpse of her feelings and her cheating had proved his deepest fear. Josh simply wasn't good enough.

He'd taken the long route back to his car, along the tourist path and Stanislaus Road, keeping out of her view. The same path they'd taken today. He just hoped it didn't end the same way.

Em touched his arm, pulling him back to the present. 'Can I show you something?'

She led him anticlockwise around the crater. Wind tugged at his oilskin and tossed Em's hair. A goshawk hovered on a thermal, hunting, then wheeled away with a screech, the sound disturbing in the morning loneliness. Josh concentrated on his footing and tried to push aside the wariness clenching his stomach.

Glancing behind to check he'd understood, Em dropped off the path and eased down the slope. He followed, scanning the crater for any erosion, but the rock here was solid, the footholds intact, and Em's footing sure.

The morning sun was still low enough to brighten their secret ledge. Em climbed up and eased across to make room for Josh, her legs dangling into the void below. He glanced to the side where the heart he'd once spent an afternoon laboriously carving lay between them.

Something leaden settled inside him. Josh looked at his hands, his left curled on his thigh, as it always was to hide his injury, and spoke quietly. 'If your plan is to dump me like before then I suggest you get it over with. This place has enough memories without adding that to it.'

Em drew in her breath sharply. 'No.' Shaking her head, she repeated the word, dismay drawing it out, as if she couldn't believe what he'd said. 'No, it's not that.' She paused for a moment, as though gathering herself, and continued. 'I need to explain.'

He stared out over the plain, at the idle centre pivots, pastures and crops. 'Let me guess. About why you cheated.'

'Yes.'

Josh wasn't sure he wanted to know. To what end, anyway? 'What's the point, Em?'

'The point is that you'll never trust me until I do.'

Mouth pursed, he dipped his head. She was right. He might love her but trusting her was proving hard. 'I never understood. I thought we had something magic. Then all of a sudden it was gone.'

'We did. And then . . .' She spread her hands, lifted them and let them fall as if words weren't enough. 'You had all these great dreams. Finishing your apprenticeship, you and your dad going into business. Getting married.'

'They were good dreams, Em.'

'I know. But to me back then they seemed so ordinary.'

He stared at her then turned away, his jaw like iron. 'Gee, thanks.'

'I was a Wallace, Josh. On top of that I was school captain, then I was crowned Miss Showgirl. I was the best rider in pony club. I'd won a dozen champion hacks and champion riders on the show circuit. I'd buy clothes that cost more than some people earned in a month. I thought all that made me special. Someone important.' She hauled in a breath. 'I was a snob. And that night at Camrick . . .' Biting her lip, she shook her head. 'You were so nervous and struggling to fit in.'

'Because that fuckwit Jacobs was trying to cut my grass. And doing a good job of it too. Jesus, Em, how did you expect me to be?'

'I don't know. Better somehow. I was young and stupid.' Liquid started to gather against her lower eyelids but Josh struggled to find sympathy. They should never have started this conversation. All it did was resurrect his anger and humiliation.

'So why bother with me in the first place? Or was our whole time together just you enjoying a bit of sport at my expense?'

'No!'

'For fuck's sake, Em. What am I supposed to think? You've made it sound like you never loved me. That all through it was just this big lie. What sort of fool does that make me?'

The tears fell.

He closed his eyes and turned away for a moment. 'Why couldn't you have just said? Why did you have to go and cheat?'

'You were so in love, Josh. All those plans . . .' She stared at her open palms. 'I got it into my mind that you'd never let me go.'

'I would have. If that's what you'd really wanted.'

Except that was a lie. He wouldn't have. He loved her too much.

'I know that now but back then I was too stupid to see how it could work. So I did what I did to force your hand.' Her eyes were enormous and sad. 'I'm sorry. You have no idea how much.' She was quiet a moment. 'I find it hard to reconcile that I could be that selfish, that cruel to someone I loved. It still shames me.'

Josh couldn't help thinking 'good', but then softened a fraction when he saw the deep remorse in her expression. Carrying around that weight of guilt mustn't have been easy. But neither was what she'd put him through. 'Why Stephen Jacobs? You knew what a fuckwit I thought he was.'

'For that exact reason. I knew it would take someone like him to stop you from trying to get me back.'

He absorbed that. Anyone else and he could have competed, but Jacobs was from an old family like Em's. His family were graziers, owned two historic sheep and cattle properties on the fertile redgum country to the north-west of town. They were part of the local rural aristocracy. An aristocracy that reality had seen long past, but still existed in the district's psyche.

'I wanted to. I had great ideas of belting the crap out of him and you suddenly realising that I was a bigger and better man than he'd ever be.'

'Really?'

He nodded. He'd had all sorts of ideas for a while, before the bitterness took over.

'So why didn't you?'

'Too proud and too shit-scared that you'd think I was a dickhead. And it would've upset Mum.'

A smiled twitched. 'Not that you'd be beaten?'

He gave her a 'you're kidding' look. He could have belted Stephen Jacobs into tomorrow if he wanted, weedy little fuck. 'No, I was just smart enough to see that I'd never be good enough for you no matter what I did. I told myself you weren't worth it anyway.'

Em hung her head. 'I wasn't. Not then.'

'And now?'

'I'd like you to think so.'

Josh thought of the mistakes they'd both made, of how they'd grown and changed. He wanted a love he could have faith in. The security of knowing she wanted the same future as him. That she wouldn't toss him over the moment she decided she wanted more from life than he had to offer.

Or someone better came along.

'I'll understand if you can't forgive me.'

The resignation in her voice had him studying her. He noted the teary anxiety, the regret, and let out a sigh and held out his arm. 'Come here.'

She shuffled across and leaned into his chest. They sat for a long time on the ledge, contemplating the landscape, until finally he kissed her hair and said he had to go. They didn't say much on the way back to the house. Josh was too uncertain and suspected she felt the same. Em kept staring at the gravel road, hands deep in her coat pockets, her mouth turned down as though she wished the morning had never happened.

Other than pausing to rehook his coat in the laundry, Josh avoided the house. They'd only end up in bed again and he needed to think.

For the first time since he'd started seeing her there was no lingering against the car door with Em settled between his legs. No teasing caresses. Instead, he opened the door and turned to cup her face and place a tender kiss on her forehead.

He stared at her a moment. 'Maybe we should have done this at the start. Got it out the way.'

'Would you still be here if we had?'

He let out a long breath and contemplated the hill, focussing on the spot where he'd learned the truth of her betrayal all those years ago. Remembering what it had done to him. 'I don't know. Probably not.' He returned his gaze to her face. 'It fucked me up, Em. For a while. I left here because of it. I chucked all my plans to go into business with Dad, moved to Adelaide. Tried to forget about here even though Levenham was where I wanted to be.'

From her breaths and swallows he could tell she was forcing tears down. 'I'm sorry.'

Josh sighed. He didn't know what to do. He wanted to forgive her but hearing her talk about it had made it harder rather than easier. 'I just wish you hadn't done it the way you did.'

'Me too.' Em bit her lip and lifted her chin. 'You've changed your mind.'

'No.' He stroked her face. 'I still want to be with you. But I'm not going to pretend that it's suddenly going to be all right between us, okay?'

She nodded and only then did Josh kiss her properly.

Trust couldn't be gained in a single conversation. It had to be earned and his already battered heart was at risk. Again.

But this was also love. There was no security, only chance.

All he could do was grab it and hope.

***

Josh strode up McArthur street, resisting the urge to whistle. The weather had remained clear, adding to his good mood and anticipation. He'd spent Sunday and Monday night with his dad at the kitchen table, turning sketches and photos he'd printed from the Internet into plans.

He couldn't believe he hadn't thought of using the cypress log for this before, instead of getting bogged down in ideas of jewellery boxes and sculptures. Em didn't strike him as a jewellery box person, no matter how well made, and he sure as hell didn't know how to sculpt. But an easel, with an adjustable work surface and side table and drawers and hollows for all her inks and paints – that was her all over.

The plans were folded in the back pocket of his work trousers. He'd tossed up whether to make it a surprise, but the net had thrown up dozens of styles. He and his dad thought they'd covered everything with theirs, but Josh decided it was wise to check. And he wanted to see her.

It wasn't only the plans for the easel that Josh took with him. He wanted to ask Em to dinner Saturday night at that new vineyard restaurant everyone seemed to be talking about, followed by a taxi back to Rocking Horse Hill, and some serious love-making. And on Sunday morning, he'd wake early and cook her breakfast. Bacon, eggs, grilled tomato. Maybe pancakes. Spoil her for once.

A proper date to start a proper relationship, now they'd got all the shit out the way. He was different now. As was she. They were too old and too experienced for games, and only too aware of how fragile hearts could be.

PaperPassion's bell rang out as he took the plans from his pocket and pushed the door open. A woman rose from behind the counter, but it wasn't Em. This woman was older, perhaps in her fifties, and wore narrow gold-framed glasses and her blonde-streaked hair in short spikes. He halted, confused, and glanced towards the bead curtain, expecting Em to rattle through it but the beads hung still and quiet.

'Hello,' the woman said. 'Looking for something special?'

Not something, someone. 'I was after Em.'

'I'm afraid she's not in today. Perhaps I can help?'

'Is she sick?'

'No. I believe she's gone to Adelaide.'

He blinked, still confused. Em hadn't mentioned anything about going to Adelaide. 'Do you know when she'll be back?'

'Not until the end of the week I think.'

'Right.' He nodded and tapped the plans against his curled-up left fist, feeling foolish. 'Right.'

The woman stepped closer. 'I'm not in often but I have a fair grip on things. Are you sure I can't help?'

He tapped a few more times then realised what he was doing and shoved the plans back into his pocket. 'Yeah, I'm sure.'

'Did you want to leave a message for her?'

'No. No message.' He turned for the door, then remembered his manners. 'Thanks. I'll catch her another time.'

On the street, he stood for a moment, staring down the road to the cenotaph. Cars passed by on either side, people going about their business.

He didn't know why he hurt so much.

Sixteen

Em's mood didn't bear speaking about. She drove with her fists clenched around the SUV's steering wheel and her attention deliberately fixed on the road. Beside her, Granny B appeared unperturbed, which somehow made it all worse.

'I trust you aren't going to be like this the entire trip.' Granny B shifted in her seat. 'It should make for a rather boring journey.'

'I should be in the shop.'

'Indeed you should. However, I'm not about to take a taxi all the way to Adelaide.'

Em sighed and relaxed her hands. Gran was right. They had another three hours' drive ahead of them and holding on to her temper was childish. She'd already expressed her displeasure many times, but her family had been unmoved. Granny B had an appointment that couldn't be missed in Adelaide with her eye specialist. Digby had too much work on, Adrienne had an important Arts Committee meeting and although Em was sure Felicity was perfectly capable of making the trip, both she and Granny B had made excuses as to why she shouldn't. Which left Em.

Normally she wouldn't have minded. Granny B could be an excellent travelling and shopping companion, and combining a trip to Adelaide with a visit to her suppliers to inspect new ranges and also see what her city counterparts were up to made the journey worthwhile. Except this time Adrienne refused to cover the shop and Em was forced to engage Helen, her casual, who she could ill afford. The tree removalists were due Thursday and the stump grinder Friday, which meant more time off and expense. The last time Em had taken so many days off in a row was three years ago, when she, Teagan and Jas had trucked Lod, Ox and Teagan's old mount Trumper to Melbourne to compete at the Royal Show.

At least Granny B was paying for fuel and accommodation, albeit grudgingly.

The news came on the radio, distracting them for a while, then Granny B reached across and turned the volume down. She sat back with her hands in her lap. 'We need to talk about your mother, Emily.'

'What about Mum?'

'I believe she's drinking.'

'She enjoys a glass of wine. So do I. So do a lot of people.'

'In secret?'

Em frowned. 'Surely it's no more than a glass in front of the telly or with Samuel?'

Granny B pursed her lips. 'Perhaps. But I don't believe so.' She turned to look out the side window, where the magnificent red gum country of the lower south-east sprawled verdant and fertile. In another fifty kilometres or so, the country would begin to change with the rainfall pattern, the flora shrinking to more drought-hardy species. 'I would never have expected it of her.'

Em wouldn't have either. Adrienne was too filled with grace to allow herself the release of control that alcohol gave. 'But why?'

Her grandmother hesitated before answering. 'I think she might be having second thoughts about Felicity.'

'Surely not. They've been getting along like a house on fire.'

Granny B shook her head. 'Haven't you noticed?'

'Noticed what?'

'Open your eyes, Emily. There's more to that girl than either she or Digby is letting on.'

'Like what?' She stared across at her grandmother. 'Come on, like what?'

'I don't know, but I intend to find out.'

Em caught the thrust of Granny B's jaw and her heart sank. 'Oh, Gran, what have you planned?'

But her grandmother turned to the window and, despite Em's frustrated pleas, refused to say another word on the subject.

***

Granny B exited the specialist's with a disdainful tilt to her nose. 'Waste of money,' she declared as they walked to Em's car. 'Just keep using the drops. Ridiculous. He could have phoned that through.'

'Still no discussion of a trabeculectomy?'

'He deems it unnecessary at this point. The eye drops are doing their job.'

'Do you think we should get a second opinion?'

'No. I've had quite enough of these doctors as it is. And none of them will restore the vision I've lost. I might as well ignore them and get on with living.' She stopped at the car door. 'And we have more important things to worry about.'

Em looked at the sky. It was only four. They could be home by eight, but Granny B had insisted on an overnight stay. Nice hotel or not, Em would rather be sharing her night with Josh. She slid into the car. 'Right. To the Hyatt? Or did you want to do a bit of shopping first?'

'Neither.' Granny B pointed through the windscreen. 'You and I are going for a drive.'

Em narrowed her eyes. 'Where?'

'You'll see. Straight ahead and then right onto Dequetteville Terrace.'

Em gave her grandmother a warning look but did as she was told. Past the Royal Adelaide Hospital, the road slipped through Rundle Park, lush with winter grass. 'At least give me some idea of where we're headed.'

'Springfield. I'll tell you where to turn.' At Em's expression she gave a dry laugh. 'I still possess one good eye, you know.'

The address to where Granny B directed Em wasn't far from the Adelaide University's Waite Campus, famous for world-renowned agricultural research. This was moneyed Adelaide. The houses were large and expensive-looking, with tasteful tall fences enclosing manicured gardens and well-established shade trees. Sleek cars were parked in paved driveways, many European-brand SUVs that made Em's old car look shabby and out of place.

Granny B ordered her through the open gates of a red-brick driveway. Over the top of a green and silver pittosporum hedge, Em glimpsed a magnificent two-storey Georgian-influenced mansion. The drive curved, giving her a full view of the house. Camrick it was not, but it still possessed plenty of majesty.

The drive widened into a parking area. Em switched off the car and alighted with Granny B.

'What are we doing here?'

'Meeting a friend of mine.'

'Who?'

'You'll see.'

'I'm not enjoying this game, Gran.'

'It's not a game, Emily. We have a problem and I intend to solve it.'

The front door opening halted their discussion. A man appeared, his arms spreading in a warm gesture of welcome.

'Audrey, how wonderful to see you.' He looked her up and down, eyes twinkling. 'Still haven't lost any of that famous Wallace glamour.'

Despite his years, he looked fit, and had intelligent brown eyes, a generous smile and hair as silver as the woman's whose hands he clasped with obvious delight.

'And you're still the charmer.' They exchanged kisses, before Granny B stepped back. 'Charles Markham, please allow me to introduce my granddaughter Emily.'

His gaze ranged over Em with the same appreciation he'd given her grandmother. 'Another beauty. Those Wallace genes are quite something.' He held out his hand. 'Enchanted to meet you.'

'And you.' Although Em still had no idea where the man fitted into her grandmother's life or her schemes.

Charles beckoned them into the house, talking over his shoulder as he led them to a sitting room. 'Tea? Or is it time for an aperitif? You were always partial to a Tom Collins, Audrey, if I recall.'

'I was indeed, but I'm quite happy with a G and T to save you trouble.'

'And you, Emily? What can I tempt you with?'

'Emily will have a glass of white wine.'

Em clenched her jaw but manners prevented her from arguing. 'White wine would be fine.'

'Chardonnay? There's riesling in the cellar, if you prefer. Eden or Clare Valley.' He frowned a touch. 'I don't believe I have any New Zealand sauvignon blanc, sorry. So popular these days among the younger set. Can't stand it myself, far too cloying.'

His pained disdain reminded her momentarily of Uncle James, who'd made no effort to hide his wine snobbery. 'Chardonnay will be fine.'

Charles indicated a floral three-seater lounge and beckoned them to sit. After the cool of the fading afternoon, the room was cosy and cheerful. Partly from a well-tended fire crackling behind a brass grate, partly from the plush soft furnishings in warm colours and textures.

She waited until Charles had left to fetch their drinks before turning on her grandmother. 'Okay, what the hell is going on?'

'What does it look like? I'm meeting an old friend.'

'There's more to it than that.'

'Of course there is, but you'll have to wait.'

Not in the mood to sit, Em remained standing, leaving her grandmother alone on the three-seater. Not that Granny B appeared the slightest affronted. She sat with her legs together and angled to one side, princess-like, and her hands in her lap, graciously smiling on Charles's return and accepting her tumbler of gin and tonic like some latter-day lady of the manor.

'Please,' he said, handing a wine glass to Em and sweeping his arm towards a wing-backed chair to the side of the fire. 'Sit down. I won't be a moment.' He headed back out again, returning quickly with a tumbler of something amber on ice, and a manila folder. He sat next to Granny B. 'To old friendships,' he said, raising his glass and drinking.

Charles placed his tumbler down on the timber coffee table, and leaned forward. 'Shall we get down to business?'

'Excellent idea.'

He removed a pair of reading glasses from the pocket of his shirt and perched them on the end of his nose, smiling at Granny B. 'Old age, hey, Audrey? Gets to us all.'

'Sadly, yes. But fortunately our minds remain sharp.'

'They do indeed, thank goodness.' He opened the folder, slid out some pages, and picked up the top sheet. 'The story's rather sad, I'm afraid.'

Em couldn't hold back any longer. 'I'm sorry to interrupt, Charles, but what's all this about?'

'Ah,' said Charles, glancing at Granny B for direction. At the old lady's nod he turned his attention to Em. 'I'm a journalist or, rather, I was. Retired now.' His eyes lit with secret knowledge. 'Mostly. Your grandmother contacted me to do some research on Felicity Townsend, to whom I understand your brother is now engaged.'

Em felt a shrinking inside. On top of her being Digby's fiancée, Em also regarded Felicity as a friend. It was a nascent friendship, to be fair, but one she hoped to nurture. Engaging a journalist to snoop into Felicity's past stank of dishonour.

'How could you, Gran?'

'If you're worried about privacy,' said Granny B, ignoring the accusation, 'I can assure you Charles understands the meaning of discretion.' A look passed between them, something cryptic and intimate, which left Em suspicious as to how close their friendship actually was.

'This is a gross betrayal of trust.'

A row of fine lines appeared around Granny B's mouth but her expression was unapologetic.

Charles simply watched them, though Em knew he was making as many judgements of her as she was of him. After a few beats of tense silence, he continued with his findings.

'Your suspicions were well founded, Audrey. The Townsends have quite a long history of criminal behaviour, mainly to do with the manufacture and distribution of amphetamines, although they're out of action for the time being.'

'For what reason?'

'Jail tends to make the drug business difficult. They were small time, anyway.' He paused meaningfully. 'Unlike Mark Ainsley.' His gaze met Em's. 'The man Felicity attempted to kill.'

Em straightened in shock. 'Kill? What do you mean, kill?'

'Two years and seven months ago, Felicity Townsend stabbed her fiancé with a kitchen knife.'

With shaky hands, Em placed her glass on the table and pressed the tips of her fingers against her mouth. Felicity? It couldn't possibly be true. She dropped her hand. 'You must have the wrong person.'

Charles reached into his folder, removed a newspaper cutting and passed it over. The photographer had caught Felicity looking wide-eyed and vulnerable as she was bustled into the courthouse. Em skimmed the text then dropped the clipping on the table as though the ink contained poison.

'Did you know about this?' she asked Granny B.

'Not until Charles told me.'

Em still couldn't believe it. Felicity? She was too sweet, too delicate to inflict that kind of violence. She loved animals. She loved Digby. Brutality wasn't in her nature. 'It must have been self-defence.'

'Most likely it was, but the court didn't see it so cleanly,' said Charles. 'Ainsley was not a pleasant man, regardless of what his family believes, or what was shown in court.' He made a rueful gesture. 'He and the Townsends were in business together, albeit briefly. Lance Townsend was never a particularly smart operator and the son Brett, Felicity's brother, was even worse. When their relationship turned sour and the Townsends couldn't pay up, Mark Ainsley effectively demanded Felicity as payment.' He picked up the clipping and studied the photo. 'She didn't know. She was seventeen, poorly educated and, according to those who knew her, an inveterate dreamer. All around her she saw hopelessness. Families on welfare, drug addictions, friends getting pregnant. She only had to look to her own mother to see what awaited her. Ainsley lived in a nice suburb, dressed well, drove a good car. When her father introduced her to him, she didn't see drug money. She saw a middle-class respectable world, filled with things she'd be denied if she stayed in Elizabeth.'

'In other words,' interrupted Granny B, 'all the things she has now, thanks to Digby.'

Em was too horrified to speak. Felicity's own father had sold her to a drug dealer?

Charles considered her. 'It's difficult to fathom, isn't it?'

Em nodded, sick with shock, her head overloaded with questions. 'So what happened?'

'Ainsley became obsessed with her, violently so. She was young, very beautiful and immature. All she saw was a man who appeared to value her more than any one else ever had, but the reality was that Ainsley regarded her as his property, to do with as he liked. Which he did. What was meant to be an escape for her turned into five years of hell. The one time she fought back cost her nearly two years in jail.'

Em shook her head. How could she have not gotten away? At seventeen Em could understand her staying – just – but Felicity was older when she stabbed Mark Ainsley, a grown woman. She could have walked out. Run interstate. Contacted a shelter. *Something.*

Except Em had read enough newspapers and books, and watched enough television to know that's not how battered women behaved. The trouble was she couldn't picture Felicity as a helpless victim.

Granny B sat back. 'A girl whose father could trade her like a piece of livestock must have had a shocking upbringing. She'd have to be mentally disturbed.'

'You'd think so, but no. She was assessed as part of the trial and deemed traumatised but with no underlying mental issues. There were some problems in jail, which I've listed in the report, but since release Felicity has been living quietly in assisted accommodation in Gawler without incident.'

'Where Digby met her.'

'Yes.' He smiled understandingly at Em. 'In innocent circumstances.'

Which only made Em feel sicker about what she'd discovered. If Felicity wanted to keep her past a secret then she had that right. That Digby knew was obvious now; the way he'd covered up when Felicity mistakenly revealed she'd worked in a commercial kitchen, how he helped change the subject whenever her life in Adelaide was brought up. And if Digby understood then so could they. People were allowed to start new lives, free from their pasts.

'We didn't need to know this, Gran.'

'Your grandmother asked for my help with the best of intentions, Emily. She's always been protective of the Wallace family name.'

'Someone has to be,' said Granny B, her chin lifted. 'And I appear to be the only one with the gonads to do so.'

Charles laughed, momentarily breaking the tension, although not Em's deep disquiet. 'You are a warrior among women, Audrey. William was a lucky man.' He held up his glass to chink it against hers. 'To your formidable Wallace gonads. Long may they fire in your loins.'

***

'I hate what you've done,' said Em on the drive home the following lunchtime, after a morning spent snooping on PaperPassion's rivals to prevent the trip from being a complete business waste.

'Feel free to dislike it all you like, Emily, but we are better off knowing.'

'How are we better off knowing?'

'It helps give us some understanding of her motives.'

'What motives? She loves Digby. Digby loves her. They're happy. Tell me, what can possibly be wrong with that? How does knowing her past change that?' When her grandmother didn't respond, Em stared hard at the road. 'You're just a snob, that's all. You're scared about everyone finding out and it ruining the Wallace family's precious name.'

'Don't be so ridiculous,' snapped Granny B. She watched the road for a long moment, her mouth tight, until finally she released a long sigh. 'It's not snobbery, Emily. I'm worried. Camrick has changed since her arrival, the whole family has. That girl is causing problems, only for some reason you refuse to see it.'

'That's because there's nothing to see.'

'Dressing like your mother, wearing the family jewellery as though she already owns it? That's nothing?'

Em didn't answer. The jewellery had annoyed her too. But if Adrienne wanted to loan her favourite earrings or any other item to Felicity, Em could hardly bitch about it. Doing so would only make her look sour.

'What worries me most is how she's changed since her visit to the hill. Something connected with her that day and now it's you she's emulating. Every conversation seems to be about the farm and Digby's spending a small fortune at Campbells. She's even imitating the way you speak. As for Digby buying her a horse —' She sniffed loudly. 'I don't like that business at all. It sets a precedent you would be wise to be wary of.'

'I'm not thrilled about the horse thing either, or Digby telling her she can visit whenever she likes, but I'm not going to read anything sinister into that or anything else. So she likes animals? So do a lot of people. As for the rest, she's just trying to fit in.'

'And your mother's newly acquired drinking habit?'

'That could be caused by anything. Maybe she and Samuel are having troubles.'

Her grandmother harrumphed before turning away to stare out of the window.

Of course Em had noticed the clothes and accent, the way Felicity's pronunciation of the 'a' in words like plant and dance had changed, switching from a nasal 'ant' to a more refined 'aunt'. But all the Wallaces spoke that way, and Em could see how Felicity would want to fit in. She was to be Digby's wife; it seemed obvious that she'd have a fear of embarrassing him, and what better way to avoid that than copy his mother and sister? Anyway, for all they knew it could be Digby giving her the elocution lessons.

As for Adrienne's drinking, Em would simply have to talk to her.

From the cropping zone, the landscape passed back into the rich grazing lands of the south-east. As they headed towards the famous vineyards of the Coonawarra, they passed an Italianate double-storey limestone mansion, once the centrepiece of a vast station and home to one of the Wallace's great business and agricultural rivals. The house reminded Em of the connections between the district's various families, and her mind drifted to Charles and his intimacy with Granny B.

'You and Charles . . .'

'Yes?'

'Did you have a relationship?'

'As it so happens, we did,' she said, a wistful look softening her face, 'although a long time ago, before I knew your grandfather. Charles was a fine man, but William was a better one.'

'And after Grandpa died?'

'That, dear Emily, is none of your business.'

Em smiled and looked back at the highway. She'd suspected as much from their conversation once the business of Felicity was closed. The table cleared and their drinks freshened, Charles and Granny B had fallen into a nostalgic discussion, reliving the glamorous parties and scandals of the fifties and sixties. They'd moved in similar, privileged circles. Granny B was a frequent visitor to Adelaide. With her wealth, breeding and good looks, she must have had enormous fun.

'You'd have been quite a catch in those days.'

'I was rather.'

'Poor Charles. He must have been very disappointed.'

Granny B smiled. 'Indeed he was. But he would never have left Adelaide for Levenham, and I wasn't about to forsake my life there. He was an excellent journalist. Very good at wriggling out secrets. He so easily fooled people, you see. They always believed him far too aristocratic for such a grubby activity.'

'I can imagine. So will you take up his offer?' she asked, referring to Charles's proposal that Granny B return for an extended stay.

'No.' But there was a sentimental edge to her voice. 'Perhaps a few years ago I may have, but not now.'

'Why not?'

'Someone has to watch over your mother, Emily. And the rest of the family.'

Em stared back at the road. 'We can take care of ourselves.'

'Indeed. But never discount the wisdom of old eyes. Even half-blind ones.'

They arrived back at Camrick soon after four and Granny B disappeared to her room with Charles's folder. Em had every intention of heading straight home to the hill but she was still too disturbed by the revelations of the previous afternoon.

Beyond feeling enormous sorrow and sympathy for Felicity, Em wasn't sure how she felt about her future sister-in-law's past with regards to her family. Felicity had almost killed someone. She'd been to jail. Now she was engaged to one of the district's most eligible bachelors, heir to the famous Wallace name and wealth. She would be scrutinised and Em's family, which had always fiercely guarded its privacy, would have to somehow cope with that.

The trouble was that this was a secret with no chance of staying that way, and Em was well aware of Levenham's communal failings. Her father Henry had experienced his own share of prejudice for marrying a woman above him in station. Em had experienced a little of the same with Josh, but being young and in love she'd barely noticed at first, or cared. It had existed, though, the disdain and sly looks, the barbed comments from schoolmates. Gradually, it had worn her down, made her question something that was pure and right.

What affect would Felicity's past have on Digby, on Adrienne? How would Felicity cope when people shunned her or made their whispers obvious, when women Digby had turned down raked cat's claws over her reputation? Was she strong enough to face it? From what little Em knew about battered women their sense of self-worth was fragile. Jail wouldn't have helped either. Who knew what vulnerabilities existed behind that beautiful facade.

Felicity was curled up on the lounge reading a Jilly Cooper novel. She marked her place as Em came in, smiling hello as she leaned forward to put the book down. 'How was your trip to Adelaide?'

'It had its moments.' The cover of Felicity's novel showed a curvy woman wearing tight breeches and holding a riding crop while having her bum felt up by a disembodied male hand. 'Good book?'

'It is, actually. It's horsey and fun. Full of posh people.'

Em nodded and glanced around the room. Other than some clothes hanging from the knobs of the bedroom robes, the made bed and clean kitchenette, Felicity appeared to have made little impact on Digby's bachelor decor. Perhaps it was because she spent so much time in the main house, keeping the stables for sleeping and private moments.

'Did you want to sit down?' Felicity tilted her head as Em hesitated to answer. Em wanted to stay, to talk about what she'd learned, but to do so would give away that Felicity had been spied upon. 'Em?'

'Thanks, but I need to get home to the animals.'

'Of course you do.' When Em still didn't move, Felicity frowned. 'Is there something wrong? Something I've done?'

Em shook her head. 'No.' Then she let out a deep sigh. 'Yes.' She glanced around for a chair and took the closest, sitting very straight with her hands clasped on her knees, her troubled gaze on Felicity. 'I don't know how to approach this.' She looked down for a moment. 'I learned something in Adelaide.'

For a heartbeat, Felicity's puzzlement kept her together. Then her body seemed to collapse in on itself. A mewl of distress escaped her lips. She hugged her chest, eyes filling with tears. She placed trembling fingers to her mouth, then lowered her hand and with a couple of deep breaths gathered herself. 'How did you find out?'

'It doesn't matter.'

Felicity's watery gaze slid towards Camrick. 'It was your grandmother, wasn't it? I sensed from the start she didn't like me.'

'No. Don't think that. It's just hard for her. She comes from a different generation, one where you always knew the background of the people marrying into the family. In her eyes, learning about you was a normal thing to do.'

Felicity's head dropped. 'She must hate me now.'

'No one hates you. None of it was your fault. The man was abusing you.' Em paused, then carried on gently. 'We all make mistakes, Felicity. I've made some terrible ones, hurt people I loved. That doesn't mean I should be condemned forever.'

Felicity regarded her with hope. 'It doesn't upset you, that I've been in jail?'

Aware of how much their friendship rode on this and, potentially, her relationship with Digby, Em chose her words carefully. 'It's not ideal, but the reason why at least gives it perspective. Digby knows, doesn't he? All of it?'

'I told him everything when he asked me to marry him. He said it didn't matter, that he'd love me no matter what I'd done.'

Em's chest swelled with pride in her brother.

Felicity fixed her blue eyes on Em's, her pain and plea-filled gaze locking them together. 'All through my life, my dad and brother, even Mum, used to treat me as though I was worthless. Like I was nothing.'

'You're not nothing, Felicity.'

'I know that now, thanks to Digby. And with him I have a chance to show the world that I'm worth something.' She touched her neck and smiled dreamily. 'He's wonderful, you know? Like no one I've ever met. It's like he looks at me and sees only good things. How can I not love a man like that? He makes me want to be different, to be as special as he sees me.' Her focus returned, flowing with determination. 'To be the wife he deserves.'

Em embraced her. 'You already are.'

***

Em contemplated Felicity's words as she walked across to Camrick. When word got out, Digby and Felicity would still face a rocky path, but Em had confidence that the way they felt about each other would see them through. She smiled to herself. It was incredibly romantic when she thought about it. Perhaps she'd make *Cendrillon*, Charles Perrault's seventeenth-century version of the Cinderella tale, her next project.

Halfway across the yard, Em noticed Granny B pacing the back lawn, trailing smoke, the glow from her cigar weaving cosmic lines in the dark. The evening wind was glass-sharp and far too chilly for an old woman, even one with the constitution of a stud Hereford.

'Don't tell me you've been waiting for me?'

Granny B jammed her cigar between her teeth. 'What else would I be doing out here without a decent malt? You'd better come inside.'

'What's up?'

'You'll see.'

She followed Granny B into the hall. Distracted, Em took three strides before she realised the floor wasn't right.

'Now do you see?' asked Granny B.

Thick cream carpet now lay where the beautiful floorboards had ranged in warm golden hues. It spread like a hayed-off lawn to the end of the house before blanketing the stairs to the floor above. The effect was not as Em had expected. The hall was brighter, but it also had a sterile feeling. Too much cream, too much blankness. The doctor's surgery of Granny B's warning.

For the first time Em could recall, her mother had an interior design wrong.

Seventeen

Friday morning saw Rocking Horse Hill once more fogged with noise as workers arrived to grind the cypress stump.

Em had observed the previous day's tree removal with a kind of morbid fascination, the drone of machinery vibrating in her chest, worsening her heartache, yet she couldn't stop pacing the yard and paddocks, watching. The men used their chainsaws and chains with honed skill, fluoro work shirts and hard hats flashing bright against the wall of remaining pines. The truck's haulage arm lifted the heavier pieces to the tray where they were quickly secured by straps. Piece by piece, the space in the Avenue of Honour widened. By the end of the day, the tree line appeared more gap-toothed than ever.

Afterwards, Em had waved them off and stood back, her sense of loss acute. Sawdust left pale patches on the grass and darker layer of pine needles, and channelled the eye to the tree's low wide stump, a stark and sad grave marker against the shadows.

After this morning it, too, would be gone.

Tiredness didn't help. She'd woken early to move a highly recalcitrant Kicki and Cutie to the hill paddock where they were less likely to be spooked by the grinder noise, then Lod, who was much more cooperative. A quick breakfast and shower, and Em had rushed into town to collect Granny B and install her at PaperPassion. Neither was enthused by the idea of a morning with her in charge of the shop. With her impatience and intolerance of fools, Em's grandmother made a less-than-ideal shop assistant and, after the carpet episode, both would have preferred she stayed at Camrick to watch over Adrienne. But Em simply couldn't afford the expense of more casual wages. She could only pray that Granny B wouldn't cause too much damage.

The new carpet at Camrick still bothered Em. All those classic floorboards, with their handsome grains, covered with that pile. Whatever her mother had envisaged, surely it hadn't been that travesty?

'I can only imagine she made the decision after one too many glasses of wine,' her grandmother had whispered as they'd headed towards the kitchen.

Em had kept her voice equally low, although, given the carpet's thickness, any sound was unlikely to carry. 'It's not bad . . .'

'You certainly couldn't describe it as good.'

'Has she said anything?'

'No. But I can tell she's not pleased. A little tick appears at the side of her mouth whenever it's mentioned.'

'What did you say when you saw it?'

Granny B's gaze shifted sideways for a moment then she raised her chin. 'I told her it was very nice.'

Em had lied too. Hugging her mother hello, she said that the carpet lightened the entire area.

'So much better than all that timber.' Adrienne gave a shallow, twitchy smile. 'I know the boards were lovely but they were old-fashioned and made the area so dark. And it's so much safer for Mum on the stairs now.'

It was all so worrying.

Despite her fatigue and a morning's opportunity to work on *The Ballad of the White Horse*, Em stayed outside, wandering the yard and paddocks, observing the grinder as it chewed the last of the tree to scrap.

Finally the job was complete and the workers and truck departed. Arms folded tight across herself, Em trudged back to the car. The tree was done. In the spring, a sapling would take its place, the scar would heal and Second Lieutenant Stanley would be memorialised once more, as was right.

She drove into Levenham, mind skittering from subject to subject: Josh, the lost cypress, Felicity and Digby, her illuminations, the message she'd left for Teagan that was still unreturned, the shop. Her thoughts returned to Josh and settled there. Em hadn't heard from him since Sunday, which seemed odd, but he was most likely as busy as she.

Em could have called him but she was scared of hearing the same resignation in his voice as on Sunday. They'd parted that morning with their relationship unresolved. If anything, it was even more tenuous than before. What if she rang him and his voice held the tone that told her forgiveness might never come?

Em glanced at the dashboard clock, assessing how much longer she could leave Granny B in charge of PaperPassion. Surely half an hour wouldn't matter, and her grandmother was the one who'd encouraged a visit to Michelle in the first place. Em may as well make the most of her spare minutes.

She took the road to the eastern side of town, winding her way through the rabbit-warren streets of the old public housing quarter, noting with satisfaction that the area had, as the local paper and others suggested, experienced a renaissance. It was still nothing like the southern side of town, where large houses clustered the high ground, or the inner north, where Camrick maintained its grand footing, but it had a new air of pride and tidiness. More well-maintained houses and gardens lined the streets than ill-tended ones. Newer-model cars held pride of place in the drives. On roofs, satellite dishes turned their faces to the day like sunflowers, a more telling sign than any of the east's changed fortunes.

She almost missed the Sinclairs'. Where once the fence was chainwire and steel tubes, a picket fence painted British racing green now marked the boundary. The limestone house had changed too. It used to be a weathered grey with bluish mortar peeping between the joins; now it was rendered smooth and painted a sandy white, its frames and guttering the same green as the fence. The front garden remained the same: standard roses against the fence line, a trimmed and well-weeded lawn, and a swept concrete path lined with winter blooms. Michelle hadn't lost her gardener's touch.

The sight of Josh's ute, parked to the side of the house under a dark green Colorbond carport, caused Em's heart to skip in anticipation, even though it wasn't him she was here to see. Not really.

She pulled up across the street, remembering sweet times. She'd adored Josh's family, its simplicity and deep love. Its wholeness that made her own somehow lacking, especially after her father left. The Sinclairs argued and occasionally yelled, but without losing the love in their hearts. Michelle mothered her family with both indulgence and firmness. Tom, Em didn't know so well – he was always working. But she could see how much he and Josh loved each other. They were alike, too, both in looks and manner. Kind-hearted men any woman would be proud to call husband.

Em lowered her head. When she'd broken up with Josh she'd lost them all, a repercussion she hadn't comprehended until it was too late. Shame had kept her away since. She hoped it wasn't too late to reconnect now.

At the gate, she hesitated. Before, Em would have walked round the back, knocked and pushed the door open, calling out the way Karen, Sally and Josh did. But she wasn't a teenager any more, and that degree of familiarity was a privilege she'd forsaken. Straight shouldered, she opened the latch, walked down the path and knocked.

The front door opened. A puffy-faced woman with an orange satin scarf tied around her head regarded her with bewilderment for a half-second before flinging her arms open.

'Em!'

Em fell into her embrace, eyes itching as she felt the fierceness of Michelle's hug.

Finally, Michelle released her hold and stood back, her hands still gripped on Em's arms. 'Look at you!'

'How are you, Michelle?'

Josh's mum smiled. 'Oh, you know.'

'I'm sorry, I should have been in touch —'

'Oh, shush. You're here now. That's all that matters.' Michelle stood aside, her face now suffused with colour and excitement, and beckoned. 'Your timing couldn't be more perfect. I've just finished a batch of fairy cakes. They're for Karen's baby shower tomorrow but she won't mind if we pinch a couple.' She pressed a hand against Em's shoulder. 'Go on. Off you go through to the kitchen where it's warm.'

Em tried not to stare at the hallway walls as she passed. The collection of collaged photos had multiplied in the years since her last visit. Frames of varying sizes hung in three loose rows, at her eye-line. Most of the new additions were of babies and grinning children, but there were wedding photos too. Em was unable to hide the falter in her step when she spied a large frame filled with several pictures, all images from Josh's big day.

Michelle stopped, giving Em the freedom to pause and stare. A freedom she wasn't sure she wanted.

'She was a nice girl, Bianca.'

Em sensed Michelle's assessing gaze but couldn't respond. Jealousy had squirmed its way into her gut and tightened her throat. Bianca made a radiant bride: pink-lipped, blue-eyed, and stunning in a simple strapless gown, her pale hair expertly piled to show off the lightly freckled skin of her neck and upper chest. Her face was tilted upwards, regarding Josh. He was grinning at the camera, handsome in a dark suit, one arm around her bare shoulders, his eyes sparkling with pride and happiness. The way, a long time ago, they had with Em.

'He looks happy,' said Em, to break the silence.

Michelle caught her eye and smiled sympathetically. 'He was. But that was then and this is now.' She looped her arm through Em's. 'Enough of that. Time for tea and cake, and you can tell me all about what's been going on.'

***

Em glanced at her watch. She needed to go. Any longer and Granny B was liable to walk out in a huff, leaving the shop door open and the register unsecured.

She smiled apologetically at Michelle. 'I'm sorry, I'd love to stay but I really need to get back.'

'I know, I know. I can rabbit on, but it's just so good to see you.' Michelle put her hand around Em's forearm. 'Almost like the old days.'

Em was disappointed to leave the cake-scented fug of the kitchen but glad she'd called in. As they rose, Michelle cocked her ear. Her eyes slid to Em's. 'Ah, now he took his time.'

'Mum?' A door banged. Josh strode in, his expression surprised when he spotted Em before turning cool. 'Hey.'

'Hi.' Em's skin flushed at the sight of him, masculine and capable. Josh wore work clothes, similar to what he'd worn in the shop the first time she saw him. Sawdust clung to the sleeves of his jumper. His hair was mussed, his beard untrimmed. He smelled earthy, of timber and oil and work.

'I thought you were supposed to be in Adelaide or something.'

'No, only Tuesday night.' Em tilted her head. 'How did you know?'

'I went to the shop. The lady there said you were off until today.'

'It's been one of those weeks, unfortunately. Gran had a specialist's appointment in Adelaide that no one else could take her to and she insisted on staying the night. Then Thursday I had to be home for the tree people and this morning it was the stump grinders.' She smiled and touched her ears. 'I think all that noise has given me tinnitus.'

Josh lifted his chin in acknowledgement but didn't return the smile.

Silence fell. They stood awkwardly. Em didn't know how to behave. She didn't know where she stood with him and Josh exuded an air of annoyance she didn't understand.

'I really have to go,' she said, adjusting the bag on her shoulder.

Michelle frowned at her son, seemingly perplexed by his behaviour. 'Why don't you take Em to the shed and show her your work?'

Em glanced at him and shook her head. 'I really don't have time.'

'Go on. A few minutes won't hurt.' When neither moved, Michelle pushed again. '*Go on.*'

Josh sighed and gestured towards the door. 'There's not that much to look at.'

Railroaded but also curious, Em bent to kiss Michelle's cheek. 'It was lovely to catch up.'

Michelle squeezed her hand tightly. When she spoke again her voice had a tremor to it. 'You'll visit again?'

Em glanced at Josh, who was frowning at his mother. 'Of course.'

'Good,' said Michelle, swiping at her leaky eyes. 'Now, off you go.' She attempted to shuffle them from the kitchen but Josh wasn't so easily moved.

'Mum, you okay?'

'Just tired from the excitement of seeing Em.'

His eyes narrowed. 'Are you sure?'

'Yes, I'm sure.' She gave him a gentle push. 'Go. And behave yourself. Em has to go back to work.'

'Is she really all right?' Em asked as they walked down the drive to the garage. The sliding door was open now, exposing a workshop filled with tools, timber and projects.

'I hope so. She keeps trying to do too much. She should be resting.'

Em wasn't sure if that was a rebuke and decided to ignore it. 'It must be hard for her, though. She was always so active, and she loves looking after everyone.'

'Yeah, but now it's time for us to look after her.' He paused, the mineral scent of oil stronger despite the open door. 'So how did the tree removal go?'

'Good. Efficient.' Em's mouth twisted. 'Sad.'

'Yeah, I guess it would be.' He indicated the rear bench. 'Come have a look at this.'

She followed him across the garage, admiring a beautifully crafted kitchen trolley as she passed. On the floor, protected from the concrete by an off-cut of carpet, sheets of jarrah were laid out. Even raw, the colour was rich and vivid, the grain fine but with interesting, artful loops.

A thin stack of papers lay on the bench. She stared at the top one, trying to work out what the drawings represented, unsure until Josh slid a sheet from the bottom and laid it on top. A strange swooping feeling came over her. It swung through her body and disappeared, leaving a deep warmth in its place.

She glanced at him, heart fluttering. 'It's an easel.'

'Yeah.'

Em looked back at the plans, carefully drawn in fine pencil, the dimensions and notes written in precise numbers and uppercase letters. 'You did this.'

'And Dad.'

'Is it . . .?' She swallowed, afraid to say it in case she had it wrong.

'It's for you. Using the cypress timber.'

'Oh, Josh.' Em looked back at the plans and pressed her lips together but the tide of emotion kept coming. Embarrassed, she put her hand to her mouth but the urge to cry at the perfection of his idea remained.

'Hey.' He wrapped her in his warm arms as though the prickliness of earlier had never existed. 'Don't.'

'I'm sorry. It's just . . . after this morning.'

'I know.'

'It's perfect.'

'Don't be so hasty.' He smiled down at her. 'We haven't even started it yet.'

She pointed at the kitchen trolley. 'Men who can make that won't have any problem with an easel. You're just being modest. I know talent when I see it.'

Josh brushed the knuckles of his damaged hand down her cheek, causing Em's heart to do a slow tumble. 'Thanks for coming to see Mum.'

'I've been meaning to and this morning I had a few spare minutes.' She lifted her sleeve to check her watch again and groaned. 'Gran is going to kill me. I really have to go.'

'Okay.'

He didn't release her.

'Josh?'

'I missed you, Em.'

In the security of his arms, with her heart soothed by his embrace and thoughtfulness, the words resonated deeply. 'I missed you, too.'

He kissed her tenderly and pressed his forehead to hers, smiling in a way that made her heart somersault even higher.

'So we're okay?' she asked, hopeful but still uncertain.

'We're okay.'

***

Granny B was pacing the street at the front of the shop, the tails of her tweed coat flapping out like bat wings, when Em arrived.

She regarded her granddaughter with an expression as steely as her hair. 'And where have you been?'

'At the hill.' Em paused. 'And I called in to see Michelle.'

'I have been waiting for over an hour!'

'I'm sorry.'

'A rather inadequate word: sorry.'

Em gave the street a quick scan, noting the pension-week shoppers, the people hurrying towards the banks and the post office, and made sure to keep her voice neutral. 'I didn't mean to take so long. The workmen finished early so I thought I'd use the time to catch up with Michelle.'

'Catch up with that son of hers, more like.'

'Josh was in the shed for most of my visit, working.' She glanced at the shop door, reluctant to enter. Boredom and Granny B never mixed well and her grandmother had that look, a sly smugness underlying her anger. 'So how was it? Busy?'

'No. Dull as dishwater.' Granny B's eyes narrowed as she looked past Em. 'Ah, if it isn't Barry McClintoff, our illustrious mayor. Must have a word to him about this ridiculous cut to the Seniors Month budget they're proposing. Completely unacceptable. You can call me a taxi on my return.' And with that, Granny B strode off.

Gingerly, Em pushed opened the door and stepped inside, her shoulders immediately sagging. The shop's air-conditioning had been cranked up to tropical, but that wasn't the worst. As she feared, idle hands had been at work.

The bins containing the small impulse-buy items had been shoved to the side, blocking the racks of practical notebooks, folders and stationery. In their place, rising precariously from the floor, Granny B had constructed a notebook tower using stock from the expensive new jewel range. It looked amazing: a spire of glittering colour. Em had to concede the design was impressive, as was the effort taken in its assembly. But that was where her admiration ended. All that pile represented was stock shrinkage and loss of profit.

Almost too afraid to breathe lest she cause the structure to topple, Em stepped around the tower and headed for the storeroom to stow her bag. What a morning. First the cypress, then Michelle and Josh, and now this.

At the thought of Michelle, an intense bulge of sadness welled in Em's chest. She pushed it away. Time to rescue her books.

The door's bell tinkled, followed by a whoosh of air and rattle of the storeroom's bead curtain as the outside cold sucked the inside warmth towards it.

'Emily! I'm ready for that – oh.'

Em closed her eyes as the sound of forty collapsing notebooks reached her ears. When the noise finally ceased, she rubbed her mouth and walked stiffly back into the shop.

Granny B stood regarding the mess, her face screwed up in a mixture of disbelief and contrition. She pursed her lips before lifting her chin in defiance. 'Sorry.'

It took all of Em's self-control not to throw Granny B's comment about the inadequacy of the word back at her. Instead, she pointed at the door. 'Out. Now.'

For once her grandmother obeyed.

Eighteen

Hands deep in her jacket pockets against the Sunday early morning cold, Em trudged through the thick grass of Lod's paddock. Wet leaves left slick trails along her rubber boots, a few of the longer stalks painting damp streaks along her jeans. The ground was soggy from overnight rain but the sky glowed a glorious winter blue. The sort of sky that raised hopes and made the world feel peaceful.

Lod waited at the paddock's far end, head raised, lower legs camouflaged in the long grass as though he'd been cut off at the knees, his ears swivelling at her approach. She greeted him with affectionate rubs before sliding a halter over his nose and leading him back towards the house, Muffy trotting alongside, her belly hair hanging in thick dregs from the damp.

Lod bunted her as they walked, seeking scratches and attention. 'You're a darling boy,' she said, indulging him.

Her friends were scheduled to arrive any minute. Jas with sweet, dopey Ox and Teagan with fractious Astra. After a week of no contact the sound of Teagan's voice on Em's answering machine Friday night, saying she could make Sunday's scheduled clipping session, had relieved some of the week's tension. That and Josh nuzzling her neck from behind as she listened.

He hadn't acted like a man conserving his energy for football the next day. Within minutes of his arrival at the hill they were making love. Expecting at least a scratch from her new friend, Muffy had curled up in a sulk in her basket when Josh had ignored her and reached straight for Em.

Afterwards, she'd grilled two well-marbled steaks that she picked up from Horrigan's on the way home, and served them with homemade thick-cut chips, long green beans and buttery tarragon-scented béarnaise sauce. They'd sat at the table with the television murmuring in the background, discussing inane things – town politics, sport, Karen's pregnancy, Sally's boys, the cliffhanger ending of the latest episode of a TV series. Nothing about the future. But after the intimacy of his dad's shed, the promise they were okay, it somehow didn't seem to matter.

Friday night football had followed. Em would have preferred a movie but Josh asked to watch it, and she hadn't minded. Being with him, his arm slung along the back of the couch, fingers toying with her hair, felt enough. As did their slow wander to bed afterwards, the caresses, whispers and gasps. The way he'd lingered on Saturday morning, making her late for work, seemed enough too.

Only this morning when she woke, wishing he was by her side, smiling his lazy early morning grin at her instead of waking at his parents', no doubt hungover from the buck's party he'd gone to the night before, did she realise how shallow it all felt.

Em wanted more from him. That special magic that Felicity and Dig had. The thing that made the world sparkle and the future seem like it couldn't come fast enough. All the things she could have had already if she hadn't been so stupid the first time round.

He could kiss and caress, make her tremble with want. He could make her heart stumble and flutter, and gaze at her with those molten, desire-filled eyes. He could design easels and press his forehead to hers and whisper that he missed her, but would he ever trust her enough to love her like she was beginning to love him? Because, in his shoes, having suffered the indignity and hurt that he had, Em didn't know if that was something she could do herself.

She released Lod into the stable and left him to snuffle at the feed she'd set for him. With a morning of clipping ahead and lunch to cater for, Em had woken at dawn to bake and prepare. Both stables were mucked out, the concrete slab in front swept clean. A bucket of brushes sat near the hitching rail along with two heavy-duty crates. On one lay a set of clippers, long orange extension cord snaking across to the external power point at the stable. A new under-rug for Lod was slung over his half-door, his old rug folded alongside for Teagan, should she need it for Astra. With the nights and mornings still cold, and without their extra layer of woolly coat, the horses would need protection from the chill. Teagan couldn't afford new rugs, not with the Bliss's money troubles.

Satisfied everything was in order, she headed back towards the house for a quick cuppa. She was halfway across the garden when Teagan turned her white tray-top Toyota and dented aluminium horse float into the yard. By the time they'd hugged and lowered the float's tailgate, Jas had also arrived. The farm came alive: Muffy dancing around the cars and floats, releasing the occasional yip, Astra whinnying and Lod returning the call, Kicki and Cutie bellowing plaintive hee-haws from their paddock gate in the hope their greatest fan, Jas, would pay them attention.

Neither Em nor Jas made any comment about Teagan's birdlike bones or the dark hollows under her eyes, made even more vivid by her winter-pale skin. They shared a look though, an agreement that the situation needed probing, and Em was glad she'd put an extra bottle of wine in the fridge for lunch. An afternoon of girl talk was needed, and the way Em was feeling, she could do with some advice about Josh.

Hoping she might learn from the others, or at least calm a little, the girls agreed to leave fractious Astra until last. The filly paced the stable, poking her head out of the half-door before jerking back inside to wheel another agitated circuit. Lod paid her no attention, content to stand dutifully on the concrete in the sun, waiting for his clipping, off-hind leg cocked and his hoof resting on its point. His head was down and eyes half-closed in a doze like his old friend Ox, now equally slumberous in Lod's stable.

'Honestly, you'd send her to the knackers if she weren't so stunning,' said Jas, shaking her head as Astra embarked on yet another restless round.

'She just needs to mature,' said Em.

Teagan reached up to scratch Astra's nose. 'She's only four.'

'Ox was calm at four.'

'Yes, but Ox had no balls.'

Jas grinned and blew a kiss at Ox. The big grey twitched his ears and blinked across the half-door before returning to sleep. 'Poor thing. I wonder if he misses them.' She turned back to Em who was perched on a crate, clippers in hand, palm pushing over Lod's mane so she could clip the top-side of his neck. 'Speaking of balls, how are things with Josh the Sexpot?'

'Okay,' said Em, starting the clippers.

'Just loads of great sex then?'

'Something like that.'

'So you're definitely back together?' asked Teagan.

Em brushed a swathe of cut hair away, screwing her nose up in concentration as she guided the clippers close to Lod's ears. The darling horse barely flinched, allowing her to work carefully around the area and down his jawline.

She stepped off the crate to attack the underside of his neck. 'Looks like it.'

'What do you mean, "looks like it."? You either are or you aren't.'

Em turned the clippers off and leaned into Lod's warm solid body, one arm crossed over herself. 'I don't know if he'll ever really forgive me for what I did.'

'It's only early days,' said Jas, without any sign of the jokiness she'd displayed previously when discussing Josh. She knew Em well enough to recognise her uncertainty. 'He's being careful. You can't blame him.'

No, Em couldn't.

'How are Digby and Felicity?' asked Teagan.

'Now, that's a whole other story.' She met their eyes in turn. 'Promise me you'll keep this to yourself? For a while, at least, until she's properly settled. She's terrified about it getting out.'

Jas exchanged a worried look with Teagan and turned back. 'About what getting out?'

'She did time in jail.'

Teagan's eyes turned enormous. 'Jail?'

'Too many parking fines?' asked Jas.

'Not exactly,' said Em, fiddling unnecessarily with the clippers. 'Attempted manslaughter.'

'Oh my God.'

'Are you serious?'

Em rushed on. 'It's not as bad as it sounds.'

'How can it not be?' said Teagan. 'We're talking manslaughter.' She glanced at Jas, looking for support, but Jas's attention was fixed on Em.

'Attempted manslaughter,' corrected Em.

'Oh, right. Like that makes all the difference.'

Finally Jas spoke. 'I'm guessing extenuating circumstances?'

She'd anticipated censure from Teagan but Jas had a suspicious look she didn't appreciate. What Charles had revealed about Felicity's life with Mark Ainsley was sickening. The man deserved what he got. Em couldn't prevent her sharp tone. 'She stabbed her fiancé to stop from being hurt, again. So yes, you could say there were extenuating circumstances.'

'And how long was she in jail for?' asked Jas, still not softening her expression.

'Almost two years. Why are you looking at me like that?'

'Because I think you should be careful of her.'

'Why? She hasn't done anything to me.'

'Except maybe get a bit too fond of the hill.'

Em dropped her arms and moved away from Lod. 'God, you sound like Gran.'

'What's your gran saying?' asked Teagan.

'That she's causing discontent in the family. That she has some sort of agenda. Which is ridiculous.'

Jas glanced over her shoulder at Teagan, and some sort of message passed between them. Em bit her lip against the hurt that look caused.

'But you've mentioned yourself how much both she and Digby have changed since she arrived,' said Jas.

'Yes, and for the better.'

Lod shuffled backwards. Em reached out a hand to calm him, using the strength of his body to try to calm herself at the same time.

'Look, I know she did something awful. But she's paid a terrible price. And now she's found safety and happiness with Digby' – she slapped a palm against her chest – 'with us. Who are we to judge anyway? None of us could ever fathom what she's been through. We've all done shit things in our lives. That doesn't mean we should be condemned forever. It's unfair.' Her voice turned husky as she willed away tears that were more for herself than Felicity. 'People deserve second chances.'

'All right, all right,' said Jas, holding her palms up. 'We were out of line. You're right, we shouldn't judge.'

Teagan stepped forward to touch her arm. 'We're sorry, Em.'

She nodded, but the hurt of her friends' betrayal remained.

***

The morning crept by. A newly clipped Lod, his coat a silvery-brown, was led to his stable and swapped with Ox, while Astra continued to ignore Teagan's soothing tones and pets, and merely traded her pacing for quivery-lipped stares and head-bobs.

The air filled with the hum of insects and bees, attracted by the row of flowering golden wattles Granny B had planted along the northern fence line of the hill paddock. The sun rose higher, deliciously warm, evaporation from the wet plants and soil turning the air unseasonably muggy. Rocking Horse Hill's crater seemed to surge as though reaching, its outcrops poking rocky fingers into the stunning azure sky.

Leaving Jas to Ox, Em leaned against Lod's half-door, absently stroking his velvety muzzle as she watched a tourist pick her way around the crater rim. The woman paused every so often to admire the view and point a camera at the broad sweep of fertile land below. The sight made Em smile. No matter how many times she'd climbed the hill herself, the thrill, the sheer pride in her history, never diminished.

The tourist made her think of Josh and the emotions she'd experienced during their first climb together, when they were young. The satisfaction of seeing him stand at the top, puffing from the effort, his hands on his hips as he stared first outwards, drinking in the clean air and scenery before him, then turned inwards to marvel at the crater's sheer walls.

She'd led him down into the volcano's heart, worming along the secret route she'd known since her mother had taken her to the centre when she was small. They'd stood at the bottom, near the lake residue, and he'd taken her hand and squeezed, a silent thank you. Like he understood now how she really felt about Rocking Horse Hill.

'What are you smiling at?' asked Teagan, sliding to her side.

'I was thinking about the first time Josh and I climbed the hill.'

'Must have been romantic.'

'It was. Back then.' She smiled at Teagan, not wanting to let their earlier confrontation come between them. She valued her friends too much. 'How are things at home?'

Teagan crossed her arms. 'Not great.'

'You can talk to me, you know.'

'I know.'

'I'm worried about you, Blissbomb,' she said, using Teagan's teenage nickname.

'That's because it's your nature to worry about everyone.' She gave a hint of smile, but there was no stealing the desolation from her eyes. 'I loaned Dad the money.'

Em inhaled deeply. 'I thought you would.'

'I had no choice.' She stared at her feet. 'Everything's so fucked up.'

'I know. But it'll get better, I promise.' She waited until Teagan lifted her head and held her gaze. 'Promise me you'll come to me if you need help. Any time, day or night.' She reached across to squeeze her hand. 'I'm here for you, okay?'

Her eyes glistening, Teagan nodded.

'Promise?'

'Promise.'

'Good.' Not quite what Em hoped, but it would do for now.

As expected, Astra threw a tantrum as soon as Em switched the clippers on. The filly skittered about, legs going everywhere, eyes boggling at the clippers. Even with three women holding her and trying to keep her calm it was hopeless. After being trodden on for what felt like the tenth time, Em jogged off to the shed, returning with a piece of poly pipe that had a loop of twine threaded through the two holes of one end. She handed it to Teagan who hooked her hand through the loop and, with Jas gripping Astra's halter and one ear, grabbed a handful of soft muzzle. Rapidly twisting the pipe, she coiled the loop tight until the point of Astra's nose was squashed into a tight flesh bubble.

Teagan stayed at her head, stroking her neck and making soothing noises, waiting for Astra to calm. None of them liked to use the twitch, but the restraining device didn't harm the horse unless left on too long. Instead, it gave the horse an almighty endorphin rush, which calmed them.

'Ready?' asked Em, holding up the clippers.

Teagan nodded. Astra's bottom lip showed a telltale droop, and her eyes were glassy.

They worked quickly, taking turns to clip and hold the twitch. Lod and Ox regarded them with clever old eyes from their warm stables. By the time they'd finished, everyone, including Astra, was exhausted and messy with hair and dirt.

Em joined Jas and Teagan in heaping praise on Astra, and complimenting each other on a job well done. Astra, for once, took the attention with composure, either still on a high or simply tired of playing prima donna.

'You're a good girl,' said Teagan, leaning forward to give her a last proud kiss on the nose. But as she bent close, Astra suddenly jerked her head up, connecting hard with her mistress in the process. Teagan let out a yelp, further scaring the horse, which barrelled backwards, loose lead dragging.

'Grab her,' yelled Em to Jas, who was closest.

Teagan held her hand cupped over her face. Blood was already seeping down her wrist and soaking the edges of her windcheater.

'Here, let me look.'

'Not broken,' Teagan managed. 'Just bleeding.'

A quick glance as Teagan pulled her hand away and Em agreed. The blood was from one nostril only and already the flow was beginning to ease. Em patted her on the back. This wasn't the first time one of them had been nose-punched by a horse. It came with the territory, and they were country women who didn't get overexcited about a bit of blood.

'Just keep your head dropped forward for a minute until it stops.'

Disobeying, Teagan watched her horse, still backpedalling up the slope, dragging Jas with her. 'She was being so good. I wonder what set her off.'

'They're donkeys, you twit of a horse,' yelled Jas. 'Not bloody zebras!'

Donkeys.

Planting her hands on her hips, Em stalked past the edge of the stables and came face to face with two stumpy and extremely smug looking equines.

She threw her arms up at them. 'How?'

They shuffled closer, heads down and ears drooping like a pair of naughty dogs who knew they'd been bad but were equally certain of forgiveness. Lod gave a whicker of welcome that Kicki and Cutie took as a signal to shamble even nearer.

'Bad donkeys,' said Em, glaring at them. 'Bad, bad donkeys.'

Teagan gave a clotted-up snort of laughter. 'They're not dogs.'

'They bloody well behave like a pair of them. They were locked up.' She narrowed her eyes at Kicki. 'And they were meant to stay that way.'

The jack bunted her in the hip, big ears twirling, before raising his head to regard her with eyes that had melted her sook of a heart from the first emailed photograph. Safe now Kicki had paved the way, Cutie stepped closer, looking for a scratch too.

'Troublemakers,' Em sighed, before indulging them. 'I can't figure out how they do it. It's a hook-and-eye gate latch.'

'They take after their godmother,' said Jas, huffing as she led a still-skittish Astra back to them. 'Clever little darlings.'

'Here.' Teagan reached out for Astra. 'I'll take her.'

Jas looked her up and down. 'Absolutely not. You look like Dracula's bride with all that blood. Go inside and wash. I'll sort your horse out.'

'Better do as you're told.' Em smiled at Teagan's red-streaked face, the result of trying to clean herself up with her hands and the front of her jumper. 'And you do look pretty bad.'

Outnumbered, Teagan held up her arms and trudged off.

Em watched her go. 'God, I hope she's okay.'

'She'll be fine. It's you I'm worried about.'

'Me?' Keeping her tone unconcerned, Em began to gather equipment. 'You're seeing trouble where there isn't any.'

'Maybe, maybe not. But it can't hurt to watch your back.'

'That's what Gran said.'

'Wise old woman. Maybe you should listen to her.'

Nineteen

Em met Granny B at Camrick's laundry door. The old lady's hair was stiffer than normal, matching her posture and mouth. She wasn't looking forward to tonight's dinner. Between the carpet, the claim about Adrienne's drinking, and Felicity knowing that Granny B had had her investigated – news she'd no doubt shared with Digby – it was bound to be awkward.

There was also Em's own uncertainty. An insistent unease left by Jasmine's warning that she couldn't shake, no matter how much she chided herself for it. What she hated most was how it reminded her of what had happened with Josh. The way the sly arrow-barbs about Josh's unsuitability had at first bounced off her love, but had over time worn away at her armour and begun to lodge. Hear something often enough and you'll begin to believe it.

Except Em was older now, smarter, and she sure as hell wasn't going to make the same mistake again. Felicity had demonstrated nothing but courage and friendship towards Em since her arrival. Jas, Granny B, Josh and everyone else could say what they liked. This time around Em's defences were strong.

'You look amazing,' she said, as her grandmother helped Em out of her coat and hung it up. 'Been somewhere?'

Today Granny B's elegance had reached an even more impressive height. A pair of navy cigarette pants showed off long legs enhanced by a pair of low-heeled patent pumps. Her gold silk shirt sported a high collar, the neck fixed with a tasteful but expensive pearl brooch that matched the triple-stranded pearl bracelet around her left wrist. Her make-up was deftly applied: rouge adding colour to her heavily powdered cheeks, eyes smoky with eye shadow and liner.

'A late afternoon tea with Barry McClintoff and that idiot new councillor, Herriott.'

'I gather it wasn't fun.'

'I do so loathe vegetarians. Ridiculous people.'

'Could have been worse,' joked Em, desperate to keep things light. Granny B's tumultuous mood did not bode well. 'She could have been vegan.'

'Indeed.' Granny B maintained a special dislike for vegans. 'Hard to trust these people, though, isn't it? As I pointed out, if nature had wanted us to be vegetarian she would have given us a rumen. Anyway, how does the silly woman think we grew brains the size we did?' Granny B huffed. 'And she refused wine.'

'She probably had to work.'

'That may be true, but it's hardly supporting local agriculture. Barry and I made up for it. Enjoyed a rather nice pinot from Ryan's. That winery is doing very well for itself. I proposed to Barry that we host a local wine festival to run concurrently with Art Week, but the Herriott woman thought the idea "unwise in light of the town's youth drinking culture". What about the rest of us? Just because she's part of the lunatic greenie fringe doesn't meant the rest of us should suffer.'

'Gran.'

Granny B rolled her eyes. 'Don't start, Emily. I'm seventy-nine years old. I'm permitted my prejudices.' She cocked her arm. 'Come along. Let's get this dinner over with.'

Em tried to ignore the new carpet as she made her way to the kitchen but the awfulness of it was impossible to not notice. Granny B eyed her with thin lips, worry etching deeper lines across her forehead.

Em glanced warily towards the kitchen door. 'Is she still drinking?'

'Yes.' Granny B's mouth wobbled. She wrung her hands, the movement causing Em's unease to tighten. 'It's that girl!'

Em shushed her. 'Please, Gran.'

'Don't "Please, Gran" me. You of all people should understand what's at stake.'

'There's nothing at stake.' Except maybe Digby's heart, but given Em's conversation with Felicity on her return from Adelaide, that seemed pretty safe.

'And the hill?'

Mention of the hill brought Em to a halt. She looked up the hall, where light sliced a sharp diamond across the carpet from the half open kitchen door, and from where a soft tinkle of laughter could be heard. The sound wrenched at the anxiety already coiled slimy and malignant through her insides.

'Yes, Emily. Now you're beginning to understand.' Granny B clasped Em's arm. 'She means to take it from you.'

Shrugging from her grandmother's grip, Em lifted her hand to her temple, where the edge of a headache had started to form. 'I don't know where you get that idea from.'

But she did. Deep down, she did.

'Listen to her closely over dinner, then you'll see.'

Em swallowed and resumed walking. She had to maintain faith: in Digby's promise, in her friendship with Felicity, in her own sense of fairness and charity. In the belief that they'd sort this out like they sorted all their problems out.

She paused at the kitchen door and inhaled theatrically. 'Something smells amazing.'

'It does,' said Samuel. 'Adrienne's treating us to her famous *gigot de sept heures*, aren't you, sweetheart?'

'And *crème brûlée* flavoured with sauternes.'

Em kissed her mother, her hug lingering for longer than normal. 'You spoil us.'

Adrienne patted her hand, her smile lacking its normal energy. 'I just want everyone to be happy.'

'Can I get you a glass of wine?' asked Samuel. 'I brought a new viognier for us to try.'

'Yes, please,' replied Em, thanking God for Samuel. He'd keep things in check. 'I'd love one.'

He bent to Adrienne. 'Top up?'

'Please.'

Em felt Granny B's gaze but chose to ignore it. She walked over to Felicity and Digby, kissing them both hello. Tonight, Felicity wore an almost identical outfit to the one Em had worn to the drinks party. The high-heeled boots gave her extra height and stature, but her hands were set low in front of her belly, wrapped tight as though in comfort and self-protection. The gesture rallied Em's sympathy and calmed the irritation she'd felt upon seeing Felicity's clothes – irritation that had worsened at the sight of the sapphire necklace around Felicity's neck, a piece that had been in the family for generations.

She bent close to avoid being overheard. 'Chin up. It's just a dinner. If you can make it through jail, you can make it through this.'

Felicity's huge blue eyes flooded with gratitude. 'Thanks.'

Digby cast an unpleasant look his grandmother's way and spoke with his voice also lowered. 'We need to have a chat later.'

They did, if only to clarify where Em stood when it came to Rocking Horse Hill.

She nodded and turned to accept a glass of wine from Samuel.

'Everything all right?' he asked, glancing between the three of them.

'Everything's fine, Samuel, thanks.' She took a sip and raised the glass. 'This is very good.'

Samuel bowed. 'I aim to please.'

'And please you do, mightily,' said Em, determined, like Samuel seemed to be, to ease the awful tension clogging the room. Throwing Felicity another encouraging smile, she followed him back to Adrienne's side. 'Anything I can do?'

'No, no. I'm all organised. Felicity has been a great help, as usual. Why don't you all head into the lounge so I can set out plates?'

Em hovered as the others left. She didn't like the way Adrienne's glass was close to empty already, or the nervous smile that kept twitching her mouth. Even her attire, normally perfect, seemed somehow amiss. It lacked polish: those little finishing flourishes that took an ensemble from everyday to chic. Adrienne wore a pair of camel-coloured trousers teamed with leopard-print brown loafers and a dark brown silk shirt that matched her piled-up hair. A gorgeous outfit, except there was no matching belt, and her earrings were diamond instead of pearl or the smoky quartz pair passed down to her by Grandma Agnes. Little things, but they mattered.

'You don't have to stay, darling,' said Adrienne, laying a trivet on the centre bench. 'I have it all sorted.'

'I'd rather be here. The kitchen's my favourite place, remember?'

'How could I forget? You were always under my feet when you were small.' Adrienne smiled fondly. 'Of course, that all changed the moment James bought you Beaver. Then it was all horse, horse, horse.' She regarded the stove and sighed, and Em noticed the puffiness around her eyes, the tightness of her mouth that no make-up could cover and only sleep or relaxation could cure. 'Well, I'd best get this lamb organised.'

There was so much Em wanted to probe her mother about – if Granny B had said anything about Felicity, what was troubling her that was leading her to drink more than usual – but it wasn't the right time. Perhaps on Saturday, after the shop closed, they could have lunch together, talk. Wash this worry away the way they'd done so many times before.

'I love you, Mum,' Em said out of nowhere, startling Adrienne.

Her mother smiled hesitantly. 'And I love you, Em.' She pulled on a pair of thick oven mitts. 'Are you okay?'

'I'm fine.'

'No problems with Josh?'

'Nothing like that. I just wanted you to know I love you, that's all. We don't say it enough.'

This time, Adrienne's smile was genuine. 'We probably don't, but we know it's there, all the same.'

Em laid out plates as her mum removed a casserole pot from the oven. Lid off, the dish smelled even more delicious: aromatic with herbs, tomato, vegetables, wine and the all-important garlic. Em held a wooden chopping board steady while Adrienne lifted the boned leg of lamb from the pot and placed it down, taking care to keep the meat intact. The seven-hour cooking time had left it melt-in-the-mouth tender. While the meat rested, Em helped

Adrienne sieve the fragrant jus from the cooking vegetables before retrieving a tray of roast vegetables from the oven.

They worked in tandem, the way they often had before, sharing brief smiles across steaming plates, and Em felt a little comfort return. Tonight would be all right. Of course it would.

Leaving her mother to finish serving, Em carried the gravy boat to the dining room, calling the others as she went. Samuel's voice sang back as he ushered them all to dinner and Em again said a silent thanks for this nice man and his skill at keeping harmony intact.

Over dinner the conversation centred on the hill and the horse Digby planned to buy for Felicity. It was almost as if Digby wanted to deliberately provoke his grandmother. Adding to the tension, Felicity appeared to have taken Em's 'chin up' to heart and was joining in.

Granny B's face grew increasingly mutinous as the talk of competing in shows and even buying a new truck, one of those expensive models with a kitchenette and bunks for overnight stays, continued. She swapped a look with Em who could only hide her increasing disquiet with a shrug. Besides, if Digby wanted to spend a stupid amount of money buying Felicity a horse truck for them both to use she'd be mad to complain.

'We could build more stables, too, couldn't we, Digby? For when we have more horses.'

Em's spoon lodged in her *brûlée*. She stared at it, feeling it curdle in her stomach, along with her thoughts. A horse was one thing, so were expensive trucks, but disrupting Em's life by building stables was in another realm.

It was almost as though Felicity really did have ideas about taking over the hill.

'And when, pray tell,' said Granny B, her voice taking on the high, articulate edge that signalled an unravelling temper, 'were you proposing to consult Emily about this?'

'Em's all for it,' said Digby. 'Aren't you, Em?'

Stalling for time, Em raised her napkin and pretended to dab at her mouth. She searched for something diplomatic to say. 'Well, I'm not sure —'

But the fight was between Granny B and Digby, and neither was letting go.

'Rocking Horse Hill is Emily's home, not yours.'

'Last time I looked it was my name on the deeds.'

Granny B kept her cold glare on Digby. 'More's the tragedy.'

'Please don't,' said Adrienne.

Samuel wrapped an arm around her shoulders. 'A discussion for another time, perhaps?'

'When?' snapped Granny B. 'After he's broken his promise and stolen Emily's home from under her? A property, mind, he never once showed an interest in until she' – Granny B stabbed a finger towards Felicity – 'came along.'

'Samuel's right, Gran,' said Em, throwing Felicity a sideways look. This was a conversation she and Digby needed to have in private. Not now, with everyone het up and festering with other secrets and betrayals. 'Another time.'

'No. I will not let this continue.' Granny B threw down her napkin and bent across the table, finger jabbing at Digby. 'You need to open your eyes to what's going on around here.'

'The only thing going on is your prejudice.' Digby hurled his own napkin down. 'You're nothing but a bigot, Gran. An intolerant throwback who belongs to another time.'

'Think what you like, Digby, but I am protecting this family.'

'From what?'

'Her!'

'Audrey, please!'

But Granny B wasn't listening to anyone, least of all Samuel. Her cheeks were flushed, her eyes sparkling dangerously. She raised herself from her chair, her gaze locked on Felicity's. The girl shrivelled even further into her seat. 'You are nothing but a cuckoo in the nest. A rotten creature come to do evil. Well, I won't let you. Do you hear me? I will not let you.'

Granny B straightened, her body rigid with fury, and stalked from the room.

Silence fell. For a moment, Em could only stare at her grandmother's vacant seat while her heart thumped. Then she breathed in hard and faced Felicity. 'I'm so sorry.'

Felicity's eyes were enormous and brimming. She blinked, setting fat tears rolling. Even in distress, her beauty seemed to grow, as though an angel had begun to weep.

Recovering from his shock, Digby moved to cradle her, whispering soothing words. Samuel's voice joined in as Adrienne dissolved into sobs. Only Em remained unmoving, too stunned at events to react.

What her grandmother had done was unconscionable, yet even Em could now see the subject needed airing, that the liberties being taken were too much. But to call Felicity some sort of usurper, here to do evil? That was not only unfair, but deeply cruel.

Casting tight smiles at her family, Em left the table. Given all their ragged tempers, this might not be the best time but her grandmother was going to get a talking to regardless. She crossed out into the hall and took a few steps, pausing to look back. Felicity remained in Digby's arms, the top half of her face above his shoulder. She was looking at the ceiling, as though trying to penetrate to Granny B's rooms above, the corners of her eyes pinched with vicious focus.

A dizzying deluge of cold washed through Em. She turned away in disbelief, breathing hard. But when she looked back, Felicity's face was again soft with anguish.

And the heart-chilling expression of vengeance Em thought she'd seen was gone.

Twenty

Em murmured and turned over but the noise came insistent again, prodding her to full consciousness. She sat up, heart slugging hard, and frowned into the dark. Another ring echoed. Real. Not a dream.

She reached for the bedside phone and checked the number on its screen. 'Mum?'

Her mother's panicked voice came in rapid, breathless bursts. 'It's your grandmother. She's on her way to hospital.'

'Hospital?' Em's insides lurched as any number of terrors flooded her mind. Heart attack, stroke, a fall? Not Granny B. Please, not Granny B. 'What happened?'

'Hypothermia. She locked herself out on the balcony.'

Em blinked. The balcony? Impossible. Granny B kept a key hidden as insurance for such an event. 'How bad?'

'I don't know.' Adrienne began to sob, the sound frightening and half-choked, as if she were fighting nausea as well as distress. 'She looked awful, Em. So pale and still.'

Em threw off the doona and flicked on the light, snatching up clothes one-handed. 'Could she talk?' When her mother didn't answer she asked again, her tone made harsh with dread. 'Mum! Could Gran talk?'

'She could, but all her words were slurred.'

Em forced her voice back to normal. 'Okay. Where are you now?'

'With Digby. Following the ambulance.'

'Where's Felicity?' Em didn't know why she asked; all she knew was that a mean, suspicious feeling had slithered into her gut.

'We thought it best to leave her at home.'

The suspicion tightened its coils. She shrugged it away. Felicity wouldn't hurt Gran. The idea was insane. She tugged on the other sock. 'She must have called out. Why didn't anyone hear her?'

'I was asleep.' Her mother's breath was rough with tears and something else. Remorse? 'I went to bed early. I haven't been sleeping well, especially after what happened Tuesday night. I had a couple of glasses of wine to help and they put me out.'

Em pulled on jeans. Camrick was old and solid, but surely her mother would have heard Granny B's calls. Unless it was more than a couple of glasses of wine.

'Where was Digby?'

'At a grape-growers' meeting. He was caught up. By the time he came home she'd been out there for hours. He only noticed because her lights were still on.'

'What was Felicity doing? She must have heard something.'

'I don't know!' Adrienne began to cry more freely. Em closed her eyes, reining in her need to blame.

'Shh, Mum. It'll be all right. Gran's tougher than any of us.' The sobbing eased only a fraction but Em didn't have any time to offer more solace. 'I'll meet you at the hospital, okay?'

She hung up, and finished dragging on clothes. Muffy stood at the doorway, watching, her tail swinging and stopping, aware something was going on.

Em paused to quickly stroke her head. 'It's okay, Muff.' Except she knew it wasn't. The memory of Felicity's eyes two nights before, that narrowed expression of vengeance turning her pretty features dark, fuelled the disquiet within Em.

There was a key secreted under the coir mat at the front of the balcony door. It had been there since Em could remember as protection against the deadlocked door swinging shut. Everyone knew about it. A favourite family tale was of Uncle James shimmying up the side of the house and climbing over the balcony to let himself in one afternoon when he'd locked himself out, only for the police to turn up five minutes later, tipped off by a passer-by who'd noticed his 'break in'.

Why hadn't Gran used the key? It must have fallen somehow – been accidentally swept or kicked over the edge, or lodged between a crack in the floorboards.

Conjecture kept Em occupied as she rushed into Levenham. Better than the alternative, which was fretting over the severity of Granny B's hypothermia, a condition that could prove fatal for a woman of her age. Fatal for anyone, if bad enough.

Fatal. Em didn't want to think about that. Or about an idea that kept circling: that Granny B had been deliberately locked out.

Even later, when the emergency team had done their work and she was waiting with her mum and brother beside Granny B's bed, their panic eased by the doctor's promise that her grandmother should make a full recovery, it kept nagging.

Em took Adrienne's hand. 'I told you she was tough.'

Adrienne looked terrible, her eyes bloodshot, her hair dishevelled. Her hands, to Em's alarm, were trembling. Was it worry, hangover or fear? So many questions, none easy to ask. None that could be asked there, in the sterile hospital, in front of Digby.

She eyed her brother, wondering if he suffered similar doubts. Where his loyalty might lay if the question arose. But all she could detect was fatigue and concern.

At three a.m., Digby left them, citing his worry at leaving Felicity alone, promising to return in the morning. Em tried to get Adrienne to go with him but her mother refused. Now was the moment to ask her mother what was going on. Now was the moment to take her trembling hand and hold it tightly. But Adrienne's eyes were so tired and sad that Em couldn't. Together they sat through the night, watching Granny B's frail curled-up form, preoccupied by their own thoughts.

***

Granny B was declared out of danger the following morning, and transferred to a ward. Her breathing was hoarse and laboured, and cause for concern, particularly given her smoker's status, and there were still threats, the doctors said: pneumonia and pulmonary oedema.

Granny B said little, but scrutinised them all with her pale hazel eyes, especially Em. She coolly thanked Digby on his return, for his part in her rescue, then patted Adrienne's hand and ordered her home to rest. Em received a series of meaningful looks, which kept her lingering in the room after her mother and brother had gone, even though she had animals to tend and a shop to open.

Granny B watched the ward entrance for a long moment. When no one reappeared she beckoned Em close to the bed. Her voice was weak but clear. 'It was her.'

'Did you see her?'

'No.'

'Then how do you know?'

Granny B swallowed then coughed. Em passed her some water and watched her sip, her chest tight with concern. Granny B lay back, breathing hard. 'The key was gone.'

Not an indictment in itself. There were any number of reasons for the key not to be where it should have been. 'Couldn't it have fallen over the balcony edge? Become lost in the garden or in the gravel?'

'Check if you like. You won't find it.'

'But how would Felicity even know about it?'

'Adrienne told her the story about James.' Granny B took a few wheezy breaths. 'It was her. You know it was.'

'To what end, Gran?'

'To get me out of the way. What else?' Another band of ragged coughs engulfed her body. Eyes watering, she sank back onto the bed. 'You don't want to believe. You just want to keep your head in the sand.'

'That's not true.'

'Isn't it? You know what she's done to this family since she arrived. You've seen the rifts she's caused. And you know she's capable of violence.' Granny

B closed her eyes, pain etching her face. Without her make-up and expensive clothes, with her skin pale and her hair in stiff, wayward spikes, she appeared old and breakable. 'Damn Digby. Damn him for everything. None of this would be happening if he'd kept his trousers on.'

'The only thing Digby did was fall in love.'

'With a girl who has the power to take everything from us, even our homes.' A bony hand gripped Em's arm. 'And last night proved she will do anything to keep that power.'

*****

Em picked up a notebook off the storeroom bench, where she'd stacked the damaged stock from Granny B's tower-of-notebooks sculpture, and put it down again. Enough tiptoeing. Now was the time for answers.

She crossed her arms and addressed her brother. 'I don't want to believe Felicity had anything to do with this either, but I need to know where she was.'

Digby's eyes were bloodshot from lack of sleep, his clothes wrinkled, as if he'd picked them straight off the floor. Stubble darkened his jaw. He kept checking his watch, his movements jerky, his gaze sliding away from Em. He'd taken a sick day, a luxury Em didn't have, so she'd requested he call in on her at the shop. Alone.

It was late morning and already Em felt clumsy with exhaustion. Her eyes were scratchy, her muscles leaden. She had no idea how she'd make it through the day. On nerves and caffeine, she supposed. After two cups of extra-strong coffee since her arrival, she'd swapped to tea, but neither she nor Digby were in the mood for it. Tea meant congeniality and the small room was devoid of that.

'Watching television,' replied Digby. 'Like she said.'

'You weren't home. She could have easily snuck across and locked Gran out.'

Digby glanced at her and quickly looked away. 'She wouldn't.'

Em closed her eyes. Every part of her wanted Digby to be right but only twenty minutes ago a highly confused and agitated Adrienne had rung to say said she'd found the key lodged in the corner of the balcony, an arm's span from the door. No matter how black the night or poor the light, Granny B couldn't have missed it. It was one of those old-fashioned keys, with a decoratively curled end, long shank and blocks of distinct square teeth. A quick search would have located it. The only explanation was that the key had been put there after Granny B had been taken to hospital, when the house was empty.

'Then how else did it happen?'

The sulky, stubborn expression remained on Digby's face. 'You just want to blame her for everything, like Gran.'

'That's the thing, I don't. I want it to be an accident as much as you.'

'I'm telling you: Flick had nothing to do with it. She was upstairs watching *The Hannigans*. She told me everything that happened in it.'

As alibis went, it was pretty weak. 'She could have found that information on the Internet.'

Digby looked her up and down, his face screwed up in distaste. 'This is all about the hill, isn't it? You being shit-scared that she'll take it off you.'

Em dropped her arms and held her palms open. 'How can you say that after all I've done to welcome her?'

'Then why can't you believe she had nothing to do with Gran's accident?'

They stared at one another, Felicity's past suspended unsaid and toxic between them.

'She has a history, Dig,' said Em softly.

'I'm not listening to this.' He banged his mug into the sink, slopping tea over his hand.

'Dig . . .' She reached out for him.

He shook her off, his face twisted and ugly. 'Fuck off, Em. Just fuck off.'

Aghast, she let him go. The storeroom's bead curtain rattled and stilled. She leaned shakily back against the bench, taking in deep breaths, but her shock didn't fade. Tilting her head back, she willed the tears to stay away. The last thing she needed was a customer to walk in and find her red-eyed and snivelling.

All she wanted was the truth. A truth she hoped and prayed didn't involve

Felicity. But someone had locked Granny B out. Of the others who knew of the key's existence – Adrienne, Samuel, Digby, Josh, if he remembered the Uncle James story – none had reason for such action.

Which only left one person.

The threat of tears over, Em picked up a notebook. Its wire coils remained intact and the cover was remarkably undented, but the delicate pages inside were crumpled beyond saleability. And in that frustration-filled moment, all she could think was how like her family it was.

The Wallaces might have a rich, glittery shell, but flip back that hard cover and flick through those pages, and their story read no differently to any other.

Just another tale of human frailty and fragile, crushable hearts.

Twenty-One

'Adrienne's very confused over how the key came to be where it was,' said Samuel, when Em rang him later that morning. 'To be frank, so am I.' He made a noise in his throat. 'With Felicity's background . . .'

'You *know*?'

'I've known for a while.'

Em dragged out the photo she kept hidden beside the till, felt a headache crashing at her temples as she digested this new revelation. The frame held a picture of her family, perched like birds along the highest ledge of Rocking Horse Hill. On the far left, her dad, Henry, his arm around Em's shoulders. To Em's right, her mother, smiling in that dazzling way she had. Next to her, Granny B, in a queenly pose, and on the far end, Digby, brow furrowed and head half-turned as though expecting some monster to come lurching out of the crater behind.

The fear that they might never be like that again sapped what little was left of her energy.

'How did you find out?'

'The prosecutor was on my Timor trip.'

'You never said.'

'Not to you, no.'

She closed her eyes as the realisation dawned. 'But you told Mum.'

'After a great deal of thought, yes.'

Em let the silence linger for a moment, wishing she'd found the time to have that lunch with Adrienne, talk to her, let her know they'd all be fine. 'That's why she's been drinking.'

'She worries. About you all.'

She pushed the photo back into place and crossed to PaperPassion's door and scanned the street. Shoppers bustled along the footpaths. Friends chatted in weak patches of sunshine. A couple of workers in fluoro polar fleeces strode towards the Arms for an early knock-off beer or counter lunch. Normal Levenham people going about their normal lives. She pressed her head against the cool glass and wished she was one of them.

'So, do you think we need to talk to the police?'

Samuel was silent for a moment then let out a slow breath. 'No, I don't think so. A formal investigation would only set the gossipmongers off and your mother has enough to cope with. Plus if it was an accident, this could cause a rift between Digby and the rest of the family that might never heal.'

'Gran swears the key wasn't there.'

'I'm sure she believes that, but we mustn't lose sight that we could also be dealing with a garden-variety accident.'

'Then what do you suggest?'

'Leave it with me. I have a friend who might help.'

Samuel's friend turned out to be a retired chief inspector who spent half an hour late Friday afternoon looking around Camrick before pronouncing the incident an accident. Granny B was elderly, her enjoyment of a drink well-known. The key, he said, had probably worked its way loose from under the mat and been flicked, unnoticed, to the side. Perhaps it had been inadvertently dislodged during cleaning. Its dull surface acting as camouflage against Camrick's weathered timbers, easily missed by someone who'd had one tipple too many.

Em clung to the result. Of course it wasn't Felicity. How ridiculous that they could have thought that. Her grandmother was mistaken.

Except the memory of Felicity's eyes the night of the argument at dinner refused to fade.

***

Em slid the door open for Josh and was engulfed by the comforting scent of fresh chips. Her stomach rumbled, reminding her of how little she'd eaten that day. Aware of how sleepy a proper meal would make her, Em had stuck to coffee and PaperPassion's supply of homemade macadamia shortbread biscuits. They had kept her awake but done nothing to calm her exhaustion or emotions.

Josh stepped inside with a large butchers'-paper-wrapped parcel. 'Fish and chips. And a couple of potato scallops because I remembered you used to like them.' He lifted his right hand. 'And a bottle of verdehlo from Pikes of Levenham. Bloke at the bottle shop promised me it was good.' He leaned forward and kissed her. 'And this because you look knackered.'

'Thanks. But I could have cooked.'

'No, you couldn't have.'

A wave of emotion caused by his kindness threatened to set Em crying, but she tucked it away alongside everything else, and forced a smile. 'I'll fetch some plates.'

'No, you won't.' He nodded towards the lounge. 'You sit down. I'll sort everything.'

'But you don't know where —'

'I'm a big boy. I can figure it out.'

Arguing would take energy she didn't possess. Leaving him to it, Em dragged her weary body to the couch and sank into it, watching Josh hunt for plates and glasses. He looked handsome and comfortable in a pair of faded jeans and a zip-neck fleece with the sleeves pushed up. Sexy stubble, the length she liked it, coated his jaw and his hair curved cutely where his cowlick lay. Em wished he could take her to bed now, make gentle love to her, then hold her in his strong arms while she slept, but her stomach growled in protest.

He brought plates and glasses over, sneaking a light kiss before returning to the kitchen for the food and wine.

'I don't suppose you have any sauce?' he asked, standing in front of the fridge with the door open.

Em threw him a look.

He grinned. 'Thought not.'

'I'll make some come tomato season.' She yawned widely. 'If I don't sleep through it. God, I'm tired.' She stroked his arm as he settled down next to her. 'Don't expect too much tonight.'

He stilled, before leaning over and unwrapping the paper parcel. 'I'm not here for that, Em.'

They ate with the television tuned to the football, the turned-down volume made up for by Josh's one-eyed commentary. After, he cleared the plates and wrapping, feeding Muffy a few leftover chips in her basket.

Sleepy now she was full, Em snuggled under his arm with her legs curled up and her arm hooked around his muscled stomach.

Josh kissed the top of her head. 'Better?'

'A bit.' She closed her eyes and pressed her cheek against his chest, listening to the steady thump of his heart.

He rubbed her shoulder. 'Your gran's a tough nut. She'll be out of hospital before you know it.'

'It's not just Gran. It's everything else.' Her throat began to close as tears brewed. She swallowed hard to force them away but they lingered, held in place by tiredness. 'Mum's drinking and I had a horrible argument with Digby this morning.'

'What about?'

'Felicity. He thinks I believe she locked Granny B out.'

He leaned back to study her face. 'Did she?'

'It seems not.'

Em sat up, crossed her legs, and explained the inspector's findings. Of Felicity's past she made no mention, afraid Josh would succumb to the same suspicions as Em had, much to her shame.

Josh watched her closely as she spoke but other than the intensity of his gaze, she had no further clues as to what he was thinking. No nods, no agreeing noises, just solid eye contact and a fixed jawline.

'I'm not sure that rules her out,' he said when she'd finished. 'Your gran doesn't strike me as a person who'd be easily duped. If she says the key wasn't there, I'm inclined to believe her.'

'It's a big call, accusing someone of deliberately locking an old lady out in the cold.'

Josh reached for his glass of wine and took a sip. 'People are impulsive. Maybe she only meant to give her a fright.'

'But why?'

'Didn't you tell me they had a full-on argument at dinner?'

'Yes, but that's not a good enough reason to do something like this. Granny B's still Digby's grandmother.' Suddenly Em's energy died. Emotion swept over her, stinging the backs of her eyes with tears and her throat with gravel. 'I don't want to blame her, Josh. She's been through enough. She deserves a second chance.'

'What do you mean?'

Em reached for her wine glass and took a long drink, then put it down and stared at it, scraping the nail of one thumb down the hard surface of the other. 'She's been in jail.'

Josh stiffened. 'For what?'

'Attempted manslaughter. She stabbed her fiancé with a kitchen knife.'

'Jesus, Em.' He scraped his hand over his head. 'Jesus.' He looked at her. 'And you want me to believe that she's not capable of hurting your gran?'

'You don't understand. It wasn't like that.'

'Then what was it like?'

'It was self-defence.'

'Then why did she go to jail at all?'

Em had no answer for that. She only knew the broad picture, from what Charles and Felicity told her. The whole affair had made her feel so dirty she hadn't wanted to probe. Or maybe the actual truth was that she didn't want to know.

She shook her head and looked out the big window, wishing she could see the crater instead of the reflected light. God, Em hated this feeling of doubt. She knew what it was like to do something terrible and carry the burden, to know that some people would never forgive, no matter how much she changed or tried to atone. But Felicity's past wasn't Em's.

Perhaps it was time to stop comparing them.

***

Even with Josh by her side, his warm body wrapped against hers, the deep rest Em hoped for failed to come. Exhaustion had put her to sleep readily enough, but she woke in the early hours with her mind whirling. She lay on her side, staring across Josh towards the window and the moonlit orchard, fretting, until she finally dropped into a restless sleep that broke with a clammy sweat and dawn's first light.

A frost had fallen overnight, coating the landscape in sparkling white. The air smelled sharp as though flavoured by billions of spiky ice crystals. Kicki's and Cutie's breath plumed as Em threw them hay. Heat rose like a miasma off Lod's body as she stripped him of his thick night rugs and replaced them with lighter rugs in preparation for the predicted fine day ahead.

Josh helped with hay and gates, and played with the donkeys and Muffy when he wasn't needed, but she sensed his constant keen appraisal.

'Gerrinton's playing at home,' he said, standing by his car, preparing to go. 'Do you want to come? Might be good for you. Take your mind off things.'

'I'm going to visit Gran. Then I'm going to Camrick to check on Mum, and see if I can talk to Digby and get this mess sorted.'

'Okay.' His farewell kiss was light, a far cry from the drawn-out goodbyes of other weekends. He settled in and wound down the car window. This time there was no mistaking the worry in his expression. 'Be careful. Please.'

'I don't need to be. Everything's fine.'

He reached out for her hand. Em let him take it, comforted by his touch.

She squeezed his fingers, wanting him to understand. 'I know Felicity's been to jail for a terrible crime, but that doesn't mean she's to blame for everything that goes wrong now. The inspector did his investigation and said she had nothing to do with it. Unless we discover something else, I have to believe him.'

'He spent half an hour at the house. Hardly enough time to work out anything.' His mouth turned flat. 'I don't trust her, Em.'

She withdrew her hand and crossed her arms. 'That's hardly fair. You barely know her.'

Disappointment flickered across his face. He hesitated, as though wanting to pursue the conversation further, then reached for his seatbelt and started the car. Radio noise jolted the air but Josh didn't turn it down. Instead he waved, his smile thin and worried, and wheeled away from her, tyres crunching on the frozen ground.

Em crouched down to Muffy's height and held the warm collie to her chest, watching the cloud of Josh's exhaust and the flash of his ute through the tall grass until his car disappeared around the bend in Bradley Road.

At the feel of a rough tongue on her hand, Em forced cheer when she felt none. 'Don't you worry, Muff-Muff. We'll be okay.'

The dog answered with a whine that had Em clutching her tighter.

***

The frost dissolved into a brilliant, springlike day that brought out Levenham's Saturday-morning shoppers. PaperPassion's door swung open regularly, welcoming customers on the hunt for Father's Day gifts and gossip. Several locals tried to probe her about her grandmother, but Em maintained the Wallace account: Granny B had a minor accident and would make a full recovery.

Most were satisfied with that. But when Mrs Callahan – a contemporary of Granny B's and a pinch-faced woman Em had never warmed to – made a loaded comment regarding Felicity, Em realised Felicity's secret was out.

She watched the old lady's proud back as she left, keeping her own manner aloof and untroubled until she was out of sight, then sank onto her stool and pressed her face into her palms. Felicity's secret could never have been maintained for any period – too many people had family in Adelaide; too many had a good memory for scandal – now the news would spread like a virus.

It wouldn't be anyone's fault but the way Digby had been in the shop yesterday, he'd probably blame Em for it.

Despite the glowing day, Camrick appeared closed up and cheerless when Em arrived at lunchtime. The curtains were drawn on Granny B's floor, as were those of the front lounge, normally left open to let in light to that shaded, south-facing side of the house. In contrast, across the carriageway, the stables' blinds were all open, with the kitchen and bedroom windows ajar.

Em found Adrienne in the kitchen, her eyes puffy and red-rimmed from fatigue, tears or both. A scrunched-up tissue was held tight in one hand. A cup half-full of milky tea sat on the table in front of her, a gingernut biscuit with the edge nibbled out of it alongside.

'Mum,' said Em, leaning down to kiss her cheek. 'How are you feeling?'

'Oh, I'm not too bad.' Adrienne smiled, but her fingers plucked at the tissue, leaving a trail of tiny dandruff-like scraps on the granite. 'It's been a worrying few days.'

'It has.' Em slid a stool next to hers and sat down, placing a hand over her mum's to still the nervous movement. 'Samuel told me you know about Felicity.'

'She frightens me, Em.'

'How? I thought you got on well.'

'We did, at the start.' Adrienne gave a watery smile. 'I thought it was fun to have her borrow my clothes, like playing dress-ups. Then she started to talk differently. Even walk differently. Mum said she used to study me all the time. I just laughed it off. It was all so harmless.' She closed her fist around the tissue. 'Then she went to the farm and it all seemed to grow worse. The clothes, all that talk of riding; it was almost like she wanted to be you.'

'She just wants to fit in.' Even to her own ears the excuse sounded lame, but Em hated seeing her mother like this, so stressed and frightened.

'It's more than that.' Adrienne dabbed at a leaky eye. 'I think she really did try to hurt Mum.'

'But the inspector checked.'

Adrienne dismissed the comment with a flick of her hand. 'He hardly looked. He thought we were being hysterical.' She sniffed. 'Mum always said the man was a fool.'

Em stared hollowly at the benchtop. 'She told Dig she was watching *The Hannigans*. She told him everything that happened.'

'Oh, darling, she could have found that out from —'

'Still spreading your poison, Em?'

Em whipped around to face the voice. Digby stood in the kitchen doorway, an ugly flush rising up his neck.

'I haven't been spreading anything. I'm just trying to find out what happened.'

'Sure you are.'

'Look, Digby,' Emily said, stepping towards him, her tone calm and reasonable. 'Maybe you should check your computer, see what comes up in the browser history.' She glanced back at her mother. 'For our peace of mind.'

'She didn't do it!'

Em's temper snapped. 'Then prove it!'

'Stop it!' Adrienne rose and slammed her palms on the granite bench top. 'Just stop it!'

Her children stared at her in horrified silence. Even as a teenager Em had never heard her mother yell. Adrienne's fury seemed to blaze from Em to Digby and back again, until she abruptly collapsed back down as fast as she'd risen. She slumped forward, crimson-faced, and buried her face in her hands before breaking into loud, hiccoughy sobs.

'Mum,' said Em, attempting to wrap her arm around her mother's heaving shoulders.

Adrienne shrugged her off and ran for the door, still sobbing, and collided with Samuel.

'Shh,' he said, holding her and stroking her hair as he glared across the kitchen. 'What's going on?'

Em stared at the bench in shame.

'Nothing,' said Digby.

'I doubt that.'

'It's all right, Samuel.' Adrienne pulled away and used what was left of her tissue to swipe beneath her eyes. She sniffed loudly and looked at both Em and Digby. 'Please don't fight any more. Things are difficult enough.' She pressed the tissue to her leaking nose and hauled in a staccato breath. 'Your grandmother's safe. That's all that matters.'

Em could only pray that was true.

***

Jasmine proved as disbelieving as Josh. It didn't come as a surprise to Em but her lack of support still hurt. Yes, there was doubt, but surely there was a chance Felicity was innocent too? After Saturday night – which had again seen Josh and Em argue, then make up with sex that for the first time seemed to leave them both unsatisfied – Jasmine's reaction only added to Em's misery.

Sunday was a fine day, perfect for a beach ride and an opportunity for Em to unburden her heart. She'd started, like she had with Josh, carefully describing all that had happened, taking special care to keep to what was known. Gut feelings, personal anxieties and prejudices weren't facts, and the facts pointed towards an unfortunate accident.

'I'm sorry, Em, but Josh is right.'

Em found herself unable to look at Jas, instead focusing on the white line of breakers off Admella Beach.

Tension riddled the remainder of the ride. Changing subjects didn't alter either Em's temper or Jasmine's dismay, and the horses, picking up on it, played up, shying at flotsam and jetsam, waves and seaweed.

By the time Em reached the hospital Sunday afternoon, the self-doubt that had been building with each encounter had the crushing weight of an avalanche.

'They're refusing to discharge me,' Granny B snapped as she came in, as if the situation was Em's fault.

Although maintaining her regal posture, without make-up and hairstyling, Granny B looked like any other grandmother – old, frail and impotent. A state that didn't sit well with her. Em's shoulders sagged at the realisation that she would be the one to bear the brunt of her grandmother's mood.

Em sank onto the bed and rubbed at her pounding temple. 'With good reason. There's still a risk of pneumonia.' And blood clots, but Em didn't add that. The thought of pneumonia was bad enough. Besides, her grandmother was safe here. 'You need to stay here and rest.'

'I've had quite sufficient, thank you.' Granny B leaned forward and peered at Em, her old face softening. 'Not well?'

'Headache.' Em let her hand drop. 'I haven't had a lot of sleep these last few days.'

'No. I imagine you haven't.' She let out a raspy sigh that ended in a disturbing cough. 'None of us have.'

Em plucked at the waffle blanket. 'I don't know what to think any more, Gran. Everyone except Digby seems to believe it was her, but I'm trying my best to be fair and not point the finger without proof. Jas says I'm being naive and Josh looks at me like . . .' She shook her head as her eyes prickled, unwilling to give voice to what she feared Josh really felt in case that somehow made it real. 'Mum's on the verge of a nervous breakdown and Digby hates me because I want proof that she *didn't* do it.'

Bony fingers tightened around her arm. 'Don't worry about your brother. He'll come round.'

'But Gran' – Em couldn't help the hot spill of tears – 'what if it was her? What will happen to us all then?'

'I don't know. But this family has endured bigger scandals than this. Wallaces are survivors. Always have been. She won't beat us.'

Granny B's answer did nothing to ease Em's anxiety. This wasn't about beating anyone. This was about holding a family together.

She swiped at her tears. 'It's not worth it, Gran.'

'What's not?'

'Pursuing this. It's destroying everything. Our family, my friendships. Josh.'

Granny B's expression turned fierce. 'The only person destroying anything is that girl.'

But as Em stared blankly at the pale green ward wall, remembering Digby's fury and her mother's sobs, she couldn't help wondering if the truly destructive person was herself.

Twenty-Two

The workshop's fluorescent lights countered the falling night but still Josh felt the gloom. He'd been in a funk since Friday night, when the evening with Em he'd thought would see them back on track hadn't turned out that way. Saturday night was the same, except then even sex hadn't made things right.

He couldn't help the sick feeling that kept churning through his guts like sour milk every time he thought of what happened to Granny B. Her 'accident', so soon after what sounded like a pretty massive argument, was too much of a coincidence.

What he didn't get was why Em was being so stubborn about it. Sure, people deserved the benefit of the doubt, but if something walks like duck and quacks like a duck . . .

Josh let out a sigh, wishing he could stop thinking about the whole mess and get on with his work. He flicked a look at his dad. 'I don't understand women.'

Tom glanced up from the shed's front bench, where he was tidying one of the legs of Em's easel. A few more days and it'd be ready for assembly and oiling. Josh hadn't decided how he would present it yet. The way their relationship was deteriorating, he wasn't sure it'd ever happen.

'Isn't anything new in that, son.'

Josh reset his dad's thicknesser to the size he wanted. At some point he'd have to invest in a larger machine, but that would take a cash outlay he couldn't afford right now, and the twelve-inch machine did a good enough job. 'Em's acting weird.'

Tom didn't reply. Josh supposed there wasn't a lot to say. All the women in their lives were acting weird. His dad placed the leg down and came over. Josh turned on the machine and readied his piece of timber – some blackbutt he'd discovered going cheap at a clearing sale, and thought to recycle into a coffee table.

Protective glasses lowered, Josh guided the timber into the machine, his dad at the other end, ready to hold the milled plank steady, the noise blocking further conversation. Satisfied the plank was planed to an even smoothness, they placed it on the growing pile.

Josh ran his hand over the surface. Stained, with the right layout, the coffee table would make a great centrepiece. There was more timber for other items too. A simple entertainment unit. A small bookshelf. Perhaps matching lamp tables. He'd put the table on the website, use it as an enticement for commissions to match. Investing in that much timber stock was a risk, but it'd been too cheap to pass up and he had enough faith in his business that it would sell. Maybe not immediately, but soon enough.

The milling complete, Josh followed his dad back to the bench, where the easel pieces were laid out, the cypress warm and pale against the marked and stained bench surface. Once again Josh lamented that he hadn't had the foresight to scrounge enough timber for a matching stool. The easel would still be beautiful, though – a mix of utility and craftsmanship.

From a square base, the easel rose up on adjustable legs to form a work surface split into two distinct parts. The left and larger side consisted of a large board, modifiable to any angle and height, with a wide lip at the base to keep pencils and rubbers handy. To the right was a side table, flat but also height adjustable, and cut down one edge with a wide, square furrow to keep ink bottles in place. Another circular well had been cut to hold a metal or glass cylinder, suitable for storing pens and brushes, or a drink if Em wished.

Josh planned to fix castors to the base so she could roll it wherever the light was best, even outside if she wanted. An equally mobile stool would have finished the easel perfectly.

'Don't suppose you know of anyone with a spare cypress tree?'

'Keep your eye out. There'll be timber around.' His dad looked him up and down. 'You should ask your mum about Em. She was around visiting when you were at footy training last night.'

'Mum never said.' Neither had Em, but that didn't surprise him as much. Since the incident with Granny B and their unresolved arguments, she was keeping closed-mouthed about a lot of things.

'No. She's a bit secretive about it all,' said Tom.

'Think they're up to something?'

'Doubt it. From what I overheard they talked cooking and gardening.'

Like they used to when Em was young. Josh picked up a piece of timber and admired the turning – his dad's expert work. The legs were square at the top, before tapering into elegant rounds, the design stylish, curving in all the right places, very much like Em.

'Looks good.'

'Think she'll like it?' asked Tom.

'Yeah, she'll like it.'

His dad caught his eye. 'Hope you two don't break up before it's finished.'

'Me neither.' Josh said it with a laugh but there was an edge to his words that even his father caught.

He studied Josh for a long moment before gripping his shoulder. 'Take it from me, son. If you love her, tell her.' Tom turned his pensive face towards the house. 'Just don't leave it too late. Nothing sucks a man's soul drier than regrets.'

***

Though his parents' bedroom door was open and he could see the outline of his mum's feet at the end of the bed, Josh still knocked before poking his head around the edge.

'Joshy.' She held out an arm, beckoning him in.

His stomach clenched at how ill she looked. This latest dose of chemo seemed to be more debilitating than all the others, making her nauseous and weak. She swore it was no worse, that it was the hair loss that made it frightening, but Josh wasn't convinced. Before, his mum had kept her humour and natural cheekiness. Now, she seemed too exhausted.

She curled onto her side to create a space for him. He perched carefully, not wanting to disturb the bed too much in case it caused her pain or made her ill, and took her hand between both of his. Her skin felt moist and cool, as though all the blood was circulating further inside, fighting an internal enemy intent on killing her.

'How much more to go?' she asked.

'Just a matter of making sure the joinery is right. The height adjustment is the hardest bit.'

She smiled sweetly but tiredly. 'She'll be so thrilled.'

'Will she?'

'Of course.' Michelle threw him a look of puzzled amusement. 'Why on earth would you think she wouldn't be?'

Josh looked towards the window. A gap in the curtains exposed the garden and the glow of streetlights beyond. A shower had passed through a few hours before and the world still glistened with raindrops. Tuesday night. He wondered if Em had gone to Camrick for dinner or boycotted it. He hoped the latter. Bad things had a habit of happening in that house.

'What's up, my sweet?'

He looked down at her hand and toyed with her fingers. Some days he felt as if there was too much going on in his head. That morning, Karen told him that the mastectomy woman had to postpone her trip a week, which meant yet another week of uncertainty and sweat-filled disturbed sleep. The only time he seemed to sleep normally was with Em, but the weekend had seen even that scrap of grace disappear.

'The usual. Worrying about you.'

Michelle's lids half-closed. 'I'll be fine.'

'That's the trouble. You won't. And you know it.' He fought a shameful urge to cry. Losing Em, should it happen, he would handle, the same as he handled losing Bianca, but not his mum. Not his precious mum. He *needed* her. They all did. She held them together, made them a family. 'Why do you want to leave us?' His voice choked. 'Is it because we've done something wrong? Disappointed you somehow?'

'No! Don't you dare think that. You're all gorgeous and perfect and I love each one of you.' She clutched at him. 'And I am deeply proud of you all.'

'Then why?'

Grip loosening, she turned her head to the side. 'Don't, Joshy.'

He looked at her in despair. What was the point? No matter how much it hurt them, she'd made up her mind. And it made him even more miserable to acknowledge that a little bit of him hated her for it.

Television noise drifted in from the lounge. Josh thought about sitting in front of it for a while and zoning out or maybe phoning a mate and heading out for a beer, but where he really wanted to be was with Em. Normal, sexy, smart Em, not the one from the weekend.

He ran his hand over his beard, remembering his dad's advice. The trouble with Em was he didn't know what her response would be. That day on Rocking Horse Hill he thought he knew what she wanted. Now, he had no idea.

Josh wasn't so sure of his own feelings any more either.

'Why don't you go and see Em?' said Michelle, reading his mind.

'It's Tuesday night. She'll be at Camrick.'

Michelle glanced at the bedside clock radio. 'It's after eight. She'll be home by now.' She nudged his leg. 'Go on. You two need each other.'

'I'm not so sure about that.'

She regarded him as though he was nuts. 'Joshy, darling, she loves you.'

'Told you that, has she?' His mother couldn't hold eye contact. 'Yeah, I thought so.' He let out a long sigh. 'Dad said she was here yesterday.'

'For a while.'

'Did she tell you about what happened to her grandmother?'

'Yes. And the rest. She didn't want to, but she seemed so not herself that I insisted she tell me what the matter was.'

'I don't like it, Mum.'

'I know. I don't either.'

Not words Josh wanted to hear. Needing to be alone to brood, he rose and looked down on the bed. 'I don't think it's going to last anyway.'

'Of course it will. If you want it to.'

'Wanting isn't enough if the other person doesn't love you back.' He shook his head. His mum was the last to talk about false hope. 'I've got to go.' He planted a quick kiss on her clammy forehead and headed for escape before his anger and self-pity took over.

'You're wrong,' she called out as he reached the door. 'She hasn't said, but I know how she feels about you.' Michelle thumped her chest. 'I *know*.'

'Right. And why should I believe you?' Anguish at his failing relationship with Em, at his mother's refusal to save herself, infected his words with bitterness. 'You don't even know how to live.'

Twenty-Three

Em folded her arms and leaned against the balcony rail at Camrick. 'I really wish you'd reconsider.'

Em was desperate for her grandmother to relocate to the hill, a move Granny B was equally determined to refuse. Jack the Ripper could be living in the stables for all she cared. She was staying put.

'And I rather wish you weren't such a nag.' Smoke caressing the front edges of her severely lacquered hair, Granny B savoured her cigar for a moment, a dreamy expression on her face, before once more turning her focus to the stables. The upstairs lights were on, filtering through the blinds. A shadow flickered near the bedroom as someone moved around, and was gone.

Her grandmother had been discharged that morning and, ever since, Em had been on edge. Reluctant to take more time off from PaperPassion, she'd stayed at work, leaving Adrienne and Samuel to collect Granny B. She'd driven straight to Camrick from the shop, nervous at what the night might hold but with the hope it would encompass some sort of welcome back, conciliatory dinner, only to discover that for the first time in years Tuesday dinner had been cancelled.

Samuel was taking Adrienne out for a counter meal, while Digby and Felicity were making their own arrangements. Em had stood awkwardly in the kitchen with a carton of eggs from the hill in her hands, feeling like an intruder in the place she'd always considered her second home, while her mother suggested omelettes or a frittata as a solution to Em's and Granny B's dinner problem. It was as though no one wanted to acknowledge the trouble the family was in.

She tried again. 'Please, Gran.'

Unmoved, Granny B removed the cigar to inspect its tip before delicately picking a scrap of something off her tongue. She coughed, an awful hacking that had lodged in her lungs the night she was locked out. Em's fingers twitched with the urge to rip the cigar from her grandmother's hands and toss it into the garden below.

'And I wish to God you'd stop smoking! The doctor said it'll be the death of you.'

'I'm seventy-nine, Emily. Everything will be the death of me.' Granny B took another defiant puff and watched the smoke float across the space separating the house from the stables.

The first wisps of a descending fog were curling around the lower reaches of the yard. The rose bushes, yet to be pruned, struck thorny fingers through air that felt sickly cold, wrapping around Em like a clammy flu fever. She rubbed at her temple, wondering if she needed to see a doctor about her headaches, knowing the appointment would be wasted. Stress, worry, lack of sleep. Everyday triggers, easily cured if she could find a way.

'You needn't worry about the usurper. She won't try that trick again.'

'I'm not worried about Felicity.' She cast sad eyes towards the stables. 'It's Digby more than anyone. He won't forgive you for the argument. Or me.'

'As I explained before,' said Granny B, regarding Em over her shoulder, 'your brother will come round in time. Besides, I'm safer here. There are a lot of places one could do away with an enemy at the hill, and far easier to make it look like an accident.'

A man's shout carried from the stables. In unison, Em and Granny B swung towards the noise. Em surveyed the windows, hunting for a gap in the blinds or movement to tell her what was happening. The shouting continued in staccato bursts. Em listened hard, trying to make out the words, but it was impossible. Walls and distance muffled the sound, allowing them to read nothing but the anger.

Suddenly the voices dropped. Em's eyes strained on the blinds. Then a sorrowful wail trailed off into more silence. She waited, her breath caught, but it was clear the stables show was over.

'Arguing,' said Granny B. 'Now that's a turn up.'

'For Felicity, I imagine, but not for me. You should have seen Dig in the kitchen. I can't remember him ever being so combative. Jas reckons all that sex has raised his testosterone and given him balls the size of an elephant.'

Granny B's bark of laughter descended into a coughing fit, her eyes watering as the catch in her lungs refused to dislodge.

'God, Gran.'

'Oh, be quiet. It's just the stubborn residue of a cold.' She headed unsteadily for the cast-iron table upon which she'd left her tumbler and raised it to her lips. 'There, that's the way to cure a tickle.'

'Drowning it in Scotch?'

'You should try it, Emily. Rather amazing what a good malt will cure.' She raised the glass in a toast and drained the rest, uttering a satisfied 'ahhh' as she returned the glass to the table.

Em watched the lights go out in the windows above the stables. Whatever their argument, Digby and Felicity had obviously made up. An ache went through her as she imagined Digby holding Felicity, calming her, telling her he loved her no matter what.

Sharing something she and Josh once had, and now might never find again.

'Thinking of Joshua?' asked Granny B, moving alongside and cutting the dense air with the softer, comforting scent of fragrant tobacco and alcohol.

'A bit.'

'Growing old isn't fun, Emily, but it does have one advantage.'

'What?'

'Wisdom.' She took another puff. 'I might be able to help.'

Em studied the balcony's weathered timber floor. 'It's complicated.'

'I rather enjoy complicated. Keeps one's brain active. Very important in the prevention of dementia.' Granny B regarded her slyly. 'You wouldn't want that to happen to your grandmother now, would you?'

Despite her despondency, Em laughed. 'No. You're impossible enough as it is.' She sobered and considered for a moment, then sighed. 'I cheated on him, Gran. With Stephen Jacobs. That's why we broke up the first time.' Even in the cold, shame flushed her with heat. 'And I made sure that Josh found out about it.'

Granny B took a slow puff on her cigar and studied the smudged air. 'I can only assume you thought you had a good reason for such betrayal.'

'I wanted to break up with him.'

'And you were too much of a coward to tell him to his face?' Her lips pursed in disappointment. 'I thought you were better than that.'

'Not back then I wasn't.'

The night air was painfully cold against Em's hot cheeks, but she talked on. Explaining, in excoriating detail, why she ruined a love she realised too late was unique and precious.

'And now?' asked Granny B.

Em sighed. 'He thinks I'm being naive about Felicity.'

'He'd be correct on that front, as has been proven.'

'But that's it, Gran. Nothing has been proven. What if we're letting our ingrained Wallace snobbery get in the way of seeing the good person that Digby does? What if we're pointing fingers because her history and background makes her such an easy target?' She held her grandmother's gaze. 'I don't want to do to her what I did to Josh.'

Granny B took a last puff of her cigar and flicked it out into the night. Em watched it fall onto the gravel below. A glow filtered through the fog and was gone.

'We are all snobs in our own way, Emily. Even people like Joshua and his family, who hold onto their working-class roots with pride. We all need someone to look down on to make us feel better about ourselves. It's a sad fact of life. But with Felicity, it's not because of snobbery or prejudice. That girl has always wanted a different life. She wants the fairytale and will do anything to get it.'

'But Digby's given her the fairytale.'

'Yes, but without Rocking Horse Hill, the castle isn't complete.'

***

Car lights swept along Bradley Road, igniting the south-western side of the lava vent. For a fanciful moment, Em imagined the rock as a tall black monster, a Tolkienesque stone giant, heaving itself from the soil. Then the car slowed for the corner and the lights swept left and the vent melted back into darkness.

Hands burrowed in her pockets, head down, she stepped off the road. The car accelerated, passing her, and travelled a short distance before sliding to a sudden standstill. Reversing lights lit the gravel, followed by the whine of the engine as the car backed up Stanislaus Road. A window wound down. Em winced and kept walking without looking up. She didn't want to talk to a yahoo or drunken idiot, not at this time of night.

'Em?'

She stared at Josh. It was after eleven when she'd begun her descent from the hill, which must make it close to half past now. He shouldn't be here.

'What are you doing out? It's freezing.'

'I've been up the hill.'

'At night? Jesus, what were you thinking?'

She shrugged. 'I know my way.'

He raised his eyes in disbelief and indicated the passenger seat. 'Come on, get in.'

Em obeyed, though she didn't particularly want to. She'd returned from Camrick with Charles's papers, and settled down with a glass of wine to study them, seeking the facts about Felicity's trial, anything that might show that what she did was in self-defence and without any hint of premeditation. If the incident with Granny B required anything, it was planning. Proving a difference between the two events would help assuage some of her fears. Instead, Charles's notes had left her head pounding.

The notes revealed a pattern of violence. Two suspensions from school for fighting, one that left the other girl with a broken elbow. An incident in jail involving Felicity and another woman that was logged as an accident. Fourteen stitches from a laundry mishap? Em didn't think so. There were others, too, and in every case Felicity was let off.

Deeply rattled and realising sleep would be unlikely, Em had rugged up and headed for the one place she felt calm and right.

The car was warm and smelled of timber and oil, and a faint scent of something she took a moment to recognise as beer. Em leaned against the door with her frigid fingers pressed against her mouth, staring out at the vent.

Josh put the car into gear and his hand on her thigh. 'Are you okay?'

'Yes.'

'You're not acting it.'

Neither was he, turning up late and unannounced with beer on his breath. It reminded her too much of the other time he'd turned up late, after the club, when Em had been convinced he wanted to end it. Between her talk with Granny B and Charles's papers, she was too raw for this.

Em glanced at her watch as they turned into her drive and shifted to look at him. 'What are you doing here?'

He returned his hand to the wheel and wrapped his fists around it, and guided the ute to a halt. Muffy stood in front of the bonnet, tail wagging, brown eyes glowing devil-red in the lights. 'I had a bit of a fight with Mum. Went to the pub for a while.'

'I'm sorry.'

His mouth tightened. 'The doctors say she needs a mastectomy.'

'I know.'

'You know?'

'She told me on Monday when I was there.'

'Did she also tell you she's refusing to have it?'

Em nodded, careful of the emotional territory on which they trod. She and Michelle had shared intimacies that weren't for others. Although very much friends, they also enjoyed a sense of distance brought on by time and circumstance. In this neutral space they'd been able to confess their innermost feelings without fear of bias or judgement.

'Did she say why?'

Em eyed Muffy through the windscreen. The dog stared back at them, head swivelling from one to the other. Catching Em's stare, she wagged her tail and then stopped, uncertain. Em reached for the door. 'Muffy's getting cold. Let's go inside.'

The fire had burned down in her absence. Em waved Josh towards the bottle of red she'd opened earlier and concentrated on reloading the stove with logs.

She stayed kneeling, watching the rising flames, when he brought over her glass. She thanked him with a smile and waited until he'd perched on the arm of the lounge before turning back to the fire.

'I can't tell you about your mum. We spoke in confidence.'

'I couldn't give a shit about confidences. I just want her to live.'

Em assessed him over her shoulder, the angry clench of his hand around his wine glass, the spread of his legs. 'She'll come round.'

'When? She needs the operation now, Em.'

'Give her time.'

He leaned forward. 'She doesn't have time.'

'Do you think I don't know that? Do you think I let her tell me how bad things were and didn't try to convince her otherwise? She's *frightened*.' At his confused look she steepled her hands against her mouth, considering. She'd revealed too much already but Josh needed to understand. 'A mastectomy isn't a guarantee.'

He looked away, blinking hard. 'But the risk of not having it . . .'

'She knows.'

He took a slug of wine. 'It's Dad, isn't it? She thinks she's going to die no matter what and wants to stay whole for him in the time they have left.'

'She loves him, Josh.' Em rose and went to stroke Muffy. The dog's coat still held traces of the cold. 'People don't think straight when they're in love. You only have to look at Digby to see that.'

She only had to look at herself.

***

To Em's surprise, Josh was already up when she roused. The climb up Rocking Horse Hill, followed by their talk and the glass of wine had given her a much-needed full night's sleep. They'd cuddled instead of making love, seeking simple comfort from the touch of bodies, and Em had drifted off curled against his chest, her head cradled in the strong curve of his arm.

She wrapped herself in her fluffy terry gown and shuffled up the hall, rubbing sleep from her eyes. She stopped at the door, anxiety surging through her stomach.

Josh was at the dining table, a mug by his arm and Charles's papers spread before him. He turned to look at her, his expression ravelled with something that tugged hard at the tight knot in her belly. 'Hey.'

Em pressed her lips together and headed for the kitchen and flicked on the kettle. 'Good morning.'

'I've already let the chooks and Muffy out.'

'Thanks.' She peered through the window at the orchard and drive. 'Another frost. Should be a fine day, though. Might bring a few shoppers out. If it stays fine I'll be able to get in a ride after work. Lod's so unfit at the moment. Which reminds me, I need to ring Teagan.'

'Em?'

Em kept facing the window. She closed her eyes, knowing what was coming. The kettle clicked off but she made no move to pour tea.

Josh's chair creaked with movement. 'Em?'

She opened her eyes and looked further out. To Kicki and Cutie scratching each other's necks in the rising dawn. To Lod covered from neck to tail in his bright new rug, breath steaming as he plodded a well-worn path to his gate.

And beyond, to the right, with the rising sun peeking over its stony ridges, Rocking Horse Hill.

'Where did this come from?'

She didn't need to look at him to know what he was referring to. 'A retired journalist friend of Gran's. She asked him to investigate Felicity for her. Those are his notes, along with the trial transcript.'

'And you've only decided to read it now?'

'What Gran did was wrong.' She turned to face him, her chin high. This wasn't about Felicity any more. This was about him and her. About trust and forgiveness and second chances, but the conviction she tried to inject into her voice came out flat. 'We should accept people for the way they are now, not for something they did in the past.'

He scrubbed his hand down his face, the gesture pained and frustrated, and stared at the papers. 'You know it was her, don't you? I can hear it in your voice.'

'I don't know anything. And neither do you.'

'She's dangerous, Em.' He swept up a series of pages and thrust them towards her. 'Read her history. She hurts people. People that get in her way. People like your Gran. Like you.' He dumped the pages on the breakfast bar. 'You say you need proof before condemning her? There's your proof. Page after page, from school to jail. It's scary.'

'That isn't proof!'

'Jesus Christ. What is wrong with you?'

'I'm being a decent person,' she said, slapping a hand to her chest. 'Unlike you.'

'Oh, right. *You* want to lecture *me* on decency? The person who cheated? Decency, like fuck.'

Em blinked. There it was. The words that proved it. That, like Felicity, she'd never be forgiven.

Josh closed his eyes. 'I didn't mean that.'

'But you did.' She walked on stilted legs to the sliding door and opened it, standing aside as cold air blasted the room. 'I think you should go.'

He said nothing for a long while, his expression tired and incredibly sad. Em wanted to go to him, to make things right, but they never would be. The words had been said now.

'Don't, Em.'

She swept her hand towards the outside, her jaw clenched against tears that were so close to bursting.

Josh stepped to the threshold, staring out at the kaleidoscope colours of the sparkling, dawn-lit frost. Em held her breath, willing him to leave quietly, wanting him to stay.

'I promised myself I'd fight this time.' He looked across his shoulder at her and she could see him working hard to keep his emotions in check. 'But it turns out there's nothing to fight for.'

Em wanted to ask what he meant but her throat was closing over with pain. A single tear slid. His gaze traced it. A muscle in his jaw flexed but he didn't move. It was as though he was fixing her in his mind as she was fixing him. The man she loved.

The man who would never forgive.

Muffy's basket creaked, severing the silence. She crossed the floor, the taps and scratches of her nails on the slate impossibly loud. Josh broke from Em's gaze as the collie pressed against his calf, eyebrows furrowed as though not understanding why he was leaving so early.

Josh crouched, stroked her cheek and placed a gentle kiss on her head. 'You be a good dog and look after your mistress.'

Then he was gone.

Twenty-Four

Em stared at her drawing of G.K. Chesterton's king and traced her finger around a face she'd touched in real life only the night before. Lips she'd kissed with passion and meaning, softly tilted eyes that had, for a few short weeks, held an emotion she'd hoped was love.

But hoping didn't make things real.

She placed the drawing back down and sank her face into her hands. Sorrow crept through bones already weak with defeat. Since learning the true cost of selfishness and pride, Em's ego had never been huge but today she actually disliked herself. For so many reasons.

Traffic noise filtered through PaperPassion's door. As predicted, the frost had burned off, leaving Levenham crystal bright. Too bright. She wanted rain, wind that slashed through thick clothing, treacherous, slippery footpaths, anything to keep customers away and leave her alone with her broken heart.

After Josh left Em had walked outside, oblivious to the cold, and stood at the edge of the hill paddock, watching the crater come to life.

Its majesty never changed. Hundred-metre-high slopes were shadowed a deep dark green, the crater edge gnawing at the peach and blue sky with rocky teeth. The quarry scar was a proudly shown off war wound, the volcano the victor against the battles of man.

The morning smelled earthy and raw. Across the sky, birds wheeled. The lowing sounds of dairy cattle drifted on a zephyr. Lod whickered from his paddock. Yet as idyllic as the morning seemed, Em wondered if it was worth it. All this pain, all this fear and for what? A strip of land at the base of an extinct volcano.

No one's castle. Not even for Em. Just a home, now empty of the one thing that kept it warm.

The shop door chimed. Em took a moment to compose her face before looking up.

'Felicity, what are you doing here?'

If it weren't for her fair hair and blue eyes, Felicity could have been mistaken for a Wallace. An expensive navy trench coat swirled around her small frame and cut with military precision across her shoulders. Wool crepe trousers draped her legs, the fabric flowing with each step. A printed blouse billowed softly from the waistband. She'd styled her hair into a piled-up loose knot of the sort favoured by Em and Adrienne, showing off a pair of large diamond earrings. Another family heirloom. Make-up completed the picture of wealth and refinement.

But Felicity's smile was fragile. Fake, Em thought. Fragile and fake. 'I wanted to talk to you.'

Em leaned her hip against the edge of the counter. 'About what?'

'Digby. He's so upset, Em.' Felicity's blue eyes began to pool but, like the smile, Em couldn't bring herself to believe the tears were real. 'Your family was always so close and now . . .'

Something shifted in Em. Something cynical and mean, a monster roused by the breakdown of her and Josh's relationship. Her mind flew to Charles's notes, still scattered on the table at Rocking Horse Hill. The disturbing facts they contained, facts a part of Em still resisted. She thought of Granny B, of Adrienne. The harm that had befallen her family. She thought of Josh, Jas and Teagan, their warnings. Lastly, she thought of Digby and the hill, and the monster shifted again, growing claws.

'And whose fault is that?'

Shock turned Felicity's eyes enormous. For a long moment she could only stare at Em, then she stiffened and tugged at the cuffs of her jacket. 'I haven't done anything except fall in love with your brother.'

'No?' Em took a step forward, surprised when Felicity stood her ground.

But jail had probably taught her the danger of backing down. 'Where were you that night?'

'At the stables, watching television, like Digby told you.'

'Watching what, exactly? You must have had the sound turned up loud not to hear Granny B calling out. Strange when we could hear you and Dig arguing last night.'

A mascara-stained tear slid down Felicity's cheek leaving a grey streak through her make-up. 'I was watching *Montague Manor*. It's a good show. Australian. Set after the war.' Her lip wobbled. 'I've always liked stories about families. Especially proper ones, different to mine. What?' Her eyes widened even further. 'What?'

Em felt as though she was made of ice. Felicity had lied and now Em had caught her. 'I know you did it.'

'No.'

'And I'm going to make sure Digby knows it too.'

'No.' Several more trails of mascara wound down her cheeks. 'You can't.'

Em strode behind the counter. She didn't trust herself to remain close to Felicity. The monster inside wanted to hurt something, to make this woman pay for all she'd done.

'Em . . .'

She regarded Felicity coldly. 'Get out.'

At the computer, the screensaver's colourful starburst gave way to her email program.

Keyboard taps became the only sound in the shop.

When she'd finished she glanced up. Felicity was standing in front of one of the display bins, swiping her cheeks with a tissue. A sudden rush of guilt raked Em's chest. She dropped her head to take several deep breaths and remind herself not to be fooled. This was the woman who'd locked her grandmother out on a freezing night. Who'd left Granny B with a cough that still ripped at her lungs. Who'd cleaved a family and destroyed a relationship that could have been forever. Who'd taken Em's warm, caring heart and turned it savage.

Em raised her head again and kept her gaze straight.

Felicity turned and met it with one as equally unwavering. She placed the tissue in her coat pocket and, with her spine rigid, opened the door. Street noise and cold rushed in. For a long moment Felicity kept her back to Em, then she turned, her husky voice filled with conviction. 'He loves me.'

Em aligned the mouse curser over the send button and clicked.

'Not for much longer.'

***

A dirty, unwholesome feeling crept up on Em in the mid-afternoon and refused to let go. She kept checking her email, hoping that her message to Digby would bounce. It wouldn't. She'd used his Department of Agriculture address.

Fear of how he would react made her nauseous. Nor could she stop the sick feeling when she remembered Felicity's expression at Em's parting remark. The distress in her eyes, as if she knew that single click would mean the end of her happiness. What if Em had been wrong?

Home and solitude couldn't come fast enough but it was after six when she turned into her drive. At first her heart soared as her headlights lit the reflectors of another car, then she recognised Teagan's beaten-up Toyota and knew something was horribly wrong.

Em found her on the back verandah, huddled up like a street waif with Muffy in her lap. Teagan looked up, her eyes hollow, her freckled skin pale and taut over bones that seemed to have sharpened to painful edges. A thin wool jumper with holes in the elbows hung off her frame and her jeans were mud-streaked around the cuffs. On her feet were a pair of cheap slippers, also mud-covered, as if she'd run from home in panic.

Em took her hand. 'Why don't we get you inside?'

'It's all gone, Em. Everything. All that work. Gone.'

'Come inside where it's warm first, then you can tell me everything that's happened.'

It took a bit more coaxing to get Teagan to her feet. She held Em's hand like a child, allowing herself to be led inside to the couch where Em tucked a woollen rug around her. As though sensing she was needed, Muffy huddled by Teagan's feet, offering her body for comfort like a breathing fluffy toy.

Em stoked Teagan's hair away from her face. 'I'm going to make us some tea, okay? And then we'll talk.'

Teagan nodded. She looked shell-shocked.

Em kept watch while she waited for their tea to brew. She contemplated food but suspected it would be a wasted effort. Perhaps later, when Teagan had revealed her secrets and let her anguish go.

In the meantime, sweet tea would do.

She handed Teagan her mug and sat down alongside her, blowing on her tea as she waited. The fire spread warmth she didn't seem to feel.

'He's lost it all,' Teagan said eventually, staring at the glass front of the fire and the dancing flames within. 'Everything. The farm, my money. It's all debt. My life, all my dreams, gone.'

'What happened?'

'Gambling.' Teagan's voice was bitter. 'Although he doesn't call it that. He calls it trading contracts for difference. A perfectly legal financial derivative, no different to trading shares. What a load of bullshit. It's gambling. And he lost.'

'I'm sorry.'

'You know what I can't believe? That we never suspected.'

'Not even your mum? He must have been spending a fair bit of time on the computer.'

'Oh, he was, but here's the real clanger: she thought he was surfing porn sites and was too embarrassed to confront him about it.'

'Oh, Blissbomb.'

'The bank's foreclosing. He told us this afternoon.' She swallowed another mouthful of tea, as though fortifying herself. 'I'm leaving, Em. I have to get out, away from here. I can't stand another day.'

'Where will you go?'

'To my aunt, in New South Wales.' She breathed out. 'Astra will have to go. My horse gear and the float. They're not worth much, but . . .'

'I'll buy her from you. Take care of her here, and when you're back on your feet you can have her back.'

'I can't ask you to do that. It's too much.'

'No, it's not.' Em smiled. 'You mightn't think so right now, but you're worth it.'

The floodgates opened. Until then Teagan had been holding it in but with Em's words her grief poured out in great wracking sobs. Em took their mugs and placed them safely on the floor before cradling her friend and soothing her as best she could, stroking her hair against the howls and self-recriminations, shushing her, promising a new life, a new future.

Wishing it for them both.

***

Although Em asked her to reconsider, Teagan was determined to leave as fast as she could. Em made an emergency call to her casual, Helen, to look after the shop the following morning so she could help her friend.

While Teagan was at the farm fetching Astra, Em headed to the building society, where Jas helped her organise the transfer of seven thousand dollars to Teagan's account. Astra was worth double that, but it was all Em had spare. She could sell shares but trades took three days to settle and Teagan had refused a cent more. Em had done enough. Seven thousand would see her through.

'I'll buy her float,' said Jas. 'And the saddles.'

'You can't afford it.'

'I know, but I want to help.'

'Then you can store both at your place and look after buyers when we advertise.'

'Tell her I'll call and hug her for me, please?' Jasmine's eyes filmed. 'I'll miss her.'

'I know. So will I.'

Em was prepared for more tears at the hill when Teagan said goodbye, but the previous night seemed to have exhausted her supply. Except for some brief wateriness as she farewelled Astra, who appeared delighted with her new home, Teagan remained remarkably calm.

'It's weird,' she said to Em, who was standing by the ute's open door. The rear tray was half-packed with suitcases, a couple of faded canvas duffle bags, an equally faded swag and two hastily taped boxes. All her possessions. 'But I feel liberated somehow, like the world's lifted off me.'

'You've been under a lot of stress.'

'And now I'm going to start anew.'

'You'll make a great go of it too.' Em hugged her tightly. 'Call me if you need anything.' She shook her gently for emphasis. 'Anything, you hear?'

'I hear.' Teagan hugged her back. 'You did the right thing, telling Dig about Felicity. Don't think otherwise.'

They'd talked into the night, about the Blisses, about Teagan's ruined dreams, about family and ties that could turn into nooses. About right and wrong and the grey in between. About friendship and love, and that elusive state called contentment.

'And don't worry about Josh. You can try again, when this is all over and everyone's safe.'

Em smiled at her optimism. 'I'll miss you.'

'I'll miss you too. But we'll see each other again.'

'Absolutely. You have a horse to collect.'

Teagan laughed and somehow Em knew she'd be okay. 'She won't want to leave here.'

'Of course she will. Astra knows who her true mistress is.'

They hugged again, fiercely, relaying thanks for a friendship that was impossible to articulate with words. That strong bond forged from liking, and life's ups and downs.

A precious thing to be cherished. Like proper love.

Twenty-Five

Josh made yet another restless circuit of the shed as the first of the afternoon's forecast showers began to patter the roof. What a dick he was. He should have known this was going to happen. He should never have grabbed Em's hand at Camrick, never thought that they could resurrect what they once had.

He stopped in front of the easel and stared at the finished design. At the work he and his dad had spent so many hours on, enabling them to reconnect, to talk, to fuse a friendship that had loosened in the years he'd been gone. Josh wrapped his fists around the cypress board and braced himself with straightened arms, his head lowered. He breathed in hard. If nothing else, Em had given him precious moments with his dad. He had to at least be a little bit grateful for that.

Josh released the easel and stood back. The timber was soft and warmly coloured, with almost pinkish hues. It was also an awkward shape, which made getting it to Em problematic. Easy, wrapped up and laid flat in the back of the ute, but that would mean handing it over in person. Briefly, Josh considered asking his dad to deliver it to the hill, then dismissed the idea. His days of cowardice were over. He'd face her, talk normally and hold his chin up.

Plenty of other women in the world. Plenty.

'Fuck,' he said, and strode out of the shed.

His mum was at the kitchen table, scribbling in one of her notebooks. Better today, although Josh worried it was an act for him, to prove his accusation wrong. On his arrival home from the hill yesterday, he'd immediately apologised for his outburst. One rift in his life was enough, and he had a better understanding of his mum's motives now. Thanks to Em.

Something else he owed her.

Michelle looked up, her smile faltering as she took in Josh's face. 'What's the matter?'

'Nothing.' He scraped out a chair and sat down. Drumming his fingers on the table, he stared around the room. He rose again and filled the kettle, aware all the time of his mother's assessing gaze. 'Do you want a cup of tea?'

'What I want is for you to tell me what's wrong.'

Josh leaned against the kitchen bench with his arms crossed, head tilted towards the kettle as though his mood alone could bring it to the boil.

'It helps if you turn it on,' said Michelle, rising and reaching around him to flick the switch. She joined him along the bench and leaned her shoulder into his. 'Is it Em?'

He nodded, his teeth clamped to stop himself from swearing.

'Have you broken up?'

'Something like that.'

His beard began to itch. He scratched it, thinking he might shave it off, and then remembered how sexy Em said she found it.

Em. Jesus. When would it end?

'Oh, Joshy. What happened?'

He shrugged. How to explain? He didn't really know himself. He dropped his arms and crossed the room to the sideboard and stared at all the happy faces trapped in his mum's precious photo collection. He'd thought there would be one of him and Em one day. Now that would never happen.

'We argued.'

'About what?'

He spread his arms a little before letting them slap back against his thighs. 'I don't know. Us. Her. I thought we could make a go of things but all this crap with her family got in the way.'

Michelle sighed. 'That Felicity has caused so much damage. Poor Em has tied herself in knots over that girl.'

'Hardly. All she does is defend her.'

'Yes, because of you.' At Josh's uncomprehending look Michelle went back to the table and sat down. 'Do you know she still hasn't forgiven herself for what she did to you?' She nodded, and answered his unspoken question. 'She told me. You never admitted what really happened.'

'You and Em were close,' said Josh, sitting with her again. 'I didn't want you to think badly of her.'

'I guessed that. And you're right, I wouldn't have been terribly forgiving if I'd known.' She let out a sigh. 'I'm still not greatly impressed but at least I can see how much she's learned and changed from it. And she's so very sorry.'

'What's that got to do with Felicity?'

'Nothing as far as I'm concerned, but Em is convinced there's some sort of parallel between herself and Felicity. If Digby can give Felicity a second chance after the terrible thing she did, then maybe you could do the same with her. All it would take was understanding and forgiveness.'

Josh stared at the window. Of all the things he could have said to Em, the dig about her cheating was the worst.

'She loves you, Joshy. You need to sort this out.'

'How?'

She gave his cowlick a yank. 'By talking to her, you silly boy.'

Josh stared at the table. He wasn't sure he wanted to sort it. The relationship had been veneer-thin from the outset. Lots of sex, food and nothing much deeper. The closest they'd come to talking about their feelings was the morning they'd climbed the hill.

Hardly the behaviour of a woman in love.

His mother sighed. 'You know your trouble?'

'What?'

'You're too scared of getting your heart broken again.'

If Josh wasn't feeling so crap he would have laughed. It was too late to save his heart. Anyway, she was wrong. He'd decided the day they climbed the hill that when it came to love there was no security, only chance. 'I'm not scared.'

Michelle raised an eyebrow.

'I'm not.'

'Joshy, Joshy,' she said with a sigh, 'how many times do I have to tell you? You can fool yourself, but you'll never fool your old mum. The whole time you were with her you were scared of what she could do to you. So you held back. Poor Em never knew where she stood. For all she knew you were using her. This business with Felicity just gave you the excuse to get the out you were looking for.'

Josh couldn't believe what he was hearing. Using her? If anyone was being used, it was him. 'How could I be using her? I love her.'

'We all know that, but does she?'

Josh looked away, a sick feeling inside as he recalled his dad's advice: Nothing sucks a man's soul drier than regrets. Josh's already felt like a desert.

Smiling, Michelle patted the table. 'You stay here. I'll make us tea.'

He slumped, his head in his hands, remembering Bianca and the way she'd stared at him with her cool blue eyes and told him she wanted to separate. That she didn't love him any more and she was pretty certain he sure as hell didn't love her. He had, but something had broken between them and he hadn't wanted to face it until that day. Just as he hadn't wanted to reveal how he felt to Em.

His mum placed a steaming mug in front of him. 'Now, Joshy, my sweet, let me tell you a little bit about women . . .'

***

Oily puddles shone on McArthur Street, lit by headlights and shop lights. A shower had passed through, enough to slick the bitumen and scent the air. The puddles swirled with rainbow colours as the surface scum shifted with the wind and traffic vibration.

'Off to see Em?'

Josh stopped. He'd been so deep in thought he hadn't noticed Digby's approach. He smiled and reached out to shake hands. 'Digby, how's things?'

Digby shrugged. 'Could be better.'

'Don't tell me. Women.'

'Yeah.'

'Join the club.'

Digby looked back over his shoulder towards PaperPassion. 'If you're after Em, she's not there.'

'Where is she?'

'The hill. She had most of the day off apparently, then when she was coming back in, Malcolm Fuchs rang to say her donkeys were out on Bradley Road.'

Josh glanced across the street and then at his watch. It was after five-thirty. Early enough for a drink and Digby looked like he needed one more than Josh.

He nodded towards the pub. 'Feel like a beer?'

Digby scratched the back of his neck and brooded for a moment. 'Okay. Why not.'

They crossed back in front of PaperPassion, Josh unable to stop himself looking inside. The woman he'd met when Em had been in Adelaide stood near the bin of rubbers and pencils. She looked up, smiled and resumed her rearranging.

'Just so you know, Em and I split up,' said Josh when they'd settled in the front bar at a corner table with their beers. The pub was beginning to crowd with Thursday payday workers. Half an hour later and they'd have been unlikely to score a table. Josh nodded to a couple of footy mates but Digby had barely looked around.

'I thought you and her were full on,' he said.

Josh took a good slug of beer, enjoying the slide of the alcohol. 'I said something stupid. Now she thinks I don't trust her.'

'Shit of a thing, trust.'

'Yeah.'

For a long moment Digby didn't say anything. He sat staring at his beer, working his bottom lip between his thumb and forefinger. When he finally spoke, he kept his eyes down. 'I think Flick's been lying to me.'

Josh put down his beer. 'What about?'

Digby shook his head, clearly unhappy about the discussion. A buzz was humming through Josh, the buzz of something being severely wrong.

'Dig?'

He looked up, his eyes shiny. 'What happened to Gran. I don't think it was an accident any more.' He swallowed and looked away, his mouth twisting. 'I think Flick deliberately locked her out.'

'Jesus. Are you sure?'

Digby shook his head. 'I don't know.'

'What do you mean, you don't know?'

'I want to believe her, but . . .' He lifted his glass and drank heavily.

Josh wrapped his fingers around Digby's shoulder and dug them in hard. 'If what you say is true then your gran could still be in danger.'

'Em sent me an email yesterday. Flick had gone into the shop to talk to her. We've been arguing a bit, me and Flick. Mum's a mess. Gran spends most of her time on the balcony smoking. Samuel isn't happy with any of us and Em . . .' He let out a long breath. 'At first I thought she was on our side, but then she kept questioning me about it, asking to find proof that Flick didn't do it. Then I caught her talking to Mum and it made me wonder if she was right. Which only made me angry because I felt so shit for being suspicious.' He trailed off again.

Josh wasn't about to let him drift. 'And?'

'Em wanted me to check the computer. She reckoned Flick could have looked up online what she said she watched that night, but I wouldn't do it. I thought there was no way Flick would hurt a member of my family. She loved it here.' His mouth turned down and Josh had a lurching feeling that Digby was going to start crying in the pub. 'She loved me.'

'You said Em sent an email.'

Digby took several quick breaths and a sip of beer and when he continued the crack in his voice had gone. 'She said she had proof about Flick.'

'What proof?'

'In the shop, when Em asked what she watched that night Flick told her it was *Montague Manor*.' He stared bleakly into his drink. 'She'd told me it was *The Hannigans*.'

'So you checked the computer.'

'This morning, while Flick was in the shower.'

'And?'

'Nothing in the search history.'

Josh looked at him in puzzlement. 'Em was wrong then?'

He shook his head. 'I checked the PVR hard drive. There was a partial recording for *The Hannigans* that night, like what happens when you pause live sport and the drive automatically keeps recording.'

'So she could have left the stables and gone to the house.'

Digby nodded.

Josh took a moment to catch his breath. He stared around the pub. The intensifying hubbub of chatter as the pub reached capacity barely registered against the pound of his thoughts.

'Did you ask her about it?'

'Yes.'

Frustration had Josh wanting to shake him. 'And?'

Digby began working his lip again.

'For fuck's sake, Dig.'

'She accused me of not loving her any more.' His eyes shone with tears. 'She said I was being poisoned by Em. That she was just like my grandmother, wanting to break us up.' His voice turned hoarse. 'Yet, all throughout, not once did she deny it.'

A wave of cold washed through Josh. 'Okay, answer me this. Do you think she'd hurt Em?'

Digby didn't reply.

'I'm losing my patience here.'

Digby looked up, his eyes desperate. 'I don't know.'

'Fuck.' Josh pulled out his phone and dialled. Whatever had happened between them didn't matter now. He needed to know she was safe. The phone rang five times before switching to the answering machine. He hung up and tried her mobile. He almost slammed his own phone onto the table when it went straight through to voicemail. 'Call Felicity,' he ordered Digby, dialling Em's home number again. 'Find out where she is.'

Once again Em's phone rang out. Maybe she was still fetching Kicki and Cutie, or out with Lod. Perhaps she'd gone to climb the hill and he was panicking over nothing.

Digby slid his phone from his ear and frowned at it. Then tapped the screen and returned it to his ear. 'There's no answer. On either number.'

'You,' Josh got up, 'come with me.'

He didn't wait to see if Digby followed. He strode out of the pub, breaking into a jog the moment he hit the footpath. His ute was parked further up the street, a few minutes away. Minutes he didn't want to spare.

Already the sky was beginning to darken with the final farewell of day. A strong southerly brought clouds scudding across the sky, further blocking the light. Em should have been home.

'Wait,' yelled Digby, standing beside a silver Jeep. 'My car's just here.'

Digby drove erratically towards Camrick, tyres locking as he braked hard in the driveway, spraying stones that pinged loudly off the stables' roller-doors. Josh stepped out, waiting close by as Digby swung open the door and leapt up the stairs, calling as he went.

Twenty seconds later he was out, looking ashen and frantic. He ran into the main house. Josh tried Em's number again, his teeth gritting as the call remained unanswered.

Digby appeared at Camrick's back door. 'She's not there.'

'Could she have gone for a walk?'

Digby shook his head and ran back towards the stables, and disappeared inside again.

Adrienne stepped from the house as Digby re-emerged. 'Digby, darling, what's the matter?'

Digby ignored her, speaking instead to Josh. 'Mum's car's gone.'

Josh tried to stay calm against the wildness infecting his brain. He addressed Adrienne. 'Is your car meant to be here?'

'Of course.' Her gaze snapped towards the stables' first floor. 'Where's Felicity?'

'Come on,' said Josh, yanking open the Jeep's door. 'Now, Dig.'

Digby paused long enough to hold his mother's shoulders and kiss her cheek, saying something that Josh missed but which he guessed was reassurance. From the way she wrung her hands and kept glancing at the stables, Adrienne seemed far from convinced.

The drive out to the hill seemed to take forever, even with the speedometer hitting close to 140 kilometres an hour. Josh didn't care. All he wanted was to get to Em.

The Jeep's rear swung out as Digby skidded onto the loose gravel of Bradley Road. He slowed but his speed was still dangerous.

Not wanting to distract Digby, Josh said nothing. His eyes were on the hill, scanning the skyline, hoping to spot Em's silhouette in the fast-falling dusk. The Jeep slid onto Stanislaus Road and he checked the side mirror and the road back towards the tourist car park, then whipped back as Digby began to swear.

'Oh fuck, oh fuck, oh fuck.'

Ditched into the gutter opposite Em's house was a bronze BMW.

Josh unclipped his seatbelt.

Digby swung through the gate. Josh was out before the wheels had stopped turning. He shouted Em's name but the wind caught his voice and flung it aside only to replace it with the rapid barking of a dog.

He looked at Digby, frozen at the side of the car, until a cry had them both running.

Twenty-Six

Em cocked her head and listened, but the howling of the wind blocked everything. She crossed to the kitchen and peered out through the window above the sink but there was nothing but the swaying fruit trees. Though the rain had been sporadic – light showers that dampened the ground and made outside chores tiresome – the sky was still thick with sodden clouds that cloaked the sunset and brought the night in fast.

She listened for a few seconds longer but discerned nothing out of the ordinary. She thought she'd heard a car door slam but it must have been her imagination, the hankering of a heart that wished for impossible things. If he did come, Josh would park at the side of the house, and the drive remained empty.

She turned away, spying the half-finished bottle of red wine left over from Josh's last visit, and poured herself a glass. She should have gone back to the shop after sorting Kicki and Cutie. It was too easy now, in the warm fug of Rocking Horse Hill, to wallow in all the things she'd done wrong.

Her mobile, its battery dead, sat on the end of the kitchen bench alongside the house phone and answering machine. Sipping wine, she stared at both, aware that no matter how much she willed it, Josh wouldn't call. Nor would she call him. It was over. Sometimes the baggage was too heavy for a second chance to fly.

Loneliness engulfed her. She placed her wine down on the sink drainer and pressed her hands into her eyes. The heels of her palms were wet, but she fought against sobbing. Of her closest relationships, only the ones she shared with Granny B and Teagan had survived the winter. The others were all damaged or ruined, perhaps irrevocably.

Muffy came to sit by her feet. Em looked down and smiled, sniffing as the dog looked at her with sweet brown eyes. She crouched and cuddled her close. 'What would I do without you, Muff-Muff?'

The question was barely out when Muffy jerked away from her hands and released a furious torrent of loud barks. Em fell back against the kitchen cupboards as Muffy raced for the sliding door and clawed it with both paws, the barks interspersed with threatening growls.

Josh. And from Muffy's reaction, he must be in a temper.

She shushed her collie and wiped her eyes before rising. Muffy had her nose to the glass, but from what Em could see no one stood on the other side. The dog let out a whine and pawed at the edge of the door, trying to hook it open.

'Shh, Muff,' she said again. She slid open the door, frowning as Muffy darted out into the night and vanished. 'Josh?'

Em stepped out and squinted to the left where the porch extended to the old laundry. Nothing moved in the shadows. Her frown deepening, she moved to the edge of the timber deck and peered into the garden. From the house came the shrill ring of the phone.

'Josh?' She moved to the porch's top step. 'Come on, this isn't funny.'

The ringing ceased.

Em looked back at the house, still frowning. She glanced at the garden again and took two steps back as a prickly heat threaded through her skin. Someone was definitely here and maybe it wasn't Josh.

A gust of wind shook the yard alive with noise. Em listened hard as she peered into the shadows, jumping in fright as the house phone started again.

'Oh, for God's sake.' She walked back towards the door, body half-turned to keep checking behind her. Though she wanted the phone, nervousness made her whistle for Muffy.

Only the wind-rustled trees answered.

The prickling of her skin worsened.

'Muffy!'

Quiet returned as the ringing stopped and the gust faded. Em's breathing sounded hoarse and heavy. Where the hell was Muffy? Uncertain, she glanced at the kitchen and back towards the garden before taking a hesitant step further out along the porch. 'Muff-muff?'

There was movement at the side of the house. Em spun around, her hand flying to her chest. She cried out in a sort of half-laugh as relief washed through her. 'Felicity, you scared the living daylights out of me.'

Felicity stepped further into the light. 'Why?'

Em's relief faded as she registered the pain in Felicity's voice. She cast around for Muffy and found her half a metre to the side, her hackles raised, sidestepping on careful paws as she tracked Felicity's unsteady walk towards the porch.

The wind licked Felicity's hair around her face. Marks like bruises darkened the hollows beneath her eyes. Despite the temperature, she wore only a plain red T-shirt and the same turned-up cuffed jeans and gym shoes that she had on the first time Em met her at Camrick.

Digby had read the email, and acted. Now Em had to deal with the consequences.

Guilt made Em hold out her arm in welcome. 'You must be freezing. Come in.'

Felicity continued her disturbing zombie walk and plaintive question as though she hadn't heard. 'Why?'

'Come inside and we'll talk.' Em stepped back to give her room. Felicity took the two steps up to the porch as though her bones ached. Her mouth was horribly turned down, her eyes anguished, but even in her distress she maintained that fragile beauty that had attracted Digby and brought her crashing into their lives.

'All I wanted was what you had.'

'I know. I know you did.' Em gestured towards the door. 'Please, come inside.'

'A family. A proper one. With people who love me.' She lumbered closer to Em. 'All those things that you take for granted but I've never had.' She tilted her head, eyes streaming with tears. 'I thought I'd found it, with Digby.' She sprawled her fingers over her heaving chest, stretching the material of her shirt. 'He loved me.'

Em regarded her with pity and hurt. 'Then why risk it all?'

'She was poisoning everyone against me.' Felicity's mouth twisted. 'You would have done the same.'

'To a vulnerable old lady? No. I don't go around hurting people.'

'But you do! You took Digby from me. He was my hope. He was going to give me everything!' She sobbed, the sound heart- wrenching. 'Now I'm nothing again. Nothing!'

'I'm sorry. So sorry.' Em reached for Felicity, wanting to hold her, to prove that it would be all right. She could have her family, the love she sought. They'd get her the counselling she needed, make her whole so all this could be put aside. Start again.

For a brief moment, Felicity allowed the embrace, then a growl escaped her mouth. She pushed with surprising strength, catching Em off guard. Em lost balance, stumbling over Muffy who'd raced to her side. She reached out her left arm to break her fall, but Muffy was beneath her feet. She twisted, hoping to avoid the dog and fell awkwardly. A loud surreal crunch seemed to cloud her head. Then the pain started.

Somewhere between the groans and Muffy's barks Em registered the cut of headlights through shadows. She thought she heard Josh. Car doors slammed.

'Flick!'

Felicity's chest heaved. 'Not Dig, please not Dig.' She looked down at Em, her hands twisting against one another. 'They'll think I did this. They'll think I wanted to hurt you. They'll send me back to jail.'

Em tried to sit up. Pain shot her eyes closed. 'They won't.' She gritted her teeth, panting as she tried to move. 'It was an accident.'

'No. No. They'll say it's my fault.'

'Em!' This time the voice was definitely Josh's.

Felicity whimpered again. And then she ran.

'Felicity, no!'

Cupping her elbow, Em forced herself to her feet. Ignoring Josh and Digby's calls and Muffy's hysterical barks, she stumbled down the garden path after Felicity. Starbursts of pain shot behind her eyes, but she kept going.

Em burst through the shrubs at the end of the path and searched frantically, finally focusing on the hill paddock. The gate hung open and ahead, up the slope along the fence line, a golden-haired woman was climbing the stile.

'Oh, God.' Em stumbled onwards, Muffy at her side. 'Felicity, stop!' She ran, away from Josh's and Digby's stricken yells, ignoring the sickening throb of her shoulder.

The stile was agony. She had to let go of her elbow to negotiate the climb and the pain was excruciating. Felicity had too great a head start. Already she was across the slope where the old track curved towards the quarry.

Behind her, Josh's and Digby's shouts became louder as they gained ground. Muffy barked as though urging her on and galloped ahead. Em kept going, slipping and stumbling on the slick track, her warning yells swept away by the wind.

Felicity's hair acted like a beacon. Em consoled herself that as long as she could still see its moonlit glow Felicity was safe. All Felicity had to do was stay away from the quarry edge.

Another wind gust brought a terror-filled cry.

'Felicity!' Em ran harder, sliding onto her side as her feet gave way. One-handed, she crawled back onto the wet grass. Bracken whipped her face and blackberry thorns dug through her clothes, but she barely felt the sting. In front of her the path was intact, just, but further up the hill it had disappeared, cut away by landslip. Felicity stood on an isthmus of unstable land, chest heaving as she stared up the steep slope where her escape route lay.

'Felicity, please,' panted Em, pushing upright. Taking careful steps, she moved through the tangle of overgrowth and worked her way sideways before tracking towards the trail edge. Moving as close as she dared, she beckoned with her good arm. 'Come back this way, towards me.'

Felicity pressed a knuckle to her teeth. 'They'll send me back.'

'They won't. We'll protect you. Digby will protect you.'

'He doesn't trust me any more.'

'He still loves you. You can earn it back.'

Felicity's mouth twisted, her voice like a child's. 'I just wanted a proper home.'

'I know. I know you did.' Em felt a shudder beneath her feet, like the groan of a rousing giant. 'Please, we don't have time. Take my hand.'

For a harrowing moment, she didn't move, then, with a hesitant step, Felicity reached out for Em. The shudder worsened. The ground lurched.

'Now!'

Felicity lunged, but the earth was already giving way beneath her. Em thrust forward, catching her hand around the crook of Felicity's elbow as she slid. Em was pulled forwards as Felicity's weight dragged her to the ground. Pain exploded across her shoulders but she screamed through it, her grip as fierce as her yell. Around Em, the ground continued to heave. She braced herself against the soil, her face at the edge of the slip, looking into Felicity's terrified eyes.

Digby's voice roared out of the darkness. 'Flick!'

'Stay back!' But Em's order had no effect. Hands grabbed her legs and worked their way up until they hooked into the back of her jeans.

'Get back. The ground's too unstable.'

But Digby wasn't listening. He knelt beside her, and reached towards Felicity. The grip on Em's jeans tightened and she realised that it wasn't Digby's body across her legs, but Josh's.

Josh risking his life for her.

'Let go, Josh. It's too dangerous.'

His voice came back steadfast. 'No.'

Tears of pain and emotion burned her eyes as her grip on Felicity began to fail. The air was filled with the smell of ancient peat and decaying plants.

Digby stretched further out. 'Take my arm, Flick.'

Em's grip slipped again. She stared at Felicity, willing her to hang on. Her angel's eyes were huge and dark in the moonlight.

'Come on, Flick. Just reach across. I won't let you go.' Digby leaned forwards, reaching out. The movement caused a chunk of soil to break away and tumble down the dark wall that had opened like a monster's yawn across the side of Rocking Horse Hill.

'Dig,' warned Em.

'Come on. I'm here. Like I promised I always would be.'

The ground began to lurch in earnest. Panic and pain made Em cry out for Josh. The pull on her jeans tightened. An arm scooped around her legs like a pincer. The earth was slipping and she didn't know how much more would fall away.

'I have you.' Josh's voice was steady and promise-filled. 'I won't let you go.'

Desperation turned Digby's voice hoarse. 'Flick, please.'

Tears had streaked lines across Felicity's muddy face. She let out a sob. For a moment she tilted her head downwards, then she looked directly up at Digby. 'I love you.'

'I know, baby. I love you too.'

Em began to sob. 'I can't hold on.'

Felicity wasn't helping. Her arm had relaxed, her grip faltering. As she held Digby's terrified gaze, her expression filled with a strange serenity.

Realising her plan, Em began to plead. 'Don't. Please don't.'

The mud began to slide, a pulse of soil that moved like a wave under her stomach.

'No!'

Digby lunged, catching his knee on Em's injured shoulder. She screamed and suddenly the land was gone and Em was being dragged painfully backwards, her shoulder on fire.

'Digby!' Strong arms held her but her shrieks kept coming. 'Digby!'

Her voice subsided to a wail. She dropped her head, uttering his name one last time, a pitiful sound, barely heard in the torrent of the night, until its last sorrowful trail was swept away by a roar and unholy tremor, as though the heart of Rocking Horse Hill had heard her cry and reached out through the earth to reply.

Except this time its voice was all fury.

Twenty-Seven

Josh's feet sank into the spongy grass as he crossed the garden cemetery. The lawn had become so over-thatched some of the memorial plates appeared buried themselves. A few were completely overgrown, their black-and-brass-lettered faces reduced to tiny dark eyes peeking from the surrounding green.

The day was funeral glum, as though Mother Nature had sensed a family's grief and donned mourning clothes in sympathy. Grey clouds hung over the landscape, some with charcoal bellies, threatening rain. Unlike in Adelaide, where Josh had been the last few days, spring had yet to cast its hope and sun-drenched spell over Levenham. Not that he or his family had much chance to experience the sunshine. Their view had been of hospital walls and the stoic face of the woman they all adored.

Though the operation had gone well and Michelle was recovering, surrounded by the rest of the family, Josh itched to be back there. After resisting for so long, they were all afraid of her emotions after the double mastectomy. The removal of tissue from Michelle's other breast wasn't necessary but the knowledge that she'd taken this preventative measure gave enormous relief to them all. Josh hoped it did for her too. On the surface, except for occasional spontaneous bouts of weeping, it seemed like it did. On the inside was anyone's guess, and Josh wanted to be there, to reassure, to show his love.

But he burned to be here more.

Across the park, outside the low fence, reporters gathered in clusters, chatting among themselves while keeping an eye on the far corner of the cemetery. Levenham's burial ground was split between old and new. Nearest the road, taking up several acres, were the low graves of the new garden cemetery, where Josh's grandfather and other relatives were buried. But in the corner, rising up a slope and backed by a row of magnificent grey-trunked English elm trees, were the headstones, angels and raised marble slabs of the old plots.

As Josh neared, he could hear the words of the vicar as he spoke about a woman none of them really knew. Josh sought out Em as he hurried closer, silently apologising to the dead upon whose grassy graves he accidentally trod. Roadworks along the Duke's Highway had delayed him and he'd missed the church service. As soon as the funeral was over he'd be straight on the road back. Unless things had changed.

Christ, he hoped they had.

He found her next to Granny B, the pair stiffly alike. Their backs were wooden, chins raised, looking across the grave and artificial turf-covered dirt mound towards nothing. Not disdainful, more defiant. Wallaces in body and soul. A light breeze curled the ends of their long wool coats and brought with it the sound of sobbing.

Josh entered the old cemetery and paused near a moss-covered gravestone, breathing steadily from his rapid walk. Granny B shot him a sideways glance before looking away again. The dismissal made Josh falter. He glanced at Adrienne, weeping into Samuel's chest. One of the local policewomen he recognised from the investigation stood nearby, her watchful gaze on him. He nodded at her and received a small acknowledgement in reply, an action that made him breathe out hard. There was a possibility the Wallaces had restricted the funeral to family only, ruining his chance to talk to Em.

He looked at her again and for a brief moment she shifted her gaze until it connected with his. She didn't smile. Not with her mouth, not with her eyes. Nor was her expression cold. She simply assessed.

Sixteen days after the tragedy and this was the closest he'd come to her. In the chaos that followed the landslide and its aftermath – the family's grief, the recriminations and media swarm – she'd exiled herself and Muffy to Camrick.

Untouchable. Jasmine had come for the remaining animals. Footage of her, grim-faced and silent, loading Kicki and Cutie into a horse float, and several cranky chickens and a furiously paddling white duck into a wire cage on the back of an old ute, appeared on the television. Lod and another horse were the last to go, then a large padlock was fitted to the gate and Rocking Horse Hill was left to loneliness.

As he was.

At PaperPassion, the door remained locked, a blind pulled down over its glass panel. A typed card proclaimed the shop 'closed until further notice'. He didn't know if it would reopen. He didn't know anything, least of all where he stood in her life.

Em looked away as the vicar began to recite the 23rd Psalm.

The Lord is my shepherd . . .

Josh lowered his head, fists curling, hating this impotence. Hating what had happened to them. Muttered 'Amens' followed the psalm's last line. He was determined to at least talk to her, and took a few steps closer.

He halted as Granny B narrowed sharp eyes in his direction, then murmured something to her granddaughter. Em shook her head, the movement tiny. Granny B persisted and this time Em's gesture became more distinct, as she jerked her head towards the road and the news crews. Her mouth thinned and she stared steadfastly across the grave, as though Josh didn't exist.

An ache spread across his chest and into his throat. He didn't need much more proof. Whatever they'd once shared died completely that night.

Granny B's mouth formed a moue, then she marched straight for the headstone where Josh stood and turned once more to the open grave, where Felicity's coffin still hung by its straps over the hole below. 'Joshua.'

'Granny B.' He gestured towards Em. 'How is she?'

'Rather well, considering, although I suspect her shoulder still gives her some grief. She was lucky it was only a slight dislocation.' Granny B paused and contemplated the grave. 'Lucky in other ways, too, of course.' She threw a filthy look towards the road. 'The parasites have been giving us hell, but after today we should find some peace.' Her gaze shifted again and her voice lost some of its loftiness. 'Although I fear Digby never will.'

Unlike Em and Granny B, who'd chosen navy and deep burgundy as their funeral colours, Digby was dressed in black. Black wool coat, black suit, black shirt. Stark against his clothing, held together with a simple white bow, was a large bouquet of pure white tulips, petals folded into delicate cups that trembled with Digby's grief. His forehead still bore the pink line from the stiches he'd received and a pair of crutches leaned nearby against another grave. But it was his eyes that revealed where the real damage lay. A haunted, unfocused gaze that stared inward instead of out.

Suddenly Digby raised his head. For a long moment, he did nothing but stare blankly at Josh, then he straightened and nodded. Josh nodded back. They didn't need words. Tragedy had tied them forever.

He turned back to Granny B. 'He'll recover.'

Felicity had made Digby a different man. In a strange way, she'd made them all different.

'Yes, I suppose he will. He is a Wallace, after all.' She gestured to the surrounding graves, some new and glossy, others lichen- covered and stained with age. 'This was Emily's idea, to bury her here among Wallaces. Can't say I'm happy about it. Not sure Adrienne is either but Emily was adamant. She said it was the right thing to do. Odd attitude to have towards an attempted murderer in my opinion.' She eyed him up and down. 'And you? How are you holding up? You endured as much as my grandchildren that night.'

'I'll be fine. Once I talk to Em.'

'Oh, you will.'

'When?'

Granny B didn't answer. Instead she dug into her pocket for a cigar, checking the end before lighting it with an expensive-looking rose-gold lighter. She puffed, the fragrant smoke drifting softly in the crisp air. 'She's protecting you, you know,' she finally said.

'Me?'

'You and your family. From the vultures.'

'I don't need protection.' All he wanted was Em. A chance to talk. A chance to apologise for what went before.

The media weren't bothering Josh much now anyway. After the initial bombardment, news of Michelle's cancer had caused them to ease off, and like Em's family, his had closed ranks. With the exception of Karen, who, at over eight months pregnant, was uncomfortable, fiercely combative and couldn't help taking swipes, no one was talking. Besides, the media weren't really interested in him, not when they had the Wallaces.

'You probably don't, but she's granting it regardless.' Abruptly, Granny B lifted his hand, his damaged one, with not a trace of distaste affecting her powdery features, and patted it. 'Patience, Joshua. Patience.' And with that she marched off, back to Em's side.

The two women murmured together for a moment. He hesitated, desperate for some sign, and was at last rewarded with the faintest curve of Em's mouth. Then her eyes slid to him. And this time there was no mistaking their softened edges.

Josh raised his gaze to the sky and inhaled a deep, shaky breath. Relief and hope made his eyes smart. He blinked several times and flexed his jaw until the emotion passed. Patience. For Em he would find plenty. Aware of her, but without looking, he headed across to Digby and gripped his shoulder.

'I'm sorry.'

Digby's eyes were bloodshot and heavy. He acknowledged Josh with a grimace before reaching for his crutches, and hobbling to the edge of the grave for his final goodbye.

Josh left them to their mourning, passing back across the lawn with his hands in his pockets and his head down, but his gaze was angled sideways to survey the journalists. One followed his progress as closely as he followed theirs. A hundred metres from the fence, near to where he'd parked his car, the journalist broke from the group. Josh maintained his long pace. He wanted to run, but it would only draw more attention.

They intersected at his car.

'A word, Mr Sinclair.'

Josh didn't answer. He yanked open the door, slid in and slammed it shut. The journalist pressed his face close to the window, continuing his questions. Josh started the car. The radio was pumping out the latest Pink single. He turned it up, loud, and put the car into gear.

The journalist stepped back. After all, Josh was a nobody.

But a nobody high on hope.

***

Tom waited by the open door of the garage while Josh lined the tray of his ute with a thick removalist's blanket. In the sun, the easel's timber glowed an even richer hue. So it should, given the layers of oil and hours of polishing Josh had put into it.

Excitement fizzed within him. It had been nearly three weeks since the funeral, five weeks since he'd last spoken with Em. Spring had finally come south and the day felt glorious. Thanks to Em's text message it was about to get a whole lot better.

Though he could have lifted it himself, Josh allowed his dad to help him load the easel and secure it in its blanket. Together they replaced the tonneau cover, clipped it in place, and stood back with their hands on their hips. Maybe in a few months, once his mum was in the clear and his dad had the peace of mind he needed to leave Flanagan's, this would be something they'd do often.

'Have a look at you two,' called Michelle from the back door. 'Like a pair of proud cockies.'

Josh grinned at her. 'That's because we've a lot to be proud of.'

He didn't mean the easel either. They were both proud of her, and thankful. No one knew what the other cancer and mastectomy survivor had told Michelle, what they'd shared, and in the end no one cared. Not even Karen who, with the joy of her first baby approaching, had felt the most let down by her mother's defiance. All that mattered was that their plan had worked.

Even now, Josh still felt swollen with admiration. Proud of the way his mum gritted her teeth against discomfort, the way she'd adapted, the way she still managed to boss them all around without effort. And they adored her even more for it.

It hadn't been easy for Michelle. Post-operation there was the shock of seeing her chest for the first time. The hideous drains and tight compression bra. She'd promised them the pain wasn't as bad as she'd expected, until the injections of saline into her skin expanders began. That had proved to be agonising. Agonising but worth it. Within a few months she'd have new breasts that defied gravity and age. Better than her daughters', she liked to tease them.

She still couldn't do much. No lifting, pulling or pushing. Josh and his dad found themselves almost elbowing each other out the way to help her. Best of all the notebooks were gone. 'For another time,' she'd said when Josh inquired after them during her first week home. If it weren't for the fluid drains and bandages, he would have bear-hugged her until she squirmed and squealed in delight like she used to when he was a teenager.

'She's going to love it,' said Michelle.

'I hope so.'

His dad's hand curled around his shoulder and squeezed. 'No point standing around.'

'No.' Josh jangled the car keys. This was it. Five weeks of waiting about to end and now he couldn't seem to move.

Michelle eased her way down the back step and to his side. She took his left hand and held it between hers. 'Don't be scared.'

'I'm not.'

She sighed and gave him her favourite sceptical look.

He jangled his keys some more. 'The text just asked if I'd mind coming to the hill. It didn't say anything else.'

'Of course it didn't. Em understands that some things are too important for a silly text message.' Her gaze softened. 'She loves you. Now it's time for you tell her the same.'

He'd come close, that night, but like everything else the chance had been lost in the drama. As soon as Em was safe, he'd left her with Muffy and his phone, yelling at her to dial emergency while he began his panicked scramble down the quarry in search of Digby and Felicity. He'd found Digby almost immediately, dangerously perched a third of the way down the quarry face. He was unconscious, with blood and mud stuck to his face. Beside him, protruding ghostly pale from the dirt, was a slim hand and forearm, already turning cold.

Josh had half-dragged, half-carried Digby to firmer ground before climbing back down for Felicity, but as soon as he began to scoop soil from above her body, the wall of dirt and rock shifted again. More weedy clods broke away. Small avalanches of earth cascaded either side of him. He waited until they steadied, and began again, only to set off a larger slide that swept Felicity's arm away and, if not for a last-second lunge to the side, would have taken him with it.

The realisation of how close Em had come to the same fate didn't sink in until later, when he'd climbed back from the quarry and found her near an ambulance, her arm in a sling and Muffy at her feet, waiting, as they all were, for news of Felicity.

'They found her,' he said.

She regarded him with pitiful hope then looked away, her expression almost unbearable to witness. She swallowed and spoke, her voice hoarse. 'Thank you.'

'For what?'

'For pulling me back.'

He crouched down and took her hand, careful not to bump her damaged shoulder. 'I'd never have let you fall.' He held her gaze, ready to tell her what he should have weeks ago. For the second time in his life Josh had almost lost her. There would be no third time. He'd make sure of that now. Except she'd begun to cry and the paramedics had arrived back, along with the other emergency services, and the moment was lost.

His mum squeezed his fingers, bringing him back. 'Go on with you now.'

Smiling, Josh bent down to kiss her cheek. 'Don't wait up for me.'

She laughed, a sound that warmed him and brought his anticipation back to life. 'Believe me, Joshy, my sweet, we had no plans of doing that.'

Twenty-Eight

Em rested on the top of the porch step and gazed across her bedraggled garden. After their beachside holiday, the chooks appeared happy to be home, clucking and scratching contentedly around the tangled mess of plants, tearing up any surviving seedlings with sharp claws and beaks as they searched for grubs. Chelsea was even more delighted. Jasmine's windswept stone and sand garden held little joy for a water-loving duck.

Em didn't mind the damage. In a few days she'd sort it out: dig out the wasted winter vegetables and toss them on the compost and replace them with spring and summer seedlings. She smiled. In a few days it'd be Monday. How easy it was to forget that she needed to go back to work, reopen the shop, somehow make up for the losses of profit and goodwill over the last five weeks.

She wrapped her arm around Muffy and hugged her. 'Next weekend then, hey, Muff-Muff.'

The mug of tea she'd brought out was long emptied but Em stayed studying the garden, wallowing in being home. Camrick had felt like an exile, and perhaps a little cowardly. But with the media camped on their doorstep in the aftermath of the quarry's collapse and with so much for their family to come to terms with in the weeks following, it proved necessary. The time away had given her some perspective. A chance to reconcile what her beloved hill had done.

And, more importantly, what she had done.

She turned to look at the great maw left by the quarry's subsidence. The old greying scar had been replaced with an almost blood-dark fresh mark. Around the rim of the collapsed edge, emergency stabilisers had been hammered in place, an ugly substitute for what plants and trees would have done over time. A furore over the area's management had erupted, with competing interests blaming each other. All it had achieved was to fill the letters-to-the-editor sections of newspapers with vitriol, along with news websites and social media.

From her balcony at Camrick, Granny B had peered south, smoked her cigars and harrumphed over it all.

Em spent her time very differently.

For a long while she blamed herself, until Samuel sat with her one day as she worked on *The Ballad of the White Horse* in the kitchen and talked about human fallibility. How easy it was for the tiny decisions to cause tragedy. How they built against one another, until it took only a small flick or careless touch to send them scattering like dominoes.

Such had been the case with his son. His whingeing dismissed as merely that of a boy hankering for a day off from school. Missed symptoms, a misdiagnosis of flu. Overworked emergency staff. And suddenly a child was in a coma, never to recover.

'But what I did . . .' Hot tears built as Em remembered the email she'd sent, the almost triumphant way she'd crushed Felicity's dream. 'It wasn't an accident. I did it deliberately, with malice.'

'Not completely,' Samuel had replied. 'You sent that email because you loved your brother and feared for your family.'

It was a tragedy towards which they'd all contributed, but blame also lay with Felicity herself. She who'd locked Granny B out. She who'd seen all Em had at Rocking Horse Hill and coveted it for herself, urging Digby to break the promise he'd made his sister and reclaim Rocking Horse Hill for her, causing arguments and the germination of distrust. She who'd seen what the Wallace name meant, its history and cachet, and misinterpreted it as a kind of power. Power that she'd never had, that could transform her from worthless to worthwhile.

That idea was the saddest for Em to absorb. Felicity didn't need the hill or a new name or anything else to stop being nothing. She had Digby, who loved her, and that made her infinitely precious.

Muffy rose, her nose lifted, sniffing and listening. Em listened too, her stomach fluttering as the sound increased. She let Muffy go, watching her closely as the dog trotted the path to the side of the house.

The engine decelerated, a gear was changed. The flutters turned into wingbeats. Em formed her hands into a steeple and pressed the edges against her mouth. The car accelerated out of a corner, travelled on, and then slowed.

Muffy's tail began to wag.

Em remained seated on the porch step. Casual, that's how she wanted this. Softly, softly with their damaged hearts.

Muffy ran ahead of Josh like a puppy, halting to look up at him with her big happy-dog grin while he caught up, then twirling in excited circles before running off again. Em wanted to do the same: run to him and wrap herself around that strong body, but the fear that he'd stand stiff and unresponsive held her back. She hadn't even been sure he'd come.

He stopped near the corner, where the path turned towards the porch steps. 'Hey.'

'Hey yourself.'

His delicious treacle eyes raked her body before returning to rest, intense, on hers. 'You look good, Em.'

'So do you.'

He did. A pair of faded jeans, his broad shoulders accentuated by a blue-and-white checked shirt, the sleeves rolled up to expose his strong forearms. But it was his face she couldn't stop looking at. His beautiful, masculine face.

God, she loved him.

He scratched at his beard and studied the garden for a moment before swinging back. 'You sent a text.'

She placed her hand on the space beside her. 'Come sit with me?'

He assessed her for a moment then approached and eased down, the porch timbers creaking mildly under his weight. His body beside hers felt like security.

The hill's new wound drew his gaze as it had hers. 'I have nightmares about it sometimes.' He refocused on Em. 'I dream that no matter how hard I grip, you keep slipping away. That it's your arm I see reaching out of the dirt. Makes me wake up crazy.'

'I'm sorry.'

He shook his head. 'Not your fault.' He squinted at the sky. 'Anyway, I'm the one who's sorry. For saying what I did. I should have stayed. Talked it out. By leaving . . .' Josh held up his hand and dropped it. 'I should have been here.'

'None of us owns a crystal ball, Josh.'

'Maybe not, but I knew she was dangerous. I knew it from the start, the way she watched you.' He looked at his boots. 'I let you down, Em. I don't know how I'm supposed to come back from that.'

'There's nothing to come back from.' She placed her hand on the porch rail. 'Stay here. I won't be long.' Seconds later Em was back. She settled down at his side and balanced the cloth-wrapped parcel on her knees, her hands flat on top. 'I've had plenty of time to think lately. About a lot of things.' She smiled at him. 'I also had a lot of time to work. This is for you.' Love and hope in her gaze, she passed him the parcel. 'I thought it only fitting that the star should have his own copy.'

Josh stared at it, uncertainty furrowing his brow, then he began to unfold the cloth.

The book was bound in fine dark leather, with a patina that made it seem smudged with age. Running across the cover's middle third was the title and author, the letters stamped and then painted in gold.

The Ballad of the White Horse by G.K. Chesterton.

He opened the cover as though it were a precious manuscript, and stilled when he saw Em's painting of the king. In daylight, Alfred appeared more alive than ever. His cape billowed as though windswept, the ancestral jewel holding it in place glittering, as if she'd painted it with real quartz dust. His armour shone under a sky as blue and real as that which shone over Rocking Horse Hill. The king was mesmerising, proud, a warrior and saviour, and regarded the world with Josh's eyes.

He swallowed and tilted his head back, breathing hard. 'You were working on it all the time.'

The show of emotion left Em mystified. 'Of course.'

'I thought you'd abandoned it. I thought . . .' He regarded the illumination once more and traced his finger over the king's armour, before looking at her. 'Thank you.'

'You're very welcome.' She held her breath, willing him to turn the page. There was more, so much more, but Josh kept holding her gaze, the way he always used to, as though if he tried hard enough he could peel away her skin and see into the heart inside. He didn't need to try; all he needed to do was turn the page.

Finally, he turned back to the book. Em's world seemed to still as his fingers slipped under the parchment corner. Slowly, the page lifted and dropped, revealing a blank sheet. Blank except for an ink inscription penned in Em's normal handwriting.

To Josh,

Thank you for taking my hand.

I love you,

Em.

Josh kept his head bowed and his eyes closed for an uncomfortable period of time. Muffy sat on her haunches, panting in the warmth. Sensing Em's anxiety, she moved closer, Em reaching out for her at the same time as Josh spoke.

'Come here.' He cupped her face and held it, then his mouth curved and Em's heart flew skyward. 'Remind me to never doubt my mum again.'

She laughed, but it was brief, the sound smothered by a kiss that blanked her mind to everything but Josh.

When they finally pulled apart, Em felt lightheaded and breathless. Muffy was on her belly with her head on her paws and a resigned expression on her sweet face. The chooks were still scratching, Chelsea was waddling her way through a messy row of beans, oblivious to the drama on the porch, while in front of them all the hill stretched into the sky.

Josh took her hand and tangled his fingers in hers. He smiled at her, eyes shining. 'This time I'm never letting go.'

***

Em smiled lazily as Josh kissed his way across her collarbone before nuzzling her neck. Sleep had done nothing to diminish the way she felt. She was full of him, his scent, his taste, his touch, his breath.

His love.

And yet neither of them had said it out loud. Em supposed they didn't need to. Their feelings vibrated everywhere, like some skittish electric force.

'I missed waking up next to you,' he said, curling his arm around her belly, a smile in his voice. 'You're all warm and soft.' He stroked the skin under her breast with his thumb, the caress shooting a trill through her groin. 'And sexy.'

'You could wake up here all the time. If you wanted.'

She breathed in as he shifted onto his elbow and studied her face. 'Are you asking me to move in?'

Was she? The offer wasn't planned. It just came out, a half- distracted verbalisation of the want she'd felt. The want for this to be more than what it was before, more than sex, more than the resurrection of a past long gone.

'It seems I am.'

'I don't know. I was kind of getting used to my old single bed.' Josh broke into a grin. 'I had lots of good dreams in that bed.'

'I bet you did.'

'Yeah, and they were all about you.' He rolled and pressed his forehead against hers, a cheeky sparkle in his gaze. 'Emily Wallace-Jones, offering to live in sin with a bloke from the east side. What would your grandmother say?'

'Knowing my gran,' said Em dryly, 'she'd probably tell us to hurry up and breed.'

He laughed. 'I'm not so sure about this breeding business yet but I'm more than happy to practise.'

A sentiment Em could only agree with.

Later, after they'd made love and lain drowsy and content in each other's arms, Josh once again kissed his way up her neck. 'My turn for presents and your turn to stay put,' he said when he'd reached her mouth and teased her lips. He slid out of bed and began to drag on clothes. 'And no peeking out the window.'

Amused, Em flopped back, listening to the movement of the house. The contentment of having Josh back in her life, the smug joy of knowing he was staying.

She could hear movement outside. A hushed expletive, followed by a growled 'out the way'. The back door slid open, Muffy's toenails clicking on the slate as she trotted inside. Josh's footsteps followed, heavier than normal. There was a strange rolling noise, then quiet followed by Josh's approach up the hall.

He kneeled on the bed and kissed her. 'You can get up now.'

Em tugged on clothes, anticipation fizzing inside her. Josh waited at the door with Muffy at his feet, watching her with a satisfied smile.

At the door he took her hand. 'Close your eyes.'

'What are you up to?'

'Something special.'

With her eyes closed, the house felt familiar and strange at the same time. For a fanciful moment in the hall, Em thought she heard breathing before realising it was only her own excited breath. The slate was cold under her feet, then warm as she passed in front of the fire, heat still radiating from the previous night's coals. Though spring had at last brought bright skies and sunshine to the hill, the nights remained fresh and occasionally frosty.

Josh took her shoulders and directed her sideways. She shuffled, relieved when she felt the thick pile of her favourite shaggy rug.

'You can open your eyes now.'

In front of the window, lit by the sun as it topped Rocking Horse Hill, the timber lustrous with polish, was the easel. Em reached out and ran her fingertips reverently over the main board, feeling its finish, the slide of the timber. Her touch dropped to the lip and skated across to the flat desk, running in and out of the inkwell hollows. The craftsmanship was superb. Beautiful, tight-fitting joints, rounded edges of silky smoothness.

She turned to Josh. His back was to the window, the sun creating a halo around his head as he watched her. And Em remembered another time, a moonlit man who'd gazed at her with passion that went deeper than physical want.

'I love you.'

His mouth curled. 'I take it that means you like it.'

'I do. It's perfect.'

'Good. Now come here.' He wrapped her to him, arms enveloping, protective, possessive. 'I'm not without faults, Em. I've got plenty, but one thing I promise. There will never be any fault in my love for you. Never.'

***

The wheelbarrow's rusty front wheel squealed all the way down the slope from the shed to the road. Josh wanted to fix it, but Em had already loaded it with the cypress sapling, spade and organic fertiliser, and knowing Josh's perfectionist nature when it came to handyman work, he'd take forever.

'Here, muscle man,' said Em, passing him the spade, 'show me how good you are.'

Josh grinned. 'Want me to take my shirt off? Give you a perve like in that TV ad?'

'You're forgetting I've seen your chest before. Many times.'

He tutted. 'A couple of months in and you're jaded already.'

Em crossed her arms and arched an eyebrow. She'd proved perfectly well only an hour before how unjaded she was. Practising breeding was what they'd come to call it – a secret nod to Granny B. One day soon they'd be doing it for real.

It felt fitting for Josh to be the one helping plant the new cypress. He may not be a war hero, a Second Lieutenant at eternal rest, but he'd saved her life. Without his determined grip Em could have been lost with Felicity, swallowed up by the place she'd loved since childhood. He'd also filled another void, that in her heart, and now he was helping to fill this one.

She watched the thread of Josh's muscles as they moved under his T-shirt, grateful once more for the luck that had brought him back into her life, and for the love that now kept him there. Life wasn't entirely without complications. The media never seemed to leave off in its tricks to get them to talk. Women's magazines were the big ones now, spying a circulation winner in their love story, and both she and Josh had faced down customers who'd turned out to be anything but.

Love cocooned them, a luxury poor Digby didn't have.

Blinking the sting in her eyes away, Em crossed her arms and turned to regard the hill. Her relationship with Digby had changed irrevocably. The closeness they'd shared had been destroyed the first day Felicity came to the hill, when Digby was left torn between the love he'd discovered and the promise he'd made his sister. What had been done could not be undone and now guilt at their actions kept them both restrained.

Digby hadn't set foot at Rocking Horse Hill since that night and she doubted he ever would again. Two weeks ago, without telling anyone his plan, Digby signed the property over to her.

Granny B had raised a toast at the news. Adrienne bowed her head and apologised yet again for her failings as a mother. No matter how many times Samuel and Em tried to comfort her, she bore Felicity's death and Digby's grief as her cross. She should have done more to make Felicity feel welcome, to make her feel secure. At least the days of deadening her culpability with wine were over. Samuel moving in had halted that. Such a pity he couldn't work the same magic on Granny B's vices.

Em turned back to find Josh leaning on the spade, watching her. His brow was speckled with sweat, his stubble lazy-weekend long.

'You all right?'

'Just thinking how sexy you look when you're sweaty.'

'Liar. You weren't looking at me, you were looking at the hill.' He sobered. 'Is it Digby still?'

She swung her toe at a half-decayed cypress cone. 'A bit.'

'He'll be all right, Em.'

'I worry about him.'

'I know, but the only thing that'll help him is time.' He smiled gently. 'And maybe another woman.'

Em smiled back. 'Perhaps we could set him up with Jas now she's free.'

He laughed. 'Too much of a handful for Dig I'd have thought.'

Em wasn't so sure about that. Jasmine seemed to have lost her bouncy edge since ditching Mike for good, but Jas was never one to stay down. Plus it might only be with her that Jasmine was subdued. As with all of Em's closest relationships, Felicity had left a scar on theirs too. They'd come back though. Em would make sure of it. Friendships like theirs were too special to lose.

By the time Josh had finished digging, a large mound of rich soil and pale, partially rotted cypress chips had grown beside the hole. Muffy snuffled through it, sniffing out mice and stinky dead things to roll in. Em helped Josh fetch fresh soil from the back of the garden to fill the space, Josh glowering at the wheelbarrow as it protested under the load.

The tree was well past seedling stage and had cost Em more than was comfortable, but the need to complete the avenue overrode any protest over the price. So much had happened since the lightning strike that it was as if the hill's circle of life had been broken and now, more than ever, Em felt it her duty to repair it properly.

For the future's sake. For contentment.

For her life ahead with Josh.

She stood back and leaned against Josh's chest. Wrapping his arms around her, he settled his chin on her shoulder to admire the new planting. Alongside its brothers, the cypress appeared small and skinny, but its trunk was straight and sturdy, its needles bright and healthy. In time, the gap would fill and Rocking Horse Hill would be whole once more.

It felt whole now.

'Look,' said Josh, pointing towards the road paddock.

Em watched, frowning, and then laughed. For as long as Em could remember, there'd been a gap between the paddock's gate and the fence's strainer post. Wide enough for Muffy to pass through but nothing larger, Em had paid it little attention. But where a dog could fit, a sneaky donkey's head could also weave.

Like a mediaeval criminal in stocks, Kicki had his head jammed between the space, eyes half-closed in concentration, rubbery little mouth working furiously at the latch. Cutie stood close by his shoulder, fluffy ears twirling as she nudged him on.

'He won't do it,' said Em, as Kicki attempted yet again to align the latch's metal eye over its hook.

'You think? That's one determined donkey.'

'That's one very naughty donkey, you mean.'

'He just wants to show his girlfriend a good time.' Josh nuzzled her neck. 'Bit like me.'

Em turned in Josh's arms and draped her own around his neck, breathing in the delicious scents of soil and pine and hard-working man. Smiling, he bent and kissed her, only to pull away seconds later. 'Brace yourself. We're about to have company.'

Em closed her eyes and groaned. 'He hasn't?'

'He has.' Josh kissed her forehead. 'Don't worry, I'll fix it for you.'

'And then?'

He regarded her with confusion. 'I'll fix the wheelbarrow?'

'What happened to showing your girlfriend a good time?'

Josh locked his intense molasses gaze on hers. 'I'm already having it.'

And as a donkey bunted her backside Em realised that, at last, so was she.

The End

Now celebrate Em and Josh's wedding in…

***It's Levenham's wedding of the year but unlucky-in-love
Harry Argyle has more on his mind than being groomsman.***

After yet again nearly colliding with an escaped horse while driving home to the family farm, Harry Argyle comes face-to-face with its pretty owner, and doesn't hold back his disapproval.

Confronted by a bad-tempered giant on a dark country road, beautician and new arrival in town Summer Taylor doesn't know who to be more afraid for: herself or her darling horse Binky. It's not her fault Binky keeps escaping. The alcoholic owner of the paddock she rents won't fix the fence and Binky can be sneaky when it comes to filling his stomach. But no matter how big and muscled the bully, she refuses to be intimidated.

When Harry's wedding party book a session at the day spa where Summer works, both she and Harry are horrified to be paired together. Grudgingly, they agree to make the most of it - only for the session to spiral into disaster. Realising he's made a dill of himself in front of sweet Summer yet again, Harry vows to set things right.

Summer isn't about to easily forgive the man who called her horse stupid, no matter how brave and kind, but with everyone on Harry's side, even fate, resistance is hard. Can these two find love or will Summer's wayward horse put his hoof in it again?

Buy *Summer and the Groomsman* now in ebook or print from your favourite retailer and fill your heart with fun!

A vivid, moving and passionate story of love and redemption set in the gloriously rich landscape of Australia's Hunter Valley.

Brooke Kingston is smart, capable and strong-willed, and runs her family's property with dedication and skill. More at home on horseback than in heels, her life revolves around her beloved 'boys' – showjumpers Poddy, Oddy and Sod.

Then a tragic accident leaves Brooke a mess. Newcomer Lachie Cambridge is hired to manage the farm, and Brooke finds herself out of a job and out of luck. But she won't go without a fight.

What she doesn't expect is Lachie himself – a handsome, gentle giant with a will to match her own. But with every day that Lachie stays, Brooke's future on the farm becomes more uncertain.

Will she be forced to choose between her home and the man she's falling for, or will the very things that brought them together tear them apart?

Purchase your copy of *Heart of the Valley* from your favourite ebook or print book retailer today. You might want to grab some tissues while you're at it. You'll need them!

*

If you'd like to know when my next release comes available plus gain access to exclusive content, news and giveaways, and a couple of sweet short stories to enjoy over a cuppa, please sign up to my newsletter at cathrynhein.com.

Dear Reader

Thank you so much for buying and reading *Rocking Horse Hill*. I hope you enjoyed Em and Josh's journey to love and happiness. If you'd like to discover what happens next, please check out the fun, sweet novella *Summer and the Groomsman* or *Rocking Horse Hill*'s deeply emotional full-length sequel *Wayward Heart*, which follows Digby and Jasmine's journey to recovery and happiness.

If you'd like to know when my next release comes available plus gain access to exclusive content, news and giveaways, please subscribe to my newsletter at cathrynhein.com. You can also connect via Facebook and Twitter using @CathrynHein. More information about me and my books, including the inspiration behind *Rocking Horse Hill*, along with plenty of other cool stuff, can be found at cathrynhein.com.

Help others find their next read by leaving a review of this novel on your favourite book website.

*

My other rural-set romances include:

Wayward Heart
Santa and the Saddler
April's Rainbow
Summer and the Groomsman
The Falls
Rocking Horse Hill
Heartland
Heart of the Valley
Promises

Romantic Adventure:
The French Prize